The
SCOURGE
EMACULUM

WESTMARCH ✦ PUBLISHING

The
SCOURGE
EMACULUM

ROBERTO CALAS

Acclaim for Roberto Calas and The Scourge Trilogy:

"I expected it to be powerful and terrifying, and Calas did not disappoint. What I did not anticipate, however, was the degree of brooding menace that would envelop me as I read, or how much I would come to invest in the fates of the characters. With such terrific tension and so much at stake, *The Scourge* was nearly as hard to endure as it was to put down."
　　—*Melissa F. Olson, author of the Scarlett Bernard series*

"This story has everything: plague, war, mad kings, ravenous zombies, heroic knights, wise jesters, true love. Rarely have I been as haunted and moved by the closing pages of a novel."
　　—*Stant Litore, author of The Zombie Bible series*

"A well-researched, well written story with characters you can't help but love."
　　—*Roberta Trahan, author of* The Dream Stewards

"Calas' writing style is crisp and tight and yet the world he has created is rich and full of color and horror."
　　—*Adam Haviaras, author of* Children of Apollo

"The author has a knack for imagining just how bad a particular situation could be for the characters—and then makes it a whole lot worse. Suffice it to say, the numerous plot twists and cliffhangers kept me turning the pages to the very end. Imagine mixing a Bernard Cornwell novel with the zombie apocalypse, and thanks to Roberto Calas' considerable research and attention to historical detail, it really works."
　　—*Joseph Finley, author of* Enoch's Device

ISBN-13:978-1942458005
ISBN-10: 1942458002

Published by Westmarch Publishing

Other Works by Roberto Calas:

THE SCOURGE:
PUBLISHED BY 47NORTH
The Scourge (Book One)
The Scourge: Nostrum (Book Two)
Wages of Sin (A Scourge short story published by StoryFront)

THE BEAST OF MAUG MAURAI:
The Culling (Book One)
Feeding the Gods (Book Two)
Stars and Graves (Coming Soon)

KINDLE WORLDS
Kingdom of Glass (A Kindle Worlds Novella)

Learn more on **robertocalas.com**!

To our children, Cesar, Lucia, Drew and Charlotte.
And to the children of Sandy Hook Elementary School.

Acknowledgments

This book would not have been possible without the help of my readers, many of whom contributed directly to the expense of its production. Most notable among those readers is Jay Bidwell, who stepped in when Sir Edward was faltering. I would also like to thank Chris Pourteau, Mary Wikswo and Joseph Finley for their generous support of Edward's campaign.

I should, of course, offer my gratitude to my beta readers: Jeff Fuller, Robert Duperre, Patie Polczyk, Kathy King, Randy L. Johnson, and Susan Johnson Crowe. And to my development editor, Stant Litore. This book would be a shadow of what it is without their help.

I would be remiss if I didn't mention my lovely fiancée, Annabelle Page, who is my editor, art director, project manager and counselor. She is my Elizabeth, so it is only fitting that I used her image as Sir Edward's Elizabeth on the cover of this book.

I would like to thank the Knights of Calas for your hard work and brilliant suggestions. Together we will conquer the world.

Lastly, I would like to thank my parents, Nick and Rina, whose eternal support keeps me from the ditches of life.

Episode One

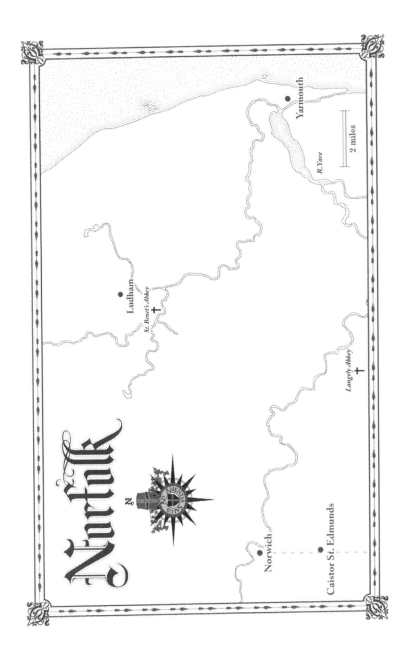

CHAPTER ONE

MEN WILL FOLLOW ANYONE. I have watched fools lead battalions and cowards command armies. I have met lecherous bishops who guide flocks upon the paths of morality, and madmen who rule entire kingdoms. And I have learned in my days upon this earth that it is not the wisest or bravest or even the most sensible who lead; it is the loudest.

And Sir Gerald of Thunresleam is loud enough to wake the dead.

His shouts echo through the sparse forest. "No!" he screams. "In a line! *Stay in a line!*"

Sir Tristan and I pause at an ivy-draped alder to recover. I unsling the leather sack from my shoulder, and Tristan does the same. Each breath I take sears my lungs, echoes in my helm. I am too old to be running in armor. Hounds howl, and the deep thud of hoofbeats sound behind us. The rain applauds on the leaves above.

"Tell... tell me that lovely story again, Edward," Sir Tristan pants as he speaks, one hand on his thigh, the other holding a crossbow against his shoulder. "You had a... a cannon pointed at Gerald... a flame... inches from the touchhole. I... I forget the next part. Tell me again what you did?"

I take great gulps of air and grunt at Tristan. He knows what happened next; I lowered the cannon and let Gerald escape. I have run from Sir Gerald from the time his master, Sir John of Muckinge, died in battle. Sir John was torn apart by the mindless victims of this new plague that has rotted England. I suppose Sir John's death is my fault—I led the plaguers to the battlefield where he died—but neither apologies nor denials will sate Sir Gerald's lunatic thirst for revenge. The madman has tried to kill me more times than I care to recall. And when I had him in my power, I let him go. I thought it my finest act as a human. But I think now it was my worst.

Sir Gerald does not seem to appreciate my act of mercy. Tristan and I left St. Benet's Abbey two days after capturing it, and we caught sight of our old enemy after less than three miles of traveling. Ten horsemen and two dozen footmen appeared on the horizon, every one of them sworn to Sir Gerald.

Men will follow anyone.

Father Aubrey, a priest back home, once told me that men are like wolves. He said we hunt in packs so we can slaughter more lambs, and the man with the loudest howl leads us all. I smiled and asked if women were the lambs in his metaphor. A peculiar look came over him as he shook his head. "No," he replied. "A woman is the hunger that burns in the belly of the wolf. The hunger that makes him slaughter the lamb."

Father Aubrey is a strange man.

My woman, Elizabeth, lies plagued in the cathedral of St. Edmund's Bury, and my belly rages with hunger for her. I have slaughtered an countless number of innocent lambs while trying to get her back, and I fear there will be more butchery before my journey is done.

And I will not give Sir Gerald another chance—he will be the first on that butcher's block.

A stocky man in ring mail and a flat-topped nasal helm stumbles through shrubs and draws up only a few feet away.

His eyes grow wide when he sees us. "They're here!" He draws his sword. "Sir Gerald, I have them! They're—"

Tristan's dagger catches the man in the throat and the shout becomes a gurgle. I sigh.

Sir Gerald will have to be the second on the butcher's block.

The man's body relaxes and Tristan lets it fall to the sodden earth. I notice a red ribbon tied around the soldier's arm. His lady's favor. A sign of the hunger that burned in this man's stomach.

I catch a strong scent of lavender—an odor I have detected several times on our journey. But I do not have time to question it. The wailing of hounds grows louder from the east. Horsemen bob through the trees, and footmen crack branches with their footfalls as they shuffle through dead leaves.

Tristan cleans the blade of his dagger on the wide, red ribbon. He squints at the oncoming men and tries to smile. "I have an overwhelming urge to visit the west side of this forest. Now, really."

I take a last look at the dead man, sling my shoulder sack, and lurch westward through the forest. The sack is heavy with supplies: a three-foot-long hand cannon; food for our journey; a large jar full of dragon's blood; and a jar of miraculous healing salve called Malta fungus.

I shove at the grasping branches with my shield. Cold water from the wet leaves sprays my cheeks through the perforations in my helm. We cannot outrun our pursuers forever. My hope was to lose them in this forest, but there are too many, and the dogs have our scent. I wonder how Sir Gerald will kill us. On our last meeting, he threatened to skin us like rabbits and piss on our pulp. He may be mad, but he is creative in his madness.

I glance back at Tristan and think of all the times I have put his life in danger. Death's skeletal fingers have scratched our shoulders too many times to count, but today I can feel his bony hand on my throat. Tristan sees me looking and blows a kiss, then picks up his pace so he is directly behind me.

Men will follow anyone.

CHAPTER TWO

THE FOREST DIES OUT SLOWLY, coughing clumps of hawthorn and acacia, until there are only the empty chalk plains of Norfolk. A goshawk cries out and circles above.

Tristan shakes a fist at the bird. "Insolent bastard." He sights the creature with his crossbow even though it is far out of range. "We're not dead yet!"

But the goshawk knows better. A horn sounds behind us. Shouts rise again in the distance.

The soldier we killed gained us time. The other men must have paused at the body because, for a time, Sir Gerald's cries grew more frantic. "Leave it! *Just leave him there!*" It was a long time before we heard the crash of their pursuit again. I almost believed we would escape.

But now there is nothing but open ground ahead. If we try to run across the plains we will stand out like ticks on a pig. And if we hide in the forest, the dogs will root us out like truffles.

I tug at edge of my breastplate, adjusting the sharp weight on my shoulders. Sweat makes my fingers slip across the metal. Tristan pants beside me, hunched with hands on his legs.

A hind leaps from the hawthorn a dozen paces away, no doubt driven from the forest by the distant cacophony of Sir Gerald and his men. She stops when she sees us, her ears taut as sails in a gust.

"You rode a cow to safety once, didn't you?" Tristan's voice is tinny in his great helm. The hind hunches low then springs away. I track her flight.

"Hinds are Saint Giles's animals," I say.

"Not even the patron saint of the insane can stomach Sir Gerald," Tristan replies.

"He's my saint, Tristan," I say. "He's my saint."

East Anglia is so flat you can watch your horse run away for three days, but I cannot watch the hind for three days. I cannot watch her for even three heartbeats because Sir Gerald is behind us. We have gained ground on our enemies, but they have not given up.

Something moves in the distance, far past the running doe. A horse pulling a two-wheeled cart northward along a worn path in the grass. The hind runs directly toward the wagon, but if Saint Giles wants me to follow, he is a fool. The cart is nearly a mile away and there is nothing but flat chalkland between us and it. We would be defenseless on the field, and the even ground would allow Gerald's horsemen to hit us at a full charge.

I spot something else in the distance.

An old mill lies to the south, half hidden by a line of overgrown hedges. The tall structure sits on a narrow channel of water, about three hundred paces away. A scattering of thatched cottages rot on the opposite bank.

I glance back toward the forest. The men are still a long way from us, but they are relentless in their pursuit. I look to the mill. Tristan and I have killed oceans of men. It is a trade we know well, and the crumbling building will give us a place to work our craft. Elizabeth's cure hangs on a cord around my neck. She is the hunger in my belly, and I will slaughter every one of Gerald's lambs if they get in my way.

I run south, calling back to Tristan. "The mill!"

My armor clatters with each stride. I hear the shudder of Tristan's plates behind me as we sprint toward the waterway. The ceaseless Norfolk wind makes flutes of our helmets and tugs at my shield. My breath comes in great ragged bursts.

The mill is not crumbling as badly as I had imagined. In fact, it is not crumbling at all. Rain beads upon fresh linseed oil on the walls. Rose bushes grow in neat lines along a footpath leading to the doorway. Someone is living in the house.

Something hisses through the air and strikes the bevor at my throat with enough force to make me gag. I stagger and crash heavily to the grass in a jangle of plates, gasping. Tristan dives to the ground beside me, skids on the wet grass, and covers us with my shield as I strip off the dented bevor and cough. The wooden shards of a broadhead arrow lie on the grass beside me.

A thin archer with a six-foot war bow stands twenty paces away, using the hedges for cover. Time has robbed the brown from his temples, but his arms do not tremble as he draws back the bowstring. Two quivers hang from his thick belt, one at either hip.

The blare of a horn trembles in the Norfolk wind. The archer glances toward the forest, then scowls at us and draws the bowstring to its full length. It is no broadhead nocked on the bowstring this time. The arrow bears a thin bodkin tip, meant for piercing plate armor. My shield is nearly useless against such a weapon. The horn blows again from behind us, louder, ever louder.

I gaze toward the Heavens for guidance.

The goshawk circles lower.

We could charge him; a middling bowman might only get one well-aimed arrow away before we closed the distance. But a good bowman could fire two or three shots in that time. I look at the man's posture. At his broad shoulders and the steadiness of his gaze. I have no doubt that he is a good bowman.

Tristan points to the garden. "Lovely roses."

No one speaks. The spinning mill wheel splashes in the channel. Rain tinks off my armor and beads on the archer's bow. The horn sounds again. Gerald's men have a bloody affection for that horn. If I live through this, I will never hunt a fox or boar again.

The archer glances again at the forest. Our pursuers will push through the hawthorn in moments. The fingers holding the bow twitch and I know the man is uncertain of what to do. Uncertainty is good. There is certainty behind us, and certainty nocked upon his bow. At this moment, Elizabeth's life depends upon uncertainty.

I rise slowly and remove my great helm, hold my arms out to the sides. It takes all of my will to keep from looking back toward the forest. "Those men will kill us," I say.

"And piss on our pulp," Tristan adds.

The archer's fingers twitch again. He flicks his gaze toward the forest and tenses suddenly. The first of our pursuers must have emerged from the forest.

I catch movement at the upper window of the millhouse. A woman stares down, her hand over her mouth, her shoulders hunched in terror.

I meet the archer's gaze. "I have a wife,' I say. "She is… ill. I just want to go to her. Please."

Our land is plagued by flesh-eating corpses, and still men fight against men. If humanity is to survive this calamity, then we must show ourselves to be human. That is why I let Sir Gerald live when I could have killed him.

I raise my arms into the air and walk toward the archer. "This plague has left so few of us," I say. "We are all brothers, now."

Tristan jerks his head back toward the forest. "Except for the madman in the forest. He's more like a distant cousin. Three or four times removed."

I wave him silent, my eyes locked upon the archer's, and take another step forward. "Please. Help me reach my wife."

The archer looks back toward the woman in the window. His hands clench tightly around the bow, then he lets out a long breath and releases the tension on the bowstring. He gestures with his chin toward the channel. An old rowboat sits upon the water, downriver from the spinning waterwheel.

"He will kill you if he knows you helped us willingly." The archer looks toward the gathering soldiers and licks at his lips. I touch the hilt of my sword. A tooth is embedded in the pommel, and that tooth is said to have come from the mouth of Saint Giles himself. I run a finger over the molar. In these times of madness, only the patron saint of madness will save us. I tap the hilt of the sword and nod toward the archer. "I'm going to pretend, do you understand?"

The archer half draws the bowstring again so I stretch my hands out to the sides. "I won't harm you."

He turns to look at the woman in the window again, then relaxes the bowstring again and nods.

I glance back. A cluster of men push out of the forest. Sir Gerald's black destrier pushes past the acacia.

I draw the sword and point it at the archer. Tristan does the same and the man hustles toward the rowboat. I nod toward the sobbing woman in the upper window.

A great rectangle of hay bales has been stacked to shoulder height beside the mill house. There are no bales at the center of the stack. I peer in, and I forget about Sir Gerald.

CHAPTER THREE

THE MOCKERY OF A CHILD snarls within the hay pen.

A boy, no older than seven, afflicted with plague. There is no white to his eyes, only black—slick almonds of ebony that reflect my face as the child hisses. Bleeding boils rise along one of his cheeks. Clumps of his hair have fallen out, leaving ragged patches of red scalp. The skin on the backs of his hands and arms has split, revealing bone and raw, bloody meat. My gaze falls, and I note his shoes. They are not much longer than the palm of my hand. He shrieks, claws at the wet walls of hay, and my soul weeps.

"Leave him be!" The archer aims the bodkin tip at my head. His face twists with rage, tears glimmer in his eyes. *"You leave him be!"*

A rain of thudding hooves sounds behind us as Gerald and his men race across the wet grass. Another horn blast reverberates across the plain.

Elizabeth and I have wanted a child for years. If it is a boy, I will name him John. He will inherit the great castle I am building at Bodiam, and will bring glory upon our family name. I am certain this poor archer and his woman had hopes for their boy, too.

I reach into a poke on my belt and draw out a ceramic ampoule, extend it toward the man.

"Edward!' Tristan snatches the ampoule. "We only have three!"

"One more than we need." I pluck the ampoule back from his fingers. The thunder of horsemen draws nearer. I have no time to explain it all, so I lay the cure on a hay bale and run to the rowboat, calling back: "Give it to the boy. Perhaps it will heal him."

Tristan unties the line from a wooden post on the bank. "Or perhaps it will make him worse," he adds.

The rowboat, hidden from the horsemen by the line of unkempt hedges, rocks from side to side as I get in. Tristan steps onto the planks with one foot and shoves off with the other. The rowboat slips quickly down the rain-dotted stream. Tristan takes the oars and quickens our pace. I nod my thanks to the archer, who takes the ampoule and studies it, then glances back at me. I nod again and point toward the cage of hay. He watches me silently, his brows furrowed.

"Are you mad, Edward?" Tristan says. "You gave that complete stranger one of the cures. A complete stranger. Now we have none to spare."

We cut swiftly downstream. Tristan continues to natter about the cures, and what will happen now if one of us gets plagued, and why we shouldn't just hand out the ampoules like festival garlands.

I do not reply. The ampoules came from Syria, and were, most recently, hidden in the floorboards of an alchemist's workshop. They are a Muslim cure for our Christian plague, and they do not always work properly. One of these ampoules turned the alchemist's wife into a monster—a shriveled and insane abomination. But another cured one of the alchemist's guards. The world always seems to hinge upon two opposite outcomes. A cure or a curse. Joy or grief. Life or death. Heaven or Hell. If this Syrian cure heals her, I will have the first of each. And if I fail, it will be the last.

Seeing Elizabeth with the plague nearly broke my mind. But seeing her as an abomination would break my soul. If the cure turns her into something worse, I will hold her tight, kiss her snarling mouth, and drive my sword through both our bodies.

I look back toward the millhouse. The archer has allowed my quest to continue. If I can bring joy to him and his wife, then I have a duty to do so. We have no cures to spare now, but a son might return to his family and, for the moment, the weeping in my soul has been silenced.

Now, if I could only silence Tristan's nattering....

Gerald does not pursue. He did not see us enter the rowboat, so perhaps he thinks we crossed the stream and are hiding in one of the old cottages. The current whisks us toward the northeast and I spot the horse and cart again in the distance. One man sits on the driver's platform, the other in the cart. I wonder where they are from and what errand brings them out of hiding.

Tristan rows us eastward. I reach into the shoulder sack and draw out the jar of dragon blood. It is wrapped in a half dozen sheets of leather-bound linen. I squeeze the bundle to make sure it has not cracked. England's fate might well depend on this jar. I tuck it carefully back into the sack.

The stream we are on joins the River Bure. The Bure flows toward the North Sea, and the North Sea is far from St. Edmund's Bury, so we beach the rowboat and walk south for a time, our boots squelching in the waterlogged soil.

I smell lavender again. The odor seems to emanate from Tristan.

"Are you wearing a scent?"

"What do you mean?"

"I mean, have you put something on that makes you smell like a woman?"

"Of course I haven't," he replies. "What a strange thing to ask. Why would you ask that? It's ridiculous."

I lean toward him and sniff. "The smell is coming from you, Tristan."

"No it isn't."

I sniff again. "It's coming from your hands."

He lets out a sharp breath and takes off one of his gauntlets, holds his wrist to my nose. "Is that what you smell?"

"Lovely scent. Are you hoping to attract a nice earl or duke?"

"These gauntlets have sharp edges on the inside." He shows me a jagged ridge on the inside edge. "Scrape my wrists awful. I wasn't going to wear them anymore, but Elizabeth gave me an ointment. Now, the sharp edges just glide over the skin. Haven't bothered me since."

Elizabeth. The name slashes through me. His Elizabeth, not mine.

"You don't have to make excuses, Tristan. I've known many girlish knights. I could introduce you to a few if you'd like."

"I shouldn't have said anything."

"Your coat of arms has a flower on it, doesn't it?" I ask.

"It's primrose," he snaps. "Bringer of good tidings."

I nod.

"I'm finished with this conversation," he says.

We walk in blessed silence for a time.

It does not last long.

"What a very strange world we live in," Tristan says.

I do not reply. Frustration has replaced my humor. We had to abandon our horses when we fled into the forest, and now we have rowed another three miles farther east to rid ourselves of Sir Gerald. I am three miles farther from Elizabeth, I have to walk to St. Edmund's Bury, and I am in no mood for Tristan's silliness. Not that it matters. His silliness is a force of nature and my silence will not stop it.

"I stabbed a man in the throat a short time ago," he says. "The man wasn't attacking me. He obviously had a woman at home. Maybe children. I stabbed him in the throat and he died, and I feel no remorse. And yet, I feel terrible when I kill one of those mindless, savage plaguers. And they want to crack open our skulls and slurp out the jelly."

His words are not silly after all. It is the great irony of our current existence. The plague has made enemies of our loved ones. It was easier before we found a cure. The priests and bishops told us that only death could set plaguers free. And because God wanted us to kill the afflicted, we killed with a righteous confidence. We sent the dead to Heaven on the edge of our swords and shouted "Hallelujah" as we did. We thought we were saving them.

We were fools.

There is a cure. We can bring the afflicted dead back to life, but we found only three ampoules. Three cures, nothing more. So precious little. We hold life in our hands, but give death, instead. And with each death, the world loses a little more humanity. It is a terrible weight for a soul to bear.

I wish Tristan had spouted silliness.

"I hope Elizabeth is well," he says.

My heart leaps at the sound of her name, but I realize he is speaking of his Elizabeth, not mine. The woman we knew as Belisencia accompanied us for a week on our journey to find the alchemist. Tristan fell in love with her and she with him, before it was revealed that she was actually Elizabeth of Lancaster, daughter to John of Gaunt and sister to the exiled Henry Bolingbroke.

Tristan insisted that she wait at St. Benet's while he and I journeyed to St. Edmund's. It was a long and terrible argument, but she finally relented. She slipped a cross around his neck, a relic that once belonged to Sir Morgan of Hastings, and told Tristan not to visit any plaguer brothels. It was a jest—a reference to a man we found whoring out plagued women in Corringham—but the tears had brimmed in her eyes as she watched us go.

I do not blame him for making her stay. The foul wind of this plague has churned England into a storm-swept sea, and only the fortified islands of castle and church can keep the waves of plaguers at bay. I do not blame him for making her stay. But when I heal my Elizabeth, I will keep her beside me for every moment of every day. I will chain myself to her side and cherish my imprisonment.

If the cure works.

"Edward." There is a sharp edge to Tristan's voice. "We have guests."

Shapes lurch toward us across an overgrown field of rotting cabbage. They bear the unmistakable, lurching gait of the afflicted. Others approach from our right. A stream on our left blocks our only way around them. I don my great helm and draw my sword from its sheath.

"Let's rid the world of some humanity," I say.

We walk calmly toward the plaguers, swords held low and away from our bodies. I glance at the tooth in my pommel. Saint Giles is the saint of madness, but he is also the saint of cripples and healing. I do not have enough ampoules to cure these plaguers, so Saint Giles will have to heal them instead. I raise his sword and sigh as an afflicted man in a filthy tunic approaches.

Be healed, brother. Be healed.

We walk for miles before finding the old Roman road that leads south from Norwich. I am glad that we did not see that city again. We had to ride through it when searching for the alchemist, and the horrors I saw there crawled into my mind. Horribly swollen and disfigured humans attacked us from all sides. We thought them demons, but they were lepers who had contracted the plague.

The Church says that lepers are cursed. I once believed that to be true, but an army of lepers helped me capture St. Benet's Abbey. And I know now that they are not responsible for their affliction, any more than the victims of this new plague are responsible for theirs.

But the plagued lepers of Norwich still haunt my sleep.

My feet ache from walking, and my shoulders burn with the weight of my breastplate. I think wistfully of the two horses we left at the edge of the forest and curse Sir Gerald. A kiln burns in the pit of my stomach when I think of him. He has no honor. If ever I have the advantage again, I will not hesitate to kill him. The world has no need for his sort of humanity.

"Edward?" Tristan stares at a group of people standing beside something large. It looks like a wagon, but I've not seen a wagon of that size before.

"We should get off the road," I say. "We should take cover before they see us."

Tristan nods. "We should."

I make out more and more details as we approach. "It's a wagon I say. With a cage built into the bed."

We both draw our swords quietly. "We should definitely take cover," I say.

Tristan nods and follows me off the road. But it is too late. We have been spotted.

CHAPTER FOUR

"HELP!" THE VOICE IS DEEP and desperate. "Please! We require assistance!"

There is no trap more effective against knights than the plea for charity. Such pleas are more often bait than desperation in these dark days, so I try to ignore them. But I rarely succeed. If I ignore the cries of suffering men, who will answer my cries when I suffer? Are we to become a kingdom of suffering men, crying out to deaf ears? I do not want Elizabeth to wake to that sort of kingdom.

I walk toward the wagon, ignoring Tristan's stare.

A man walks toward us holding a staffed crucifix, the steady rain pasting his white robes against him. There are many others around the wagon, twenty or thirty souls in rain-sodden white robes.

"We are rutted," the man says. "The oxen cannot pull us out."

I am not certain what Tristan and I can do that thirty men and women cannot, but I will offer what help I can.

The wagon is enormous, and a rain-carved furrow has trapped one of the wheels. The two red Devons strain and grunt and toss their heads but the rut is too steep. A man shouts at the beasts, whips them hard enough to draw blood.

I note this absently, because my attention is on the massive cage built into the wagon bed. Tall, thin logs stand on end to form the bars of the prison. A rugged square of canvas is threaded with leather cords through holes in the tops of the logs, forming a roof. Beneath this roof, reaching through the bars with bloody, rotting arms, are more than two dozen plaguers. They growl and moan and snap their teeth, decaying bodies writhing against one another. A woman wearing a filthy green bonnet thrusts her face against a gap in the logs and screams. It is the scream of a plaguer—a cry that sounds as if it is inhaled instead of exhaled, a feral scream that holds no trace of humanity.

I point to the wagon. "What is that?"

"It is our sorrow," the pilgrim with the crucifix replies.

"Your sorrow looks a lot like people with plague," Tristan replies. "Edward, doesn't his sorrow look like people with plague?"

"It does," I reply. "Tell me pilgrim, why does your sorrow look like people with plague?"

"Because God is testing us," the man replies. "He has sent this scourge upon us to test our faith, like he tested Job. So we must stay strong in our righteousness and show our mettle. So sayeth the Lord."

"Hallelujah," Tristan replies. He says it in irony, as he always does when anyone claims that dark events are a test. But a chorus of shouts rings out from the others around the wagon, startling Tristan.

"Hallelujah!"

"Are you traveling south?" The rain makes the man's black hair sit flat on his head. "We could use two more warriors."

Two men wearing chain mail and nasal helms step forward. The castle-and-lion crest of Norwich is sewn onto the left shoulder of their black cloaks, and they each hold the reins of a chestnut gelding. Garrison guards hired to protect the pilgrims, no doubt. They grip their poleaxes nervously and study us.

"Who are you?" I ask the man with the crucifix. "And stop dodging my question. Why are there plaguers in that cage?"

"I am James of Wymondham," he replies. "The afflicted in the cage are the people we love. God has cursed them. And there is only one way to remove a curse: Through faith and prayer. So sayeth the Lord."

"And did the Lord sayeth you should wheel them around England as you pray?" Tristan asks.

"We are taking them to the shrine of Saint Edmund," James snaps. "There we shall pray for them, in the sight of England's Patron Saint. And through our devotion, they will rise again, like Jesus Christ, our savior, and be given wings of gold and allowed to suckle from the love-milk of Mother Mary's breasts. So sayeth the Lord."

"I'm not an overly religious man," Tristan says, "but I'm fairly certain the Lord did not actually say that."

Pilgrims have wandered England for as long as we have been a kingdom. The most popular destination is, of course, Saint Becket's tomb, in Canterbury. Mounted pilgrims used to gallop recklessly for the last mile of that pilgrimage, but too many un-mounted pilgrims were being trampled. An edict was passed forbidding any horse from being taken into a gallop near Canterbury Cathedral. The pilgrims have since approached at a lively trot. A canter. Named after the cathedral itself.

But James and his flock are not going to Canterbury. They are traveling to Saint Edmund's tomb under a mistaken premise.

"Edmund isn't England's patron saint anymore," I say. "And St. Edmund's Bury is flooded with plague. You won't get near his shrine." Anxiety claws at my stomach when I think of St. Edmund's Bury. My Elizabeth waits there, her flesh rotting, and I am wasting time.

The pilgrims whisper to one another. James stares at me for a long moment. "What do you mean?"

"I mean there is no way to get a wagon full of the afflicted into the monastery," My voice is harsher than it should be, but I am impatient to continue my journey. "There are more plaguers than you can count around its walls."

"No, about Edmund. You said he isn't our patron saint?"

"Saint George is our patron saint now." Why did I stop for these people? "King Edward made the change about fifteen years ago."

A man with enormous ears steps forward. He is elderly for a commoner, probably in his sixth decade, at least. "I told you, didn't I, James? I told you it was Saint George. No one listens to an old man, though, do they?"

"No!" One of the pilgrims shouts in horror. "*No!*"

"It was bound to happen," Tristan calls to the screaming man. "How can a dead king compete with a dragon slayer? Edmund's still a saint. He's just not England's saint. And while we are on the subject, do you know that Sir Edward and I slayed a dragon?"

We did not slay a dragon. We tried to slay one, but we only scared it onto someone else's spear with our cannon fire. Tristan has claimed the kill anyway.

But the pilgrim's shout has nothing to do with dragons or Saint Edmund or Saint George. One of the plaguers in the cage, a tall woman, batters a young man with her hands. The young man snarls at her but cowers against the bars and does not fight back.

"William, you need to bind your wife!" The pilgrim gestures angrily toward the female plaguer. "How long must I suffer this? Look at my poor son's face. Look at him!"

"There's nothing to be done, Henry," William replies. "Just look away."

I turn to James. "Prayer will not help these people. I prayed for my wife at Saint Edmund's shrine for two days without pause, and nothing came of it. Going to that monastery will only bring you death. Return to Wymondham. A cure for this plague exists, and if God wills it, your loved ones will be healed. We will help you free your wagon and you can return home."

James sweeps wet hair from his forehead and sniffs at the air. "Do either of you smell lavender?"

Tristan folds his arms and tucks his hands beneath them. "Let's get this wagon free."

James nods, but hesitates. "You wouldn't... you wouldn't know where Saint George's shrine is, would you?"

James is an idiot. I glance at the pilgrims he leads and shake my head.

Men will follow anyone.

"William!" The pilgrim named Henry points again to the bullying woman in the cage. "She's biting him! Simon's song, she's going to kill him!"

"She's just gnawing, Henry," William replies. "She's doing no real harm."

The old man with the big ears waves to get my attention. "Did you say there is a cure?"

"Yes," I say. "We have seen it."

The pilgrims whisper to one another, cast hopeful glances toward us. One, a tall man with wisps of black hair pasted to his forehead, calls out: "What kind of cure?"

Tristan and I glance at one another. This is where things will fall apart. God and science live in warring kingdoms.

"It is an elixir," I say. "It heals the afflicted and completely removes the plague. Now let's get this wagon free." I walk toward the oxen but no one follows. A silence settles among the pilgrims as they think about what I have said.

"An elixir for the plague?" James says. "Do you think we're fools?"

Tristan nods. "Yes, but he's telling the truth."

The wagon rolls forward two feet, strains and shudders, then rolls back again. The drover shouts that they need to put something into the rut to ease the wheels out. He whips the Devons again drawing more blood and the plaguers in the cage shriek and reach wildly through the bars toward the bleeding beasts.

"A holy elixir?" James asks. "Water blessed by the Pope?"

"Which Pope?" Tristan says with a grin.

I nudge Tristan into silence. He is joking about the great schism that has shaken our Church. Two men have claimed the papacy; Pope Urban VI and Pope Clement VII. I have heard it said that this schism is the cause of our plague. But I have also heard that horse buggery is the cause, so I do not give such talk much credence.

"It is not a holy cure," I say. "The elixir was made by an alchemist."

Gasps rise from among the pilgrims. It is as if I had said Satan made the elixir. The wagon rolls forward, creaks as it rises a few inches, then falls back again.

James tries to speak but can only sputter at first. "Alch… alchemy is a *sin*! We shall not be tempted by such evil!"

"I don't care what you will be tempted by and what you won't," I say. "I only want to free your wagon and continue on my way."

The elderly man with the large ears scratches at his cheek and looks into my eyes. "You say it works? You say the elixir has cured people?"

James turns on the old man. "Shut your mouth, Joseph, lest evil get inside! Alchemists are the devil's monkeys! So sayeth the Lord!"

Tristan shakes his head. "You can't just make up things that the Lord said."

The old man shrugs. "These men said the cure works, so they did. Maybe God sent this elixir. Don't the Bible tell us that 'Every good gift is from above, coming down through the Father of Lights?'"

"So sayeth the Lord," Tristan adds.

"Do not try to twist the word of God, Joseph. Alchemy is a sin. If even one among us falls to temptation, we all fail. We must remain united in our faith."

"I just think we should maybe listen to these young gentlemen, so I do," Joseph replies. "If they know of a cure, it might be—"

One of the pilgrims steps forward, a thick-chested man with a red beard. "Shut that toothless mouth, Joseph. Why must you be so contrary? Always an argument from you. You heard James." He jabs a finger toward the plaguers in the cage. "All the afflicted will be lost if even one of us loses faith."

"I want to cure my Agatha, Martin!" the old man's shout warbles with defiance. "If something can bring her back, then it can't be bad, can it? I love God with all my heart, and if He sends us a gift, who are we to refuse it? 'Can you fathom the mysteries of God? They are higher than the Heavens. They are deeper than the depths of the grave.'" He looks at Tristan and nods curtly. "So sayeth the Lord!"

The old man's feistiness makes me grin. This grizzled wolf is half in the grave, but the hunger for Agatha still burns in his belly.

Martin's face grows redder than his beard. He clenches and unclenches his fists. "You will stop using the words of the Lord to defend Satan's works! I am tired of your mouth, old man! We've had nothing but grief from you since we started. And I'm through with it. Do you hear me?"

Tristan points at the old man's ears and smirks. "I'm fairly certain he hears you."

"This man is an elder," I growl to Martin. "Don't speak to him like that. Show him respect."

A wiry peasant holding a thick walking staff steps forward. "The knight speaks the truth! Leave him alone,

25

Martin. You oughta be ashamed, bringing shouts against an old man."

"It's him should be ashamed, Thomas," Martin says. "He'll bring doom down on all our families!"

James of Wymondham snarls at me, then raises his staff and shouts to the peasants. "Look at yourselves! See what Satan has wrought? This is what these men of Satan want. To drive us apart! Joseph, will you take the apple they offer? Will you side with the Serpent?"

"You obviously don't want our help," I say. "Come, Tristan." I walk past the wagon, looping wide around the reaching arms of the afflicted. The fresh blood from the backs of the oxen has worked the plaguers into a frenzy. The bars creak as more and more bodies push against the front of the cage. Trembling, blood-spattered arms extend toward the animals.

"I wouldn't whip them anymore," Tristan calls to the drover.

The drover whips the oxen one last time and the wagon rises, creaks loudly, then rolls free of the trench. The drover whoops and, at the same moment, terrible shouts rise up from the pilgrims behind us. Shouts so loud and so panicked that Tristan and I draw our swords as we turn.

The pilgrim with the walking stick, Thomas, is on his knees in the mud, staring at the road. Martin, the burly man with the red beard, holds his side with one hand and stares toward the road as well. In fact, all of the gathered pilgrims stare at the same spot—the rut that had trapped the wagon's wheel. And in that rut lies the old man, Joseph. His body has been driven deep into the mud, but his shoulders are propped against the walls of the furrow so that his head juts forward. His eyes are tightly shut, his mouth open in a four-toothed, silent death scream.

I push my way to the body and stare at him like everyone else. It takes a long moment before I can speak. "You... you pushed him under the wagon."

"No," Martin and Thomas both say it as one.

"He hit me with that stick." Martin gestures to Thomas.

"He shoved me!" Thomas replies.

Tristan sheaths his sword and brings his ear to the old man's shattered chest.

James falls to his knees and covers his mouth with one hand. "They... they were pushing and... Martin... he shoved Thomas into Joseph..."

And Joseph became traction for the wagon.

Tristan shakes his head slowly and stands. Bile rises at the back of my throat. More humanity gone from the world.

"It was them." James's voice is almost a whisper. He rises to his feet and points a trembling finger at me. "It was their fault. They brought the devil with them!"

Heat rises in my cheeks. I try to calm myself with deep breaths. "We did nothing of the sort."

"They did this!" James's voice grows louder, more confident. "Joseph's blood is on their hands!"

"You're a lunatic," Tristan says. "We had nothing to do with his death."

But the pilgrims make a loose circle around us, scowls on their faces.

"Whoever takes a human life," James shouts, "shall surely be put to death! So sayeth the Lord!"

Tristan draws his sword again and glances at me. "I think He might actually have said that one."

CHAPTER FIVE

"THIS NONSENSE STOPS NOW!" I use my battlefield voice, shouting so loudly that it makes my throat raw. "If you want to know what killed him, then look to yourselves! Your foolish squabbles led to this!"

Thomas points toward us. "It was them," he says. "They did this."

Martin nods. "They are not men, they are demons."

Tristan and I try to back away from the pilgrims but hands shove us forward. They have encircled us.

James raises the crucifix high into the air. "God has punished Joseph for listening to the devil. And now we must cast these demons back to Hell."

A few of the pilgrims shout their agreement, but most just cast wary glances toward us.

"What will you do?" I shout. Rain patters of my breastplate. Thunder rumbles in the distance. "Will you try to kill us? Will that bring Joseph back?"

The two mercenary guards push their way through the crowd and stand beside us. "This ain't right!" one of them shouts. "These men are knights! They didn't kill nobody!"

A man in white robes stoops and digs a flint from the mud. He holds the flint up so everyone can see. "The guards are demons as well! The Lord says all demons must be stoned!"

"Amen!" James shouts.

More pilgrims pry stones from the road. "Death to the demons!" Martin shouts.

"Mary's tits!" shouts the guard. "This is going to be a misery of shit."

"So sayeth the Lord," Tristan calls. He hunches low and raises his sword high.

A flint clatters off the back of Tristan's breastplate. He whirls and glares at the crowd.

"Enough!" I raise my shield and the four of us try to hide behind it. "Back away! No one is going to stone anyone. No more blood will be shed here today. Is that understood?"

Most of the pilgrims still look uncertain, even the ones holding flints. Stones will not harm armored men unless the armored men are on the ground and being bludgeoned. I do not think these pilgrims have the mettle to do such a thing, but I would rather not find out. I balance my sword against my knee and slip my helmet on. Tristan pulls his on as well.

"We're going to shove past them and run," I say. "On my signal."

Tristan shakes his head. "I'm not running from pilgrims, Ed."

"You're not going to kill any of them," I reply. "No one else dies today."

A scream slices through the rainy afternoon like a shard of broken glass through parchment. I turn toward the wagon.

"Stupid son of a whore!" Tristan shouts.

"Almighty Father," says one of the guards.

Henry, the pilgrim whose son was being bullied in the cart, has opened the cage door. A river of plaguers tumble from the wagon onto the muddy road. Some of them have already gotten to their feet. And three of these are fighting over Henry. They tear at him with teeth and nails. His linen robes rip loudly. Blood spatters onto the wagon in a red spume. Two of the pilgrims rush to Henry's side—their shouts sounding flat in the rainy afternoon—and try to pull the plaguers off. But they too get swallowed by the afflicted wave.

Tristan smacks the guards' horses with his gauntleted hands and the animals run, snorting, toward the south.

"Get the door!" I shout. "Get the door!" But it is too late for that. There are a dozen plaguers outside the cart and more stumbling free. A half-dozen of them gather around the oxen and leap like hunting dogs on bears. The Devons roar and buck, then lope forward dragging the cart with them. Plaguers throw their arms around the necks of the beasts and drag along the road, teeth tearing strips of flesh from the panicked oxen.

"The wagon!" James chases the cart down the road and is knocked off his feet by the plagued woman who was bullying Henry's boy.

I run to his side but I am not fast enough. The woman bites off a strip of James's scalp. He screams wildly and beats at her as my sword shaves off a quarter of her skull. She looks at me with eyes of angry nothingness and chews, brain and blood glistening above her brows. Locks of James's hair poke out from her mouth like half eaten spiders. I swing again and this time she falls back and stops chewing. James screams again and again. His hands touch his scalp and when he sees the blood on them his screams grow louder. There is nothing for him now except pain and the slow onset of plague. I drive my sword through his throat and pray that Saint Giles gives him peace.

A pilgrim stumbles away from me and collapses onto the road. "He... he killed James! *He killed James! The knight killed Father James!*"

"I had to!" I shout, but my voice is drowned out by other pilgrims taking up the call.

"The knight killed James!"

"I had no choice, you stupid bastards," I shout. "He was going to plague or bleed to death."

But I cannot press my argument because a wave of plaguers lumber toward us. Most of the pilgrims scream and run northward. An old woman trips and splashes heavily upon the road. She raises a hand toward me as a bald plaguer with thick black brows takes hold of her hair. I leap forward and Saint Giles sends him home. I have no time to help the woman to her feet. Three more plaguers reach me. Their teeth clack against my armor. Their hands pull at my helm.

Tristan's sword flashes at my side. He has his own plaguer problems. One of the guards lies a few feet away, his mail coat pulled up, his hand twitching as the afflicted tear at his stomach.

A fat man with a leather apron throws his arms around my head. His face is gray and spotted with red boils. The man's blood-stained mouth grows larger and larger until the jaws latch on either side of my visor. Teeth grate against metal as he gnaws. Another plaguer gets beneath my shield and takes hold of my arm. I feel pressure against the mail at my wrist and gasp. Elizabeth dies if this creature gets its teeth under my gauntlet.

I drop my sword and roar. Draw my dagger and drive it up through the fat man's chin, into his skull. The jaws stop sawing at my helm. I stab at the plaguer holding my arm as the fat man's body crashes to the ground in a trembling mound of flesh and boils. Two of the afflicted shove at my waist and crack their teeth against my cuisses. I kick one of them—a woman in a long grey dress—and she falls backward onto the road, sending up a spray of brown water. I drive my dagger into the shining, night-river eye of the other—a man with curly blond hair. He convulses and falls twitching to the mud.

A plaguer crawls on hands and knees toward Tristan and he kicks it in the mouth. A half-dozen others kneel in a circle around a pilgrim's body and feed. The remaining guard screams and buries his poleaxe into the side of a plagued man's head. But two other plaguers drag him down. Tristan and I leap at the same time. I grab a wiry man's worn boot and pull him back away from the guard. The plaguer hisses and lashes at me with his hand. I step on his back and use both hands to drive the sword into his cheek as he cranes his neck to face me. The blade splits his cheek with a crack and pins him to the muddy road. His hand claws at the sword, so I step on his neck, pull the sword free, and let Saint Giles taste his brain.

Tristan is on one knee by the soldier, his sword tip in the mud.

"He hurt?" I ask.

Tristan's helm pivots to face me and I can see one of his eyes behind the visor. There is a grim assessment in that eye. He shakes his head softly.

The guard pushes himself to a sitting position and stares at his hand. Blood seeps down from beneath his gauntlet. I think about the plaguer biting at my mail and glance at my wrist to make sure there is no blood on me.

"No," the guard whispers. "No, no." His voice is so low that I can only just about hear the words. He throws off the gauntlet and stares at the torn flesh on his wrist. "Oh, Mother Mary, no." He turns to me, his eyes wide under the rim of the nasal helm. His hands clutch at my tabard. "I don't want to die. Oh, Christ above, I don't want to die."

"I'm sorry." My words hardly rise above a whisper. "I am so terribly sorry."

His breathing is ragged and fast. "I don't want to die." He looks toward the circle of plaguers tearing the pilgrim apart, a few paces away. The rain washes the dead man's blood from their hands as they feed. "I don't want to die."

I put one hand behind his neck and touch his helmet with mine. "You will go to the Lord. You will have peace and eternal reward for your deeds today."

His head jerks away from mine. "A cure!" he paws at my tunic again. "You said there was a cure! You said there was a cure! I can be healed. Yes?"

Three cures, nothing more. So precious little.

I touch my breastplate and feel Elizabeth's ampoule poke my chest. Tristan catches my eye and shakes his head. We only have the two left, and the second belongs to Morgan.

"Please, do you have it?" the guard asks. "Do you have the cure?"

My soul withers and rises to my throat as I shake my head. "We have none to give you."

"I have a horse." The guard's head shakes with desperation, his hands tighten around my tabard. "I can go. I can get the cure. Where... where can I find it? *Where?*"

I close my eyes. "Syria, perhaps. Nowhere near, my friend. Nowhere near."

My words murder the hope that lies in the man's eyes. He throws off his helmet and weeps, hands over his face. "Make it swift," he sobs. "Please, make it swift."

I draw my dagger. The rain makes swirling patterns of the plaguer blood on the blade.

We hold life in our hands, but give death, instead.

"Make it swift," he says again.

I drive the blade into his throat and cradle his head as he sputters and chokes. The guard looks into my eyes and clutches my arm. Blood washes from his mouth and over his lip.

And with each death, the world loses a little more humanity.

His hand falls limply onto my breastplate, making the wet metal squeak, but his eyes do not close. His dead gaze pierces me and I wonder if he knows about the ampoule hanging from my neck already. If God has whispered it to him yet.

...a terrible weight for the soul to bear.

I lower my head and listen to the rain beating on my helm.

But there is no time to mourn the man. Tristan jumps to his feet and stares northward.

"Riders," he says.

I look backward. Four mounted knights are stopped on the road, less than a quarter mile to the north. One of them speaks to a fleeing pilgrim who points in our direction.

I stare upward toward the Heavens. "Satan's beard. Sir Gerald's men."

"Tell me that story again, Edward," Tristan says. "You had a cannon pointed at Gerald, a flame inches from the touch hole. What did you do again? I always forget the next part."

CHAPTER SIX

ON OUR JOURNEY SOUTH I have tried to avoid roads whenever possible, but the rain has made marshes of the countryside. We have no choice but to seek a dry path. Sir Gerald is aware of my ultimate goal, so he knows where to search for me. He will follow me all the way to St. Edmund's Bury. I am certain that he would have entered the monastery there already and killed Elizabeth, if not for the sea of plaguers circling the abbey walls. She is an angel, and the Lord protects his angels. There is no army in England mightier than the one God has stationed around my Elizabeth.

But that army is in St. Edmund's Bury and we are here. And Gerald's men are on their way.

I glance to the south. The horses that belonged to the guards mill on the grass a few hundred paces away. I pick up the dead man's discarded helm, then slip the mail coif off his head and unfasten the black traveling cloak. Tristan watches me, then nods and finds the other dead guard. He kills two plaguers to get to the man's helmet, coif and cloak, and we run for the horses.

A mass of plaguers feed on the two oxen. One of the animals is still alive. It lies on its side mewing softly, its eyes rolling. I kick a plaguer from its back then slit the ox's throat. The afflicted shriek and bathe themselves in the gush of blood. They drink as if from a fountain of wine.

A plagued man with broken spear lodged in his shoulder reaches for me and I finish the work that the spearman began. The man falls backward, his throat shredded by my blade.

The splatter of hooves on mud grows louder as the knights gallop toward us. Tristan and I approach the horses belonging to the mercenaries. The long-legged geldings back away from us as we approach. I yank the reins of the nearest one and pull myself into the saddle, hang the dead guard's helmet from a metal hook in the leather. Tristan leaps onto the other horse and we wheel the animals south before driving our spurs into their flanks.

And they run.

Two of the knights stop at the wagon, but the other two give chase. Tristan motions to me and slows, then turns to face our pursuers.

"We don't have time for a fight," I shout. "And the cannons won't fire in the rain."

He unslings the crossbow from his back.

"The string is wet, Tristan!"

"I wrapped the bow in one of Elizabeth's scarves," he replies.

My heart aches at the sound of her name. His Elizabeth, not mine.

He must have kept the bowstring cocked since our forest run, for he slips a bolt into the groove, raises the weapon to his shoulder, and sights one of the approaching knights. When they are within two hundred paces he fires. The bolt wavers in the air and falls miserably short.

"Your damned bowstring is wet, Tristan!" I slap the reins, kick back my heels and my gelding races southward. Tristan follows.

"Silk," he shouts, "is not a proper barrier to water!"

I do not answer him. The knights are too close behind us now to speak. I hunch low in the saddle and snap the reins again. My horse thunders along the Roman road, sending up daggers of mud behind and gouts of white breath ahead. Tristan rides behind and to my right, slapping his horse's flank.

The knights slow their horses after a mile or so and turn back toward the wagon, but Tristan and I do not stop. We run the horses for another mile, then slow to a trot. My gelding tosses its head and blows but I will not allow it rest yet.

Tristan twists in his saddle to look back. "They just gave up."

"They don't want to pull too far from their friends. They must have been the vanguard of Gerald's force." I thank Saint Giles and the Virgin Mary. If they are the vanguard, then Gerald is behind us. I had feared that he would ride south quickly and beat us to St. Edmund's Bury. But I do not think he has. Sir Gerald is behind us, and now nothing stands between me and my angel.

Nothing but a thousand bloody plaguers around the walls of the abbey. I wonder if God might call off his army long enough for me to get through.

"Edward?"

I follow Tristan's gaze southward. Something moves on the southern road. I take my horse onto the wet grass and give it the rest it has earned.

"Can you make it out?" I ask. Tristan's eyes have always been better than mine.

"Looks like a cart," he says. "A small one."

"Is there a bloody fair somewhere?" I ask. "This road holds a damned nuisance of carts." I watch the cart for a time. It is small, so there cannot be many men on it. No riders seem to accompany it. I do not imagine it will pose a threat to us, but I am too close to Elizabeth to take any risks. "We're going to canter past. Do not slow down, do not stop. Just ride past quickly. And when we are past, break into a gallop and get away from them as quickly as possible. Understood?"

"And when they see two armed men bearing down on them, what do you suppose they will do, Edward?"

"They will do nothing," I reply. "Keep your hands on the reins and stay in a swift canter. We may scare them, but they won't risk a fight if we don't bring one to them."

It is a pitiable world we live in now, one in which we must fear the men of reason more than the mindless masses. Perhaps it has always been so.

I take off my helm and bevor and don the mail coif I took from the dead guard. It fits snugly but wool trim along the edges keeps the links from scraping my chin. I tug the nasal helm onto my head and tighten the strap until I can shake my head without the cap rocking. The thick traveling cloak is heavy with rain, but I tie it across my shoulders anyway.

I took the guard's helmet and cloak in case Sir Gerald was waiting for us to the south, but the disguise will be useful here, too. Tristan dons the other guard's cloak, helm and coif and we look at each other. If Gerald questions the men in the cart, they will say they saw two garrison guards riding past, not knights. Gerald may suspect it was us, but there will be uncertainty. And Elizabeth's life may well depend on uncertainty.

My horse grunts when I snap my calf against its flank. I have to whip the damp reins and shout to get the animal walking forward, and it takes a jab of my spurs to make it canter.

We close the distance swiftly. My eyes pick out more details as we near the cart. Two people. One in the wagon bed and one in the driver's box. The one in the wagon bed wears a white robe with the hood pulled up against the rain. A thick blanket is draped over his shoulders. The driver wears a brown cloak with the hood up. It is the same cart I noticed near the mill, where I gave the archer a cure for his son.

Stakes have been affixed along the outside edges of the cart. A forest of stakes pointing in odd directions, so that an advancing plaguer will impale itself no matter what direction it approaches from.

The figure in the back of the cart cranes his neck at the sound of our horses. I think it is a man, although I cannot be sure because his face is obscured by a white veil. Only his eyes are uncovered.

"I don't like the look of that one," Tristan calls. "There's something terribly wrong with him."

The man in the robe speaks to the driver, who hands back a long bundle wrapped in canvas. The veiled figure unwraps the canvas and raises a thick, wooden crossbow to his shoulder.

Tristan veers his horse away from me so we present smaller targets and calls to me, "Canvas is probably better than silk."

"Make way!" I shout at the cart. "Make way!"

The cart drifts to one side of the road and the crossbow follows our approach. I glance at the men as we canter past. The driver wears a leather gambeson under the cloak. The hood shadows his face, but I can see that he is dark and bearded. Perhaps an Italian. Tristan pretends to doff his cap, and we are past.

One of the men in the cart calls to us. "Wait!"

I do not wait. Elizabeth has waited too long already. I lash the reins, shout at my horse, and break into a gallop. I will not wait. I will not stop.

I stop after three miles.

I do not want to stop, but darkness swallows the countryside. Clouds smother the crescent moon and the air becomes blacker than a plaguer's eye. I cannot see the road ahead. My horse stumbles and I realize I can go no farther without risking its life. I consider walking the rest of the way, but it would take me all night and all the next day to reach St. Edmund's Bury—and a battle awaits.

A battle against an army that has neither horses nor spears. Their weapons are sheathed in fingers and lips, and their banners are the tattered shreds of robe and tunic that hang from their rotting bodies. But there is no army in England more dangerous. They are a thousand strong, have a poisonous bite, and do not know fear. They do not rout and they do not surrender. Their war cry trembles with the savage echo of evil, for in their illness they take orders from Satan himself. And if they win, Hell will claim another acre of God's earth.

I do not want a forced march before I face that army, so I will rest tonight and fight every plaguer in St. Edmund's Bury tomorrow if I have to. The saints will rise from their graves and fight at my side. Angels of war will hurl lightning, and God himself will help smite the legions of dead and bring them home to Heaven. For tomorrow I will heal the most beautiful of his creatures.

Tomorrow I will wake my Elizabeth.

Tristan lights one of his firing cords and we use its flickering light to guide our horses off the road. We walk in the dark, our boots sloshing in ankle deep water, the night's chill drawing gooseflesh on my rain-soaked back. There are a cluster of priories and convents on the border of Norfolk and Suffolk, east of the Roman road, and I intend to find one.

It feels like we walk for an eternity before a distant light appears. An orange glow that promises warmth and perhaps food. And most of all, safety. We pick up our pace, tugging at the horses and taking long, hopping steps through the flooded fields.

There are only two structures, but they rise high into the night sky. An abbot once told me that monasteries were built as high as possible to remind the inhabitants that a monk is not bent over, but stands erect before God. And this priory stands taller than anything around it, starkly out of place on this flat, sodden land of marshes.

Smaller wings and apses jut from the lengths of the two buildings giving the impression of many buildings. And every wall is graced with tall, arched and latticed windows.

The lights we noticed come from several of these windows, and from a massive wheel window piercing the highest floor of the tallest building.

Small groups of plaguers mill around the monastery. In these days of plague, the afflicted gather around places of life like flies around dung. Tristan ties his horse's reins to my horse's and we draw our swords. I touch my breastplate and feel the guilty reassurance of Elizabeth's cure. We kill six plaguers quietly, but not quietly enough; more shapes lurch toward us in the darkness. I pound on the door while Tristan uses a windlass to pull back the wet cord of his crossbow. The horses toss their heads and back away from the approaching plaguers.

"I'm beginning to hate abbey doors," he says.

Tristan and I have found ourselves fighting for life outside churches and monasteries too often. But it is not the doors that are the problem.

"I'm beginning to hate slow monks," I say.

Tristan nods his agreement. "So sayeth the Lord."

More and more shapes draw toward us. Men who were once monks. Men who were farmers and haywards. A nun, and a young boy wearing the skirts of infancy. All of them bleeding and rotting, like the victims of a Hellish war. A bald farmer with a nose half torn off gets too close and Tristan fires the crossbow. The string is wet, but the man is only ten feet away and even a water-logged cord can bring death at that distance. The bolt carves through a boil on the man's forehead and buries itself in his skull. The farmer's head snaps backward and he crumples to the ground. Tristan attaches the windlass to the crossbow and begins winding the cord again.

I raise my fist to pound once more upon the oak but a resonant clanking echoes from inside. The towering door creaks open a few inches and a soldier's hard face peers out. "What?" he says.

I motion toward the mass of afflicted staggering toward us. "What do you think?"

The man sighs and watches Tristan miss a plagued nun with his next shot. I step forward and drive the tip of Saint Giles's sword through her eye socket, then kick her lifeless body backward.

"Alright," the soldier says. "Inside, quickly."

CHAPTER SEVEN

THE ABBEY IS FULL OF MEN, women and children. It is the same throughout England. The houses of God have become the houses of man, and while monks may stand upright before Him, the families I see do not. They slouch and stare downward, huddle together and cast prayers toward the floor. I would pity them, but most of the families look complete. Husbands hold wives, and I envy them.

The abbot is named Peter and he does not look into our eyes when he speaks. Monks are an odd breed. Mother Mary is the only woman they are allowed, so Jesus becomes the hunger in their bellies.

The abbot rings a hand bell and tells us there is little food at the abbey, and no beds available. A young postulant holding a basket trots down the long gallery hallway and bows to us. I take a loaf of raveled bread from the basket and thank Abbot Peter for the safety of his walls.

Tristan and I follow the postulant back along the gallery, leading our geldings. A monastery is no place for a horse, but horses are worth more than silver these days, and I need mine to reach Elizabeth. We leave our steeds to graze in the cloisters and find an empty corner of the dormer to sleep in.

I dream that night of armies clashing. The forces of Heaven and Hell meeting in a seminal battle, and England is the prize. But in the dream I cannot tell which side is which.

Cannons with demon mouths erupt, three quick bursts, and the battle begins. I am caught in the middle of the battlefield. Another three cannons shake the skies and the armies rage toward one another. I crouch and cover my head as the next cannonade fires. And as the armies collide, I wake and take deep gulps of air.

The cannons erupt once more. Four, five, six bursts. I do not know how the cannons from my dream can follow me back to the abbey. It takes a moment for sleep to fall away completely and for me to realize the sound is not cannons, but a pounding on the monastery doors.

Tristan is already on his feet, buckling his sword. I do the same and, with a glance at our armor on the floor, we hurry down the stairs and through the galley hallway that leads to the great double doors.

The door is partly open when we arrive. The soldier that allowed us into the abbey peers out. Abbot Peter is behind him, rubbing his fingertips together and trying to see through the small opening. A dozen sleepy families watch from their makeshift beds along the gallery.

"What about him?" the soldier says to someone outside. "Is he plagued?"

I can only make a few words of a reply from beyond the door. "... fine! ... sake! ... the door!" Snarls ring out from outside. The voice grows much louder. "We. Are. Going. To die!"

The soldier glances at Peter, who shrugs. The door opens and two men stumble inside. They turn and drive their shoulders into the door as hands reach through. They are the men who we passed earlier, on the cart. Tristan and I push past Peter as the soldier jabs at the afflicted with a shortspear. The weight of the plaguers drives the door open further. Two of the afflicted slip inside: A tall man with a leather cap tied under his chin, and a naked woman. Tristan and I drive our swords into the man's stomach at the same time, then realize our mistake.

"I'll get the woman," I say. But Tristan is already drawing his sword out of the man's belly and our blades clang as we both stab her. He laughs but the situation is not humorous. Both plaguers are still alive and we have no armor. The man's hands clamp around my left arm. I drive my sword into his mouth with such force that the tip drives through the back of his skull.

Tristan swings his blade with two hands and knocks the woman into me. I slip on blood and fall to one knee, my sword still in the man's mouth. Tristan hacks at the woman again and again. Blood everywhere. I leverage the male plaguer to the ground and put my foot on his throat. He flails at me with his hands and catches me in the side of the head. I grunt and drive the sword with both hands at his forehead. The blade skips off bone and gouges his temple, so I plunge my sword down again and finally break through the skull. His legs kick once, then he is still.

I glance at Tristan. He is blood spattered and panting, but unharmed.

"Now that was a storm of shit," he says.

Peter glares at him. I shake my head and gesture with my chin toward the watching children. Tristan covers his mouth. "My apologies," he calls to them. "It was a storm of ships. Like a tempest at sea. That's what I intended."

Someone chuckles behind me. "That's what I *meant*."

Tristan and I spin around so quickly that a spot of blood is fired from my tunic and splatters the door. I look at the man before me. "Zhuri?"

"My friends!" Zhuri shouts. "I was certain that was you on the Roman road!"

"God's mighty penis!" Tristan embraces him with one arm, holding his bloodstained sword at a distance. Peter hisses at the words, but I do not think Tristan hears it. "How did you find us?"

The man in the white robe and veil finally speaks. "We followed the sounds of blasphemy."

The abbey seems to spin around me. I stumble backward and look carefully at the man who has spoken. "That's... that's not possible."

Tristan's sword falls jangling to the stone floor. He touches his mouth with one hand. "How... what..."

The man removes his veil. The skin of his face is broken in places by shining red wounds, and laced with black streaks. The side of his jaw is one long, healing sore, but he grins anyway.

Tristan looks as unsteady as I do. He places both hands on his head. "Morgan?"

Sir Morgan laughs. "It seems the Lord is done testing me."

Life has come from death. The world has gained humanity.

Morgan is cured.

"Hallelujah!" Zhuri shouts.

Episode Two

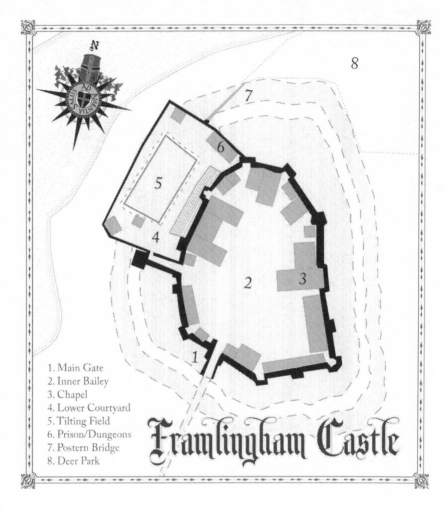

8

7

6

5

4

3

2

1

1. Main Gate
2. Inner Bailey
3. Chapel
4. Lower Courtyard
5. Tilting Field
6. Prison/Dungeons
7. Postern Bridge
8. Deer Park

Framlingham Castle

CHAPTER EIGHT

"HOW?" I THROW MY ARMS around Morgan and embrace
my old friend. "How are you healed?"

Morgan groans and pulls away from my embrace. "Still
healing," he says, wincing.

Zhuri grins a wolfish smile and opens his mouth to
speak, but Peter herds us out of the galley. The Moor tries
to speak to me once more as we walk but Peter speaks first.

"You must be hungry," he says. "Come with me to the
refectory. We don't have much, but we can take the edge
off your hunger." His voice is taut. He glances back toward
the gaping faces of the huddled families in the galley, then
shoves us onward as servants come to clean the blood from
the foyer. I believe Father Peter is more concerned with
Tristan's cursing than with our hunger.

The briny scent of stew greets us as we enter the sparse
refectory. The other monks are already at the table, eating a
leek pottage and black bread while scripture is read to them.
I am not certain how early it is, but I imagine they have just
finished matins, the first service of the day, which is
practiced two hours after midnight.

The monk reading scripture falls silent as we take seats
at the long, bare table. I smile at Morgan. I cannot stop
smiling.

Morgan has been returned to us.

He was afflicted because of me. Because I chose to involve him in this quest. A plagued animal bit him and he spiraled into the darkness. We were forced to leave him in a black cellar, at a convent in Hedingham, and Zhuri was his only light. The Moor stayed behind to watch over him while Tristan and I continued to St. Edmund's Bury.

We left Morgan in a cellar, like a wild dog, and the thought of him in that dark place weighed upon me like a dragging anvil. Like God's finger pinning my tabard to the soil.

But he is healed.

Perhaps I am being forgiven for the countless sins I have committed on my journey. I do not feel forgiven, but a ray of God's light has broken through the clouds.

Tristan claps Morgan on the back and the old knight winces.

"Heaven's gate, Tristan!" Morgan shouts. "My entire body is an open wound!"

Tristan laughs and fills Morgan's bowl to the brim with leek stew.

"What is that smell?" Zhuri asks. "Like some sort of flower."

"It's lavender." I smile at Tristan.

"I don't smell anything." He scoops out more stew.

"One ladle only, please!" Father Peter says. "We do not have much."

"This man has come back from the dead," Tristan replies. "I hardly think Jesus was restricted to one ladleful when He came back, do you?"

Peter hisses and the other monks cast angry glances at Tristan.

"Tristan!" Morgan shouts. "You are in God's house!"

"Well, God should keep His pantry better stocked."

One of the monks stands, his chair groaning across the wooden floor, and jabs a finger angrily toward Tristan.

"You have offended Father Jacobus," says Peter.

Tristan smirks. "Are your monks under vows of silence?"

"They're not monks," Morgan replies. "They're Premonstratensians."

Peter nods agreement, and Tristan barks a laugh that makes him snort. "You just made that word up. Admit it."

I know Morgan is not making it up. He is a second son, and so was sent to the priesthood when he came of age. When his older brother died, Morgan gave up the cloth and took up the sword.

"Premonstratensians," Morgan says, "are canons. Priests living under Saint Augustine's Rule."

"And they can't talk?" Tristan asks.

"Most can," Peter says. "But mine have taken vows of silence. They will not speak until God has lifted this scourge from the land."

"It's not a scourge," I say. "It's a plague. Archbishop Hartley is calling it a plague now."

Peter shrugs. "Plague or scourge. They are the same, are they not?"

Tristan holds up a hand and squints. "So God will notice that your monks aren't talking and suddenly decide to lift this plague?"

"They're not monks," Morgan says.

"Have you ever considered a vow of silence, Morgan?" Tristan replies.

"Their silence is a sacrifice," says Peter. "A show of devotion. If these devout men do not utter a word for one full year, do you not think God will notice? How can He overlook such sacrifice? I only wish more people were as devoted. Perhaps God would have lifted this curse already."

Morgan crosses himself. "You speak truly and righteously, Father Peter."

Tristan looks as if he is going to speak, but Zhuri interrupts them with an impatient wave of his hand. "Listen!"

Everyone quiets. Morgan and the Moor exchange grins. Zhuri extends a closed fist, palm up, and opens it. Inside is a ceramic ampoule with Arabic writing upon it. He laughs, shifts in his seat with excitement. "Do you have any idea what I hold in my hand?"

Tristan studies the object carefully. "Judging from the ceramic used and the shape of the ampoule, I would say it's some sort of cure for this plague. And based on the style of that writing, I assume it has come from Syria."

Zhuri's smile vanishes. "How could..."

Tristan holds up his ampoule—an exact copy of the one Zhuri holds.

"Where did you get that?" Morgan asks.

"The more important question," I say, "is where did you get yours?"

Morgan pours most of his stew back into the kettle and jerks his head toward Zhuri. "He can tell it better. I wasn't there. Besides, I get too angry when I talk about it."

I look to Zhuri, who puts the ampoule away and brings a bowl of stew to his lips. He slurps, then wipes at his mouth with a sleeve. "Gregory the Wanderer."

Of course.

Gregory the Wanderer. It could only have been him. An old man who steals relics from churches and sells them. I was told that he traded with a ship's captain from Syria for the cure to this plague, then traded a few batches of this cure to the alchemist. I recovered three of the cures from the alchemist's workshop, after he was murdered by monks.

Gregory is the source of all the Syrian ampoules we have found. But the old man had something else that he claimed could cure the plague. Phials of a liquid that he traded to us when we first met him. But those phials did not contain a cure at all; they contained plaguer blood. And through our good intentions, we infected an entire village. Morgan had fallen in love with a woman in that village, and Gregory's cure took her away.

Tristan ladles out more stew and pours it into Morgan's bowl. "You need nourishment," he says. "I don't want to argue with you while you are feebleminded with hunger. It's less fair than usual."

"Gregory the Wanderer," Zhuri repeats. "The old bastard drove…" He pauses and holds up a warding hand to the scowling canons. "The old *man* drove his wagon directly up to the convent. Wanted to trade with us."

Father Jacobus smacks Tristan's hand and the ladle drops into the kettle before yet another serving of stew can be drawn out.

"Zhuri should have blown that old thief's head…" Morgan looks at the priests and clears his throat. "He should have captured the old man and held him at the convent until justice could be delivered."

"Which is what I had set out to do," Zhuri adds. "I recognized Gregory's wagon from your description and loaded my hand cannon. Sister Margaret let him in, and the moment he stepped off his wagon I put the barrel to his forehead."

The pottage glugs and splashes as Morgan again pours some of it back into the kettle.

"And what did Gregory do?" I ask.

Zhuri shrugs and tears a chunk from a loaf of black bread. "Not much. I will give him his due. He looked at the cannon and asked me if it was a gun. I told him to shut his mouth and prepare to go to his God. Sister Margaret tried to make me put the weapon away, but I had sworn to be Morgan's protector, and to take on all debts and debtors. And this Gregory person owed Morgan a life."

"I wish I had been there," Morgan shakes his head. Tears brim in his eyes, and I know he is thinking of his Matilda. "I wish I had been there."

"So you killed him?" I ask.

"The old man looked directly into my eyes… well, looked with one eye, the other was staring toward Sister

Margaret. And he said, 'If you give me that cannon, I will give you a cure for this plague.'"

"And you believed him?" Tristan asks.

"Absolutely not," Zhuri replies. "I remembered about the last cure. The phials full of plaguer blood. And I reminded him of that. I said that his cure was the reason I was going to blow a hole in his ugly, wrinkled..." He pauses and gives the priests a tiny bow. "Ah... the reason I was going to imprison him in the convent and... wait until... until justice could be delivered."

"But this one was a real cure, Edward," Morgan says. "Zhuri had nothing to lose, as I was plagued already. He made the old man give me the cure and waited until I was healed before handing over his cannon. And he asked for a second ampoule. For Elizabeth." His eyes drift down toward the table. "I... I am truly sorry about your lady, Edward. I have prayed for her every night since I received the news."

"Your prayers have been answered," I say. "We have the cure." I look to Zhuri and give him a solemn nod. "Thank you, Zhuri, for thinking of my Elizabeth."

Zhuri returns the nod, a twitch of a smile tugging at his lips. He is proud of himself, and he should be.

The priests exchange glances with one another. Father Peter stares from one to the next, making subtle calming motions with his hands. We should not have spoken of the cures so openly. But I am beyond caution. Morgan is back, and Elizabeth will be in my arms soon.

I sit forward in my chair and address Zhuri. "When you gave him the cure, how did it happen? How long did it take?"

Zhuri chews a mouthful of bread, swallows. "Thirty breaths, Edward," he replies. "Thirty breaths before Morgan returned. It took four nuns and the porter to hold him down. I poured the elixir down his throat and held his mouth shut while he bucked like a wild horse. But I held on.

I watched the black of his eyes drain away to red, then white. His thrashing slowed. His breathing grew more regular. Then... then he spoke."

Tristan takes hold of the ladle again and draws out more pottage. "Did he speak fondly of me?"

Father Jacobus grabs Tristan's wrist.

Morgan closes his eyes.

"It was just one word," The Moor's gaze falls to the table.

I know the word.

It is the hunger that burns in Morgan's belly, and I am responsible for its absence. I am responsible for the absence of so many words. But Morgan's word did not need to die. There is a cure, but we did not know of it, so we erased his word from the world.

Tristan tries to pull his arm out of Father Jacobus's grip. The priest loses his balance and falls forward, upending the kettle. The priests leap to their feet and pull back from the benches as the green stew sweeps across the table and down in thick streams to the wooden planks.

Father Jacobus, his face red and trembling, points a hooked finger at Tristan and shouts, "Damned fool!"

A chorus of hisses erupts from the other priests. They point at Jacobus, who places both hands over his mouth.

"Damnable fool," Zhuri says into the silence.

Morgan does not move. He shakes his head softly and whispers.

"Matilda."

CHAPTER NINE

THE OTHERS MAKE THEIR WAY to the dormer after the meal, but I cannot sleep, so I wander the old monastery building. I find myself in the nave of the great church. It is a long, three-storied chamber, each floor defined by arches that rise toward the Heavens, moonlight streaming in shafts through dozens of windows. I straighten my shoulders and walk toward the carved screen that hides the high altar. Only priests are allowed in the east end of abbey churches, so I kneel on the cold stones before the wooden screen and say a prayer to Saint Giles and the Virgin.

Morgan is healed.

Zhuri saw it happen.

If I had any doubts that the cure is real, they are gone now. The Syrian elixir works and my Elizabeth will return to me.

What happened to the alchemist's wife was a mistake. Perhaps a bad seal on the ampoule made the tincture spoil. Maybe something corrupted the ceramic before the serum was added. Just a mistake. A mistake not likely to occur twice.

Nothing bad will happen when I give Elizabeth the cure. I have no doubts.

I pull on the cord around my neck and draw the ampoule out, study it closely to make certain the wax seal has not been damaged.

Elizabeth will be healed. The black of her eyes will fade—a stormy night chased away by the rising sun—and summer blue will rule my world forever.

I have no doubts.

"You should rest, Sir Edward." Father Peter's voice echoes through the nave. "The soul needs sleep to thrive."

"My soul cannot rest, Father," I reply. "It is plagued. And only my wife's smile can heal it."

He walks to my side, his soft shoes scuffling along the stones, white robes swishing side to side. "The cures. You have three of them, then?"

I rise to my feet and consider lying to him, but if God still listens to the voices of man, then it is priests who will be granted audience. And I need help to save His fairest angel.

"Yes," I say. "Three."

Peter's gaze wanders across the face of the divider. "And where did these cures come from?"

I clear my throat to buy myself time. This is where things fall apart. God and science live warring kingdoms.

"An alchemist," I say.

The priest nods, his gaze never straying from the screen. "It is said alchemists and sorcerers are unclean. That their works are the works of the devil."

"So sayeth the Lord."

"And will this alchemist make more of these cures?"

I shake my head. "The alchemist that made this cure is from Syria. And Syria burns."

Father Peter looks at me, then gazes back at the divider. Crowns and ivy and fleur-de-lis are carved into the wood.

"Christ was an alchemist," Peter says.

They are odd words, and I study the priest.

"Water to wine, no?" He grins without looking at me. "It can also be said that Moses was a sorcerer. Who but a sorcerer could part an ocean? Or turn a staff into a snake?" He runs his fingers along the screen. "If this scourge was

God's doing, then only God can undo it. And if this cure heals the afflicted, then God wants us to have it."

"If only everyone thought as you do," I reply.

"Will you find another sorcerer to make more of these cures?"

I shrug. "I don't know any other sorcerers."

He looks at me then, no trace of humor in his features. "I want you to promise that you will save one of those ampoules, and that you will give it to someone who can reproduce it."

I look into the priest's eyes and nod. "I promise."

He shakes his head. "No, do not make your oath to me."

He grasps the edge of the screen and drags it to one side so that the high altar—and the tall silver crucifix that hangs above it—are visible in the moonlight. "Promise Him. Promise our Lord and Savior that you will have as many of these made as possible. That you will distribute them across England. Promise Him. Fulfill that promise, and they will make you a saint."

I grin at the last words. Saint Edward. Elizabeth's eyes would roll for eternity.

"It would fill me with joy to find someone who could make more of these cures, Father. But I don't know where to look. And no one will help me. I find that my greatest obstacle is not the afflicted, but the healthy. Have you been out there Father? Men have become like animals. King Richard is either dead or in hiding. We carve ourselves tiny kingdoms and wage war. God is wielded like a weapon, His words used to kill and torture. We have lost our humanity."

The priest is silent for a long moment, perhaps mulling my words. When he speaks, his voice is low and sober. "The founder of our order spoke an ancient line of wisdom once, about the world outside the monastery: 'As often as I have been amongst men, I have returned less a man.' It is as applicable now as it was then. Men have always been animals. Humanity is the triumph of will over instinct."

It is my turn to think about his words.

"I am one of those men, Father. I have warred and sinned and caused great misery. I have killed healthy men and I have killed men afflicted by this plague. I have sinned more than I can recount."

He lets out a long breath. "Well, stop it."

He grins and I smile, but the scars on my soul ache.

The priest rests a hand on my arm. "I see repentance in your heart. You are ready to be forgiven. I believe God is guiding you, and I believe He wants to redeem you." The priest glances toward the altar, gazes at Jesus on the silver cross. "And I believe you are England's last hope."

"England is doomed." My grin is a brief one.

"God has shown you the truth. The afflicted are not demons. They are sick. They must be protected and healed. They are not to be slaughtered, Edward."

"Sometimes they must be slaughtered," I say.

The priest shakes his head. "You would not slay a madman would you? Or an imbecile?"

I blow out long breath. "Only when there was no other choice."

"Only when there is no other choice," he confirms. We sit in silence for a time before he speaks again. "Your salvation is within reach. Protect the afflicted, Edward. And put the cure in the proper hands."

"And where will I find these proper hands?" I ask.

"On the proper person," he replies with a smile. I fix him with a stare and he grows sober. "God gave you the cure, Sir Edward. It is you who must find that person."

"God should be more selective."

He points toward the crucifix. "Make your promise."

I kneel on the cold stones again and clasp my hands, stare at a poor carpenter hanging from a cross, and I make my oath.

We rise at the first hint of dawn and help the priests distribute bread to the families that have made the monastery their home. Tristan lets children try on his gauntlets and both his helms. The children adore his silliness. They trail after him in a long line around the monastery for the rest of the morning.

I give Morgan the jar of Malta fungus and tell him to apply it to his wounds. He argues at first and recoils from the foul smelling substance, but I threaten to have Tristan hold him down and do it myself, so he relents.

We break our fast with a loaf of hard bread and a cup of wine, then Tristan and I brush down our horses in the cloisters.

"There is that smell again," Zhuri says. "Like a woman wearing flowers in her hair."

"We're in the cloisters, Zhuri," Tristan says. "There are flowers all around us. Why would you think the smell was coming from one of us?"

Zhuri tilts his head and studies Tristan. "I never said I thought it was coming from one of us."

"How long will it take to reach St. Edmund's Bury?" Morgan asks.

"It's about thirty-five miles to the monastery." I set the saddle on my horse's back and work at the girth. "Six or seven hours at any rate."

"It'll take a bit longer than that," Morgan replies. "Our cart is not very fast."

I drape the saddlebags and work the straps that bind them to the saddle. "No, brother, it will be six or seven hours. You and Zhuri are going to Sussex." I look up at him. "Your daughter waits for you there, Morgan. I thought I orphaned her before and I won't take that risk again."

Morgan stares at me for a long time, then he lunges forward and takes hold of the saddlebags, hurls them to the ground.

"Morgan what—"

"*How dare you?*" he shouts.

No reply comes to my mind. I simply stare at him.

"How dare you?" he shoves me backward and my horse shifts nervously, its hooves scraping dully on the stone. "Zhuri and I drove that bloody cart all over Suffolk and Norfolk looking for you! Every rut or stone we hit was agony to me, Edward, but we never relented. We rode to Bure, then Norwich, then a monastery in the middle of a damnable swamp looking for you. We have ridden for four days so that we could find you and help save Lady Elizabeth. And now you have the *hocks* to send us home? I swore an oath of fealty to you, Edward. *Fealty!*" The shouts ring in the cloisters. A startled sparrow flutters out from an old oak. "You have dragged me clear across England to find your wife and, oath or no oath, I will *not* go home now, when only thirty miles separates you from her. I will not go home! Do you hear me? I will *not* go home! *How dare you!*"

"Sussex sounds nice, actually," Zhuri says.

"I'm sorry," I try to suppress a smile. "Morgan, we would be honored to have your company on our journey. Would you like to accompany us to St. Edmund's Bury?"

He glowers and crosses his arms. "No I bloody wouldn't. But you can't stop me."

"Nor will I try again." I look into his eyes so he can see my sincerity. "Thank you, Morgan."

"You're bloody welcome."

We ride double across the fens of Norfolk, our horses sloshing though calf-deep water. It takes time to find the stable where Morgan and Zhuri stowed their cart and horse. In the end, we simply follow the sounds of snarling. A crowd of plaguers shuffles around the dingy wooden structure.

"I count eleven," I say. "Let's find an easy place to defend and draw them in." I speak the words instinctively, then remember my conversation with Father Peter.

Morgan shakes his head. "Edward, those are people."

Tristan scoffs. "They're plaguers, Morgan."

"They are people," Morgan replies. "People who can be healed."

"If we had a cure," Tristan replies. "Those people will never be healed. They will wander like that until they rot. Is that truly what you want for them?"

"It doesn't matter what I want, Tristan," he says. "What matters is what God wants. And God said 'thou shalt not kill.'"

"Yes," Tristan replies. "But he was speaking figuratively."

The afflicted are not demons. I made an oath to a crucified God, and so I must defend the victims of this plague. I must become champion of the dead.

"No, Morgan's right," I say. "These are people."

"People who want to eat us," Tristan replies. "People standing between us and Elizabeth."

Tristan has fought at my side for two decades. He knows my weaknesses.

I cannot go to Elizabeth while these people surround the stable. And truly, what are a dozen more lives in this ocean of death? I touch the hilt of my sword, the leather worn and hard by years of use.

I made an oath.

"No," I say. "They are people. And we're not going to kill them. Humanity is the triumph of will over instinct."

Tristan sighs. "And death is the triumph of instinct over humanity. So what do you suggest, Ed?"

"I'm going to reason with them."

Tristan laughs, then sees I am serious. "Reason with them?"

Zhuri shakes his head. "There is no reasoning with the dead, Edward."

"They're only figuratively dead, Zhuri." I ride toward the shed, shouting at the afflicted. "You'll never get in there! Come at me instead! Come feed!"

It takes a moment for the plaguers to acknowledge my existence. They turn to face me, a few at a time. One peels itself from the stable wall and staggers toward me. Then another. Within moments every one of them lurches in my direction.

I lead them from the stable, around a patch of alders and through a field of turnips. Plaguers are lazy. They will not chase prey over long stretches, so I ride slowly and circle back close to them several times. When I am a hundred paces from the stable, I glance back. The wagon is outside. Tristan and Zhuri are hitching the horse. We have our cart and God has His peace.

A triumph for humanity.

CHAPTER TEN

MORGAN'S BLOODY CART MIRES itself every hundred paces or so along the marshy grasslands of southern Norfolk. Tristan and I must dismount each time and shove until the lumbering thing pulls free. It is a muddy, tiresome routine that slows us down and makes me anxious. Morgan insists he can ride, but I do not believe him. His skin, though healing, is still raw and new blood soaks through the white robes he wears. I give him ointment to apply to his wounds, but not even Malta fungus will heal him quickly. He should be resting. Mending at the Hedingham convent, not traveling across a plague-swept England.

Our floundering pace through the fenland is vexing, but it is not my biggest concern. My biggest concern is knowing that if we are to make it to St. Edmund's Bury with the cart, we will have to travel upon main roads. And that is a grave problem, because Sir Gerald knows our destination. Our only chance of avoiding him is by skirting roads. If we had no cart, we could approach through Thetford Forest and slip into the city at night. But Morgan has paid a higher price than any of us on this quest. He has every right to be there at the end.

We reach an old trail heading southwest and set the cart upon it. It is a worn path, thick with half-buried flints. It will not be a comfortable ride, but the ground is dry. A thick mist smolders around us, sapping color from the world.

Tristan rides beside the cart. Morgan watches him for a time, then points to the cross dangling from the knight's neck.

When we were at Hedingham, moments before the plague took Morgan, he hung the cross around Tristan's neck and spoke: "When you find your faith, this will protect you."

The carved wooden symbol is said to be made from the True Cross, upon which Jesus was crucified. Morgan traded with Gregory the Wanderer for the relic. He gave the old man a fully barded warhorse in return for the cross and a few other artifacts. At the time I thought him a fool for making such a trade, but I have seen Morgan perform miracles with that cross. Repelling plaguers. Breaking a charge of mounted knights. Tristan would say they were coincidences. But I have witnessed coincidences, and I have never felt the touch of God in them. I felt that touch when Morgan wielded his cross.

Tristan looks down at the relic, draws it off his neck and tosses it to Morgan.

"I hope it helped," Morgan says. "Did you find your faith, Tristan?"

"Yes," he replies. "Turns out I had left it at a tavern. Went back the next day and there was my faith, still on the table where I'd left it. Damned lucky no one walked off with it."

"Always joking," Morgan replies. "You try to hide behind your humor, Tristan. You think it will shield you from His sight. But God sees everything. He watches everything you do and everything you say."

"It seems to me that God isn't the most efficient of creatures," Tristan replies. "Why watch everything? If He can see anything, then why not just watch the interesting parts?"

"You are a damned miscreant," Morgan says.

"And you are faithful and devout?" Tristan asks.

"I try to be."

"So explain to me, Morgan, how you can accept the fact that an alchemist cured you."

"Tristan." I growl the word.

"It's fine, Edward," Morgan shrugs his great shoulders. "It's a fair question." He looks at Tristan. "I did not make the decision. All I can do is accept the path that God has shown me, and to do as much good as I can with the additional time He has given me."

Tristan scoffs. "But He didn't give you extra time. A magic elixir did. A sorcerer conjured you back from the dead."

"Zhuri made the decision," Morgan says. "I cannot be blamed for a decision I had no part in."

The Moor glances back from the driver's platform. "Perhaps I should have left you rotting in the cellar then."

"That's not what I meant…"

"So Zhuri, who thought he was doing good, should be damned, but you, who benefitted from his actions, are innocent."

"Zhuri is not a Christian. It is irrelevant what he did or did not do."

"So I must be Christian to be relevant?"

"You… both of you are twisting my words."

"Leave him be," I say. "I have never met a more devout man than Morgan of Hastings."

Morgan nods several times. "Thank you, Edward."

I nod back. "The poor man is reduced to wearing leper robes. Must you insult him as well?"

"Maybe he is a leper," Tristan says. "Morgan, are you leper?"

"These are not leper robes!" Morgan snaps. "They are clerical vestments. I thought you were on my side, Edward."

"Remember when those plaguers turned away from Morgan, Ed?" Tristan asks. "And you said it was the power of the relic? Maybe it wasn't the cross. Maybe they turned away because he's a leper."

"Shut that arse in your face, Tristan," Morgan snaps. "I am not a leper."

"Leave him be," I say. "Morgan has returned to us from the dead and the two of you are tormenting him."

"Let them laugh at me if they wish," Morgan says. "But know that the Lord punishes those who mock. Have you not heard the story of the children who mocked Elisha? 'He went up from there to Bethel, and on his way, some small boys came out of the city and jeered at him, saying, 'Go up, you baldhead! Go up, you baldhead!' He turned around and cursed them in the name of the Lord. And two she-bears came out of the forest and tore forty-two of the boys apart.'"

"So sayeth the Lord," I reply.

"I hope those children learned their lesson," Tristan says. "Perhaps the kind and merciful Lord should have had them tortured first."

Zhuri looks from Morgan to me. "Your God slaughtered forty-two children because they taunted a bald man?"

"Don't be absurd, Zhuri," Tristan replies. "Our God would never slaughter children. He sent two bears to do it."

"I do not understand your religion," Zhuri says. "I thought Christ preached forgiveness and kindness."

"He did," Tristan replies. "Kindness is the most important aspect of Christianity. And if anyone in the community is not kind, they are murdered in horrible ways."

I tell Tristan to ride ahead of us, a half-mile or so, in the hopes his keen eyes will spot any danger before it spots us. But we do not need his eyes; all we need are ears. A horn blares in the distance after we travel a few more miles. Two short blasts, one long. A call for action.

"Get the cart off the road!" I shout.

Zhuri lashes the tired horse. The wagon rattles up the lip of the path and northward, toward a sparse forest. Morgan winces and holds the edge of the bench with both hands. Tristan gallops back to me and reins up, his horse blowing and lifting its forelegs off the ground.

"I couldn't see them," he calls. "But they're close."

I slap my knees against the flanks of my gelding and send him after the cart, with Tristan close behind. We catch up to Zhuri and Morgan and ride alongside until we reach the precipice of the forest. A thick mist rises in coils, like ghostly serpents.

"Hide the cart in there, and stay with our horses." I dismount. "Tristan and I will slip through the forest. Maybe we can get a look at them."

Tristan vaults from his saddle and takes position at my side. Vision is more important than protection right now, so we leave the nasal helmets on instead of donning our great helms. Tristan touches the leather-wrapped hand bombard jutting from a saddlebag, then glances up at the drizzle and shakes his head. He unstraps the crossbow from the saddle instead. I wait as he clamps a bolt between his teeth, puts his foot through the weapon's stirrup, and cranks the windlass handles until the bowstring is locked in place. Then I run through the misty forest, keeping my eyes on the old road in the distance. The horn sounds again, louder, and hoofbeats rumble in the distance. We are more than a hundred paces north of the wagon trail, but I hunch low and step cautiously. The clank of our armor is muffled by the thick traveling cloaks we wear.

I hold out a hand to stop Tristan and we listen. The hoofbeats grow louder. I can hear voices in the distance, and then, much closer, the sound of weeping.

Cold water spatters my face as I sweep away a leafy branch and scan the forest. A figure stumbles through the brush and nearly falls. It is she who weeps.

The woman glances back toward the road as she walks, then scans the forest floor, her gaze sweeping wildly among the hawthorn and gorse. Someone has tied a cord around her waist and attached a fox tail that dangles from her backside.

A maiden walking alone, looking frightened, and weeping. I want only to reach Elizabeth, but how can a man of honor ignore such a scene?

Tristan and I rise and push through the wet sprigs toward her. I give a whispery shout: "Do you require assistance?"

She shrieks and backs away from us, thick tears tumbling from her dark lashes. The perpetual drizzle has soaked her clothing. She is young, her black hair unbound. The thin chemise she wears is wet and torn. It clings to her and hangs off one shoulder, revealing smooth skin on a bony frame.

"I haven't found it yet!" she screams. "I need more time!"

I hold a finger to my lips and make calming motions with my other hand. "What haven't you found?" I take a step toward her and she backs away, shaking her head.

"The arrow." She pants as she speaks, the panting of someone about to fall into desperate sobs. The white chemise is soaked through, revealing every feature of her reedy frame. I wonder when she last ate. "I can't find it," she continues. "You arrived too soon. *I didn't have a chance.*"

I glance back at Tristan, who sneers at me. "You couldn't give the poor maiden more time, could you?"

"That's not helping, Tristan." I take another step toward her, pull my cloak off and place it over her shoulders. "I know nothing about an arrow. Why must you find it? Are you in danger?"

She stares at me, tilts her head and sniffles. "You're... you're not part of the hunt?"

"I'm just trying to get home," I say. "Which hunt do you speak of?"

"Witch hunt, indeed," Tristan says.

A horn sounds, loud and very close. Men shout. Boots crash through the forest. The woman flinches at the sounds, the tears flowing again. "Please, help me."

I look toward the road. At least five or six men. Tristan and I glance at one another. He raises his crossbow as I draw my sword. No knight with any honor could do anything else.

"Thank you, sirs." She lifts her skirt and walks away from the road slowly. Her shoulders hunch as she scans the forest floor. Tristan and I look to one another, then back at her. She scowls at us. "Hurry! We must find the arrow. Red fletching and stripes painted on the shaft. Anon! Anon!"

"What fun," Tristan says. "I hope we find it."

"What game is this?" I ask her. "Are you in danger or not?"

"There! Is that it?" Her voice rises, then strains with anguish. "No! It is a branch!"

I look back toward the road. Shapes plunge through the mist-drenched scrub. They will see us soon, if they have not already. I take hold of the woman's arm and turn her to face me. "Are those men going to harm you?" She shakes her head and I sheathe my sword. "Let's go, Tristan."

He lowers his crossbow and we crash through gorse, northward away from the men.

"They will take my maidenhood," the woman cries. "They will fill me with their seed and leave me to starve."

My sword flashes out from its sheath and Tristan's crossbow rises. We lurch back toward her.

"Perhaps," Tristan says to me, "you should have been more specific in your question."

"Rape is harm, maiden," I mutter. "In case this sort of thing comes up again in the future."

The first two men push through wet leaves, laughing, but what they see is not funny, and their humor dries up. Tristan and I stand shoulder to shoulder. My sword is pointed forward in mid-guard. His crossbow is strung and loaded and aimed in their direction. We are not thin, we are not dainty, and neither of us wears a fox tail.

"We can't seem to find the arrow," Tristan says. "Care for a war-bolt instead?"

They both step back. One, a tall man with long black mustaches, draws a dagger. The other, a thick slab of a man with hair so blond his eyebrows are almost invisible, unslings an axe from his shoulder. Both wear coats of mail, but no tabards or arms that could identify them or their master. I do not think they are Sir Gerald's men.

"The young maiden doesn't wish to be raped today," Tristan says. "You evil bastards."

The tall man looks at the crossbow and sniffs. "Are you wearing lavender?"

Tristan fires.

"I didn't say they would *rape* me," the woman cries.

CHAPTER ELEVEN

THE BLOND SOLDIER SHRIEKS and falls to his knees. Tristan's bolt has lodged in his thigh. Three more men crash through the branches.

I take a step back and straighten my arm, putting Saint Giles between them and me.

Tristan drops the crossbow and draws his sword. "Did that harpy behind us say what I think she said?"

The new men are dressed in the same fashion as the first two. Mail and round helms, no tabards. They draw weapons and glance nervously at the tall man who spoke to Tristan.

"No one needs to die," I shout. "Back away and everyone lives!"

Tristan glances backward. "She's gone. When will we learn to stop being so bloody chivalrous?" He smiles at the soldiers. "Hello. I believe there's been a misunderstanding." He tries to laugh but it sounds more like a cough. "Terribly sorry."

The tall man with the mustache kneels beside the wounded soldier and touches the bolt. "You aren't sorry yet," he says without looking up. "But you will be, soon. Your short, misery-laden lives will be the very definition of the word."

I draw myself to my full height. Elizabeth waits in a monastery not thirty miles from here. She is the hunger that burns in my belly, and not one of these lambs will keep me from her. "I am Sir Edward Dallingridge, Knight of the Shire and friend to King Richard. I have killed more men in France than you have seen in a lifetime, and I will kill the lot of you with my bare hands if you don't leave here at once!"

Confidence is a parasite that feeds upon the courage of your foes. If you show no fear, your enemy will hesitate, no matter how badly they outnumber you.

The tall man twirls his mustache with his little finger. His arrogant posture falls away. "Can you prove what you have said?"

"Course I can," I say. "Come closer and I'll show you."

"Not that," he says. "Can you prove that you are who you say you are?"

I let my blade drop a few inches. "I can."

"And you are not with Bolingbroke?"

I exchange a glance with Tristan. "Bolingbroke? Henry of Bolingbroke?"

"The very same. Are you allied with him?"

"I don't know what you are talking about," I reply. "The last I'd heard of Henry Bolingbroke was that he had been banished to France."

The man nods and gestures to the other men, who put away their weapons with reluctance. "Then we are not enemies."

"God's Teeth we're not!" the blond man cries. "He put a bolt in me!"

"As a point of fact," Tristan says, "it was the crossbow that put the bolt in you. And to be fair to the crossbow, it was acting under a mistaken premise."

The tall man extends his hand toward me. I remove my gauntlet and clasp his arm. We shake vigorously and grip each others's forearms to make certain there are no hidden weapons.

"I am Sir Simon of Grimsby," the man says.

Two men help the wounded soldier to his feet and support him as they walk toward the road.

"There was a woman here," I say. "She said that if she didn't find an arrow, you and your men would rape her. That's not true, is it?"

He smiles and rolls his shoulders in a slow shrug. "Rape is such an ugly word. We were playing a game, nothing more."

"Here's another ugly word." Tristan rests his hand on the hilt of his sword and steps toward Simon. "Eviscerate."

"What type of game were you playing?" I ask Simon.

"She wanted something." He twirls his mustache. "And we wanted something. So I made a wager with her."

I understand what occurred here, now.

"You fired an arrow into the forest," I say. "And if you found her before she found the arrow, you and your men could take her maidenhood."

"That is absolutely untrue," Simon replies. "Maidenhood can only be taken once. And that honor would be mine. The rest of my men would simply fuck her."

He laughs, and the men laugh with him.

My heart pounds a deadly rhythm. "And what would be her reward if she found the arrow first?"

Simon nods to one of the soldiers, a boy no older than fifteen. The boy tosses a moldy loaf of bread to him. "She would eat for the day," he says. "Although we pissed on the loaf when she ran into the forest."

More laughter.

The rage rises slowly in me, coiling around my soul like a red mist. I feel the leather of Saint Giles's hilt against my bare palm but cannot remember reaching for it.

"You've spoiled the game," says Simon. "Now she won't eat and I won't fuck, and we'll have to take you to Framlingham."

"And why," I hiss, "would I go anywhere with you?"

"Because someone wants to see you," he replies.

There is no one on Heaven or earth who could make me go to Framlingham on this day. Not a soul. I tighten my grip on Saint Giles's sword. "And who would that be?"

"Your friend," he replies. "King Richard. I am his new marshal."

My hand falls away from the sword. His words are like a gale, scattering the red mist of my fury. King Richard!

Something crashes through the forest behind us, but I do not look back. I stare stupidly at Simon of Grimsby.

"I found it!" the woman calls. "I found the arrow!"

The boy throws the loaf of bread to her.

Richard is alive.

We have a king.

England is saved.

"This doesn't smell right," the maiden says.

"No," Tristan knocks the loaf from her hands. "It certainly doesn't."

Framlingham Castle is close, only ten miles to the south. But ten miles is a third of the way to Elizabeth, and we are heading in the wrong direction. I try to protest. To tell Simon that I will go to Framlingham only after I reach my wife in St. Edmund's Bury. But he draws a tattered parchment from a poke at his belt and shows me Richard's seal upon the bottom. Simon has been tasked with bringing any knight he finds directly to Framlingham, without exception.

I can ignore the order. Cut my way through these men and continue to Elizabeth. But I cannot make an enemy of the one man who can give my Elizabeth a peaceful home again. And Richard will no doubt have an army. Men who can help me reach my sleeping angel. The king's men would sweep Gerald's soldiers aside and I could march unmolested into St. Edmund's Bury. Seeing Richard is a delay that may do more good than harm. So I swallow my protests and prepare for the journey to Framlingham.

Simon of Grimsby has ten more men waiting at a crossroads, where the wagon trail meets the Roman road leading to Norwich. All of the men have horses, and Simon sends one of them northward to collect Morgan and Zhuri. We wait in the misting rain for them to return. The woman from the forest eats a new loaf of bread that I hope has not been pissed on.

"Why does King Richard sit at Framlingham?" I ask.

"Because he grew tired of standing." Simon laughs with his men and my hatred of them grows. This knight thinks he is a clever chicken.

"Why isn't he in London?" I ask.

"Because he's at Framlingham," says Simon. "He can't be in two places at once, can he?"

The men's laughter is like stone scraping glass.

Tristan looks as if he wants to say something, but not even he is careless enough to insult the king's marshal.

Morgan's wagon rattles down the path and stops beside us upon the Roman road.

"Is everything in hand?" Morgan asks.

I nod to him. "We're making an excursion before St. Edmund's Bury."

"An excursion?" Morgan crosses his arms over his chest and studies the gathered soldiers. "What sort of excursion?"

One of the soldiers reaches up and touches the olive skin of Zhuri's face. Zhuri slaps his hand away and there is more laughter among the soldiers.

"We're going to Framlingham Castle," I reply. "To see the king."

"Which king would that be?" he mutters.

Simon yanks the woman by the arm toward the forest. The woman walks with him, tearing at the bread with her teeth, tears welling in her eyes.

"What are you doing?" I ask.

He pauses and grins back at me. "Something ugly."

I reach for my sword hilt but two spears flash out toward me. The leather flexes beneath my grip until I can feel the wood beneath, grinding into my palm.

I look at the young woman, who takes a strip of dried meat from Simon. She sees me looking and shrugs. "It's only rape if you fight." She sniffs at the meat. A tear rolls down one cheek as she bites off a piece. "Maidenhood is... such a small thing. And hunger is so very large."

Something in my heart shatters.

Simon takes a grip of her hair and kisses her savagely. She wipes her lips with a forearm and rips at the salted meat with her teeth again as they walk, again, toward the forest.

"Who is that?" Morgan asks, pointing to Simon.

"That," Tristan replies, "Is King Richard's man."

CHAPTER TWELVE

SIR SIMON LEAVES THE BULK of his men upon the Roman road, to await more knights of the realm. Then he and two other soldiers set off with us to meet a king.

This is the second time I have traveled to Framlingham under Richard's orders. I visited the castle a year ago to survey its defenses. To find any weakness that could be exploited by the French. I measured the depth of the ditches, suggested that removable wooden hoardings be added to the crenels along the walls, made certain that the murder holes were clean and clear. At the time, I was worried about the French. But the French have become the least of our problems. If I had known of the coming plague, my inspection would have consisted of nothing more than a short walk around the castle. Because only unbroken walls are needed to stop the dead.

I spent much of that year plodding across southeastern England, surveying castles and city fortifications. A panic had gripped the lords of England after Rye was burned, and so Richard asked my patron, the Earl of Arundel, to send me out so that I might appease the populace.

When my task was completed, I took the opportunity to ask the king's permission to build a castle at my manor in Bodiam. "Rye is only twenty miles from Bodiam," I told him. "If they can burn Rye, they can burn Bodiam."

He granted the license to crenelate immediately, but I know it was simply as a favor to me. Bodiam is not circled on any French war maps, and not enough buildings exist in my village to make a good fire. Richard knew this just as well as I, but he granted the license anyway. And I have always been grateful to him for that.

We approach from the northwest, which is the best way to see Framlingham Castle. The fortress presents its finest face from this angle; a golden line of flint and clay-stone, broken by thick rectangular towers and reflected with perfect symmetry in the reedy mere at the castle's feet. From this distance, the fortress and its reflection resemble two golden crowns. The first faces skyward, toward God. The second points the other way.

We circle around the endless pond until we find the northern road leading to the main gateway. The castle gatehouse rises before us—a broad, unembellished square of scattered flint, reinforced at the edges by great blocks of sandstone. Richard's banner, blue and emblazoned with the lion and lily, hangs from the wall. A ditch thirty feet deep snakes around the curtain walls, and a long drawbridge that extends from the gatehouse is the only easy way to surmount the trench.

"Is there no plague at Framlingham?" Morgan asks.

"King Richard will tolerate no demons at his gates." Sir Simon's voice is overly formal and dramatic. "His mighty armies drive them out."

I look in all directions and do not see a single plaguer.

"Perhaps Richard should tolerate no demons in all of England," Tristan says. "Or are his armies not mighty enough?"

"The very presence of our mighty king will drive the plague from England," Simon replies. He smiles at the two soldiers riding at his side and all three of them laugh.

I am surprised that a King's servant should be so flippant about his master. When I see Richard, I plan on speaking to him at length about his new marshal.

In the distance I spot a group of men pulling at a plow. I wonder that Richard does not have oxen to do the job. Until I study the men closely.

"Tristan."

He follows my gaze and his eyes grow wide. The men pulling the plows wear wooden masks, and their hands have been severed. They are plaguers. It is something I have seen before, and so has Tristan.

A stout dog, attached by rope to the harnessed plaguers, walks ahead of the group, tantalizing the plowmen and driving them ever forward with the heavy plow.

The masks look identical to ones I saw near Boxford, at a place called the Holy Lands. Followers of a prophet named Hugh the Baptist purposely afflicted themselves with plague and made the wooden masks before the change came over them. And when they made the transition from senseless pilgrims to mindless plaguers, a man named Matheus set them to work the fields.

But how can they be here? Thirty miles from the Holy Lands?

We are stopped at the gatehouse by a hulking constable in a leather jerkin. He is stout, with bulging shoulders and a thick brown beard streaked with the first snows of his winter.

"They'll be inspected before they can enter," he says to Simon.

We are taken into the gatehouse barracks and made to remove our armor and clothing while men in robes examine us. We've often been scrutinized upon entering fortifications in these dark days. I understand the need for such measures. Plague hides in flesh—like Greek warriors in wooden horses—and leaps out at night to conquer the living. But this inspection is more thorough than any we have had. A man spreads the cheeks of Tristan's arse and it takes three soldiers to break up the ensuing scrum.

Two robed men recoil from Morgan's ragged wounds. One asks him if he is plagued. I hold my breath. Morgan prides himself on his honesty, but we could use a good lie.

He looks at me, then at the man in the white robe. I can almost hear the struggle in his thoughts. Finally, he shakes his head and speaks: "I was dragged behind a horse."

I release my breath. It is a good lie—he looks precisely like a man torn by the road. Although in truth, he seems better than when I last looked upon his body. There is no blackness left on his skin, other than the scabs. Most of his wounds have stopped bleeding, and those that have not are nearly dry. Even the long gash on his jaw has scabbed over. Perhaps the Malta fungus is helping.

The robed men examine him carefully, but find no boils nor dying flesh, no fever nor shuddering, so they clear him to enter.

Sir Simon whispers with the constable for a time, then waves us forward and walks through the gate.

Framlingham Castle has no central keep. The interior buildings are set against the curtain walls. A great hall to the west, living chambers to the north, and a steep-roofed chapel to the east. There are no families in the castle. No makeshift tents or sleeping pads on the ground. No cooking pots hang from tree-branch tripods, and no children chase one another through the bailey. It seems empty, save for the guards upon the walls and lingering in the courtyard.

A great cheer arises from the west, outside the curtain walls. Sir Simon and four other knights lead us toward the sound, across the castle bailey, through the massive postern tower on the west side until we are outside once again. We find ourselves in the lower court, a vast outdoor yard encircled by a ten-foot wall of cobbled flint. This is where the cheers originated.

A sprawling length of tiered benches has been built here. And on those benches, clapping and shouting and whistling, sit hundreds of men and women. They are not the starving masses I have seen at other castles. They are gentry and nobility. Plump and healthy, and dressed in silks and brocade.

In front of the benches lies a tilting field several hundred paces long and a hundred paces wide. A low wall of piled stones circles the entire arena, and a deep trench about as wide as a man is tall encircles the wall. A jester stands on a log at the center of the field, looking surly and pointing at the seated gentry. He sweeps his hand to encompass the crowd, pauses, then turns around and pulls down his pants. The men and women cheer again.

Simon leads us onto the tier of benches. The odor of vomit and sweat mingles with rosemary from the Hungary waters worn by the ladies. I am not certain what to think of these new Hungarian tonics that women are using to scent their bodies. The smell is pleasing, but there is a taint of artifice and strong alcohol that repels me at the same time. I brought Elizabeth a phial of these waters from France once. We sat sniffing at it and laughing for much of the night. She has yet to put it on her skin, but I catch her with the phial to her nose often.

We shuffle past the lords and ladies. Their red faces and careless movements speak of wine and honeymead. Vast quantities of it. The whole lot of them are drunk.

The jester sweeps his hand to encompass the crowd again, then turns and pulls his trousers down once more. The crowd cheers.

It is difficult to get past the spectators because of my armor. A woman shouts insults at me as I bump into her. Another man slaps my cuisses and tells me I am hindering his view.

Tristan, walking behind me, leans in close to the man and shouts above the din: "We're terribly sorry for blocking your view of that man's arse."

Further on, a pretty woman sits on a man's lap, her eyes closed, lips parted. The man's hands are on the front of her dress, cupping her breasts, and they rock slowly.

They are fornicating.

Here, in front of everyone, they are fornicating. This is not Framlingham, it is Sodom. It is Ninevah. It is every damned village in the Bible, and I feel filthy for simply being here. I will speak to Richard quickly, and leave this loathsome place as soon as I can.

One of the woman's bare feet rests on the shoulder of the man in front of her, and most of her leg has worked free of the silk dress she wears. She has no hose, so I can see the pale skin of her thigh. The man in front of her does not seem to notice her foot, or if he does, he does not seem to mind.

No one seems to mind. I glance around. This lewd act goes unnoticed by everyone. Except for Tristan, who grins and elbows me. Morgan sees what we are looking at and tries to shove us onward but the woman's leg blocks my path. I step over the obstruction, as Simon did, and move on. Tristan steps over with one leg but, as he straddles her shin, he runs his finger up the sole of her foot. She flinches. Her eyes jerk open and she slaps at his armor hard enough to set it clanking, then spits at him. A moment later she arches her back and gasps as the man beneath her shifts position.

They continue.

Morgan scowls at the couple as he passes. I do not think they notice his disapproval. And if they do, I do not think they care. Zhuri places his hand against his temple, so that his fingers block the couple from view.

Simon rolls his arm in the air to hurry us along. He leads us toward a platform built into the center of the long tier of benches. A canopy, died blue and red and bearing both lions and fleur-de-lis, stretches above a carved wooden throne and six other chairs. The throne is empty. In fact, there are only two people sitting under the canopy. The first is a soldier wearing a nasal helm, layered leather jerkin, and a massive steel spaulder on one shoulder. The other is a thin blonde man with a wide board on his lap and a quill in his hand.

Simon steps onto the platform, slouches into the throne, and motions to the empty chairs. The soldier, who sits in the back corner of the platform, stares at Simon, but says nothing. The blond man does the same. They may hold their tongue at Simon's insolence, but I bloody will not.

"I don't care if you're the Pope," I say. "Get out of Richard's throne or I will throw you out."

"Which Pope?" Simon replies, and it is the last shred of disrespect I can take. I step forward and reach for him. His hand darts to the hilt of his dagger. The soldier in the corner rises and points at me.

"You are known to me!" The man's voice is thick with an Italian accent. He throws off his helmet and turns his head so I can see his cheek. "This you made, no? You remember, no?" His face bears scabs in the shape of my gauntlet's lobstered fingers.

I made them, yes. I struck him in the face with all my strength when we were in Hugh the Baptist's Holy Lands. He was trying to prevent our escape at the time. And I was trying to facilitate it. My shock at seeing him here freezes me. First the masked plaguers pulling the plow, and now him.

The Italian mercenary looks past me and whistles loudly, waves toward a line of soldiers a few benches down. The mailed men stand and pick their way through the drunken crowd toward us.

"I remember," I say finally. "You were holding us prisoner. And you wanted to afflict us with plague."

The Italian draws a short sword and raises it to within an inch of my face. "Now I going to make things in *you* face."

Simon laughs and dangles one leg over the arm of the throne. A half dozen mailed soldiers press onto the platform. A half-dozen blades point our way.

"Put him into your arms," the Italian calls to the soldiers.

The men look at him, then at each other. The mercenary throws his free hand into the air. "Take him. Make him not move."

Two soldiers take hold of my arms. Tristan draws his sword but finds two blades at his throat. Morgan tries to shove the swords away but another two men take hold of his arms and he groans as his wounds are stretched. Zhuri raises his hands into the air.

"I write my name in you skin, no?" The Italian grins as he surveys my face. The tip of the mercenary's sword touches my cheek. "And I am to tell you, I have very long name."

Episode Three

CHAPTER THIRTEEN

AN EXPLOSION OF TRUMPETS rings out across the lower court. So loud that I can feel the notes in my fingertips. So loud that the Italian holding a sword to my face flinches. He glances back toward the jousting field and so do I.

The sun has burned away the low-lying clouds and its rays glimmer along the bright metal horns of no less than thirty trumpeters. A herald steps out in front of the crowd. He speaks loudly, but the lords and ladies have recovered from the shock of trumpets, and the swell of their conversations drowns his speech.

"And therefore, at the king's court, my brother," says the blond man with the quill, "each man for himself, call not for your mother."

I stare at the writer, who shrugs. "It needs a bit of work."

I look back at the mercenary, who grins and points his sword at me again. "The face of you *needs a bit of work*. And I am to do it."

Sir Simon rises from the throne, lays his hand on the mercenary's forearm. "You can't carve him."

"He put the hand of him into my face." The mercenary tilts his head to show Simon the scabs on his cheek. "I get back on him."

"You'll have to get back on him some other time. If you touch him now, Richard will leg you."

I do not know the term *legging*, but it means something to the Italian. His gaze flutters from Simon back to me and he takes a small step backward. "I then ask Richard if he let me to do it."

"Don't be a fool. Richard won't *let you to do it*. This man is a Knight of the Shire and a member of Parliament. You are a foul-smelling, brainless and ill-mannered peasant who amuses the king."

"I do not smelling foul," the Italian says, but he sheathes the short sword. "I will kill this knight. I will kill him with many blood."

"Perhaps," Simon replies. "But not today."

The mercenary fixes hazel eyes on me and drags a hand over the scabs upon his cheek. He jabs his finger toward my face. "With many blood!"

Simon waves off the mail-clad soldiers and sits on the throne again. I think about Elizabeth locked away in a cathedral while I sit among two hundred drunken nobles and argue with a vengeful Italian.

"Are we here to watch a joust?" I snap. "Or to meet with King Richard?"

Simon flicks his hand as if I am a buzzing insect. "Both." He drapes his leg over the arm of the throne again. "Richard will be with us shortly. In the meantime, do try to enjoy yourself."

The blond man smiles at me. "Yes, enjoy yourself. Drink. Feast. Revel until you die."

Tristan points at the writer. "There is none other."

We all look at Tristan.

"And therefore, at the king's court, my brother," Tristan says, "each man for himself, there is none other."

"I like that." The writer strokes his lip with the feather. "There is none other. Yes, that will do. That will do." He dips quill into inkpot and scrawls on the parchment.

"So you are writing again, Geoffrey?" Simon asks.

The writer ignores him.

"Geoffrey doesn't want to be the court poet anymore." Simon chuckles. "He tried to leave Framlingham two days ago, but we can't have Richard's favorite poet leaving us, can we?" He points. A chain binds the writer to a ring on the floor.

I look at the bound man and remember who King Richard's court poet is.

"Chaucer?" I say. "Geoffrey Chaucer?"

He bows his head and makes flourishes with his hands. "Would that I was another, but yes, that is my name." He sniffs the air. "I smell lavender."

"My wife loves your poetry," I say. "She'll be envious she wasn't here to meet you."

"Never envy us," he replies. "Never envy we at Framlingham. 'Tis your wife I envy. She is elsewhere."

"His wife is plagued," Zhuri says.

"And still, I envy her."

"Why did you try to leave Framlingham?" I ask.

"Leave, now, lest you discover," he replies.

Simon laughs and waves off Chaucer's reply. "A sullen child, this Geoffrey Chaucer."

A drummer, hidden from my sight, hammers out a marching beat and calls my attention back to the field. Two knights, one with a canvas sack over his shoulder, run across the courtyard and approach a squat, tile-roofed stable that sits at one end of the tilting field. The front of the building sits only a few feet from the edge of the trench surrounding the jousting field. Planks extending from the foot of the stable entrance span the trench and lead, by a break in the inner stone wall, onto the field.

The knights take position outside the double doors and, a moment later, the trumpets silence conversation again. A lone horseman rides through the postern gate and into the lower courtyard. Strips of overlapping steel serve as barding for the horse, and these plates rattle as the animal shifts into a high-stepped prance.

The Scourge: Emaculum

The rider makes a pass in front of the benches, raising a lance into the air and receiving a smattering of cheers. He wears a suit of blackened armor, and it is perhaps the finest harness I have ever seen. The late-day sun glimmers golden across the metal and I cannot see a surface that has not been engraved. He wears a new, high-lipped species of helmet known as a frog-helm, popular with jousting knights on the Continent. Mounted on the crest of the helmet, in gilded gold, is the top half of a roaring lion's head. And upon the head of that lion is a crown of silver.

The armor is a master's work. Fit only for a king.

Richard, son of Edward the Black Prince, is going to joust.

I have won only two tournaments in all my years, but I have loved the sport since childhood. I lived and dreamed of the tilting yard when I was younger. The sight of Richard in his splendor, ready to risk his life in the list, rekindles my old love.

I cheer for my king. Tristan and Morgan do the same, and even Zhuri claps politely. But we are among the few. The jester has left and the men and women in the benches no longer cheer. They drink and play games, kiss and grope. Only a scattering of them look toward the field.

Richard canters past, lance high. A set of planks has been laid across the trench on the side opposite the stable, and he walks his horse across them. He trots through a break in the low stone wall and holds his position as squires pull the planks away.

There are no hurdles dividing the tilting field, and I find this very peculiar. I have never seen knights joust without a divider between them. The risk of horse collisions makes it dangerous to the point of stupidity.

The two knights at the stable lift a thick bar of wood and pull open the doors. I wonder if Richard's opponent will ride from the cottage. What an odd way to make an...

Realization comes to me like a shower of molten lead. I understand why there are no dividers. I stop cheering. Bile rises in my throat.

"No." I can only manage a whisper.

The first of the plaguers lurches out. An old man wearing a torn robe. Blocks of sandstone prevent the doors from opening too wide, leaving only one direction for the old man to walk—over the planks and into the tilting field. He takes a staggering step forward, his gaze jerking from one side of the courtyard to the other.

The knight holding the sack draws out a dead, bloody chicken and hurls it over the trench and stone wall, into the tilting field. The old plaguer takes a step onto the planks and raises his nose to the scent. Before he can take another step, a rush of plaguers shuffles from the stable and onto the planks. I count ten, but they are massed together so it is hard to tell. The old man is knocked into the trench as the others rumble across the makeshift bridge. His screams ring out across the lower courtyard.

Simon laughs behind me. "Stakes in the trench," he says. "We always get a half-dozen rotters falling in. I imagine they are bored to death down there, eh?" I do not laugh and he mistakes my silence for stupidity. "Do you see it? I said *bored*. The spikes?"

The trumpets ring out again. Richard's horse tosses its head. The king lowers his lance, gives a muffled shout, and slaps his knees against his charger's armored flanks. The animal springs toward the plaguers with a snort.

"He musn't do this!" Morgan shouts. "Those plaguers are not animals!"

"He's right," Tristan adds. "They're not even French!"

"Simon!" I shout. "Tell him to stop!"

Simon laughs. "Tell the King of England to stop? You jest, of course."

The king's horse picks up speed, cantering with the metallic rhythm of barding and armor. Its hoof beats are like distant cannon fire.

"There is a cure!" I shout. "Those people can be cured! *In the name of God*, tell Richard to stop! *Stop!*"

I howl the last word because Richard is almost upon the first of the plaguers—a woman in a blue dress who stumbles across the field with her arms flush against her sides. Richard's lance takes her in the chest. Blood and bones explode from her back as the steel tip slashes through her. Her shriek sounds almost human. The king releases the spear and draws his sword. The woman topples backward but the tip of the lance enters the earth, and she is held suspended over the grass. She slides slowly down the shaft, completing her fall one inch at a time.

I take great gasping breaths. "This is murder."

"We've killed scores of them ourselves," Tristan says.

"Not like this," I reply. "Never like this."

I have killed plaguers to ease their suffering or to defend myself and my friends. Never have I slaughtered them for entertainment.

Chaucer chants softly:

"And high above, depicted in a tower, sat Conquest, robed in majesty and power. Under a sword that swung above his head, sharp-edged and hanging by a subtle thread."

Richard's blade flashes in the sunlight, ends life in careless sweeps. I do not see demons dying on that field. I see sons and uncles. I see fathers too sick to care for their families. I see good men, like the mercenary we had to kill on the Roman road. But it is the women that pain me the most. Angels, like my Elizabeth. Saints, like Morgan's Matilda. King Richard's sword extinguishes hunger. Erases words from this world. He is the wolf that slaughters the lambs.

And I am sworn to stop him.

CHAPTER FOURTEEN

I VAULT OFF THE PLATFORM and shove through fondling couples and bench-side dice games. Tristan's footsteps rumble behind me. Simon shouts to me but I am not listening. I hop to the grass in front of the benches and sprint toward the trench that surrounds the tilting field. The ditch is a little wider than a horse is long, a jump I could make without much effort in a tunic and breeches. But it will take a great effort to make the jump in my armor. I hesitate at the edge, absently noting the tips of sharpened stakes that line the bottom. A group of soldiers sitting on the front-most benches watch me closely, so I try to strike a relaxed posture, and watch the action on the field. Tristan takes position at my side.

The king nearly severs an old man's head. The blood sprays in a dozen streams, like sunset rays in a misted forest. A woman wearing bloody blonde plaits at either side of her face takes hold of Richard's armored leg. He hacks off both her arms with one swing, then stabs her in the face several times. The blood flows down her cheeks like tears.

"No." My words push out through clenched teeth.

Richard cleaves the top of the woman's head and she topples backward stiffly.

Morgan's voice rings out from somewhere behind me. "This is mortal sin! These are God's creatures he murders! They can be cured!"

The Scourge: Emaculum

The king's horse falls to its forelegs as plaguers find gaps in the barding. Richard swings out of the saddle and sheathes the sword, draws a maul from the dying horse's saddle. No more careless sweeps. Death comes for the plaguers on the end of a five-pound slab of metal. Their bodies are mashed and spattered onto the field. He destroys them. Strives to rid the tilting field of all humanity.

A wounded plaguer in a herald tabard rises behind Richard. The king spins as the afflicted man crashes into him and the two fall to the ground.

King Richard roars and rolls so that he is on top of the plaguer. He holds the maul's handle at the very top, so that his gauntlets are above his head and the thick head of steel down by his chest. Another shout resounds across the lower courtyard as he buries the man's skull beneath five inches of steel and three inches of Norfolk clay.

Richard whirls to face the crowd. He raises the maul crosswise over his head and howls once more.

If there is cheering, I do not hear it.

All I hear are the boisterous swells of conversation and the sharp laughter of the nobility. The king holds his pose for a few heartbeats. The frog-helm pivots so he can take in one end of the crowd, then the other. He jogs the maul up and down a few inches again, as if the crowd might notice the motion. But they do not.

He hurls the maul to the ground. The weapon bounces, ringing off the grass. The king throws off his gauntlets and twists four bolts on his shoulder. He removes his helm and tosses it to the ground, fumbles with the cords of the leather cap he wears.

Richard is not as handsome as his father was, but he possesses a fineness of features that Elizabeth says makes him attractive. Those fine features glisten with sweat today. His body is slender, so slender that his secret nickname among many knights is, "The Damsel." He wears a mustache and trimmed beard, and a thick mass of unruly black hair falls to the nape of his neck.

The king motions toward the squires. "Come!" he shouts.

One of the young men shoves planks across the trench and another squire crosses the boards, holding his arms out for balance. Richard waves toward the stable where the two knights are posted. "More!" he shouts. "No breastplate or helm this time."

One of the knights holds up a fist toward the king to acknowledge the instructions. The squire begins unbuckling the straps of the king's breastplate.

He wants to do it again. He wants to butcher more men and women, and I cannot allow it.

I am the champion of the dead.

The wide trench stands between me and my oath. I back up three steps, take a long breath, and run at the ditch. Three paces. One. Two—

Something crashes into me. I stumble to the side and put my hand down to keep from toppling into the trench. A soldier in chain mail grabs my arm and pulls me to my feet.

"Where are you off to, then?" he asks.

"To stop a terrible mistake," I say.

Another soldier arrives, takes my other arm.

"Why don't we watch from the benches, eh?" the first soldier asks.

"Because I won't sit idly while people are butchered for sport."

"So sayeth the Lord!" Tristan shouts from behind us.

The first soldier's hand tears free from my arm as Tristan hammers him to the side. The second soldier seizes Tristan and, while they struggle, I leap.

I strike the far wall of the ditch and the breath explodes from my body. I flail wildly, remembering the spikes, dig my armored fingers into the clay. Soldiers shout behind me, but a more immediate sound draws my attention. I glance down into the steep-sided trench. The sharpened stakes are set in rows along the bottom of the shaft and, impaled upon two of these, is an afflicted woman. She is a skeleton wrapped in wrinkled flesh. The black eyes look unusually large in the withered sockets. She hisses and writhes against the spikes.

They left her there.

I see another plaguer, impaled face-down a few yards away. And yet another a little farther out.

They leave them in the trench.

The afflicted fall in and no one takes them out. They are left to rot, in agony. I wonder how long this poor woman has suffered.

Something buries itself into the earth next to my arm. A crossbow bolt. I dig my toes into the trench wall and drag myself up onto the far side, an arm's length from the wall of piled stones.

Past the wall, and far to my right, Richard stands on the field with his arms out. The squire fumbles with the straps on his shoulders. Both seem oblivious to my presence on the near side of the trench.

Sir Simon's voice calls out from behind me as I scramble to my feet.

"At this range, my bolt will cut through your armor as if it were cheese."

"Cheese can't cut through armor, Sir Simon." Tristan is held by two men in chain mail and seems to have lost his awe of the marshal.

I turn to face them. The king's marshal keeps the crossbow trained on me.

"Hop back over, Sir Edward," Simon calls. "We can drink mead and taunt the Italian until Richard is done."

I hear the squeak of the stable doors again, hear wood crash against the sandstone blocks. There is no time for strategy.

"Your bowstring's wet," I say.

There is only the briefest flicker of Simon's eyes toward the crossbow. Tristan kicks the marshal an instant before I throw myself sideways over the stone wall. The bolt clicks as it skims off the steel greave upon my shin.

I roll to my feet and run hunched toward the stable. The crowd cheers. I am certain they are celebrating my unexpected arrival on the field. And, in all likelihood, Sir Simon's unexpected attempt to kill me.

I glance back. Richard raises an arm to the lords and ladies. He thinks they are cheering him. The squire removes the engraved breastplate, and Richard slaps his unarmored chest a few times, raises his arm again.

I turn away and sprint toward the stable. One of the knights peers from behind his door at me. But I am not interested in him. What interests me is the dozen soldiers running from the benches. They sprint along the other side of the trench, pointing at me and circling toward the back of the stable.

The crowd hoots and stomps as I near the planks leading to the stable. Their wild applause is like hail on cobblestones. A dead chicken soars over my head. The second knight stiffens as he notices me for the first time.

Broken, shuffling footsteps sound from inside the stable. They are coming. The afflicted are coming.

I pass the stone wall, hop on the wobbling planks, and bound across the trench.

"You can't be here!" The chicken-hurling knight ducks behind his door and peers at me over the edge.

I take hold of the door and slam it shut, turn to the other knight.

"What do you—"

I tear the door from his hands. But the plaguers are upon me. Glinting eyes of polished ebony. Heads jerking from side to side. They come with open mouths and black, jagged fingernails stretched toward me. I know now that they are not demons. They are simply sick people.

But they are terrifying sick people.

I put my shoulder into the door and drive it back as hard as I can. Bodies thud against the oak and fall away. The doors meet and I shove my arm into two of the brackets that once held the barring plank.

The doors shudder. The steel of my vambrace takes most of the pressure, but only a few of the afflicted are pounding. I will not hold off nine or ten bodies shoving in unison.

The two knights stand motionless. They stare at me through the open visors of their bascinets. "Get the plank!" I shout. The door shudders again, and this time the steel vambrace digs painfully into my arm. *"Get the plank!"*

The first of the soldiers from the benches rounds the corner of the stable. He is young and badly trained. His instinct is to grab my shoulders, which allows me to pull his sword from its sheath with my left hand. He releases me and stumbles backward, his body taut, his hand touching the empty sheath. I hold the sword up so he can see it, then slide the blade into the brackets and pull my arm free.

The soldier points a finger at me. "You are in a mighty heap of trouble, sir." More soldiers round the corner, some with spears, some with drawn swords.

I cannot escape them. Nor do I want to. I swore to the Carpenter, upon the cold stones of a priory, that I would defend the afflicted. And I have kept my word. I am the champion of the dead.

The soldiers advance, but I do not fear them. They will take me into the castle and Richard will speak with me. I will explain why I stopped his exhibition. I will tell him about Elizabeth, about the oath I made, and the cure that exists. And, together, he and I will repair this broken land.

I hold my hands up, palms outward, so the men understand I will go willingly into their custody. I smile so they know I am calm.

A familiar face appears among them.

"Put him in your arms!" The Italian mercenary pushes forward. "Put him in your arms, and kill him! Kill him *with many blood!*"

The soldiers advance.

I stop smiling.

CHAPTER FIFTEEN

THE ITALIAN SURGES FORWARD and swings his short sword into the air. The steel gleams. His face twists as he primes for the strike, but the blow never falls, because thirty heralds shatter the sky with their trumpet song. The sound is louder than cannon fire. The soldiers fall back from me and stare toward the trumpeters. The Italian looks too, his sword still high above his head.

The king stands at the center of the jousting field, watching us with crossed arms.

It is not the wisest or bravest or even the most sensible who lead; it is the loudest. Every person in the lower courtyard stares at Richard silently.

When the fanfare ceases, there is only the sound of plaguers pounding upon the doors behind us, and the clank of the soldier's sword in the bracket.

The king stalks across the field toward me, the tip of his sword carving a long, rattling line in the earth. His body is rigid. The smile is gone. He passes the kicking body of his dying horse and halts a few paces from the trench. Jams his sword into the ground.

His voice is a winter morning. "Bring him to me."

The Italian shoves me onto the planks. I hold my hands out to the sides again and walk across the trench, toward the King of England.

He studies me for a time, squints. "I know you."

"Yes, my lord."

"No!" His anger startles me. "I am a king! You will address me *properly*." He draws his sword from the clay and points it at the Italian beside me. "Tell him, Pantaleon."

"The King, he want that you call him 'Your Majesty.'"

I stare at the Italian. "Your Majesty?"

"Also he does to allow, 'Your Highness.'"

The titles sound garish to my ears. Like something a doting minstrel might sing to his master. I have heard it said that Richard is fond of poetry and music, but this seems infantile.

I bow toward the king. "Your Majesty."

He looks into my face for a time, then waves the sword at me. "Sir Edward. Sir Edward of Dallingridge."

I bow once more. "Yes, my... Your Highness."

"What are you doing on my tilting field, Sir Edward?" He rests the sword on his shoulder.

"Your... Your Majesty." The title sticks in my mouth. "These wretched creatures you slaughter are the people of England. I swore an oath, to you, Your Highness, and to God, to protect them."

The stable doors thud, and moans rise from inside. There is no other sound in the courtyard. Richard stares at me with no expression at all, and I shift under that gaze. A plaguer howls. The twisted, high-pitched inhalation common to all of them. The king glances at the stable, and laughs.

It is a reckless laugh. Unfettered and entirely inappropriate. He doubles over with laughter, covers his face with one arm, and slashes at the air with his sword. Ice forms deep in my chest. This is not the king I once knew. I understand, in that moment, that Richard is plagued. The walls of Framlingham are thick as mighty boulders and high as ancient oaks, but there is no fortress strong enough to keep out the third plague. The scourge of madness.

King Richard has lost his mind.

"That sounded… that sounded quite dashing, Sir Edward." Richard wipes at his eyes with his fingers. He points with the sword toward the stable. "Shall we speak with those people of England? Invite them to feast with us? Will you take one as a lover?"

I clench my jaw and stare forward, think about the two-hundred men I need to reach Elizabeth.

"If those are the people of England, then my kingdom is a sad one, indeed. Tell me, Sir Edward, do you think my kingdom is a sad one?"

"There is no kingdom greater than yours, Your Majesty."

He rests the sword on my shoulder, the edge of the cold blade touching my neck. "So you agree that the creatures in that stable are not the people of England."

I do not like speaking with kings.

"Why the silence?" Richard removes the sword from my shoulder and waves it as he speaks. "My question is simple. If England is the mightiest kingdom, then how can those things be its people?"

I take a long moment to collect my thoughts.

"All kingdoms suffer calamity," I reply. "It is how we react to calamity that makes us great."

Richard laughs again. "Oh, but you are a clever one, Edward. Found your way out of that muddle didn't you? And with such elegance. You sounded like a troubadour. Are you a troubadour, Sir Edward?"

"No, Your Majesty."

"I think perhaps you are," he replies. "Or maybe you should have been. Sing those words, for me. The words you spoke about calamity."

I look at him to gauge his sincerity, but I find only madness. "I do not sing well, Your Highness. And I do not have much time. My wife is—"

"*Sing for me!*" His shout echoes across the courtyard. There is no trace of good humor on his face, only fury. "Your king *commands* you to sing!"

I clear my throat. If I live, Tristan will make certain this moment hounds me for the rest of my days. The Italian chuckles at my side and I send a withering glance in his direction. I will kill him with many blood when this is over.

I do not truly sing the words. I warble them out, like a priest chanting at mass. Elizabeth heard me sing once, and she made me promise I would never do it again.

"*All kingdoms suffer calamity.*" I chant. "*It is how we react to calamity that makes us great.*"

Richard claps his hands and laughs. "You are right," he says. "You are not a troubadour. I'm afraid I must command you never to sing again, Sir Edward."

I bow my head to hide my distaste. "Your Majesty, my wife is sick. She is plagued and waits for me in St. Edmund's Bury. I was on my way there when—"

"*Nowel, nowel, nowel.*" Richard sings an old minstrel's song. "That is singing! *Nowel, nowel, nowel.*"

His voice is rich and well-tempered, but I do not have time for this sort of madness. I force myself to relax my clenched fists. "Your Majesty, please…"

He grins and sings more loudly, waving his sword to the tune. "*Out of your sleep arise and wake, for God has made for mankind's sake…*"

"Your Majesty, a knight and his men are trying to…"

"*… all of a maid who makes me knell, of all the women she is the belle.*"

I cannot help raising my voice as he continues to sing. "They're trying to… They're trying to keep me from reaching her! *I need your help, Your Majesty!*"

"*Nowel, nowel, nowel.*"

I stop talking and wait for him to finish, but he seems to tire of the song when I stop trying to compete with it.

A silence falls and in that silence, the Italian speaks.

"Your Highness, I make question to you?"

"Pantaleon de Allesandria, do you have a song to sing?"

The mercenary raises a hand in my direction. "This man, he put the harm on my face. I may be let to put death to him? He insult my body with the fists."

"You want to kill Sir Edward?"

"With many blood, Your Majesty. *With many blood.*"

Richard takes a slow step toward the Italian. The humor drains from his face. "Sir Edward has been a loyal knight for as long as I can remember, Pantaleon. He has been just and true to me, even though some of his friends have not. He is my subject and my kinsman." He touches the tip of his sword to the mercenary's forehead. "Your words are an insult to my ears. An insult!"

The Italian takes a step back, flashes a convulsive smile. "I am... I am not want insult of you ears, Your Highness."

"You have insulted them," Richard replies. The ice is back in his voice. "Take him down below and leg him. With many blood."

"No!" The Italian whirls away from the nearest soldier. "I do not meant I kill Edward. The language has many hardship for me. Please. Please!"

Richard waves him off. "I'm tired of you, Pantaleon. You are a bore."

"Please! *Please!* Your Majesty! I make mistake!"

I try to feel good about the Italian's fate, whatever that fate is, but I cannot. Killing him in single combat would be satisfying, but to have him taken away on the whim of a madman is an injustice I cannot bear.

"My lord," I shout. "*Your Highness.* I don't know what legging is, but he does not deserve it. The Italian was making a jest. A jest we started while sitting in the benches, before you arrived. There no real threat. We are friends."

The soldiers pause and Pantaleon waves a hand toward me. "Yes! He talks what is true!"

Richard studies me. I cannot tell what he is thinking and that terrifies me.

He rubs at his bearded chin and smiles. "I have a proposal for you, Edward." He points the sword toward the rattling oaken doors. "You believe those creatures in the stable are human. I know them to be demons." He swivels the sword so it points to the mercenary. "You believe the Italian did not mean you harm. I believe he did. Let us put lance to our convictions. Three passes. If I am victorious, you stand by my side and we kill the plaguer demons and the Italian together. You will forget this silly business with your wife and remain here at Framlingham until I tire of you." He swings his sword in long, lazy arcs. I wonder if everyone he tires of gets legged. I wonder again what it means to be legged.

"And if you are not victorious?" I ask, watching him carefully.

"If I don't win, then my exhibition ends. You will have defended the good people of England, and saved a boring Italian mercenary." He cocks his head as if remembering something. "Oh, and perhaps I will help you find your wife."

CHAPTER SIXTEEN

THE LORDS AND LADIES IN the crowd thunder their feet upon the benches. Some cup hands to their mouths and shout, others whistle and clap their hands above their heads. Perhaps they are glad that Richard has an opponent capable of striking back.

I sit upon a barded white destrier—a fine horse with a restless step. The stables are behind me, as is Pantaleon di Alessandria, bound and on his knees before a dozen soldiers.

The last time I jousted was in France, nearly five years ago. So much has changed since that tournament in Normandy. I touch the helmet upon my head. Richard provided a frog helm for the joust, and it is not comfortable. I can see very little and hear even less. The entire thing hangs suspended on my head by a web of leather cords intended to keep the steel from slamming into my face when struck by a lance. I suppose it is a clever invention, but I would have preferred my great helm.

Richard waits at the far end, on a long-legged, skittish grey charger. He looks across the field and raises his lance in the air.

Fire courses through my limbs. It has been too long since I stared down the list at an opponent. And what an opponent it is. My heart pounds. Not because I face the

King of England, but because the King of England stands between me and Elizabeth.

Richard's charger lowers its head and strains, churning the grass and rattling forward. The king is sloppy. Just a hair out of rhythm with his horse, but a tilt is a contest of hairs. The difference between a master of the lists and a dead man can be slimmer than the width of a blade of grass.

I raise my lance high. It is made from carved sycamore. Far lighter than the oak shafts they use on the Continent. It feels like a thunderbolt in my hands. I grew up shattering lightweight lances like this, and would have nothing else in hand when Elizabeth's life is at stake. My blood burns hotter as I tighten my grip.

I cannot sing and I am not overly fond of dancing, but I can put the tip of a lance through a ring that fits on a woman's finger. Richard is sloppy. So I will make my horse dance and let this sliver of sycamore sing upon the king's face.

The destrier lurches forward, not as spry as the charger on the other end, but powerful and fearless. The world rises and falls through the frog-mouth slit. Leather cords creak. The cheers of the crowd become a distant ocean. I listen instead to the rhythm of my steed, and the horse listens to mine. We dance together to the rattling hymn of armored plates. Until the rattles grow steady. Until they are one. A heartbeat of steel.

Nowel, nowel, nowel.

King Richard rumbles closer. I couch the sycamore shaft in the lance rest, and tap the butt against my side so I know its precise position. I told myself I would let Richard take the first pass, but the song of the lists rages in my head. It has been too long since I threw down an opponent in the jousts.

Nowel, nowel, nowel.

There is no barrier, and his horse edges too far toward me. I use my knees to warn the destrier but the gelding is already adjusting its course. At the last instant, my steed turns its head back toward Richard. My lance rises as the king twists in the saddle. There is an explosion of soft wood upon my shield. Shards rain against my helm.

My lance does not shiver. The steel tip sings upon his helmet with the thunderous clank of metal on metal. A thunderbolt hurled at the king. The shock of it rattles the bones of my arm. But Richard takes the worst of it. He tumbles from the saddle, head back, spurs high and gleaming in the setting sun. He hits the ground with a dangerous clatter.

I drop my lance and turn to look at the king. He lies in a heap of gilded plates upon the grass. Two squires and a man-at-arms rush out to him. He is not moving. Perhaps I should not have hit him so hard.

The distant ocean surges back and crashes into me. The crowd's roar is louder than it has been all day. I look into the benches and cannot believe what I see. The lords and ladies are cheering the fall of their king.

I ride to the far side of the field and wheel my horse. The king rises slowly to his feet, slapping hands away and brushing himself off. His helmet is askew, but he looks to the crowd for a long moment. His shoulders rise and fall in a long, deep breath. A squire straightens the king's helmet and bolts it into place, then helps him onto the charger. Richard kicks his spurs into the beast much harder than he needs to and rides toward the stable side of the field.

Angry kings are dangerous. Angry, insane kings are murderous. Will Richard help me if I beat him in all three passes? He sentenced Pantaleon to a horrible fate simply because the mercenary had grown tiresome. What would he do to someone who embarrasses him in front of the nobility?

A soldier hands me a new lance. I raise it high and look to the king. He jabs his lance into the air and starts toward me. He is angry, and it throws him even more out of rhythm. I tap my gelding's armored flanks and he lunges forward, tossing his head and blowing. He is a lively old horse, strong and dependable. Together, we could throw Richard down all afternoon, but I do not know if we should.

Richard's petulance is legendary, and I am certain his madness has not improved this condition.

"We're going to lose this pass, old boy," I say. "It won't be your fault."

I would not risk losing a point if I thought Richard could beat me. But I must let him have a modicum of victory. My heart pounds at the risk I am taking, but it is a calculated risk.

Richard leans forward in his saddle and tilts his head to one side. He looks stylish, but it only makes him more unstable in the saddle. It embarrasses me to give up the pass to him, but only fools humiliate kings.

We approach. I raise my lance the width of a blade of grass. The steel coronel of Richard's weapon glances off the top of my shield and strikes my bevor hard enough to take my breath. I fall back against the saddle's cantle. The tip of my lance grazes the king's spaulder with a clink.

Sir Simon, who was chosen by Richard as the *chevalier d'honneur*, sits at the center of the piled-stone wall. He sips at a goblet and raises a banner in his left hand without much enthusiasm. Richard has won the pass.

The king shouts at his horse and sets it into a jangling, high-stepped prance.

Let him gloat. He will be on the grass in a moment.

A soldier hands me another lance. The Italian still sits on his knees by the stable, his hands bound behind him. He stares at the ground, his face expressionless, but his chest surges with swift breaths. I glance at the stable. The bar has been replaced in the door brackets. I wonder how many plaguers are left inside. How many afflicted souls are counting on me? I know of at least one, and she waits for me in St. Edmund's Bury.

I slap the frog-helm with the edge of my shield and howl as the destrier bounds forward. I am champion of the dead. My lance must be true.

Richard rumbles toward me. I do not trust Sir Simon to give me a point unless it is definitive. The king will have to be unhorsed again. I growl in my helm, and tap the sycamore shaft against my side. My feet push against the stirrups. The destrier grunts with each step.

Richard's lance rises. Too high. A dozen blades of grass too high. I dip my lance into place. I want to strike the center of his helm again. Lances rise on impact, so I aim for his throat. He leans toward me. I shift the lance to center it.

I am sorry, Your Majesty.

He leans farther toward me. I correct again. The lance feels wrong. I tap the shaft against my side. The butt is too far from me. Something is not right. Richard yanks his reins hard in my direction. What is he doing? An eye fills the frog-mouth slit of my helm. A horse's eye.

No tilt barrier.

My destrier lunges to one side but Richard's charger moves too quickly. It is a sickening blow. A horse makes a short, high pitch noise I have never heard before. The world tumbles. There is grass. A screaming crowd. Horseflesh and armor. All of it spinning end over end. A horse shrieks. The earth kicks me in the face and the distant ocean swallows me.

When the seas slowly subside, when the bell-tower clang that echoes in my head fades away, I realize that I cannot feel my legs.

A hoarse voice sounds from behind me.

"I win."

CHAPTER SEVENTEEN

IT TAKES SIX SOLDIERS TO LIFT the dead destrier off me. Two men help me stand and the numbness in my legs turns into a thousand stinging insects. God or Saint Giles or the stars of Gemini were with me today, because the horse rolled onto me at the very end of its fall. The poor destrier. I never even knew his name.

Richard's horse is still alive. It lies on the ground, head shaking, eyes rolling, until a soldier draws a knife across its throat.

The collision of horses means the final pass was a draw. I did not win. But I did not have to. I simply needed to ensure that Richard did not.

The crowd cheers as I take a few hesitant steps. Someone claps me on the back heavily and I stumble forward.

"Listen to them, Edward! Listen to them!" Richard gazes at the crowd and holds up an arm to them. He winces and clutches at his shoulder, raises the other arm instead. A thick clod of earth is wedged into the corner of his visor "They love us!" He takes one of my hands and raises it into the air. The cheers are like a rockslide. Richard laughs. "They love us!"

That we both survived and are relatively uninjured is evidence that God still watches the earth. I pull my hand out of Richard's grasp and work at the bolts that keep the helmet attached to the breastplate. "You will help me reach my wife, Your Majesty?"

Two squires rush to Richard's side and help him remove his helm.

"We had a bargain, Edward," he says. "You had to beat me in three passes. And you did not."

I give up on the bolts. "It displeases me to disagree with Your Highness, but you did not say I had to win. Only that I couldn't lose."

He furrows his brows, shakes his head. "That is not what I said."

One of the squires pries off the bolts for me and another helps me take off the helm. Of course that is what he said. His words have echoed in my mind since he uttered them: *If I don't win, then my exhibition ends.*

And Richard most certainly did not win.

He sees my expression and laughs. "Don't be sullen. We shall discuss it. Now smile for the crowd, Edward. Smile for the good people of England."

The squires work like ants, stripping off our armor, one piece at a time. Richard beams at the cheering crowd.

I force steadiness into my voice. "Why are you at Framlingham, Your Highness?" I ask.

"I was on my way to Scotland with an army." He smiles and I catch a glint of lunacy in his eyes. "Do you know what's worse than a Scot?" He waits for my answer and I simply shake my head. He barks a laugh. "A fucking dead person that tries to eat you!" He cackles wildly and tries to speak again. "Although... although only *marginally* worse."

I wait for him to grow serious. A red-haired, freckled squire pulls off my breastplate and scurries away with it.

"You fled to Framlingham?" I ask.

He looks at me with a refinement that I did not imagine he possessed anymore, raises a finger to me. "Kings do not flee. They simply change their military objectives." He laughs madly again.

"And Framlingham became your new objective?"

"Anywhere that didn't have dead people trying to eat me seemed a sound military objective."

The last of our armor is removed and Richard leads me back toward the benches.

"You're not with Henry Bolingbroke are you?" the king asks as we walk.

"Henry Bolingbroke?"

Richard waves dismissively. "Of course not. Pay no mind."

We reach the tiered benches. Soldiers shove people from their seats so that a path forms to the canopied platform. Richard walks first, smiling and holding up his good arm. The crowd applauds and whistles as we pass by, but it is me they clap on the back. Richard glances back and notices the attention I am getting and his smile flickers and fades.

Tristan, Morgan, and Zhuri stand in the platform. Sir Simon sits in a wooden chair to the right of the throne, sipping from his goblet and ignoring us.

Morgan clasps his hands together. "Thank Our Lord in Heaven that you are both alive."

Tristan grins. "Edward, were you *singing* out there?"

"I don't know what you are talking about," I reply.

"It sounded like singing to me," Zhuri says. "In the broadest sense of the word, at any rate."

The two of them laugh.

"Two knights mock the knight they serve," Chaucer says. "You should feel shame, the two of you..."

I nod my thanks.

"... what he did upon that field could never, in any sense at all, be called singing."

The three of them burst into peals of laughter.

"You've found your humor again, Geoffrey?" Richard snaps. "Perhaps you can pen a comedy for me."

Chaucer's laughter dries up. "A Divine Comedy that would be."

Richard sits on the throne and rests his chin on one hand. A squire brings two lead goblets. The king takes one and hands the other to me. He drinks and motions with his eyes toward a chair on his left. I nod to my companions and sit beside the king.

The jester returns to the jousting field and stands on the wall. He points a finger at the crowd, turns around and pulls his pants down. The noble men and women cheer.

"Can we discuss my wife, now?" I ask. "Would you lend me men, that I might reach her, Your Majesty? Two hundred men would be ample."

Richard slumps in his throne and traces a lily burnished upon his boot. "Is your wife healthy, Edward?"

"She is not, Your Majesty."

He peers at me sidelong. "Then leave her be. She is with God now."

I shake my head firmly. "She is sick, Your Highness. And she can be cured."

Richard watches the jester and says nothing.

"Is your queen here?" I ask. Perhaps Queen Anne would be more sympathetic to my request.

The king does not look at me. His eyes stare toward the jester, but I do not believe he sees the man. "She is." His hand clutches into a fist. "She is in the chapel."

Richard was roundly criticized for his choice in wives. Anne of Bohemia brought nothing with her. No powerful alliances. No fortune to fill England's coffers. Choosing her was a strategic blunder, but it is said Richard loves her with all his heart. And I cannot fault a man for that. I take a long draw of wine from the goblet.

"You knew my father, did you not?" Richard says.

"A great man." I do not lie when I say it. Edward the Black Prince was the best man I have ever known. I crossed all of France with him and fought by his side at Limoges and Najera. "If you cannot spare two hundred men, Your Highness, I can make do with half that."

Sir Gerald can't have more than a hundred men with him.

Richard stares out toward the field with half-lidded eyes.

"How many French widows did my father make?" he mumbles.

I take three deep breaths. Elizabeth tells me I should do so whenever my temper threatens to overwhelm me. "He made an immeasurable number of widows, Your Highness," I reply. "The convents overflowed."

The king leans back and his jaw tightens. "And how many towns did he burn?"

"Hundreds, Your Majesty," I reply. "France lost the warmth of the sun for all the smoke."

He turns to me, his breath coming in ragged bursts. His hand grips the goblet so tightly that the thin rim bends. "How much French blood did my father loose?"

"Enough to turn the Seine red for a year," I reply. "Enough to drown every French son of a whore three times over, your majesty."

His eyes shimmer, then tears course down his cheeks like French rivers. He wipes at his face with a bloodstained hand, takes hold of my cloak, and yanks me close to him. "Then why," he snarls, "did the King of France proclaim a day of mourning when my father died?"

My eloquence dies.

"Tell me Edward. Why did King Charles parade through the streets of Paris with five thousand horsemen, in my father's honor? It is a mystery no one has ever bothered to explain to me. The Black Prince killed tens of thousands. So why did the men and women of France weep in the streets at the news of his death?"

I am trapped by my own words. "I... your father... your father was a very special man." Edward had a grace to him that I have never known in another man. He was the embodiment of chivalry, and even his enemies loved him.

Richard shoves me backward and turns toward the jousting field again. "What will my own people do when I die? Will they even notice, Edward? Will they weep in the streets with joy? My reign was never meant to occur." He sweeps a hand to encompass everything beyond the walls of Framlingham. "England was ready for a golden age. My grandfather was nearly dead and the greatest Englishman ever to live was going to take up the crown. Edward, the Black Prince! And what happened, Sir Edward? What did they get, instead?" His next words hold so much anger that I flinch from them. "They got *me*."

He downs the wine in his goblet and hurls it clanging along the benches. I feel a touch of despair, not at the king's words, but at the memory of Edward's death. Richard is correct. No man, alive or dead, could have filled the chasm left in our hearts by the Black Prince. I touch my chest and feel the bulge of Elizabeth's cure beneath my gambeson.

"I am a crowned heartache, Edward," he says. "I am a dead prince's shadow."

"You have the chance, Your Majesty, to be a greater king than any in our history. We are facing calamity, and Your Majesty will shine."

He glances at me, and for a moment I fear he will make me sing again. I finish the wine in my goblet.

"My marriage is the only great thing I have ever done," he says. "I married a saint, Edward. A woman loved by everyone. She is the only reason the people tolerate me."

"That is not true," I consider each word carefully. "You are young and they are unsure of you, perhaps, but you are their king. They wait for you to save them, Your Majesty. If Queen Anne is loved, then let her be your strength as you lead England out of these dark times. Let her be the hunger in your belly."

He laughs, and the madness returns to his eyes.

. "No Edward, I will not do that."

"Why not, Your Majesty?"

"Because…" His voice catches and he becomes silent for a long moment. "Because Queen Anne is now a part of these dark times." He takes a long, rattling breath. "She is no better than a Scot now."

So many wives lost to this plague. We are wolves with no hunger, hiding behind stone and subsisting on grief. It is no wonder there is so much madness in the world. I touch the bulge of Elizabeth's cure again. Richard's wife, the Good Queen Anne, is plagued. It is a tragedy, and yet, I see fortune as well. Opportunity.

"I am truly sorry," I say.

Richard seems to grow smaller as I watch. "God took her from me, Edward. He is punishing me. I think even the Lord wanted my father to rule."

"God hasn't taken her," I reply. "This is test. A test of your faith."

"Hallelujah," Tristan mutters.

"You can bring Queen Anne back," I say. "There is a cure for this plague."

Richard shakes his head slowly. "There is no cure, Edward. This is God's Wrath. And only God can lift it."

I point to Morgan, who stands, cowled, behind Richard. "Sir Morgan's plague was lifted."

Morgan draws his hood back, revealing the deep, glistening wound on his jaw. Richard studies him without expression.

I have three cures left. Elizabeth's hangs from my neck, and the other two—one from the alchemist and one that Zhuri gave me—are stashed in a poke at my belt. I draw out one of the ampoules and set it on the arm of Richard's throne.

"There is a cure."

Richard looks from Morgan to the ampoule. "What sort of cure?"

I pretend to drink more wine from my goblet. This is where things fall apart. God and science live in warring kingdoms.

"It is an alchemical cure," I reply.

He sits upright and hisses. "Alchemy? That is the devil's work."

"Christ was an alchemist," I reply. "He turned water to wine. And Moses was a sorcerer."

"So sayeth the Lord," Tristan says.

"The Lord never said that," Sir Simon replies.

Richard picks up the ampoule and peers at it, glances at Morgan.

Sir Simon leans forward, shaking his head. "Your Majesty, surely you aren't considering this. Alchemy is sinful."

I think about the young woman searching for the arrow when I first met Simon, and wonder how he can speak of sin. "If this scourge was God's doing," I say, repeating the words of Father Peter, "then only God can undo it. And if this cure heals the afflicted, then God wants us to have it."

Richard taps the ampoule against the throne nervously, licks his lips. "If I give this to my queen, she will return me?"

"God will bring her back," I reply.

Sir Simon shakes his head. "Your Majesty, I do not think this is wise. God punishes alchemists and sorcerers. And he will punish you if you turn to such evil measures."

Richard laughs again, the wild laughter that truly shows his madness. He wipes at his eyes and gestures with both hands to the entirety of the lower courtyard. "Look around you, Simon. We are in Hell already. What more can God possibly do to us?"

"He can deny you Heaven, Your Majesty," Simon replies. "Do not throw away an eternity with your queen. What is that verse? 'All flesh is like grass and grass withers... I can't remember."

"'All flesh is like grass,'" Morgan recites. "'The grass withers, and the flower falls, but the word of the Lord remains forever.'"

I stare at Morgan. He shrugs.

Richard strokes his lower lip with a forefinger. He glances at Simon, then at me. No one speaks for a long time. Tristan whistles a cheerful tune.

Finally, Richard sits up and nods. "If God did not want me to heal my queen, he would not have brought the cure to me."

"We don't know if that is a cure," Simon replies. "We don't know what that is."

Richard clasps the ampoule in his fist. "Simon, my queen is plagued already. She cannot get any worse."

Tristan clears his throat. "Actually—"

I throw my empty goblet at him and he shuts his mouth.

CHAPTER EIGHTEEN

THE KING LEADS US THROUGH the lower courtyard and into the castle. He picks up his pace with each step, and by the time we are in the inner courtyard, he is sprinting and laughing.

"There is a cure!" he shouts. "There is a cure!"

I chase after him, my companions close behind. Sir Simon and a dozen soldiers stream behind us like a military parade. Richard holds the cure between thumb and forefinger, high in the air like a holy relic. He runs high-legged, like his prancing horse. "*There is a cure!*"

Zhuri runs at my side. "He's mad!"

"That he is," I reply.

"And this is your king? This is the man you have sworn allegiance to?"

I shrug and pick up my pace. "Men will follow anyone."

We sprint through the castle bailey to a chapel that juts from the eastern wall. Two pikemen stand aside as the king yanks open a thick, iron-hinged door. Richard scurries inside and the pikemen clash their staves before I reach the door.

"Let them in!" Richard calls, his voice fading and echoing in the chapel. "Let them all in!"

The pikes part and I step through the open doorway.

Richard runs through the knave of the sparse chapel, but I do not follow him. I draw up short just inside the doorway and am bumped from behind by Zhuri. He gasps and the sound echoes to the high ceiling.

There is little to the chapel. Arched windows. Corbelled pillars. An ancient font. And, hanging from a cross above the altar, writhing and hissing and painted a hundred colors by stained-glass sunlight, is the queen of England.

Anne of Bohemia, known as Good Queen Anne for her unwavering support of the common people, has been crucified.

"Bring her down!" Richard shouts. "Bring her down!"

Soldiers run to either side of the chancel and untie knots from two thick ropes coiled around iron brackets. The men, in groups of threes, slowly let out the ropes, grunting as they lower queen and cross to the flagstones.

Queen Anne was a lovely thing when last I saw her. Soft-spoken and blonde, polite and pretty.

She is still blonde.

The queen shrieks and thrashes upon the cross. Her cries echo in the church like a Hellish choral solo. Bleeding boils mar her face. The skin of her fingers and forearms is completely black, as is the flesh around her lips. And her eyes are the soulless dark of eternal anguish. But someone has cared for her. Someone has dressed her in a shining dress of blue silk. Her hair has been plaited with meticulous patience, curled around her ears and wrapped in a brocaded veil.

Richard gazes at her with adoration. I stumble back a step and recall Lord James of Dartford—a mad nobleman who removed his wife's teeth and kept her tied to a wall with silk ribbons.

"You are certain about this?" Richard asks me. "This cure?"

"I will give my wife the very same cure," I reply.

There is no greater certainty than that.

"This is a mistake!" Sir Simon shouts. "God is watching!"

Tristan looks upward and waves. "Hello!"

Feet shuffle on the flagstones behind me. Curious lords and ladies file into the chapel.

Anne shrieks and lunges against the padded cords that bind her. The wooden cross rocks from side to side, drumming against the stones. Richard leans over his queen and hugs her waist, strokes the silk dress. "All is well, my puppy. All will be well." He glances up at me. "How... how is it done?"

I look to Zhuri.

"Tip the ampoule into her mouth," he says. "And hold her jaw so she cannot spit it out."

Richard studies Zhuri. I believe it is the first time he has noticed the Moor. "Who in God's Kingdom are you?"

"I am a friend to Sir Edward, and to you, Your Highness." He waves with exaggerated friendliness. "Hello!"

"You are a Moor!"

Zhuri feigns astonishment. "Allah be good! So I am."

Richard looks to me.

I shrug. "So he is."

Sir Simon gestures angrily toward Zhuri. "Your Highness, he is a heathen!"

"He may be an infidel," Morgan replies, "but he's no heathen."

Zhuri sighs. "Thank you for that fervent defense, Morgan. I feel much better."

"Do try to get your denominational insults straight, Simon," Tristan adds.

The king gives Zhuri a last look, then turns back to Queen Anne and places a hand behind her thrashing head. The tears shine in his eyes again. "Edward, if you bring back my wife, I will grant you anything you wish. Anything at all."

"I wish only that Good Queen Anne be returned to us," I say. "So my king and the people of England can rejoice in the passing of her affliction." I lick at my lips. "And, perhaps, some help reaching my own wife, Your Majesty."

Richard nods. "You shall have two hundred men at your disposal, Edward."

"Thank you, Your Highness." With two hundred men, I will cut through Sir Gerald's men like a spear through butter.

"And I will make you the new marshal of England!" Richard stares at his wife and licks his lips. He studies the ampoule closely, then gazes again at his wife.

"I helped him get that cure, Your Highness," Tristan says.

"You made me the marshal of England, Your Highness," Simon interjects.

Richard waves him off. "Everyone will be amply rewarded and happy. Now lend me some assistance!"

I kneel next to the cross and hold Anne's jaw. She bucks and howls, and her teeth snap shut, nearly catching my fingers. I take a long breath and look at Tristan, who looks back with wide eyes and shakes his head.

"Hold her still!" Richard shouts.

I take hold of her jaw again, carefully, and clamp a hand over her forehead. My palm slides on a bloody boil. Richard breaks the ceramic tip of the ampoule.

Morgan's deep voice booms from behind me. "'We do this in your name, oh Lord. Our prayers of faith will save the one who is sick, and the Lord will raise her up.' *Amen.*"

Amens ripple through the crowd of onlookers. Some fall to their knees and hold clasped hands upward. These are the same lords and ladies who fornicated and gambled on the benches a short time ago. I can see the fear in their postures, in their expressions. If God can heal the afflicted, then He still watches over us. And if He still watches over us, what has He seen?

"You do this in the name of God, do you?" Sir Simon sputters. "You practice sorcery and witchcraft in the name of the Lord?"

"Do shut up, Simon," Richard says. He motions to the guards and two of them take hold of Simon's arms.

"Your Majesty, this is a mistake!" Simon shouts.

The king meets my gaze, takes a sharp breath, and tips the ampoule. A liquid the color of rust trickles into the queen's open mouth. She makes a rasping sound and tries to shake her head, but I clamp her jaw closed. Anne thrashes wildly, burns me with the eternity of her eyes. Her skin blackens under my grip, but I do not let go. I watch her closely, until her throat pulses.

She has swallowed it.

"How long?" Richard says. "How long before I get her back?"

"Thirty breaths," Zhuri says. "Thirty breaths before it starts to work."

"Will... will those awful black marks heal? And the boils?"

"They will, King Richard. I am told that she will bear scars where her skin has split, but most of the disfigurations will heal."

Richard clasps his hands and rocks. "I have been without her for over four months."

"More than," says Zhuri.

Richard stops rocking. "Sorry?"

"He was agreeing, Your Highness." I squint at Zhuri.

We wait silently. And as we do, more and more people shuffle into the chapel. Word of the cure has spread. The men and women from the courtyard have come to witness the miracle of life. The resurrection of their queen.

Richard rocks slowly. His trembling voice warbles out a song.

"*Nowel, nowel, nowel.*" It resonates in the high-roofed chapel. "*Out of your sleep arise and wake.*"

Ten breaths and no change.

She strains and screams and snarls like a cornered wolf.

Dear God, it won't work. It won't work and Richard will blame me. And a mad king's blame is a terrible thing.

"*For God has made for mankind's sake, all of a maid who makes me knell.*"

Another five breaths and still no change. I think of the alchemist's wife, and the horror she had become. The sweat seeps along my hairline.

"It hasn't worked," Sir Simon whispers. "You see, Your Majesty? These men are frauds. Only God may cure the plague."

But Richard does not seem to hear Simon's words. He continues to rock, his eyes closed. "*Of all the women she is the belle.*"

Queen Anne draws in a screeching breath. Her back arches.

Richard opens his eyes and strokes her dress wildly. He looks to me, then Zhuri.

The queen falls back onto the cross and her breathing grows softer, more rhythmic. Her eyes close, and the snarl she has worn since I set eyes upon her fades.

Zhuri smiles.

God is at work here. I am watching the invisible hand of God.

Richard covers his mouth with trembling hand. "Oh my puppy! Oh my lovely Anne!"

She opens her eyes and tilts her head so that she can see Richard. The black of her eyes lightens as I watch. Turns a dark, mottled crimson, then pink. A tear rolls down her cheek.

Morgan falls to his knees beside me and prays. "'Many are the afflictions of the righteous, but the Lord delivers us from them all.'"

Richard places his hand behind his queen's head and touches her forehead with his. "My puppy. My blue-eyed songbird."

"'Bless the Lord, oh my soul,'" Morgan continues, "'and forget not all His benefits, Who forgives all your iniquity, Who heals all your diseases.'"

A trembling smile breaks upon the queen's face. She tries to reach out to Richard but the padded bindings prevent her from touching him.

Zhuri's smile spans his face. "She will speak in a moment, like Morgan did."

Richard pulls back from her. Tears streak his face. "Speak puppy. Speak to me."

I look to Morgan. "Sorcery?"

He shrugs. "God."

Tristan scoffs. "Science."

I look back to Richard.

He is no longer smiling.

A clump of the queen's hair has fallen out and rests in his hand. He strokes at her head and more hair falls out. "What? What is this? Is it... normal?"

A dark, heavy, cold thing tears at my heart.

Zhuri's smile fades. "I..."

The skin of Anne's face flushes red. Blood sprays from one of the boils and spatters Richard's cheek. "What is happening? What is happening, Moor!"

Anne arches her back, bucking against the cross, her screams are so powerful that the crowd backs toward the door. She laughs and spits a tooth at Richard. Blood drips from her mouth as more teeth sag and drop from her withering gums. Her breathing becomes a series of whooping gasps that end in laughter and another scream. She throws her head from side to side, banging it against the edges of the wooden cross and tearing great gashes in her cheeks. Hair falls away in great clumps, leaving only ragged patches and bloody streaks of scalp.

"Stroke my cheek, Rithard!" her cries are low-pitched and rasping, her toothless mouth making her lisp. "Eat of my fleth, my lord!" She laughs, and her voice becomes soft and gentle. "Oh Rithard. How I have longed for your touch. Would you be a darling and break my fingerth?" she giggles and runs her tongue along her lips. "Just one or two of them. I want to hear them thnap. *I want to hear them thnap!*"

I am incapable of speech. I can only watch as her skin shrivels and blackens before my eyes.

Richard stares at her without expression, draws a knife from his belt, and jabs it into her eye. I lurch backward, breathing in great gasps. Queen Anne shrieks and laughs and bucks upon the cross. The king rocks the blade back and forth, calmly, until she stops moving.

"Merciful Allah!" Zhuri cries.

Blood wells down to the wooden cross and dribbles onto the floor. Richard releases the knife, wipes blood from his hands gingerly, with his forefingers, and turns to look at me. I cannot return the stare. I can only look at the abomination that Queen Anne has become.

"To be honest," Tristan mumbles. "My role in finding that cure was rather insignificant."

"I told you!" Sir Simon shouts. The guards still hold him. "I warned you against this! 'The grass withers, and the flower falls, but the word of the Lord remains forever!'"

Richard stands and straightens his gambeson. He smiles at the soldiers and nobles behind him, but his eyes well with tears. His voice seems almost casual when he speaks.

"Sir Simon, Edward was curious about legging." He looks at me—a fury lurking behind the tears—smiles cordially and returns his attention to Simon. "Please take him below and educate him."

Hands grab my arms roughly and bring me to my feet. I scarcely notice. My thoughts are consumed with Elizabeth and the cure.

It does not work.

Roberto Calas

The cure does not work on women.

Episode Four

CHAPTER NINETEEN

I FIND MYSELF IN THE LOWER COURTYARD again, but I do not remember walking there.

Thoughts of Elizabeth are a hood upon my mind, a visorless helm that turns the world black and washes all sound away. Two men have been healed by the Syrian tincture, and two women have been destroyed by it. It cannot be a coincidence.

The cure does not work on women.

We are taken to a stone building at the north end of the courtyard. Guards wave us through two iron-studded doors that lead into the prison chambers and down spiral stairs to the dungeon.

I note our travel absently. As if the stone belly of Framlingham is only a dream. I hear nothing. I look without seeing.

It is the smell that finally cuts through my stupor. A seeping mist of decay that drifts through the underground passageway. The armed soldiers behind us make faces and whisper to one another. I flex against the cold manacles that bind my hands behind my back.

We were stripped by these soldiers and forced into itchy white robes before manacles were clamped over our wrists. I thought briefly about resisting, but that would have brought death to all of us, or perhaps an even crueler fate than whatever *legging* is.

The Scourge: Emaculum

They took Elizabeth's cure from around my neck. I did not stop them. It is poison to her. All of my efforts at finding a cure for her have been for nothing.

The cold stone of the dungeon floor numbs my bare feet. A fat man in a woolen robe wraps a cloth around his face, turns a key, and tugs on the tiny door that leads to the inner dungeon. The wood scrapes loudly against the carved-stone floor, and a stench batters us like a rotting ocean wave. It is the smell of souls decaying. The smell of mortal bodies melting in a small, dark place. Zhuri leans to one side and vomits. I press my hand against my nose and look to the fat jailer, who still holds the cloth to his nose.

"I'd say you get used to it, but you don't." He pulls a torch from a bracket beside the door and chuckles. "Not never."

The four of us are shoved inside. I step over a puddle of carrot-laced vomit. The torchlight glistens from wet stones and thick iron bars. A moan rises from the row of dark cells to my right, a trembling moan that bespeaks suffering of biblical proportions. An old cistern, as wide as I am tall, yawns a few paces to my left. The floor of the dungeon is painted in blood, and my bare feet slip in the grime. Something barely identifiable as a rotting body lies mangled, like man-shaped meat, just outside the jailer's torchlight. A lunatic laughs in one of the cells, the peals of his laughter echoing and ringing for an eternity.

I have entered Hell's foyer. This is where I will die. God, Saint Giles, and Mother Mary have turned their faces away. My lifeless body will be hurled into the cistern and my soul will continue to fall, spiraling into the darkness of eternal misery. The devil and his demons will torment me, will burn me without respite. But I will smile as the flames lick my flesh, because their work will distract me from the true agony—the anguish of an eternity without Elizabeth.

A rat feeding on something red and wet peers at me, then continues eating. Zhuri speaks quickly and tightly in

Arabic. Morgan takes deep breaths and crosses himself. Tristan is silent, and that is perhaps the most frightening thing of all.

The jailer pushes us toward the back wall of the dungeon. A man kneels there, trembling. His arms are raised up and out to the sides, wrists chained to the water-stained wall. The torchlight falls upon him, and I realize that he is not trembling. The movement is caused by thousands of maggots and insects feeding upon his corpse. Six other sets of bloodstained manacles dangle along the wall.

"No!" Zhuri shouts. "This is a mistake! I have done no wrong!" One of the soldiers cuffs him with a gauntlet, and the Moor doubles over, sobbing. "This is a mistake!"

"Have pride, Moor." Morgan's words are harsh, but his tone is gentle. "Die with honor."

Zhuri chants in Arabic, his stuttering breaths breaking the rhythm of his words.

The jailer unlocks the manacles holding the dead man and kicks the corpse to the stones. Soldiers back Tristan and Morgan against the wall and clamp their wrists with the rusted manacles. Zhuri struggles and two guards beat him. His cry of pain pulls me from my despair, momentarily. I shove at the guards with my shoulder and one of them pounds me in the temple with a dagger pommel. The world rings. When I can see again, Zhuri is bound to the wall and bleeding from nose and forehead.

The jailer grins at me. "Richard wants you to go first, he does."

The madman laughs again in one of the cells.

Something scrapes along the floor in the cage nearest me. A body moves in the darkness. Hands dark with filth and blood grip the lowest bars of the cell door. A soiled face, bloodspattered and impossibly thin, wedges into one of the squares made by the crossed iron bars. Mud and gore have turned the man's patchy beard into slime. His mouth opens and closes several times, as if chewing, then a sound emerges. "P-p-p."

The jailer laughs and mocks the sound. "Puh-puh-puh." He kicks one of the man's hands.

The prisoner winces but does not move. "P-p-pity."

"There ain't no pity here," the jailer says. "Only p-p-pain!" He roars with laughter. One of the guards, a tall man with a forked beard, laughs with him.

"P-p-please." The man in the cell closes his eyes. "P-p-please."

The jailer kneels so his mouth is only a foot or so above the man's face. "You was high and coddled all your life, wasn't you? Giving orders to everyone. And now look at you. Now look at you."

I realize with a start that I know the prisoner. The room seems to grow darker. I lean against a cold, iron bar to steady myself and kneel in front of the gate.

"Hello, John," I say.

The man's head jerks toward me. He looks into my face for a long moment before recognition flares in his eyes. "Eh-eh-ed-w-w?"

"Yes, it's me, Edward."

I nod to Belisencia's father, the Duke of Lancaster.

I nod to my first commander and lifelong enemy.

I nod to John of Gaunt.

CHAPTER TWENTY

I HAVE SPENT MOST OF MY LIFE hating John of Gaunt.

I challenged him to a duel three times and nearly came to blows with him twice.

I simmered in a prison for days because of him, and I have watched my kingdom slide into mismanagement because of his advice. He is the loudest of Richard's advisors, and so the King has always done what he says.

But John of Gaunt is not so loud anymore. He makes tiny hisses with his breath and looks up at me, and I feel a surge of pity. Not even he deserves to rot here. I cast a sideways glance at the jailer, to see if he will put an end to the conversation, but he seems interested in our exchange.

"Did Richard tire of you, too?" I say.

He tries to speak, but no words come out, so he simply nods his head.

I have hated this man, and yet, at the end, what use is hatred? Our bodies turn to shit when we have passed through the bowels of life, and the spice of hatred only makes us smell worse.

"I'm sorry for all the trouble we have had between us, John. I know I am not blameless in our quarrels."

He stares into my face, and I notice his eyes. They are gray, with no whites to them. I recoil and look to the jailer, who laughs.

"Is he plagued?" I say.

"Hard to say," he replies. "He's headed there, anyways. Takes weeks to turn once you've been legged." The jailer stands and thrusts his torch through one of the iron squares, illuminating the tiny cell.

And I see, for the first time, John of Gaunt's legs.

He is a skeleton from the waist down. His legs are nothing more than bones, with wisps of black, rotting flesh, and brittle tendons holding those bones together. His hips, just visible beneath the shredded white robe, are swollen, pustulant, and so rotted that he left a trail of sludge when he crawled to the gate.

"What... what have you..." I cannot find a question to adequately address my shock.

The jailer laughs again, and the soldiers join him. He points toward the cistern. "Thirteen rotters in the hole. Hungry rotters, they is." Sparks erupt from the torch as he pulls it from the cage and raises it toward the ceiling. A pulley hangs over the cistern. A rope dangles from the pulley.

Dear Mother Mary.

They will dangle me in the pit and let the plaguers eat the flesh from my legs.

Two soldiers lunge forward and take hold of me. I struggle, but my hands are bound behind me. They hurl me to the grimy floor and pin my shoulders down. My face slides in the cold gore. Two other soldiers take hold of my legs. I howl and kick and try to free myself but the soldiers know their work. They have done this before.

Tristan and Morgan shout and rattle their chains while Zhuri calls down Moorish curses upon them. The jailer slips a loop of thick cloth around my thigh, pulling it high against my hip, then slips a wooden dowel between the cloth and my skin. The muck from the floor seeps through the itchy robe and chills my shoulders as I thrash against my captors. The jailer twists the dowel in the cloth, tightens the loop until the pain is excruciating.

"Wouldn't want you to bleed out and die too soon, would we?" he asks.

The jailer loops a second cloth around my other thigh and twists until my leg is numb. He binds my ankles together with a scrap of rope. The soldiers stand me up, carry me toward the cistern. I lunge against them. Bellow and curse. I scream Elizabeth's name. But I accomplish nothing. They know their work.

One of the soldiers unwinds a rope from a bracket affixed to the rear wall. It is the same rope that dangles from the pulley. Tristan spits at the soldier and earns himself a kick to the stomach. The jailer uses a pole with a hook on one end to snag the knotted end of the rope that hangs over the cistern. The soldier with the forked beard slips the rope under my arms and knots it tightly.

"Richard wants you to live for a long time," The soldier hisses in my ear. "You and the Duke of Lancaster can share a cell."

"You will burn for this!" I shout. "You will burn!"

The difficult work is over, so most of the soldiers leave the room, hands over their noses. Only four men stay behind, and two of these pull on the far end of the rope. I am hoisted into the air, the pulley squeaking like an injured rat. I flail, knowing it is useless. Knowing that I will die at the hands of the afflicted people I am sworn to protect.

I swing back and forth over the cistern, spinning slowly in the air. The rope digs under my arms. Faces look up at me from five feet below the lip of the cistern. Bloody, black faces with bleeding boils and shattered teeth. Packed tightly they can scarcely move. A forest of skeletal hands reach up. Their hisses are like a woman's tears on burning brimstone.

The soldiers let out the rope slowly, and I descend. I kick my bound legs violently, so that my swinging becomes more pronounced. The jailer reaches out with the hook and steadies me. He knows his work.

"A curse on all of you!" I shout. "God is watching!"

The chains rattle against the far wall as Morgan, Zhuri, and Tristan struggle to free themselves. The fat jailer laughs and shoves me with the hook, setting me spinning. The room passes me in flashes.

My companions yanking at the chains...

Black hands gripping cell bars...

The jailer grinning...

Four soldiers watching me as they slowly let out the rope...

The first hand touches my foot. Jagged nails scrape against my flesh. I do not think nails can spread the plague, but I curl my knees to my chest anyway. My shoulders tilt back. Plaguers grab the hem of my robe and heave. Fabric rips. I dip lower still. A cold hand brushes my back. I roar and kick downward with my legs.

A shout rings out across the dungeon, and it is not mine.

Tristan is free. He and the jailer scuffle near the cistern.

Tristan is free!

Inexplicably, the soldiers pull me upward. Up, toward God. Up toward Heaven. Up, away from the grasping, hissing mob.

I am saved!

The rope goes slack, and I plummet.

Down toward the plaguers. Down toward death. Down toward Hell.

I am damned.

CHAPTER TWENTY-ONE

THE SCREAM THAT BURSTS FROM my throat is like none I have ever made.

An instant later I realize that the scream is not mine.

I do not land on clawed fingers or snapping jaws. I land on a bucking raft of blubber and wool. A jerking, howling raft of dying jailer. The fat man is in the cistern. He lies upon the hands and faces of the plaguers below. And I lie upon him.

The world shakes and pitches. A bloody scrap of torn fabric tumbles through the air.

I am alive.

The rope digs under my arms again, and I am lifted clear of the cistern. They are pulling me out.

Two soldiers haul at the rope. Another chases Tristan around the cistern. The last guard lies on his stomach at the edge of the pit, reaching down with his hand. A torch at the edge of the pit illuminates the dying man below me. He gurgles and spasms, facedown atop the sea of plaguers. His arms flail and claw for the soldier's extended hand, but the plaguers will not relinquish their meal. They scrape and rend and bite. The fat man tips to one side and sinks, like a fleshy barge, into the grasping sea of plague. The jailer's blood spatters bright red among the greys and blacks of the afflicted horde. One of the fat man's hands reaches up from the depths of the Hellish cistern, fingers clawing at the side of the pit. But the plaguers know their work. They show no pity. Only pain.

A pinched voice rings out across the dungeon. "What happens here, now? What do you do?"

I swing my shoulders so that my body spins toward the door. Pantaleon di Alessandria stands just inside the dungeon, fingers pinching his nose. "Are you not have the sanity? What is you do here?"

Tristan and the soldier chasing him stop running. The men holding me over the cistern turn to look at the Italian. There is a long pause before someone calls back.

"They killed Sandre! Threw him into the pit."

"I am not care what they kill!" Pantaleon shouts. "I care in what is you do! Why is prisoner not with the chains? Why he is run?"

"I thought Richard wanted to leg you," one of the soldiers asks.

"King Richard, he say he sorry. And he cherish me again. So, you speak at me. What is you do here?"

Silence is the only response. Tristan stands upright and looks at me. Pantaleon shakes his head.

"Take *Cavaliere* Edward outside the rope. Your Majesty, King Richard, wants that he may put them in question."

The soldiers remain silent for a long moment. "Pardon?" one asks.

"Take the Edward away from the rope and let all him and the men meet the King."

"They've... they've met him already," the soldier replies. "That's why they're here."

"For the love of Heaven," I snarl. "Let me down. King Richard wants to speak to us."

I visit John of Gaunt's cell while the soldiers free Morgan and Zhuri from their chains. My hands have been bound behind me again, so I kneel awkwardly in front of the cage. My old enemy winces when he sees me, or perhaps it is his attempt at a smile.

"Eh-Ed-w-w…"

"I am sorry for what happened to you, John."

"H-heh-Henry."

"Henry?" I ask.

He nods. "Heh-Henry. T-t-tie-tite…"

"I don't understand, John."

"Rich-Richard… t-took way t-t…"

"I'm sorry, John. I can't make out what you are saying."

Tears brim in his eyes. He scowls and shakes his head, then lets out a long breath. "P-pi-pity. P-p-please."

I glance toward the door. Pantaleon is outside, face averted from the stench. I look toward the soldiers. They face Zhuri, who still has one hand bound. I turn back to John and nod. He thrusts his head through the iron bars. I stand, raise one foot, and do what I have wanted to do for twenty years. I break John of Gaunt's neck.

And it brings me no pleasure. Only pain.

When my companions are free from the manacles on the wall—and their hands bound behind them again—Pantaleon advises the soldiers, in his mangled English, to report the jailer's death to the constable.

One of the soldiers—the one with the forked beard—taps two of his men on the chest, and they hustle out of the room.

"Tell him Sandre was responsible for the prisoner that got free!" the blond soldier calls after them. "He was the one who manacled him! The fault was Sandre's!"

The Italian picks up the fallen torch and looks into the cistern, shaking his head.

"Sandre was having many keys," he says. "You are getting the keys, or Richard will to scream upon you."

The two soldiers peer into the cistern, and Pantaleon shoves them in. Their screams are three parts terror and one part shock of betrayal.

The Italian whirls to face us, his cloak whipping around his shoulders. "There is small time to run! We go now! With many quickness!"

I exchange glances with my companions and nod my thanks to the Italian.

And we go. With many quickness.

We walk back swiftly along the dark underground passageway.

"Well done in there, Tristan." I say.

"No thanks are needed." He is pleased with himself. I can tell by his smile. "But I expect I won't hear any more lavender jests."

"Slippery wrists," I say. "I may start using that salve myself." But I know I will not. Because my time on this earth is almost done. Elizabeth cannot be cured. I will give myself to Hell, and let Satan distract me from my agony.

We hustle up the winding stone staircase and through a door leading to the upper prison. Empty cells line both walls here. A porter paces near the door leading outside, rubbing his hands together. He draws a dagger when he sees us, his eyes wild.

"What's happening down there, Italian?" he calls. "Thomas said Sandre is dead. And why are these people out of the dungeon?"

Pantaleon makes calming motions with his hand. "I tell to you all." He draws near and, in one motion, unsheathes his own dagger and stabs the man in the throat. Blood sprays the Italian as he twists the blade and shoves the guard to the floor.

Pantaleon takes keys from the man's belt and releases us from our bonds. When we are free, he hands me the dead porter's dagger, draws his short sword, and gives his own dagger to Tristan. "Some people take the horses away from castle and we find with them later. But now, we are killing more people." He motions to the door. "Outside."

I do not want to *killing more people*, but we have no choice. The constable will be on his way to the prison chamber soon, and the entire castle will be alerted to our escape.

I let out a long breath and prepare to take more humanity from the world.

CHAPTER TWENTY-TWO

THE PRICE OF OUR ESCAPE from Framlingham Castle is four more lives: two guards outside the prison chamber and another two at the postern door leading out of the lower courtyard and into the countryside. Four more souls.

The prison at Framlingham was built beyond the curtain walls, which is a sound strategy for preventing escaped prisoners from taking over the castle. It is, however, a poor strategy for recapturing escaped prisoners. We trot across a stone bridge that spans the northern ditch, hunching low and hugging the stone ledge. Our caution is unnecessary. The men in the northern watchtower stand with their backs to us, laughing and passing what appears to be a wineskin. We clear the bridge and find ourselves on an old trail leading to the vast deer-hunting park north of the castle.

A horn sounds when we are a quarter mile from the curtain walls. Our escape has been noted.

We run faster, past thick clusters of elm and ash, a half mile into the lush hunting grounds of Framlingham.

"A friend to me hided horses!" Pantaleon calls as he runs. "And all that we are to be need!" He points to a stand of alders rising by themselves in the distance. "There! Five horses are being there, behind the trees! And six soldier men with the chain mail and the weapons. They friends to me and are to help."

More horns sound behind us. I glance back toward the castle. No one pursues yet. We round the stand of alders.

A thin donkey chews grass and stares at us absently. Beside the animal lies a large, canvas wrapped bundle—wide as a carriage wheel and high as my waist. If there are horses, and men with armor and weapons, they are cleverly hidden. I look at the Italian.

"No!" He spins in a circle, hands in the air. "No! There were to be the men! And the horses!"

"Perhaps they are in the sack," Tristan offers.

"Are you certain this is where they were meeting you?" I ask.

"Yes!" The Italian shouts. "*Sono idioti! Idioti e vigliacchi!*" He slashes the cords holding the canvas together and pulls the bundle open. Two suits of armor gleam in the last breaths of daylight. Mine, and Tristan's. Our two hand-cannons are there also, and our shoulder sacks, swords, helmets, pouches, and all of our clothing. There are also two linen sacks. I open one and discover dried strips of meat. Tristan opens the other and finds bread, cut into squares.

At the center of the pile, tied to a leather cord, is Elizabeth's cure. I lift it from the stack and clench my hand around the ampoule. How much did we go through to find this? How much humanity did I take in my quest for this cure? How much humanity did I lose? And what was it worth?

Nothing at all. Because the cure is useless to Elizabeth.

I push thoughts of her out of my mind. They will cripple me. I have a duty to Tristan, Morgan, and Zhuri. Only when they are safe can I surrender to my grief. The linen-wrapped jar of dragon blood lies at the bottom of my shoulder sack. I take it out, run my fingers across its surfaces to make sure it has not been damaged. The men of England may need this jar. Only the men. I swallow the wave of sorrow that rises in me once again.

"Couldn't they have found me something decent to wear?" Morgan asks. "New robes at least?"

The "clerical vestments" that Morgan has worn since leaving Hedingham are filthy and covered in dried blood.

"Leper robes are meant to be dirty, Morgan." Tristan pulls his breastplate from the pile. "At least Edward and I have armor again."

"You are not want the big armor," Pantaleon says. "It turn you slow."

"It does not slow us down at all," Tristan says. "My armor was designed to fit me perfectly. I can dance in it. Now ask me how I know that. Ask me."

"Quiet, Tristan, " I say. "There is no time to put the armor on. We have no horses and a dozen knights are about to storm out of Framlingham. Pantaleon, thank you for your help. Good luck in your endeavors."

"You will give to me the paid, no?" Pantaleon asks.

"Give you the paid?" I ask.

"I take you from the smelling room. I take all into the free. You give to me the paid?"

"You expect to be paid for freeing us?" I sputter my words. "I saved your life!"

"Yes. For you, there is being no paid. But the friends of you, yes. I take them into free. I put Pantaleon into the danger."

I try not to think about Elizabeth, but I know her fate colors my words, imbues them with more anger than I feel. "I saved your bloody life! Have some dignity! *Some honor!*"

"Honor?" he asks.

"Yes, honor," I snap. "Respect for others and for doing what is *proper* without seeking reward. Honor."

The Italian scowls. "*Proper* is to get the paid when I take people into the free. Only the paid makes good in the life. Only the paid." He draws Tristan's ten-shot hand bombard from the pile. "Perhaps this is the paid?"

Tristan pulls the cannon from the Italian's hands. "Perhaps bloody not!"

"Payment is the only good thing in life?" I say. "That's absurd. What about justice? What about love? What about chivalry?"

The Italian grins. "You can eat the *justice*? You can drink the *love*?" He chuckles. "This *chivalry*, can you to fuck on it?"

"You are filth," I say. "And you have no honor."

"I maybe own the honor before," he laughs. "But I sell it for the whore money, maybe. I walk beside you until the danger go. And then you will be giving to me *the paid*."

"I will be giving to you a broken skull," Tristan says.

"We don't have time for this foolishness," I say. "Take what you need from the pile, all of you, and put the remainder on the donkey."

We pull our boots on, sling shoulder sacks and strap on sword belts. I draw my shield from the stack, and Morgan finds his cross. Zhuri flips open a leather poke and takes out the last spare ampoule of the Syrian cure. We have two doses left, and no one to give them to. I think about the dying mercenary—the one escorting the pilgrims—and I clench my fists.

The last item in the canvas sack is a coil of rope. We tie the sack again and use the new rope to secure the great heap of armor and supplies onto the donkey's back.

Two horn blasts shatter the twilight silence of the deer park. Horsemen finally burst from the postern door of the lower courtyard and storm across the long bridge leading to the park. Two dozen at least, holding torches or lanterns.

We stumble in the dark, toward the northwest corner of the deer park. There is silence around us, save for our breathing and the muffled clank of armor in the canvas bag.

We reach the timber fence bordering the park. If we were deer, the fence would trap us in the killing grounds of Framlingham. But we are men, and desperate ones, so we pull down the damp stakes, push through the gaps, and slip quietly into the night.

We wind around the great mere, hunching low and swatting at the donkey when it brays. My feet sink deep into the marshy ground and squelch when I draw them out.

A great forest lies to the north of Framlingham, and we creep into it, hearing the mad tolls of distant church bells. Richard is alerting the countryside to our escape.

The forest is black as my mood, but we pick our way through, stopping every hundred paces or so to ensure that no one is lost. I have never taken a donkey through a forest, and it is an experience I hope never to repeat. The animal balks at every log, scrub or jutting stone we come to. I would release the creature, but only a fool makes decisions based on inconvenience. In this plague-swept kingdom, flesh is the new coin. Horses are the golden pound, and pack animals the shillings. This donkey represents wealth, and we need that to escape Richard's net.

Morgan winces and limps sometimes as he walks, but the damage from the plague seems to lessen with each hour. He speaks to Pantaleon often, perhaps to take his mind from the pain of raking branches and tearing scabs. Their conversation turns to the plaguers plowing the fields outside of Framlingham and how Pantaleon became acquainted with King Richard. The Italian tells him that Matheus, the man from the new Holy Lands near Boxford, became plagued. This comes as no surprise to us, since it was Tristan who secretly infected him.

Hugh the Baptist, the plaguer whose ability to speak convinced an untold number of pilgrims to afflict themselves, lost his lower jaw. Pantaleon tells us it simply rotted away. With no talking plaguer and no Matheus, the pilgrims stopped coming, and Pantaleon was forced to find new ways to get the paid.

"Your Majesty, the king, he buy many rotters from the man, Matheus. So I make path to the castle of Framlingham, for finding the work."

I have harbored doubts about Matheus since the day I met him. He was a persuasive man, and a part of me always wondered if he was telling the truth; if perhaps we are dead already, condemned to wander purgatory, surrounded by demons, until we are deemed worthy enough for Heaven, or unworthy enough for Hell. But Pantaleon's words strike the wonder from my heart. Matheus was a merchant, selling the afflicted. Profiting from the faith of pilgrims, as so many others have done before him.

"King Richard bought plaguers from Matheus?" I ask. "As if they were slaves to be sold?" It should not surprise me after all that I have seen this past day and night.

Pantaleon nods. "This Matheus, he sell the rotting people to many another. And in paid, he receive many gift."

In this plague-swept kingdom, flesh is the new coin. Even rotting flesh.

"And how did he buy you?" Morgan asks.

"With the things of important," The Italian replies. "The drink, the women, and the horses."

"Sounds like quite a night, Italian." I can almost hear Tristan's smirk in the forest darkness.

"The name I have is Pantaleon di Alessandria."

"I know your name, Italian," Tristan replies. "But it's a silly one."

Pantaleon does not reply for a long moment, and when he finally speaks, his voice is low and fierce. "It is great name. It is meaning *the lion*."

Zhuri chuckles. "In Spanish, *pantalones* means pants."

Tristan laughs quietly with the Moor. "Are you named after breeches, Italian? Did your mother name you while doing the wash?"

There is another long pause in the darkness, the only sound our footsteps shushing through leaves or snapping twigs.

"My name is meaning *lion*." There is something menacing in his voice.

"What's your brother's name?" Tristan asks. "Tunic?"

Zhuri and Tristan muffle their laughter with their hands.

"Do you mind if we call you Trousers?" Zhuri asks.

"Quiet, both of you," Morgan snaps. "Richard's men may be in this forest. And you should leave this man alone. He saved our lives."

I nod to Morgan, although I doubt he can see me in the darkness. I do not like this Italian, but he saved our lives. More importantly, I worry that he might try to kill Tristan and Zhuri if they continue. Although perhaps that would finally quiet them. The two of them are adding mirth to an otherwise dark night, but their laughter grates upon me. My Elizabeth is lost forever, and I may never laugh with them again.

A horn sounds in the distance. Am I to always flee from horns now? I do not know if Richard's men are in the forest. No sane man would send men into a dark wood, where ambush lurks around every tree. But this is the new Richard. I cannot assume he will do what is wise.

The forest thins out after two or three miles and we break onto a field made bright and colorless by a three-quarter moon. A square tower rises in the distance, black, save for a glimmer of moonlight along one side. A church, no doubt. No bells ring from it, so either Richard's men have failed to reach the place or the inhabitants do not care about his quarrels. He is the King of England, so I can imagine only one reason for them not to care.

We march through a furrowed plot that has been left fallow and, as we draw closer to the distant tower, walls become visible. Another priory.

"You English possess many church," Pantaleon says. "Many church."

It is true. We do.

When commoners commit a sin, they seek a confessor. They divulge their sins and pray for God's forgiveness. Or, if the sin is grave enough, they make a pilgrimage to beg a saint for salvation.

It is not so for the ruling class. When nobles sin, they build churches. They bury their transgressions beneath flint and oak, and the greater the evil, the greater the church. The sins of our rulers are endless, and so churches rise everywhere, usually on the very spot that the sin occurred. The churches stand like gravestones, monuments to the evil in men's hearts. Each holy site blossoms like a flower from the offal of nobility, from the fecal remains of lambs those wolves have slaughtered.

If ever I decide to bury my sins beneath a church, it will take a hundred million flints to do so. The transepts of my creation will stretch the width of England, and the spire will be seen from Spain. I will call it St. Elizabeth, and I will weep at its altar for the rest of my days. I will weep for an angel I almost saved.

And God will almost forgive me.

We approach the priory, and I realize why the bells are not ringing. A great section of the outer wall has collapsed and a shape lurches out from the breach. The afflicted have overrun the compound.

We hide behind a short line of hedges and study the broken wall.

"If we are discussing this," Zhuri says. "I would prefer not to enter that place."

"We don't have to enter," I reply. "The four of you should head south. I'll go west toward St. Edmund's."

There is a silence into which the donkey brays. The Italian smacks the animal's rump.

"Why should the four of us head south, Edward?" Morgan asks.

I peer through gaps in the hedge. The afflicted man has turned to face us. Damnable donkey. I look closely at the plaguer. He was once a monk. Or is. I do not know anymore which term is appropriate. One of the monk's arms dangles limply at his side.

"There's no reason all of us should go to St. Edmund's Bury." I reach under my breastplate and draw out the cure, hand it to Tristan. "There's no purpose to it."

"I thought we discussed this earlier." Morgan's voice is strained.

"We did, Morgan. But that was when we thought... we thought she could be healed." I curse myself for the break in my voice.

"And we think differently now?" Zhuri asks.

"Of course we do," I snap. "The cure only works on men."

Morgan shakes his head. "Edward—"

The plagued monk growls and stumbles toward us.

"What nonsense are you speaking, Edward?" Zhuri cocks his head to one side.

"It's not nonsense, Zhuri. I have seen it. Two men have been healed by the Syrian cure, and two women turned into abominations. I won't have my wife become one of those things. Best she... best she take her place in Heaven than live in that Hell for the rest of her days."

"Edward, the cure works on men and women," Morgan says.

"It's not true, Morgan! I won't do it to her. I won't let her... I won't let her become..."

I drop my head into my hands and take deep breaths.

Morgan grasps my shoulder. "It works on women, Edward. I have seen it. And so has Zhuri."

I look up, glancing from one to the other, daring them to convince me.

"He speaks truthfully," Zhuri says. "One of the nuns at Hedingham was healed, just after Morgan took the cure. She spoke and laughed and was completely sane."

"Completely sane," Tristan repeats. "This said of someone who no doubt believes that a man loaded two of every animal in existence onto a boat."

"Shut that heretic mouth, Tristan," Morgan replies. "If you doubt Noah did what is written in Genesis, then explain how all of those animals survived the great flood. Go on. Did they tread water for months? Tell me Tristan. How?"

Tristan opens his mouth, leaves it open for a long moment before speaking. "I'm not sure it's even possible for you and I to discuss this, Morgan."

"And me," Zhuri says. "'you and *me* to discuss this.'"

Their conversation seems to fade away. They argue and laugh and shout, oblivious to the impact of their words. A woman was healed by the Syrian cure. They have seen it. There is hope! There is blessed, Godly hope!

I snatch the ampoule from Tristan's grasp and study it closely. There is either Heaven or Hell in that ampoule. Life or a horrible death. The world hinges always upon two opposing outcomes.

But it might still hold my Heaven.

Women can be cured.

Joy floods through me like a hot spring, bubbles to every corner of my body.

Women can be cured.

Sometimes.

The hot spring cools, then freezes.

I will give Elizabeth something that will either save her or damn her. My heart is a smith's hammer in my chest.

I will save her or destroy her, but I have hope again. Blessed Mary, I have *hope*.

The plaguer snarls again. He is not more than twenty paces away.

Pantaleon stands and draws his short sword.

Morgan and Tristan glance at me, then at the Italian.

"Put it away," Morgan says.

Pantaleon glances at the blade, then at Morgan. "The demon, he comes to here. We must to kill it."

"They aren't demons," Tristan says. "Put the sword away."

Pantaleon scoffs, gestures toward the plaguer. "I not know why you say such. The rotter will eat upon us. It is demon." He throws his hands upward in frustration. "The bishop of England, he tell the people to kill these!"

"Yes, but he was speaking figuratively." Tristan lays his lays his hand on the Italian's arm and pushes the sword down.

Pantaleon wrenches his arm free. "Even the Pope, he is saying the sick people should be kill."

"Which Pope?" Tristan replies.

"Let's go." I stand and gauge the distance to the priory walls.

"I thought there was only one Pope," Zhuri says.

"There is," Morgan snaps. "We have only one true Pope, blessed and sanctioned by Christ Himself."

"Yes," Tristan replies. "But we're damned if we know which one that is."

CHAPTER TWENTY-THREE

THE PRIORY IS A SMALL ONE. Just large enough to bury a small cardinal sin, or to clear the assorted moral debts of a dying nobleman. The place is nothing more than a dotting of small stone buildings huddled together, surrounded by shoulder-high walls. A tiny church—not much more than a stone hall attached to a Norman tower—hunches at the center of the complex.

"There are no bodies on the ground," Morgan says.

"They must have fled before the plaguers arrived," Zhuri replies.

"What plaguers?" Tristan asks.

A thin figure shuffles aimlessly along the grassy stretches between the outbuildings and the walls. There is no other sign of plague here.

"Let's look for a safe place to sleep," I say. "If we can't find one here, then we keep moving." The lack of plaguers worries me. These days it is in the calmest of waters that the worst dangers seem to lie.

"It's strange that Richard's men haven't followed us through the forest," Tristan says.

"It's night," I reply. "It would be difficult to find us. And we could take his men by surprise in the darkness."

"We could surprise dozens of men in armor?" Tristan says.

I shrug. Despite the threat of ambush, Richard should have sent men into the forest. If I felt someone had wronged Elizabeth, I would hunt them through Hell itself. I do not know why the king's men are not pursuing, and that, too, makes me restless.

The closest building is a small thatched structure set apart from the others. A battered door lies at an odd angle, twisted back and to one side because of a broken top hinge. I take hold of the iron latch and pull. Wood grates on stone as the narrow door straightens. I shove it forward, evenly, and it creaks open. The stench of rotting flesh wafts from the room. Moonlight streams through a glazed window, creating a silver patch on the floor but doing little to illuminate the room.

Tristan kneels and strikes a flint, showering one of our last firing cords with sparks. It takes a half dozen strikes before the powder on the rope ignites. He rises and thrusts the smoldering cord into the darkness.

A body lies on the floor. There is not much left of the cadaver. Bones and fabric, an open-mouthed skull. The carcass seems to twitch, but I realize it is an illusion created by the flickering light.

"Someone's had a snack," Tristan says.

"Have you no respect for the dead?" Morgan snaps. "Such a cruel bastard you can be."

"Me?" Tristan replies. "*I* didn't eat him."

"Be prepared," I whisper. "The door was shut." Plaguers do not shut doors when they leave a building. Whatever fed upon this poor man is likely still inside.

Tristan swings the cord to the right. Shadows dance from four long-armed chairs sitting one in front of the other. Wooden boards rest across the arms of each chair. Polished oxhorns sit in round holes at a corner of each board. Tools lie neatly upon the makeshift desktops—awls, razors, pumice stones—and, tucked into a wooden stand on each, is a feather quill.

"Scriptorium," Morgan says.

A place for writing. For days on end, monks sat in those chairs, dipping their quills into the oxhorn inkwells and scrawling out line after line of text. Father Aubrey, my priest at Bodiam, told me that it takes a monk thirteen months to copy a Bible. I try to imagine sitting in one of those chairs every day for a year, scrawling line after line. Beheading would be preferable.

I take the firing cord from Tristan and step into the room. Nothing approaches from the darkness. There is no sound in the room other than the scuff of my boot against the planks. The others follow behind me. A rat darts from the darkness and Pantaleon kicks it into the corner. The creature screeches and scampers in the darkness. "These are dirty creature," he says. "They are many dirty."

Tristan kneels beside the rotting body and tugs a leather pouch from the man's belt. He looks inside and whistles. "I had no idea monks were so well paid." He tips the pouch and four golden nobles tumble into his palm.

"I am accepting one of the gold money for the payment," Pantaleon says.

"Hold onto them, Tristan," I say. "Would you really sell your honor for just one golden noble, Pantaleon?"

"You speak the word again," Pantaleon says, smirking. "Aw-nor. This is not a thing being real. I am not possible to touch it. Or look at aw-nor with eyes. I can to feel a coin. And the coin lets me to feel breast of the beautiful woman."

"Lets me feel," Zhuri says.

"Lovely," Morgan says. "A Spanish Arab is teaching English to an Italian."

"Keep quiet," I say, extending the firing cord toward one side of the room, then the other.

"Someone must have shut the door from outside," Zhuri says. "There is no one here."

My teeth grind. I force myself to relax my jaw.

Shadows bounce as the light from the firing cord flares and dims. A modest bookshelf sits against the far wall, with six or seven bound volumes upon it. Pantaleon brushes past me and pulls one of the books from the shelf, flips through it, then grabs two more of the thick tomes.

"We are needing the sack," he says. "To put inside this books."

Another rat, or perhaps the same one, scurries out from the shadows. Pantaleon stomps at it several times before finally crushing its skull with his heel. "Dirty creature."

Morgan takes one of the books from the Italian and studies it, flips open the wooden cover. "This is a book of hours," he says. "I didn't think you were a worshipping man."

"I were." Pantaleon grins. "I worship the gold. Books in this sort, they worth many gold. The paid from the books will let me to feel many…" He frowns.

"Will *let you feel* many," Zhuri offers.

"You will not sell the Word of God." Morgan places the volume back on the shelf. "And you will touch no breasts with money that came from selling sacred books. Put them back. All of them."

"What about this one?" Tristan still kneels by the dead man. He holds up a book no larger than the palm of his hand. "Is this worth anything? The monk had it."

"We're not here to read," I say. "Let's make certain this room is safe and then barricade the door."

Another pair of rats scampers from the darkness, and Pantaleon stomps at them. Morgan walks to Tristan's side and takes the tiny book. "Edward," he says. "If you would, please. Richard's men didn't return my Bible. I want to find another small one to carry."

I give him some light. He flips through the pumiced pages, reading the tight black lines of text. "It's in English," he says. "Very rare." He flips to the next page and shakes his head. "Just verses from the Bible. Must have been a selection of this man's favori..." His jaw tightens as he flips to the next page, then the next. Even in the dim light I can see his face growing red. "This... this is filth! Utter filth!" He hurls the book across the room. It strikes the back wall and bounces halfway back.

Tristan steps forward and scoops it up.

"Leave it Tristan!" Morgan shouts. "Leave it alone!"

Tristan clears his throat and reads out loud: "'Ezekiel 23:20.'" His eyes grow wide and he chuckles before reading the next line. "'There she lusted after her lovers, whose genitals were like those of donkeys and whose emissions were like those of horses.'" He laughs and holds the book up so we can all see it. "So sayeth the Lord!"

"That is filth," Morgan replies.

"But it's God's filth," Tristan replies. "Are you saying the Bible is filthy?"

"No. I'm saying that dead monk was a lewd, disgusting and debauched sinner. He collected the filthiest verses for his own sordid pleasures."

"Have you no respect for the dead?" Tristan says. "Such a cruel bastard you can be."

"Calm yourselves," I say.

But Tristan clears his throat and reads another line. "'So you longed for the lewdness of your youth, when in Egypt your bosom was caressed and your young breasts fondled.'" He raises one brow. "I had no idea the Bible was like this. It's no wonder you read it so much, Morgan."

Morgan snatches the book. "I'm going to burn this stack of excrement."

"How dare you keep the Word of God from me?" Tristan says.

"God has better Words than these."

Tristan lunges for the book, but Morgan holds it out of his reach. Zhuri and Pantaleon chuckle, and I cannot help smiling. Elizabeth will be cured. Morgan is back. And my heart sings again.

"You just want the book for yourself!" Tristan shouts.

"Shut your cave!" Morgan shouts. "If you want to read the Bib—"

"*Mashalla!*" Zhuri's shout silences both of them. The Moor kicks violently. A rat strikes the wall with a squeal. "That dirty creature bit my boot."

"Hungry, dirty creatures," Tristan says.

Two more rats scamper toward us. Their oily fur glistens in the flickering light. Zhuri hops onto one of the chairs, and Tristan laughs.

"Laugh if you want," Zhuri says. "Rats spread disease."

More of the creatures patter out from under a great stack of collapsed shelves.. A half dozen pairs of eyes, glinting red in the smoldering flame. Their fur bristles in oily spikes. Large rats. Big as shoes.

Morgan kicks one. "They must be starving to come at us like this."

I drive the point of my sword through one, pinning it to the floor with a thud. The rat squeals and thrashes. "Let's find another building. One without vermin."

Pantaleon walks to the fallen shelves from where the rats come. "I will to look here," he says. "For only the moment. I find for more books."

Tristan stomps, making another rat-shaped stain on the floor. "Maybe we should sleep on the chairs, eh Zhuri?"

"Leave it, Pantaleon," I lift my sword and stab the rat again, but the creature continues to writhe under my blade. Tough animal.

"It is just one moment." Pantaleon tugs at one of the shelves, recoils and makes a face. "I am seeing books. But such many dirty creatures here. Such many."

A thought occurs to me.

I raise the sword again. The rat drags itself toward my feet, its jaws snapping. I slash at the creature, cutting it in half. The jaws continue to snap. The forelegs claw at the wooden planks.

"Pantaleon," I call.

The rat drags itself forward toward my foot.

"Pantaleon!" My shout rings dully in the cramped scriptorium.

The stack of shelves topples with a crash and a billow of rats scurry from beneath the fallen planks. They swarm onto and around the Italian, crashing like an ocean wave, the flood of them carrying past him and toward us. So many of them. Pantaleon stumbles back and falls onto one leg, then springs to his feet again as more rats leap onto his armor. He howls and crashes toward us, slapping rats off his legs. He rocks madly as he steps on the scurrying creatures, their twisted squeals filling the air.

"They're plagued!" I bellow. "They're bloody plagued! Flee for your lives!"

Zhuri leaps so quickly that the chair he was standing on falls backward with a clatter, the tools and board jangling to the floor. Tristan accidentally slams his shoulder against the narrow doorway before stumbling out, sideways. Zhuri and Morgan plunge out after him.

I kick at rats as more and more of them pool around my feet. "*Pantaleon!*"

The Italian brushes past me screaming. He holds a leather-bound book under his arm and a rat in his hand. I shove him through the doorway and follow, feeling the scrape of claws on my boots. I brush at the vermin convulsively, panic sending fire through my limbs. Morgan yanks the door shut and leans back to hold it in place. He stamps his feet furiously at any of the creatures that comes close. Pantaleon drops the thick tome. He jerks and twists, kicks one calf against the other to knock a rat free. Tristan and Zhuri run in circles, stomping on the plagued vermin.

The Italian seems to remember that he still holds a rat in his gloved hand. He screams, a high pitched wail, and hurls the rat. The animal bounces off the ground, into the air, and scurries forward as soon as it strikes the earth again.

"*Madre di Dio!*" The Italian shuffles backward, but the rat leaps at him. I did not know rats could leap so far. It lands on his foot and scuttles up the long leather boot, winding around his leg. He runs, high-stepping and slapping at his legs. "*Farlo fuori!*" he shouts. "*Farlo...* Get it... get it from me! Get it from me!"

Zhuri and Morgan chase after him kicking lightly at his legs.

The donkey brays and flees as a rat approaches it. I take a great running kick that sends the rat into the wall of the scriptorium, leaving a red splotch on the stone.

One of Morgan's blows finally connects with the rat on Pantaleon's leg. The animal tumbles away, but charges the Italian again when it hits the ground.

"Get it!" Morgan shouts.

"Kill it!" Zhuri cries. "Stomp on it, Tristan, stomp on it!"

Tristan makes an attempt to stomp on the animal, but his heel glances off the oily fur. Morgan lunges forward and catches the rat's rump with his heel. The creature screeches but tries to staggers forward again, pinned by the tail. Pantaleon leaps into the air and stomps with both feet, crushing the rat and releasing a spatter of black blood in all directions.

A silence falls upon us as we search the grounds for more rats and breathe heavily. We look at one another, eyes wide, shoulders rising and falling.

Tristan laughs.

He doubles over, hands on his thighs, and his laughter rings out across the priory.

"This is funny thing to you?" Pantaleon's shout drowns out Tristan's mirth. "If the dirty creature had to bite me, it would give to me sickness! *And this is funny thing to you?*"

Tristan raises one hand in conciliation, but does not stop laughing. "Sorry... sorry," he takes great gasping breaths, then straightens and shakes his hands in feigned panic. "Get it from me! Get it from me!" He breaks down again, wiping at his eyes.

Pantaleon glares for a long moment, then smiles weakly. Shrugs. "Is funny a little. The animal, it does not stop at me!" He chuckles. "It come again and again!"

Zhuri chortles. "How was that, Edward?" He dons a terrified expression and mimics my accent. *"They're bloody plagued! Flee for your lives!"* He laughs and Morgan, still holding the door, laughs too.

I slash two handed at a rat scampering toward me. "And who knocked over half the scriptorium trying to get out, Zhuri?" I snap.

Zhuri hoots and falls back against one of the walls, wipes at his eyes with the heels of his hands. "The rat... the rat was on Pantaleon's *pantalones!*"

Tristan, doubled over, gasps as he laughs. "Stop... stop... I can't breathe..."

The laughter creeps into me as well. I drop to a knee and shake my head and join them. It has been a hard day, and it feels good to jest. We laugh and laugh like bloody fools, the peals of it ringing out into the darkness.

Elizabeth will be healed. I know she will. I have no doubts. And Richard's men have stopped pursuing us. All is well.

But my humor suddenly turns to something else.

I lurch to my feet and stare northward, toward Framlingham. Richard is no longer pursuing us. And I suddenly realize why.

He does not have to pursue us. Because he, like Gerald, knows where we are going. But unlike Gerald, Richard has an army. An army that can defeat the ring of plaguers surrounding the monastery.

Richard is going to kill Elizabeth.

The laughter of my companions rings around me like mockery.

CHAPTER TWENTY-FOUR

THE PRIORY CHURCH IS DEVOTED to Saint Mary the Virgin, which does not surprise me. Mother Mary has followed me on my journey—so much so that sometimes I feel like a character from one of the Greek plays Elizabeth likes to read. The ones where gods move humans like chess pieces. Mary is not a god, but I feel her hand wherever I go.

We seal ourselves into a small room built against the church walls, just outside the nave. It is the prior's chamber, I believe, and it is free of rats, so we pull the donkey inside and bar the door. Whoever left the supplies for Pantaleon only thought to give us four strips of dried venison and a cut-up loaf of bread. We eat all of it, and Zhuri shakes the bread bag over his mouth to catch the last of the crumbs.

Morgan applies his nightly coat of the pungent Malta fungus and is snoring on the floor in an instant. The others fall into the steady breathing of sleep not long after. I lie awake for a time, my body humming with exhaustion. I think about King Richard. Night makes certainty of my fears, and I almost rise and begin walking toward St. Edmund's Bury on my own. But a night's march when I am exhausted will leave me easy prey for the endless predators of Suffolk.

Richard will need time to ready his soldiers. And his men will need a night of rest. I calm myself with those thoughts and drift into a troubled sleep.

We rise when the first patches of sunlight creep under the door. My first thoughts are a jumble of dreams and regrets. Of Elizabeth and guilt. I should have been with her in St. Edmund's Bury when the plague struck. I stayed behind, in Bodiam, to work on my castle.

My castle.

What use is a fortification when there is nothing for me to defend? My Elizabeth was in East Anglia, and I was building in Sussex. The ache of it is as strong as it was the day I found her plagued.

St. Edmund's Bury lies to the west, but I want to put some distance between us and Framlingham Castle before continuing our journey. We walk south instead, among sodden fields, each sloshing step taking me one pace farther from Elizabeth. I remind myself that I cannot take any steps at all if Richard finds me, because the flesh will be stripped from my legs. And if Richard is sallying forth with his army, it will take him a long time to reach St. Edmund's Bury. Armies are slow, cumbersome things, dragging behind supplies and camp followers.

We reach a small river after a mile. I think it is the River Ore, although Morgan believes it to be the River Deben. Both rivers run mostly north to south and lie between us and St. Edmund's Bury. We will have to cross one of them at some point, so I decide to ford here, where the water is shallow. Tristan and Pantaleon have to pull together to get the stubborn donkey into the water.

Once across, we head south again, along the gently rolling mounds that East Anglians call hills.

"Why so gloomy, Ed?" Tristan asks. "We have a cure, Richard has stopped chasing us, and the *sun* is *out*. Can you fathom it? The sun is out."

I walk a few steps before replying. "Richard is very likely marshaling an army right now. Preparing to march on St. Edmund's Bury."

"Why would he do that?" Morgan has a dagger out, and a whetstone he borrowed from Pantaleon.

"Because he thinks I killed his wife," I reply. "And so he will kill mine."

No one speaks for a time. A magpie chitters in the distance.

"That is absurd," Zhuri says. "He would not risk thousands of his men to kill one woman. Only a madman would…" He trails off and clears his throat. "We should find horses."

The soft grassy swells roll downward into a shallow valley. Naked wood catches the sunlight. A palisade of freshly cut stakes rings an entire village. Someone has been busy.

There is only one break that I can see in those walls, and a gatehouse of logs guards it. Two men stand on the tower of the gatehouse, daylight flashing from steel helms.

"I'll wager there are horses in there," Tristan says.

I glance over my shoulder, then back at the fortified village. "Framlingham can't be more than five miles away. Richard's men have probably alerted them."

"If Richard is going to St. Edmund's Bury, why would he bother alerting a village five miles to the south?"

It does not matter whether Richard has alerted them or not. We need horses. And if there are horses anywhere nearby, they will be in this village.

"I will go by myself," I say. "The rest of you hide in the trees over there. There's no sense in risking all our lives."

"I thought we came to an understanding about this at the priory, Edward." Morgan runs the whetstone over his dagger blade as he talks.

"Where you go, we follow," Tristan says. "I don't want to quote the Bible, Edward, but I will." He purses his lips and squints. "In truth, I can't remember the verse, but it has to do with falling into a cesspit or something."

"'Two are better than one,'" I say. "'For if one falls, the other will lift up his fellow. But woe to him who is alone when he falls and has not another to lift him up.'"

"That's the one. Don't make me say what you just said."

It was the verse Belisencia spoke to me when I tried to sneak away from the Hedingham nunnery. I wanted to leave them there, in safety, while I finished my search for the alchemist. But they would not allow me to. I look at Tristan and he returns the stare.

We continue walking.

"If Richard's men are waiting for us there," Tristan says with a grin, "You all know what to do, no?"

Zhuri and Morgan grin. All three of them shout it at once: "Flee! Flee for your lives!"

"What possessed me to bring such fools as you along?" I grumble.

"To bring *fools such as you along*," Zhuri corrects.

"We're not fools," Tristan says. "We're clever chickens."

"And you're hopeless without us," Morgan adds.

I smile in spite of my anxiety and call back to the Italian. "Pantaleon, you can go if you want. We may be walking right back into Richard's hands by entering that village."

The Italian shakes his head. "You want that I go so you not have to give to me the paid. I follow behind. Perhaps you find for me a woman to have the pleasure with?"

"We don't even have a horse for you to have the pleasure with," Tristan replies.

Zhuri sighs. "I could use a good woman. Or a good horse, really. It has been a while."

He and Tristan chuckle.

Pantaleon laughs with them. "If you are needing the pleasure so many, you can to bugger my arse. For the paid, of course." He continues to laugh. Tristan and Zhuri grow silent. We all stare at the Italian.

"What did you say?" Morgan asks.

Pantaleon smiles nervously. "It is a thing that sometimes is done, in Italia. Men put their… their *pene* into arses. For the pleasure."

"I know what buggering an arse is!" Morgan stammers. "Do you let men do this to you often, you obscene bastard? For pay?"

"It was for joke!" the Italian shouts. A flush rises in his cheeks. "You say bugger a horse, and we are missing horses, so I offer donkey! It was joke only!"

Tristan's laugh is loud and short. "You were talking about the donkey?"

Pantaleon frowns, gestures toward the animal. "Do you not speak the English? A donkey in the English has name of *arse*."

"Ass," Tristan replies. "A donkey is called an ass. Two small letters, one enormous difference."

Pantaleon frowns. "Then what is the arse?"

"It's a filthy canal." Tristan shrugs. "That's what the alchemist called it."

"Quiet," I say. "They're looking."

The soldiers face us now, their helms dipping toward one another occasionally to exchange comments. I wonder again if Richard's men have been here. Morgan runs the stone across his dagger blade as we walk. It sounds like death's fingers scraping toward us.

A door of bound wooden logs blocks entry to the village. The soldiers peer down at us as we near. They wear flat-topped nasal helms with chainmail coifs, but I cannot make out the arms on their tabards. One of the men calls down when we are ten paces from the gate. "Are you here for the trial?"

Tristan looks to me but I do not return the glance. I keep my eyes on the soldier and nod. "Yes. The trial."

"What's that thing with you?" The soldier calls down.

I glance back at the animal Pantaleon holds. "It's a donkey."

"It is ass," Pantaleon shouts.

"I know what a donkey is," The guard calls back. "I'm not concerned with the donkey. I'm talking about the other thing. Is that an Arab? No infidels are allowed in the village during the trial."

I glance at Zhuri. "He's not an infidel."

"I'm not?" Zhuri asks.

"Tell him that you follow Christ." I whisper through clenched teeth.

"Edward, I have no doubt that Christ was a wonderful man, but Muhammad is my prophet."

"Tell. Him. You. Follow. Christ." I wave cheerfully to the soldier.

It is several heartbeats before Zhuri speaks, and I realize the turmoil I have created in his heart. "I am not an infidel," he calls. "I used to be. But I... I follow Christ, now."

The guards whisper to one another. "If you follow Christ, then quote the scripture, infidel."

Zhuri lets out long blast of breath and looks to me, then Morgan. It is impossible to relay a verse to him without the guards seeing it. But Zhuri does not seem to need my help.

He looks back at the soldiers, clears his throat, and quotes scripture: "'There she lusted after her lovers, whose genitals were like those of donkeys and whose emissions were like those of horses.'"

"So sayeth the Lord!" Tristan shouts.

The silence that falls upon us is a profound one.

"That's not in the Bible," one of the guards calls finally. "You just made that up."

"Do you not know the Words of God?" Zhuri shouts. "Perhaps *you* are the infidels."

"Those are good Words," the other guards says. He disappears, and the gatehouse shivers as he clumps down stairs that we cannot see. The door of wooden logs swings open and the guard nods to us. "The Arab can come in, but the leper has to wait outside."

"I'm not a leper," Morgan snaps. "These are clerical vestments!"

"We could give him a bell to ring," Tristan says. "Could he come in then?"

It takes us time to convince the soldier that Morgan is not a leper. The second guard climbs down and joins in the argument. Tristan thoughtfully offers to let the soldiers "bugger the Italian's arse" if Morgan is allowed in, which almost gets Pantaleon banned from the village as well. But it is the tiny book of lewd Bible verses we found in the scriptorium that finally ends the argument. Tristan hands it to the guards. One of the two can read, and he thumbs through it warily, then with more enthusiasm. The two soldiers chortle over the selected verses and wave us into the village without looking away from the book.

Tristan says something to them, but I do not hear his words. No sound comes to me at all as I stare into the village.

"Shut the gate!" I shout. "Shut the gate!"

But there is no time. Nearly fifty afflicted souls run toward us, snarling, howling, unstoppable.

The village seethes with plague.

Episode Five

CHAPTER TWENTY-FIVE

THE SWORD OF SAINT GILES SINGS as it leaves its sheath. Tristan's blade flashes in the morning light. The plaguers—a dozen paces away—stumble toward us, shrieking.

"Run!" I resist the urge to tell my friends to flee for their lives. "Run!"

The first line of plaguers jolts. Their heads snap backward. Their legs skid forward and they fall to the muddy earth. The next line does the same. And the ones after that. They fall upon each other in a groaning mass of rotting flesh, one wave after the next, until all of them lie writhing on the ground, chains clinking and grinding.

"They're chained," Morgan's breath trembles. "They're bloody chained."

The two soldiers burst into laughter.

Zhuri picks himself off the muddy track and brushes at his clothes. "Funny? Is that supposed to be a joke?"

"It's not a joke," the guard replies. "But it's funny, anyway. Don't matter how many times I see it." The two soldiers laugh again.

The plaguers have been fitted with iron collars. Long chains connect these collars to a large, metal ring driven into a sunken log.

"What is the purpose of these plaguers?" I ask.

"Their purpose," one of the soldiers says, "is to eat." They burst into laughter again.

"And they will eat, if you don't replace that rusted ring," Tristan snaps. "You've got all of them hooked to one ring? Are you mad?"

The guards wave us into the village again and return their attention to the book of lewd verses.

A thickset soldier holding a spear meets us inside the walls and introduces himself as Brian Nottynge. His surname means 'bald' in the old tongue, and it suits him. A thick brown beard runs wild about the bottom of his face, but, like a mountain, no shrubbery makes it to the upper slopes.

Brian motions for us to enter a long post-and-beam hall. A ripple of fear courses through me. I wonder again if Richard's men have been here. I wonder if we are walking into a building full of soldiers. I wonder if we will die today.

My hand rests on the hilt of my sword as I enter.

I was correct about the soldiers, but not their purpose. Six of them, wearing hardened leather tunics, order us to remove our clothing and boots. They inspect our bodies for bite marks and touch hands to our skin to feel for fever. One of them, a wiry man with a cleft chin studies the scars and scabs upon Morgan's body.

"Self-flagellation," I offer. "He suffers so that God may lift this plague."

The guard grimaces at the extent of the wounds. "He keeps suffering like that and he'll be able to ask God to lift the plague in person."

Brian Nottynge watches from a bench by the door as we don our armor again. "So you're here for the trial?"

Morgan works the straps on my breastplate. I want to ask Brian about horses, but I do not want to raise suspicions by asking too quickly. So I simply nod to him.

"I can't tell you how we laughed at that joke by the main gate, Brian," Tristan says. "Can you picture how funny it will be when they jump out at an old woman? Maybe she'll die right away and not suffer through the pain of a ruptured heart."

"Not meant as a joke," Brian replies. "The councilmen wanted them on the outskirts. But you can't leave demons untended. Up by the gate, they're guarded."

"Unassailable logic," Tristan replies.

Brian picks at his beard. "There's no chance that any of you are attorneys, is there?"

"No," I reply. "No chance of that."

"Do any of you have a familiarity with the law?"

I am a member of Parliament and know the law well enough, but I will not tell this man anything that will identify me. My first thought is to simply say no, but helping others is often the surest way of helping yourself. "I've settled disputes in a manorial court. Are you in need of advice?"

He scratches at the unruly beard and nods. "That might just help. What's your name, sir?"

"John Radynden."

Radynden is my family name, though no one knows me by it.

"Well, Sir John, you may prove quite useful today."

We leave the hall, and Pantaleon unties the donkey from the small apple tree where he left it. Brian leads us along a rose-lined track, past clean and well-tended wattle-and-daub cottages. We reach a stone church with an octagonal tower. The building sits in the crook of two roads at the village center. At least a hundred villagers have gathered around a waist-high wooden platform built in front of the church. The men and women look thin, but healthy, and I marvel that this village has managed to shrug off the plague, perhaps even thrive.

There are two men on the platform: one sits in a chair, wearing a simple knee-length woolen tunic, and the other stands before him, dressed in the long, wide-sleeved houpelande robes that attorneys wear. The two men do not speak, and I imagine they are waiting for proceedings to begin. Someone has built a scaffold next to the platform and a hangman's rope dangles from it.

"Gallows at a trial," Tristan says. "How wonderfully efficient."

"Wait here." Brian pushes his way through the gathered villagers. I mark his progress by the ripples of the crowd. Tristan points down the road, just past the church, to a metal cage hanging from an oak bough. A skeleton rots inside the enclosure. "Do you think they have five of those cages for us?"

I look at the gibbet and think once more about Richard's soldiers.

Brian returns, escorting a well-dressed fat man. This new man approaches, arms held wide to the side, a smile opening like a chasm on his jowly face. "Welcome! Welcome to Wickham Market! I am Martin, the mayor and chandler of this village." He leans forward, places a hand beside his mouth, palm out, as if guarding his words. "If you need any candles, give me a nod and I'll dazzle you with wax. Special prices for my new friends."

"Prices?" I ask. "Do you still accept coin here?"

"Why, of course we do," Martin replies with an exaggerated wave of his arms. "Plagues come and go, but coin is eternal." He reaches into a pouch and draws out a silver penny, studies it, then holds it out to us with a flourish. "This coin was stamped forty years ago. Forty years, my friends. It has seen two kings and two plagues. It has lived through the Battle of Crecy, the Treaty of Bretigny, and the death of the Black Prince." He makes lofty gestures with his hand as he speaks. "The world has changed and changed again, but the coin carries on, unaffected, like a boulder in a stream."

I unstrap the pouch of coins we found on the dead monk and toss it to Martin. "There are four golden boulders in there. How many horses can we get for that?"

He stares into the pouch, then tosses it back to me with a smirk. "Even boulders yield to water after a time. Horses, I'm afraid, are the only things that cannot be bought with coin in this village." He bows as deeply as his thick belly will allow and extends his hand. "I am at a disadvantage, good sir."

I shake the moist hand. "I am Sir John Radynden. And these are my friends." I point to Tristan, then Morgan. "Sir Ralf and Sir Thomas. And those are my servants, Peter and Leon."

Tristan pinches his face at me. "No one calls me Sir Ralf anymore. I'm known as Sir Gruelthorpe the Mighty."

I give him a brief scowl. The mayor raises an eyebrow and studies Tristan for a long moment, before turning to face Morgan. "A leper knight." Martin clasps his hands together and bows toward Morgan. "These are trying times, indeed."

Morgan scowls. "I'm not—"

"I'm sure you make fine candles, Martin," I say. "But we don't need candles. We need horses."

The mayor laughs, a hearty laugh, full of wind and thunder. "Don't we all! I'm the bloody mayor and *I* don't have a horse."

"What's all this about?" Tristan points to the platform, then scowls at me while Martin looks away. Either he's still irritated by the name I gave him or he thinks I am being careless by asking about the horses so pointedly.

"This is the second of three trials that we are hearing today." Martin laughs again, a great belly-shaking sound that makes Tristan grin. "The Lord gives us trials and trials and trials, does He not?"

"Hallelujah," Zhuri says.

Martin shakes his hands toward the sky and booms a reply. "Hallelujah!"

"Does no one sell horses in this village?" I ask.

The mayor looks at Zhuri, shakes his head in extravagant surprise and points. "Stop the wagon, my friends... you're not English. Not English at all."

Zhuri folds his arms. "The village of Wickham Market is fortunate to have such an astute mayor."

Martin roars with laughter. "A servant with a sense of humor. Such wit for an attendant. You're an Arab, aren't you? What in God's name are you doing here?"

"I'm a Moor," Zhuri replies. "And I ask myself that question every day. I can only assume that Allah wanted me to suffer before sending me to Jannah."

I clear my throat loudly. "Martin, can you tell me where I may find horses?"

"A Moor!" Martin says it as if a unicorn stands before him instead of Zhuri. "But Sir John said you were called Peter?"

Zhuri looks to me, then clears his throat. "That is the name I have assumed."

"Assumed?" The mayor waves a finger at Zhuri. "I understand! Very clever. Less problems for a Moor in England if he has an English name. But you speak well! I'm not talking too quickly for you am I?"

"*Fewer*," Zhuri replies. "*Fewer* problems for a Moor in England. No, you are not speaking too quickly."

Martin roars with laughter again. He is a cheerful, jiggling, blustery man, this mayor. "He corrected my English!" He turns and shouts to the crowd. "A Moor corrected my English!"

"It loses its charm," Morgan says.

King Richard is assembling an army to kill my wife, and this mayor prattles on about everything except what I need. "Horses." I try to keep my voice level. "Where can I get horses?"

Martin coughs out a few more guffaws, takes a deep breath, and shrugs with extravagance. "Nowhere in the village, Sir John. There are three horses in Wickham Market today. And not one of them is for sale. I might be able to find you a goat, though. How about a nice nanny goat? Two years old and full of vigor. A fine animal. Damn fine animal. I'd let you have it for one of those nobles. And sweeten the deal with a dozen of my finest candles."

"You can't ride goats," I say.

"Can't ride cows, either," Tristan replies. "But I understand people do it."

I give Tristan a sharp glance then turn back to the mayor. "Can you take me to the owners of those three horses? Perhaps I can persuade them."

Martin shakes his head, which makes his jowls quiver. "I doubt very much they can be persuaded. Doubt it very much."

"Anyone can be persuaded," I say. "Every man has something they want dearly."

"And these days, that something is horses." Martin points behind me. "Horses are a sensitive subject these days in Wickham Market, Sir John. But you are welcome to ask the owners yourself. They are walking this way."

I turn to look, and gasp. My hand flies to the grip of my sword.

Tristan hunches down, his armor rattling.

A dozen men in mail walk toward us.

"Soldiers need their horses more than ever these days." Martin continues speaking, but I cannot hear him clearly, because the words he spoke earlier ring in my ears.

The Lord gives us trials and trials and trials.

The oncoming soldiers wear tabards over their mail. And emblazoned on the bright blue linen, are the lion and lily of King Richard.

I cannot give these men what they want, because what they want is me.

Hallelujah.

CHAPTER TWENTY-SIX

I BACK AWAY FROM THE APPROACHING SOLDIERS. Tristan and the others do the same. We exchange looks, and I shake my head. Even with surprise we cannot defeat a dozen men in mail.

Martin gives me a bemused smile. "Are you afraid of metal? Those are the king's men. Here to protect us and to shower us with Richard's wisdom and glory!"

One of the soldiers wears a thick breastplate and a blue cape trimmed in silver. A knight. He walks toward me, and does not stop until he is close enough that I can smell the mead on his breath. "What's this then?" he asks.

"Visitors, Sir George," Martin replies. "They're going to buy Henry's goat. That one's a leper and the other one is an Italian named Leon. They traveled here to Wickham Market for the trial, and to spend God's good coin." He winks at me.

"I'm not a leper," Morgan says.

Sir George looks at me again, then at Tristan. "So, what are the knights for?"

"Sleeping," the mayor replies. "Looking at the stars and listening to the chirp of insects. Stop being so suspicious. Just because you keep the lands of Wickham Market free of plague, Sir George, does not mean that plague cannot flourish elsewhere. Good men need strong swords at their sides when they travel these days. Now be off, good sir, and take your men with you. One of these knights is going to help us with the anathema, and we have work to do."

Sir George stares into my face, and I stare back. I have seen him before, but I cannot remember where. There is recognition in his eyes too, but I do not think he can place me either.

"My name is Sir John." I hold out the pouch that holds the four nobles. "I'd like to buy your horses."

Sir George glances at the pouch. "Our horses aren't for sale."

"There are four gold nobles in that pouch," I say. "We also have a donkey and a paste that will cure any injury."

"I may not have made myself clear." Sir George's voice holds a hint of anger. "Our horses are not for sale."

"And I may not have made myself clear." Anger seeps into my voice as well. I step closer to the knight and my breastplate taps his. "My wife needs me. If I don't—"

"Step away from me, sir!" George's hand touches the hilt of his sword. His soldiers crowd around me. "Our horses are needed here, to keep this village clear of plague. And that is the end of our discussion. Wickham Market is a lawful village. I make certain that it remains so." He lays his finger on my breastplate. "I trust you and your men will respect that."

Tristan and Morgan push their way through the soldiers so that each stands at one of my shoulders.

"We will cause no trouble, Sir George," Morgan says.

Tristan points toward the iron gibbet hanging from the distant tree. "Is that how you keep order in Wickham Market? Is that your work, Sir George?"

"That is the Lord's work." George keeps his eyes on mine. "That sinner has been rotting in there for too long. It's time to put some new blood in the gibbet."

"He must have committed a great crime indeed," Tristan says. "What did he do? Ask to buy a mule?"

"The official charge is '*offensa cujus nominatio crimen est*,'" George replies. He turns to his men and waves them forward. The soldiers pass us in a long column, some drinking from wooden mugs, some eating bread or oily chicken, and all casting long looks at me and my companions. Sir George addresses Martin before he leaves. "I'll return for the anathema. I pray your guests behave themselves." He looks toward the gibbet and the rotting skeleton inside, then meets my gaze. "A lawful village."

George walks off, along the edge of the crowd and down the road branching away from the church. I watch, hand still on my sword grip, as they depart. Is it possible that they have not heard about us? If Richard sent a message, he would have described us as unarmored men, so Tristan and I might escape notice. But there is no way they could miss Zhuri. A Moor in England stands out like amber among glass.

"*Offensa cujus...*" Tristan squints as he tries to work it out.

"It means buggery." The mayor shrugs and watches Sir George and his men. "The man was put in there for buggery. Cows and a horse."

Tristan snorts, a short, violent sound. "Did you hear that?" he barks another laugh. "He's in there for... he... cows... and a horse... in the filthy canal..." He snorts again, but no one joins him. "*Offensa cujus nomin...*" He clears his throat, dons a more sober expression, and watches the departing soldiers.

"Sir George means no offense," Martin says. "We had a bit of trouble a week ago. A band of knights. It was not a pleasant day. George lost eight of his men. They were after horses and food."

"Did they serve anyone?" I ask. "Where did they come from?"

Martin shrugs. "We didn't recognize the device. Three cocks. They all had them."

"Lucky bastards!" Tristan says.

Zhuri chuckles and Martin, realizing the joke, laughs as well.

I do not laugh. Morgan and I exchange glances. Three roosters. Gerald of Thunresleam.

Martin wipes at his eyes, but his laughter trails off when he sees my expression "Smile, Sir John. In these terrible days, cheerfulness is our duty. The good Lord says, 'A joyful heart is the best of medicine.'"

"The good Lord is absolutely right," Tristan says. "I try to eat one or two joyful hearts a day."

They laugh again, all of them. Even Morgan chuckles, after calling Tristan a fool. But I cannot laugh. Because Sir Gerald's men have been here, and they might still be near.

"Have Sir George and his men been at Wickham Market long?" I ask.

"Weeks," Martin replies. "They helped clear the plague from around our village. And they continue to do so."

"They haven't been to Framlingham?" I ask. "And no one from Framlingham has come here?"

"Not since shortly after the knights attacked. King Richard declined to provide any payment to compensate the families of the men killed by those knights. And he also declined to give George more men to replace the ones lost. Our wise and glorious king sits in his castle, and some say he has no care for the rest of his kingdom. His men kill or drive off any commoners that seek refuge at Framlingham. I do not think Sir George is overly fond of our king, and I cannot blame him. But I will deny it to my death if you repeat that. To my death!"

A wagon, pulled by two oxen, rattles down the crossing road toward us. Five men sit inside, two of them priests. It seems like some sort of bizarre ceremony held in honor of the trial, because four pigs on lead ropes trot ahead of the wagon, and one of the priests tosses what looks like cuts of meat from a basket onto the road behind.

"What, exactly, is happening there?" Tristan asks.

"The trial is beginning," Martin replies, scowling. "Justice comes this way."

The wagon rumbles past the church and stops beside the wooden platform. The five men step down, one at a time. Martin leads us to one side of the crowd, so we can see the wagon and the front of the platform clearly.

"What crime is being tried?" Morgan asks.

"Murder," Martin replies. "Savages from our village killed a little girl. They tortured her. Tore her face off and left her to die."

"Why would they do such a thing?" Zhuri asks.

"Because they are monsters," Martin replies. "Brothers, all of them. Grew up here, in Wickham Market, with good, law-abiding parents. But there was always something evil in their eyes. I knew they would bring grief to this village one day, and a fortnight ago, they did."

Morgan makes the sign of the cross in the air. "'May we be delivered from wicked and evil men. For not all have faith.'"

"You wanted me to help with something," I say to Martin. "Is my help worth even one horse?"

Martin shrugs. "I would give you a dozen horses if I had them, but I do not, Sir John. If you help me with the next trial, I will have a word in the ear of Sir George."

"You would do that?" I ask.

"I would. No promises, of course. No promises at all. Sir George of Brighthelmstone is a man of principle. It is difficult to change his mind."

I nod my thanks, but I am not hopeful. We should leave the village. Search for horses somewhere else. But finding horses is like finding buried treasure these days. And I know there is treasure here in this village. Shining treasure with hooves and manes. Stealing is a sin, but the hunger in my stomach burns brighter than salvation. Sir George's instincts about me were correct. I will have those horses. There will be time for penance later.

The priest leads the three men to a bench at the foot of the platform. All of them take a seat next to a man and woman who hold hands.

"Shouldn't the brothers be bound?" Morgan asks. "If things go badly for them, they're likely to flee."

Martin tilts his head and squints at Morgan. "Those three men are not the brothers. They are the councilmen who will rule on the case."

"Where are the accused then?" I ask. "Shouldn't they be present?"

"But, they are present." The mayor points to the left of the platform. "There. Those four over there."

A half-dozen men stand where Martin points, but I cannot decide which ones are the accused. The wagon stands behind the men and I briefly consider making an offer on the oxen. But oxen are slow. Far too slow to beat Richard's army to St. Edmund's Bury.

"Will the brothers be brought onto the platform now?" Morgan asks.

"The attorney might put one or two of them up there," Martin says. "But certainly not all four."

"They should all be allowed to face their accusers," Morgan says.

"Don't be absurd." Martin laughs, his thick, thundery laugh. "It would be impossible to keep order. You can't put four pigs on a stage."

CHAPTER TWENTY-SEVEN

PIGS ARE ON TRIAL.

It should not come as a surprise. Trials like these occur from time to time in villages and towns, mostly in France, but we English are not above them. A dog on trial for killing sheep. A horse for trampling a man. A cow for kicking a child. I never understood such proceedings. Father Aubrey tried to explain it once. He said that trials of this sort are a way of mourning, a means of coping with tragedy. That animals are put on trial so that men and women can bring order and justice to a senseless and random event.

I have never believed that.

In my younger days, I thought animal trials were a reflex of anger. Like a man kicking a rock that he stubs his toe upon. But age has given me insights into the motivations of men. I now believe that animals are put on trial because sometimes they do not know their place. They forget, sometimes, the hierarchy of God's creatures. And nothing enrages a man—or terrifies him—so much as an inferior rising above his station. This is why the Peasant Revolt has reverberated across the world. This is why men accused of treason are publicly beheaded. This is why men like Saint Thomas Beckett are murdered.

Animals are the most inferior of the inferiors, so they are tried and executed, and man ascertains maintains his moral, spiritual, and physical superiority.

But I am not interested in superiority of any sort right now. I need horses, not absurdity.

Martin excuses himself and makes his way to the platform, where he announces the trial and relinquishes the stage to the attorney. The attorney, a young man with a trimmed mustache and a pointed beard, describes the events of the crime.

"On July 8, in the year 1385, upon the feast day of Saint Withburga, five pigs entered into the home of Reginald Fynch, a cowherd on a farm in the village of Wickham Market, and of his wife, Elenor. The five pigs encountered six-year-old Basilia Fynch inside and set upon her with furiosity, eating the face and neck of the said child, who, in consequence of the bites and defacements inflicted by the said pigs, departed this life."

The woman on the bench, Elenor apparently, sobs and covers her face. The man beside her—Reginald, I assume—puts an arm around her shoulders, the muscles of his jaw flexing.

The attorney recounts the despair and rage that Reginald Fynch suffered upon entering the home. A rage so powerful that the man killed one of the five pigs with his bare hands. It is, the attorney adds, the remains of this dead pig that the priest was scattering on the roadside "to rot and putrefy and to never enter a human body."

Two witnesses are called to the stage. The first is Reginald Fynch himself, who testifies angrily that the pigs tethered to the wagon are, indeed, the ones he saw in the house, tearing at his daughter's flesh. The second witness is a man named Salomon Daye, a bread maker who rushed to the Fynch home when he heard Reginald's screams and saw the very same pigs there.

Martin returns to us as Salamon testifies. The mayor watches the proceedings for a time, then sighs heavily. "We have but one attorney in the village," he says. "So the pigs are being defended by a church clerk."

"A church clerk?" Morgan says. "That is hardly a fair defense."

Martin shrugs. "We do what we can in these dark times." He pats me on the shoulder. "But we have Sir John now. And he will defend the accused in the next trial."

"Defend the accused?" I shake my head. "I am no attorney, Martin."

"You do not wish to help us rid the world of this foul plague?"

"And how, exactly, will defending a criminal do that?"

"You are not defending a criminal," Martin replies. "You are taking part in a solemn ceremony and trial. An anathema. We are going to excommunicate the plague."

I stare at him for a long moment. He clears his throat. "We posted notices in churches throughout Suffolk, asking the afflicted to come and be judged. And come they have! Did you see the plagued men and women at the gate? They all showed up for the trial. A few at a time. We've been keeping them here as they present themselves. They will be tried under God, Sir John. Under God! The priests say they must be defended properly in the trial or the anathema will not work. And you are a lord, well-versed in the law." He frowns. "Where is it that you come from?"

"You want to excommunicate a plague?" I ask. "Are you mad?" I say the words, knowing he is not. Or if he is, it is a common madness. Like animal trials, I have heard of anathemas. They are curses, cast against creatures that cannot take the sacrament, and so cannot be officially excommunicated.

Locust swarms, hives of rats, flies, even worms and weevils are said to be cast away or killed outright by these curses. I once witnessed an anathema trial against caterpillars, with one of the caterpillars present, and it made today's pig trial seem solemn by comparison. Yet another anathema, in France, was directed at pigeons that made too much noise outside the church during mass. The curse was so effective, it is said, that it reaped an unintended consequence: to this day, any pigeon that flies within five feet of the church falls dead. I laughed when I heard the tale, but a priest told it to me, and who am I to doubt the veracity of God's servants?

"The afflicted are demons," Martin says. "And so we must curse them back to Hell."

I shake my head. "The afflicted are not—"

"Shhhh." The mayor points to the platform. "Here comes the defense."

An old man steps onto the stage. He wears long robes, similar to the houpelande worn by the attorney.

"We didn't have another attorney's robe," Martin says. "So we gave him one of Father David's robes. It's a fortunate thing priests and attorneys wear similar clothing."

"And both occupations serve similar functions," Morgan replies. "Both represent justice and mercy, and try to shepherd their charges toward a good judgment." He grins, pleased with his metaphor.

Tristan nods. "And the more you pay them, the better the chance of a good judgment."

Morgan crosses his arms. "Must you always be so wicked?"

"My apologies," Tristan replies. "Attorneys do not deserve such cruelty."

"Shhh!" The mayor points toward the platform again.

The clerk gazes at Reginald and Elenor on the bench, and clasps his hands. "I am terribly sorry for the loss incurred by Reginald and his wife. It is a tragedy. A horrible, grievous tragedy." He turns to the crowd and holds a trembling finger to the sky. "But to try animals in a court is to imbue them with an equality to man. If beasts are capable of knowing right from wrong—and can incur praise and blame—then they are capable of being judged in the afterlife." He stares into the crowd and lets the words settle. "If that is the case, then beasts would be a species of man, or men a species of beasts. And both of these propositions are incompatible with the Word of God!" The old man's voice gains strength, he thrusts his finger higher into the sky and glares at the crowd. "Based on this argument, I call for the trial to be ceased, and these animals to be released!"

The whistles and boos begin even before he finishes the last sentence. Someone throws a carrot. Two soldiers wade through the crowd to restrain the vegetable hurler. I turn my back. The clerk is the only one at this trial who has spoken with any sort of sense, and he is being assaulted for it. I will not find horses for sale here, among this crowd. Only absurdity. It is time to search out the stables.

I glance toward the gate and spot a soldier sprinting toward us. The pommel of my sword touches my palm.

"Galfrid presents a most formidable defense." The attorney is back on stage. "Well structured and delivered. But Galfrid is a clever man. He knows very well that we are not judging the animals before us, but the demons that lurk beneath their flesh. And those demons must be expunged! I say to our honorable councilmen, find these animals and their demons guilty and justice will be done!"

The crowd roars at the words.

"An unassailable display of logic," Tristan says.

Martin clambers onto the platform and raises his hands to quiet the crowd. He turns to the three robed men sitting on the wooden bench beside the platform. "What say you, councilmen?"

The men lean in and there is much nodding and whispering. I glance back again. The running soldier stops at the far edge of the crowd and searches for someone.

One of the councilmen, a stooped man with a long gray mustache, stands.

"We find the accused porkers guilty of willful murder. We further find that the pigs killed the child and ate of its flesh on a Friday, and it is expressly forbidden by the

Church to eat meat on a Friday. Therefore, the pigs should have additional punishment before their execution."

The men and women cheer again; some wave their arms wildly in the air or shake their fists at the squealing pigs.

I glance back again. The soldier shoves his way into the crowd.

"We have to go." It is not possible to be overcautious when the King of England wants you dead.

"But you have been called to defend the afflicted," Morgan says. "Or the anathema will not work."

"Anathemas always work, Morgan," I watch the crowd ripple as the soldier pushes his way through. "Locusts eventually leave. Caterpillars die off. And pigeons grow quiet when the rutting season ends. Now let's get out of this village before it's too late." But I do not know in which direction to flee. The others look to me as I debate our choices.

The cheers of the men and women in the crowd are wild and shrill. The pigs squeal and buck, perhaps sensing the aggression of the crowd. Martin waves his hands again to silence the crowd. "The councilmen have spoken. The accused animals will receive ten lashes each, immediately, and then shall be hanged by the neck until dead."

His next words are spoken quickly—almost mumbled—his hand making a cursory sign of the cross. "We do this in the name of the Trinity: Father, Son and Holy Spirit. *Amen*."

The spectators grow reverent for a moment. They bow their heads long enough to say *amen*, then cheer savagely again.

The soldier in the crowd finds Brian Nottynge and speaks to him, gesticulating madly. Brian's gaze sweeps over the area slowly. His eyes meet mine and the surveying stops. He gives me a smile with far too much warmth, and whispers an aside to the soldier.

I set off at a brisk walk toward the gate and call back to the others. "Let's go!"

Richard's men must have arrived. They will either wait at the gate, or they will head to the platform to collect us themselves. Either way, we will have enemies at both sides. But I am guessing Richard only sent one or two men. And only two guards at the gatehouse. Much better chances.

"Edward, what's wrong?" Morgan asks.

"Wait!" Pantaleon shouts. "The arse does not moves."

"Ass," Zhuri calls.

"Leave it," I snap. "Leave it and move! Quickly!"

Brian Nottynge walks our way, his short sword out of its sheath. The soldier who spoke with him runs off in the direction that Sir George and his men walked only a few moments before.

A lashing whip cracks behind us. A pig's agonized squeal tears at the sky. The crowd roars. Tristan glances back. "That will teach those porkers not to eat meat on Friday." He grins, but there is concern on his face. "Brian Nottynge is following us with his sword out."

Another crack sounds, followed by another squeal. The crowd cheers, wild and loud. And, like a demented echo, the plaguers by the gate howl.

Brian stops following and watches us. I pick up my pace, not quite running, but not walking either. Sir George and his soldiers hurry back down the crossroads toward the platform. The time for calm is past.

"Edward, what's happening?" Morgan asks. "Say something."

"Flee," I say. "*Flee for your lives!*"

We flee for our lives, toward the gate.

Another crack sounds in the distance, and I can only just hear the squeal. The plaguers near the gate roar and yank against their chains. They pull as one… and take a step forward.

"How… how are they…?" Morgan stammers.

"The log!" I stop running, halfway between the gate and the crowd. "They're pulling it out!"

"They're going mad!" Zhuri shouts. "Why are they going mad?"

A pig shrieks again and the plaguers howl, pull the log out another few inches.

All of us turn, at the same time, toward the platform, where the pigs are being flayed. We look at one another, then at the plaguers. The blood. The afflicted smell the pig blood.

I look again to the platform. The crowd cheers. Sir George and his men are still a long way off. I look back at the distant plaguers. They strain and roar and claw at the air. They seem to lurch forward again, but it is hard to tell from this distance.

"That log is sunk deep," Morgan says. "There's no way they'll get—"

The faint, ringing sound of metal shattering silences him. Plaguers crash forward, tumbling over one another and onto the road.

They are free.

They rise like Hell's vengeance and lumber toward us, picking up speed with each staggering step. I can just make out the glitter of a long chain dragging behind each one.

"The rusted ring," Tristan says. "It's a terrible weight to bear, always being right."

"What do we do?" Zhuri asks.

I do not know what to do. We could avoid the plaguers. Race around them and escape in the madness that will soon fall upon Wickham Market. I think of Danbury, a village we doomed. One of my crowning sins.

"There are a hundred innocent men and women in this village," I say.

"And four guilty pigs," Tristan adds.

I think again of Danbury. If humanity is to survive, we must show ourselves to be human. I draw the hand cannon from my shoulder sack. Tristan watches, then draws his ten-shot hand bombard, the weapon named *God's Love*.

"I thought you were the champion of the dead," Tristan says.

"I am the defender of humanity, Tristan."

I glance back toward the crossroads. Sir George and his men reach the platform. Brian Nottynge speaks to them and shouts something that I cannot hear.

I look back again toward the village gates. The afflicted stumble closer. Not more than fifty paces. A half-dozen soldiers from the long hall step out into the street. They stare wide-eyed at the afflicted, but do nothing to stop them. A knight wearing Richard's crest on his tabard stands among them, watching as well. The cowards do not want the plaguers to turn their attentions toward them.

"This will be a misery of shit," Tristan says.

"It always is," I say.

He shakes his head. "I wish I had my helm."

All of our helmets, and my shield, are in the canvas sack on Pantaleon's donkey. Which is still by the platform.

We stand on the road, half-way between the village gate and the platform where the trial is taking place. Two hundred paces from each. Stranded between the afflicted and the healthy, fearing both.

I hand my cannon to Zhuri. "I hope you've gotten better with these." Zhuri's aim with hand cannons has been short of commendable. "It's loaded. Aim for their legs. We want them stopped, not dead. These are people, not demons."

Tristan hands Morgan his shoulder sack and the hand bombard. "Light a firing cord quickly."

"I don't want to fire a cannon," Morgan replies.

"You don't have a sword," Tristan replies. "Be helpful. Fire the bloody cannon."

"Christ is my sword." Morgan takes the hand bombard and sighs. "If this gun explodes on me, I will haunt you forever, Tristan. I will make it rain on you for the rest of your days."

"I live in England, Morgan." Tristan draws his sword. "It's already been arranged."

Pantaleon steps up next to me, his own sword out, the massive steel pauldron on his shoulder facing the plaguers. "Perhaps Mayor will give to us the paid for help?"

"Everyone in this village is our enemy, Pantaleon. There will be no reward."

I draw my sword, uncertain what I will do with it.

I am the wolf that slaughters the lamb.

But I can no longer tell the wolves from the lambs.

CHAPTER TWENTY-EIGHT

THE AFFLICTED DRAW CLOSER. I squint to get a better look at them. A man in rough linen trousers and no shirt limps at the front of the crowd. The white of a rib gleams from a bloody gash.

A girl of no more than twelve years walks just behind him and to his left. Her face is powdered black with dirt and grime, her lips drawn back in a snarl. Some lingering instinct from her healthier days makes her clutch at the hand of a woman beside her, but the woman yanks free each time.

Another woman in the marching throng wears a mesh caul that binds her hair. Through some oddity, the caul remains perfectly arranged, tidy on a head that has only one ear and massive gouges down both cheeks.

They lurch forward, all of them, along the tidy street and past the shining roses. A pair of pigeons coo and launch skyward at their approach, their wing beats like fluttering banners. I have faced more pitched battles in France than I can recall. Many times have I gazed upon the faces of my young enemies—at the humanity shining in their eyes—and felt a stirring of pity. To be born French is a curse, just as this plague is a curse to the afflicted. But the Frenchmen chose to take arms against us. The blighted enemies we face today never had that choice. There isn't a dram of humanity in the eyes of the men and women that advance on us now. But I have never pitied an enemy so much.

I let out a long rattling breath. "Zhuri, Morgan, remember to aim for their feet."

Morgan hands Zhuri a firing cord. "You'll have to light me, Moor."

Shouts rise up from behind us. I glance back. Sir George and his men are stopped on the road, fifty hundred paces from us. They have spotted the oncoming horde. One of the men crosses himself. Another places both hands on his helm. Sir George tugs at his surcoat and draws his sword.

Morgan steps forward and tips the bombard so the ten coin-sized holes point toward the plaguers's legs. He nods to Zhuri, who dips the firing cord toward the touchhole at the top of the bombard.

"Say Hallelujah," Tristan calls.

"Heavenly Father," Morgan shouts, "please don't let this cannon—"

Thunder sounds beside me. A streak of white smoke lances forward as *God's Love* showers the plaguers. Screams rip through the mist of spent saltpeter, but I cannot see the people who make them.

I glance back. Sir George is on one knee. Most of his soldiers are hunched, or lying prone on the street. One of them is on hands and knees, arms cradling his head. They look more terrified at the gun blast than they did when they spotted the plaguers. I do not imagine many of them have seen a hand cannon at work.

The smoke lingers in the breezeless morning. White haze swirls and the woman with the caul staggers forward. Her hip gushes blood from where one of the ten gun stones pierced her. Bodies, just visible through the smoke, writhe upon the ground. Four or five of them. But dozens of plaguers are still on their feet. I hope Sir George decides to join us. We cannot hold off forty plaguers on our own.

The woman with the caul is five paces ahead of the throng and closing on us quickly. Her chain rattles along the earthen road.

"Put her down, Zhuri," I shout.

"Very well," he yells back, raising the hand-cannon. "You're an ugly woman! And your caul is crooked!"

"Shut your mouth and fire."

The Moor aims the hand cannon at the woman's leg. Morgan dips the firing cord into the touchhole.

"Hallelujah!" Zhuri shouts.

The gun roars and belches a plume of smoke ten feet long. The road is smothered once again by a veil of white. We back away slowly, swords up, eyes straining into the bitter mist. Something moves toward us. The woman with the caul lurches out from the smoke. She has no new wounds.

"Zhuri!"

He glances at the hand cannon. "Something is wrong with this gun!"

"Yes," Tristan replies. "It has a faulty Moor!"

"Forgive me." The woman cannot understand my whispered words, but perhaps God will give her my message. I slash with all my strength. Saint Giles severs her leg just below the knee, and she topples to the ground, her chain clattering.

"Tighten up," I say. "Don't kill them if you can avoid it."

Tristan and Pantaleon draw closer, so our shoulders touch. I take a deep breath.

"I wish I had my helm," Tristan says again.

Sir George shouts at his men. Some of them stand and settle into a loose formation. Others back away.

We tense for the onslaught.

A crush of mindless humans—not demons, but sick humans—rush at us from the brimstone fog. They are like spiders from a web, the gossamer thread of chains dragging behind. Except they are not animals, either. They are humans. Not demons. Not animals.

But humans do not make the noises these things do. Humans do not hunger for blood. And humans fall when you cut at their legs. These things do not. I am reduced to swinging wildly, aiming for whatever is closest. I ask Christ to forgive me as I cut down the people I am sworn to defend. There are too many. We have no helmets, so we cannot risk being overrun. Nor can we allow these plaguers to wander into the village. We back away slowly, keeping the horde in front of us and taking them down however we can.

Tristan shoves an old man to the ground. "What... what now?"

"I was hoping... Sir George would arrive by now." I lop off a man's grasping hand. He wears a badge from the shrine of Saint Edmund. Elizabeth waits for me beside that shrine.

Father Peter's words echo in my ears.

You would not slay a madman would you? Or an imbecile?

Pantaleon drops to a knee and severs a woman's leg. She shrieks and clutches for the leg, then topples sideways. They do not seem to think, these plaguers, but they feel pain, as we do.

They must be protected and healed

Where is Sir George? Has he decided not to help? I cannot spare a glance backward.

Zhuri is hunched over, shaking his head and reloading my hand cannon. Morgan crouches low and drives his shoulder into the hip of a thin woman, sending her sprawling. He rises and thrusts his wooden cross at another plaguer. It hisses and backs away from him.

Tristan guts a young man whose face is mostly skull, the skin torn and rotted away. The man grabs Tristan's arm with both of his and pulls himself forward. Bony jaws open. The sword rips through the plaguer's back, but he continues forward. Tristan wrenches his arms back, but the man will not release his grip, will not stop his advance. Only the sword hilt stops the plaguer, but he is close enough to take hold of Tristan's spaulder. He leans forward, jaws snapping at the metal plate.

I kick at the young man, but a naked woman lunges toward me. Her pendulous breasts are withered and swing like half-empty sacks of grain. I hack, two handed, at her throat, releasing a spume of black blood, but she does not relent. A man whose scalp is flapping upward follows behind, and I am forced to scramble back quickly.

They are not to be slaughtered.

Pantaleon is a fiend among the plaguers. He holds his short sword in one hand and dagger in the other. Whirling, stabbing, slashing and killing with many blood. He is a lion, and he roars as he sends an old woman to the dirt with a kick. "I will have the paid for this!"

Tristan groans. He has dropped to one knee and released his sword. The weapon is still lodged in the belly of the young man, who lies writhing on his side. Two others reach for Tristan, and he shoves them back.

I drive my sword through the naked woman's throat. All the way through, then wrench it back and forth, until her spine severs and she falls to the road. The man with the flapping scalp staggers toward me. I hold him off with one hand, kicking at the side of his knee with all my strength. The leg snaps, and I am at Tristan's side before the man's body strikes the road.

Tristan wraps his arms around a stout man with a long beard and drives him into the earth. I grab the hair of the other plaguer—a farmer with boils sprouting from his neck. The blade of Saint Giles plunges into the back of his neck, and the farmer collapses with a gentle thump.

Humanity is the triumph of will over instinct.

Tristan pounds the bearded man in the face over and again with his fists, blood trails painting the arc of each blow. A stocky plaguer in chain mail dives at him, but I am quicker. I lunge at the man, and we both fall to the ground in a clatter of plates and a shiver of mail. The creature snarls and rolls onto one of my arms. I throw one leg over him to pin him down and use my free hand to drive the dagger toward his face. But the plaguer grabs my wrist. It shocks me. I have never seen a plaguer defend itself. A man and a woman leap at me. I try to pull my hand free to ward them off. But it takes an instant too long to break the plaguer's grip. Blackened teeth lunge toward my face.

And stop an inch from my cheek.

Bloody drool spatters my chin. I glance past the two plaguers. Morgan stands behind them, holding their chains. A woman with dead flowers in her hair lunges at him, but Pantaleon flashes his dagger and sends her to wherever the flowers have gone. Morgan groans and swings the chains of the man and woman he holds. The plaguers lose their footing and topple to the ground, howling.

Protect the afflicted, Edward.

Where in God's holy earth is Sir George? I still have no time to look back. A dozen plaguers march through the hazy smoke toward us.

"Fall back!" I shout. "Fall back!"

The mailed plaguer growls and cranes his neck toward me, jaws open, bloody spittle dripping down his chin.

Make your promise.

I think of a poor carpenter hanging from a cross, of the oath I made to him.

"Forgive me." I drive my blade into the man's eye. He shrieks with pain, and I turn the blade as he spasms.

Shapes rush in from behind us. We have been flanked.

It is Christ's swift retribution for my failure. I stagger to my feet and face the rear. How could we have been flanked by plaguers?

But the new shapes are not afflicted men. They are healthy, armed and armored. Sir George's men have joined the battle. Finally.

CHAPTER TWENTY-NINE

THE BATTLE ENDS QUICKLY after our reinforcements arrive. Soldiers move through the plagued mass, swords and axes misting blood into the summer air.

When the carnage is complete, Sir George sweeps his gaze from one side of the road to the other. "Is that all of them? Are they all dead?"

I stare at the bodies lying upon the road. A few of them move, but most lie still as graves. I kneel and hold clasped hands to my forehead. These were not demons. They were people with an illness, and I helped strike them down.

A deep foreboding casts a shadow on my soul. A premonition that Richard will strike down my wife in the same fashion. That Elizabeth will be the price for my broken oath. I would pray to the Son of God and ask him to take me instead. But Jesus does not make deals. His way is the way of mercy. It is the Old Testament God that strikes bargains. So I whisper a prayer, quick as a breath, to the angry, vengeful God instead, offering myself as sacrifice.

I am an unworthy substitute for Elizabeth, but if a poor carpenter can save humanity, then perhaps an old English knight can save an angel.

Zhuri finishes loading my cannon.

"Is anyone hurt?" I call. "Anyone bitten?"

Sir George approaches Zhuri. "Is that a gun?"

Zhuri nods hesitantly.

"God's Teeth, but what a weapon! Might I see it?"

Zhuri looks to me and I nod. Sir George's men outnumber us, and we are exhausted. If we are to leave Wickham Market, it will not be through force. Best to be cordial.

Sir George takes the weapon reverently.

"The powder and the gun stone go in the barrel, with wadding." Zhuri pours powder into the cannon, then wraps cloth around a gun stone and jams stone and fabric deep into the barrel with a wooden dowel. He takes the firing cord from Morgan and hands it to Sir George. "You use this to light the touch hole, there. The powder ignites, and the explosion sends the stone out faster than an arrow." He shrugs. "These cannons are wildly inaccurate, though."

"Only if a Moor is holding them," Tristan says.

The knight I saw earlier—the one wearing Richard's sigil—approaches from the gate. He is confident enough, now that the fighting is finished. He seems to be whistling, though it is hard to tell from this distance. He strays to one side of the road and casually kicks the head off a rose.

Sir George hands one of his men the firing cord and looks up from the hand cannon. "King Richard wants you dead," he says. "All of you."

I look from cannon to Sir George. Is the gun his price for letting us go? It is a steep price.

My companions gather around me, all with weapons in hand, save Zhuri.

"King Richard is a madman," I say. "We won't let you hand us over to him. We will fight. Men will die." I toss the pouch with the four nobles at his feet. "We're going to run. All I ask is that you don't chase us. And we'll need that cannon back."

Sir George's lip curls upward. "Do you think I would sell my honor?"

"We would never ask you to do such a thing," Tristan replies. "But perhaps you could lease it to us for a period of two hundred paces?"

Pantaleon scoops up the pouch and waves it toward me. "This is being the paid for me, for the lives of you." He turns to Sir George and waves toward the dead plaguers littering the road. "Are you to give to me the paid for this?"

"What?" Sir George peers at me.

"He wants payment for saving the village," I say. "Give me the pouch, Pantaleon. You'll have your *the paid* when I reach my wife."

"Payment?" Sir George glares at Pantaleon. "You will not get a penny! Not a half-penny! You will get justice, you poltroon!"

"Ave, Sir George!" The approaching knight has long golden hair. His smile is as bright as his unblemished breastplate.

Sir George lays the gun on his shoulder, so that it points up toward God, and nods to the knight. "Sir Michael."

"We've been scouring the land searching for these churls. King Richard will be pleased. Very pleased." Sir Michael addresses us in a flat, almost bored voice. "Put down your weapons and you will live."

"Put down yours, and I'll let you keep one of your legs," I reply.

Sir Michael walks toward me slowly, a grin on his face. "Are you Sir Edward? The one with the sick wife in St. Edmund's Bury? Do you know that Richard is assembling an army? He's going to kill every rotter in that city. Every last one."

"His name is John," Sir George says.

"Is that what he told you? Then he's a liar as well as a murderer." Sir Michael stops several paces from me. His eyes flit down to my drawn sword and he edges back a half step. "This man is Sir Edward Dallingridge, and he killed Good Queen Anne. Willfully poisoned her."

"Who's lying now?" I try to keep my voice steady. Somewhere, deep in the folds of my heart, I had hoped the king would not remember where Elizabeth was. I should never have mentioned it. But how else could I have secured his assistance? "I tried to help Queen Anne. She was plagued, and I tried to help her. Which is more than King Richard has done for his people. He kills peasants who come to him for protection. Executes men he grows tired of. His own uncle was in a dungeon, dying in agony, the flesh and muscle stripped from his legs. You serve a madman."

"I serve the king," Michael replies. "And the king may do as he wishes. He can torture his entire family if he wishes to, because God made him king. And he can kill as many peasants as he wants, because men follow him. He is powerful. That is how the world works now, Sir Edward. There are no laws anymore. There is only strength and weakness. There are those who take, and those who get taken. The predators and the prey. And Richard is a predator. But he is a predator with a heart. He kills peasants because Framlingham is a small castle. There is no room for the great, stinking masses. If he let the commoners in, there wouldn't be enough food. Everyone would starve. So you see? He does protect his people. He is a generous hunter. A merciful butcher."

I catch Tristan's eye and nod to him, look into the village and back at him. He turns his gaze back toward Sir Michael and nods so slightly that it is almost not a nod at all.

Sir George scoffs. "If Richard is the king, then those peasants are his people, and he owes them just as much protection as he owes his friends. So which is it, Sir Michael? Is he a king who kills his own people? Or is he simply another of the cruel warlords who have risen across England?"

Tristan watches Sir George but taps Zhuri with his hand, sending a quick glance into the village. Zhuri takes a deep breath, nods.

"He is your king," Sir Michael replies. "You swore an oath to him."

Zhuri touches Morgan with an elbow, then gestures with his chin toward the village center. Morgan nods.

"Aye, he is," George replies. "But King Richard swore an oath, too. I was there. 'True justice and equity towards the people committed to his charge.' That's what he swore, before God and the archbishop. Commoners are included in the people committed to his charge. Yet, Richard slaughters them. Is that justice, Sir Michael? Is that equity?" His face grows a brighter red with each word. He takes a step toward Sir Michael, and there is venom in his next words. "Eight of my men died here not a fortnight ago defending this town, and if it were up to Richard, their widows would have starved."

"People die for their king," Sir Michael takes a step back, holds out a warding hand. "Thousands have died for him in France and Scotland and even Ireland. Why should it be any different here in England? You are all sworn to King Richard. And that means you can die wherever he chooses. And your widows can, too."

Morgan taps Pantaleon's leg with his foot, jerks his head toward the village.

"Why is it that you kick at me?" Pantaleon asks.

Sir Michael and Sir George look at the Italian.

"But according to you, Sir Michael, there are no laws anymore." I say it louder than necessary, firing a glare at Pantaleon. "If there are no laws, then our oaths are no longer valid."

Sir Michael twists a strand of his hair between his fingers as he thinks. "*Necessitas non habet legem,*" he says finally. "Do you know what that means? It means, 'necessity has no law.' It means Richard does what has to be done. He protects his people in whatever way he can, because he is strong enough to do it. Strength. It is the oldest of all laws. Even the animals follow it. If those peasants want to get into Framlingham so badly, they can band together and try to take it by force. That is how it was done in the old days. The strong survived by doing what is necessary. It is how the Danes conquered much of England. It is how the Normans took this country from the Saxons. That is what our kingdom has become again. A lawless place where the strong survive and the weak perish. Where only the people willing to do what is necessary survive. *Necessitas non habet legem.* All softness and frailty is being wiped away. Perhaps that is why God sent this plague. To prune the weak, and to make England strong once more. God sees the necessity. Do you see it? His only law is to do what is necessary. God loves the nobility, Sir Edward, and he hates peas—"

Sir Michael's face shatters.

And God strikes me blind and deaf.

Episode Six

CHAPTER THIRTY

THE RINGING FADES FROM MY EARS. Smoke swirls.

Sir Michael lies dead upon the road.

"Oh thank God," Tristan says. "I thought he would go on blathering forever."

The cannon trembles at Sir George's shoulder. His face is twisted with red rage. One of his men stands with one arm over his face, leaning away from the cannon, the firing cord gripped in a trembling hand.

"You... you killed him," Morgan whispers.

"*Necessitas non habet legem.*" Sir George hands the cannon back to Zhuri. "God has pruned a little more weakness from England."

I stare down at the mess of Sir Michael and wipe my blade on his tabard. The acrid stench of saltpeter lingers on the road.

Tristan glances back at Sir George. "I thought you said Wickham Market is a lawful village."

"It is a lawful village," Sir George barks. "And that man was lawless. He admitted to slaughtering peasants." He straightens his tabard. "I gave him justice."

"Justice," Pantaleon repeats. "This word is like the honor?"

"It means people get what they deserve," Zhuri replies.

"I do not get the paid still," Pantaleon says. "This is justice?"

"You'll get what you deserve," Tristan replies.

Sir George turns to the soldier who holds the firing cord. "Let's get these rotters off the road. Martin will have to postpone the anathema. He'll not be pleased." He spits to one side and points with his chin toward Sir Michael. "And get this varlet's body stripped and taken to the square. Looks like we found new blood for the gibbet after all. We'll hang him outside the gate so everyone can see what lawless men will find in Wickham Market."

"The justice?" Pantaleon offers.

"Too right," Sir George replies. "Lawless men will find justice here. Wickham Market will be an island of law in the seas of tyranny." He joins his men, who drag plaguers onto the grass, crushing the roses along the path. I nod to Tristan and walk quickly toward the village gate. The others follow.

"Where are you lot going?" Sir George snaps.

Tristan and I exchange glances.

"You said you wanted horses, didn't you?" Sir George walks toward us, wiping blood from his mail with a rag. "I know where you can get them. But I'll need something in return."

"One day, I will find someone who does something for me out of simple kindness," I reply.

"Not today," he replies. "I need you to relay a message for me. Will you do that?"

"I have somewhere to get to, Sir George." I will no longer tell people where I am going. "And I have to get there quickly. Who's the message for? And what is it?"

"The message is for the Duke of Hereford. And don't fret. I believe he's more or less on your path to St. Edmund's Bury."

I breathe out a long sigh. Everyone seems to know where I'm going anyway. "Henry Bolingbroke? John of Gaunt's son?"

"Elizabeth of Lancaster's brother?" Tristan adds.

"The very same. He's back in England. The message is this: Wickham Market is with you."

"What does that mean?"

Sir George reaches into the cuff of one of his boots. "It means that we will help him overthrow Richard."

I stare at Sir George for a long time while he fishes in his boot. Henry Bolingbroke. I cannot escape that name. Something is driving me toward that man.

John of Gaunt spoke of Henry in the cells of Framlingham. And the king's new marshal, Simon of Grimsby, asked me when we first met if I was with Henry. Even Richard asked about Bolingbroke after we jousted. Has he truly returned from France to overthrow Richard?

Sir George draws something out of his boot. "Tell him we could use some soldiers, if he can spare any. And when you see him, give him this. He'll know what it means."

I reach out my hand, and he places something small and cold in it. I hold it up and laugh. Sir George and the others look at me curiously, but all I can do is shake my head.

Gleaming in my hand, carved from the finest ivory, is a statuette of the Virgin Mary.

CHAPTER THIRTY-ONE

HENRY OF BOLINGBROKE, AS FAR AS Sir George knows, is in Stowmarket with an army of two thousand men. About the same number of men that Richard has in Framlingham.

The town of Stowmarket is less than ten miles away and directly on the path to St. Edmund's Bury, and Bolingbroke will likely have hundreds of horses.

We recover our donkey and leave Wickham Market under Sir George's unwavering gaze. One of the soldiers at the gate flashes the book of lewd verses at us and grins.

The heathlands around the village are vast and open. I tug my cloak tight around me and scan the horizon as we walk across the patchwork fields and tiny slopes of Suffolk. I think about Sir Gerald's men. They were in this area a few weeks ago. Perhaps they hold a fortress nearby. If they come for us, we will never outrun them on foot.

It will take much of the day to reach Stowmarket without horses. I wonder if the king's army has left Framlingham. Richard refuses to defend England from the forces of Hell, but he will lead two thousand soldiers to destroy my Heaven.

The land stretches away from us, tumbling lightly in sea-swells of brown and green, lush forests frothing in the distance.

Pantaleon picks up his pace so he and the donkey are beside Morgan. "In village," he says, "the rotters get the scare of you."

"I don't have the faintest idea what you are saying, Italian," Morgan replies. "I never have the faintest idea what you are saying."

Pantaleon touches the cross at Morgan's neck. "This. The rotters do not like."

Morgan glances down. "Course they don't. It is made from the True Cross upon which Jesus was crucified. It is a powerful relic."

Pantaleon crosses himself and grips the artifact between his thumb and forefinger. He gazes at it with reverence and whispers: "Perhaps this is the paid for me?"

"Perhaps bloody not!" Morgan yanks the cross out of the Italian's hands.

I think for a moment on Morgan's relic. Plaguers recoil from it, much as demons would. But if the afflicted are not demons, then why would they fear the power of Christ? Could they be possessed? Could the weakness of a plague-ravaged body allow evil spirits to enter?

I am a simple knight. Such questions are beyond my understanding. All I know is that both plague and possession can be cured by the phial that hangs around my neck.

Sometimes.

Zhuri peers at Morgan's cross. "I have never understood the Christian fascination with objects."

"They are not simply objects," Morgan says. "They are objects that have come into contact with a saint or Christ, Himself. Can you imagine it? Christ's body touched this. Our Lord and Savior's flesh rested upon this wood."

"And by touching Christ, the object has gained power?"

"You have witnessed the power of this cross, Zhuri. You have seen evil turn away from it."

Not even Tristan can argue. We have all seen the power of Morgan's relic.

"And there are many relics?" Zhuri asks.

"There are. I have seen dozens of them in churches and cathedrals. An iron nail that was used in Christ's crucifixion. A phial containing the breast milk of the Virgin Mary. The finger bone of Saint Benedict. The head of Saint John the Baptist. Every church must have a relic before it can be consecrated."

"Which of John the Baptist's heads did you see?" Tristan asks. "There are two, aren't there?"

"The one in France is a fake," Morgan growls.

"Maybe there is one John the Baptist head for each Pope," Tristan says. "And if you don't mind my saying, Christ must have been absolutely studded upon that cross. I have seen at least fifteen nails that were said to have been used in his crucifixion."

"I pity you, Tristan," Morgan replies. "You will never know the warmth and the strength that comes with true faith."

"All I need is the warmth of a woman's body," he replies. "And the strength of her legs around my waist."

"Your ceaseless mockery hides a fearful heart," Morgan replies.

We walk in silence for a time, and I think of Elizabeth. She owns a relic—a brush once owned by Saint Agatha, who was imprisoned in a brothel. I chided Elizabeth once, telling her it never belonged to Agatha, that it was just a whore's ancient brush. She chided back, asking me how I know what a whore's brush looks like. So I reminded her that we both watched John of Gaunt's wife brush her hair once. She feigned indignation at my insolence, but she could not hide her smile. I think about that smile now, a hundred miles from home, and I cannot help but smile too.

Morgan holds the cross in his fingers and breaks the silence. "When I am back home, I will have a beautiful reliquary made for this."

"Reliquary?" Zhuri asks.

Morgan nods. "A case built to house artifacts like this one. Usually made from precious metals."

"Artifacts *such as* this one," Zhuri replies.

Morgan does not acknowledge the correction. "Often the shape of the reliquary indicates what is inside. For this cross, I will make a case of gilded gold, in the form of a crucifix. I have seen all manner of shapes for reliquaries. If someone possesses a saint's toe, then the reliquary might be shaped like a foot. A skull might be housed in a case shaped like the saint's head. Do you see?"

Zhuri nods. "I have seen such things."

"Morgan?" Tristan says.

"What is it?" Morgan snaps.

"What shape was the reliquary that held Mary's breast milk?"

CHAPTER THIRTY-TWO

CLOUDS MARCH ACROSS THE SKY as we continue our journey to Stowmarket. We find a wagon trail leading westward and I decide to follow it. No doubt it will take us where we want to go, and I do not think anyone but Henry's men will be near.

It takes another two hours to reach the outskirts of the town, where we see the first of Henry Bolingbroke's perimeter forces. A dozen men in brigandine sit around a pair of cooking fires, the steel squares sewn into their jerkins almost black in the cloudy afternoon. Some of the men wear the Duke of Hereford's livery. Henry is Richard's cousin, so the two men share almost identical coats of arms—lions and fleurs-de-lis. The only difference of note is that Richard's coat of arms bears a cross, while Henry's does not. It is a heraldic irony, because Henry is the more devout of the two.

The men pick up spears and long axes from the grass and rise slowly when they see us. We meet on the road. One man, clean shaven and straight-shouldered, glances at the cannon jutting from my shoulder sack. "Are you Richard's men?" he asks.

"We're Richard's enemies," I reply. "And we need to speak with Henry Bolingbroke."

He glances past me as I speak and his face brightens. "Tristan! Tristan of Rye!"

Tristan steps forward and smiles. "John Langham. I was hoping you were dead."

They grasp hands as John laughs. "I'll live long enough to see you get what you deserve, you caitiff."

"Justice," Pantaleon mutters.

"What brings you to East Anglia, John?" Tristan asks. "Did the reeves chase you out of Sussex?"

"No, sir. Henry Bolingbroke did. Thousands of men have joined him. He's going to bring order to England. King Richard has abandoned God. And so God has abandoned England. But Henry, he's got the Lord's ear. Christ wants him to be king."

"Did you hear that, Morgan?" Tristan says. "Henry Bolingbroke has the Lord's ear. I wonder if he keeps it in a reliquary made of wax?"

"Where can we find Henry?" I say. "It's urgent that we speak with him."

John Langham points westward down the road. "Half-mile down the road, in town."

"Thank you." I brush past him. The others rush to keep up with me.

"Farewell, John." Tristan grins at the soldier. "A word of warning, I'm going to kill you the next time I see you."

"A word of warning," John shouts back, "Henry will probably kill you first."

Stowmarket is a sprawling town, nestled against a forest and bordered on two sides by rivers. I know that one of the rivers is called the Gipping. I do not know the name of the other, and I do not care to know it. Richard is marching toward Elizabeth, and my only concern is finding horses so I reach her first.

"Can you imagine that?" Tristan says. "An army following little Henry Bolingbroke. Who would have imagined such a thing?"

"You do not think he should lead an army?" Zhuri asks. "Is he a bad man?"

"Not bad at all," Tristan replies. "Nice enough lad, and a fierce fighter. But he's pious and boring and a little dour. A bit like Morgan, really."

"Men will follow anyone," I say.

Morgan looks at me, then at Tristan. "I can't tell if I'm being insulted by one or both of you."

"We find the army." Pantaleon points ahead of us, toward a field beside the Gipping.

Hundreds of tents and pavilions are set up just outside of the town. But no one moves among them. Not a single soldier, priest or farmer.

"We have found their camp," Tristan says. "Still no sign of an army."

I search the field as we walk closer but cannot see a soul.

"What did that soldier mean when he said Henry would probably kill you first?" Morgan asks, his voice soft, almost reverential.

"He was trying to show wit," Tristan replies. "But you need to have wit if you are to show it."

"Maybe he... Maybe..." Morgan stares at the empty field and shrugs.

"I hope you're not implying that Henry Bolingbroke and his army are plagued," Tristan replies.

"You said you'd seen a plaguer bishop," Morgan snaps. "Hugh the Baptist, that was his name, wasn't it? So why couldn't there be a plaguer duke?"

"Stop talking foolishness," I reply. The scent of roasting meat drifts in the air. A good sign. I have yet to meet a plaguer that cooks its food. Although, the meat does not smell very appetizing.

We walk through the village of tents. Past racks bearing armor and spears and poleaxes. Past iron tripods supporting kettles over cold firepits. It is an absurd thought, that a plagued duke could lead an army. But where could Henry have gone? My heart pounds, not with the thought that Henry might have the plague, but with the possibility that there may not be horses in Stowmarket.

A stout wooden bridge leads across the Gipping. No one stands guard. We walk across it, the donkey's hooves clattering over the planks. I rest my hand on the pommel of my sword, letting my finger trace the bump of Saint Giles's tooth in the grip.

Without warning, the ghostly strains of a distant choir break the silence. Voices in harmony, raised toward God. There is no sound like it in all the world. Mortal voices uniting to create something immortal. Something that cannot be of this earth. Something that touches the soul of anyone who hears it. Something that proves the existence of God.

We pass a line of hedges and all of us draw up short and stare.

Tristan lets out a long breath. "There is no God."

On either side of us, in piles as wide as small churches and high as my waist, lie stacks of smoldering dead. Twisted piles of blackened bones that still simmer and seethe. Dark blue smoke curls toward the Heavens like the sluggish emigration of angry souls.

I know now why I smelled roasting meat.

There is no difference between the bones of the afflicted and the healthy, so I can only imagine that these poor souls had the plague. I do not dare to think of the other possibility. We stare at the charred bodies for a long time while the Heavenly voices swell, stop with perfect precision, then begin again toward a new refrain.

Something hard forms in my chest, somewhere between my sternum and throat. Perhaps the last of my soul has hardened and died. Zhuri covers his eyes with a hand, and I know he struggles against tears. He and the sisters at

Hedingham burned scores of plaguers that had gathered around the walls of the convent.

"Let's find the horses and get out of Stowmarket," I say.

The song of the choir grows louder as we trudge closer to the town center. I wonder how many families lie in those smoldering piles. How many of those bones belong to children. I tap my breastplate so I can feel Elizabeth's cure against my chest and walk faster.

Three bodies hang by the neck from a tall oak a short distance away. Two men and a woman. The piles of burning dead were likely plagued, but I am certain that these three were not afflicted. I stare at them as I pass.

The singing comes from a church, of course, a long, stone building with the typical Norman tower and walls strewn with flint. Hundreds of men—perhaps thousands—kneel in the churchyard. They are crammed into every open space. More men gather at the doorway. I can only imagine how crowded it must be inside the church itself.

We walk through an open gate of wrought iron and pick our way through kneeling men.

"Kneel, sirs!" A man whispers to us.

"You have to take a knee, my lord," another hisses.

I do not have time to take a knee. Richard's army must surely have left Framlingham by now. And we are still ten miles from St. Edmund's Bury.

I shove past a man on the carved wooden porch and push into the church. The echoing voices in the choir strike me like a crash of warm water, set my bones trembling. The singers are above us, in the gallery. And before us, kneeling at every pew, are soldiers and priests.

Up by the altar, two knights in full harness hold a man's head in a barrel. The man's struggles make water from the barrel slosh onto the floor. Four priests, standing behind the knights, chant toward the drowning man, reading words from Bibles.

And, behind the knights and priests, hanging by a rope tied around her neck, is a woman. She gags and kicks violently, the noose slowly crushing the life from her.

"What is happening here?" I shout.

A priest kneeling by the door hisses at me. "Silence! And kneel! Kneel, or you'll spoil the ceremony!"

"What ceremony?"

"An exorcism!" The priest's head jerks to one side in what I can only imagine is a tic. "They are removing the demons from the afflicted man. Now kneel! Before it's too late!"

"Exorcisms," Tristan says, "look exactly like drownings." He glances above the altar. "What about the woman? Is she part of the ceremony?"

"Don't be a fool," the priest says, his head jerking again. "The death of a heretic gives power to exorcisms."

"Has she done anything wrong?" I ask. "Or did you simply pick her at random?"

"Of course she's done wrong!" The priest snaps. "She's an alchemist."

It takes a heartbeat for the words to settle on us.

We drop our packs, as one, and sprint down the aisle.

"Stop!" My words echo, and clash with the choir's song. "Take her down! Take her down!"

The knights at the barrel pull the plaguer's head out in a spray of water. They look to us without releasing their hold. One of the priests stops chanting and another urges him to continue by glaring and chanting more loudly.

Two men wearing the arms of Hereford rise and block our approach to the altar. "Halt!" one shouts. "You must kneel and be silent!"

A priest on the foremost pew rises. "They'll ruin it! They'll ruin it!"

"You have to cut her down!" I bellow.

The hanging woman's legs kick with less vigor.

One of Henry's men drives a shoulder into me, knocking me back into Tristan.

"By order of Henry, Duke of Hereford, I command you to kneel and shut your bloody mouth!"

I crouch and prepare to leap at the man.

"Edward!" Morgan shouts. "This is a church! It is forbidden!"

Necessitas non habet legem.

I lunge and grab the man by the hair, swing him sideways. He topples into the pew, knocking two kneeling men to the ground. Tristan and Pantaleon work together to shove the other guard into the pews on the far side of the aisle. And we run toward the altar.

Soldiers rise to their feet. The knights at the barrel look to the priests, who shake their heads and continue chanting. The plaguer's head is shoved back into the barrel and both knights and priests watch as we stream past. Tristan leaps, landing on his stomach upon the altar stone. But the altar cloth slides across the polished granite, and he crashes to the floor in a rattle of plates, on the opposite side.

"That hurt," Tristan calls from behind the altar. "A lot."

Henry's men are back on their feet and running toward us.

"Stop them!" one of the men shouts to the soldiers in the pew. "Stop them!"

I lean against the altar and Pantaleon boosts me up, muttering something about "... the paid... ." The woman's feet are twitching. She hangs limply from the rope. I hug her legs and lift, putting slack into the rope.

Please don't die.

Morgan, Zhuri, and Pantaleon shove at soldiers as they approach.

"Please," Morgan shouts. "Please, we do not want any more violence. This is a church!"

But there are too many soldiers in the church. They swarm my companions. Tristan leaps to his feet with a flourish and throws himself at the crowd, shouting, "Hallelujah!" He knocks a half dozen of them to the ground.

The voices of the choir surge, as if trying to drown out our screams. The four priests shout their prayers as loudly as they can. One of Henry's men screams instructions to the soldiers. A dog howls somewhere outside the church. This is what a festival in Hell would sound like. I brace my feet firmly on the altar and grip the woman more tightly.

Please don't die.

The other end of the rope runs the length of the church and is tied to the gallery's railing. "Morgan!" I shout. "Get to the gallery! Get to the gallery and cut the rope!

Two soldiers grab at my legs.

"She's a heretic!" one of them shouts. "Let her go!"

I kick at the two men.

"Take him down!" Henry's man shouts. "Take him down!"

More soldiers clutch at me. Arms encircle my legs. I howl at them, insensible words. One of my legs buckles and I dip. The rope goes taut. *"Get off me!"* The words are ripped from my throat. *"Get off me!"*

They pull my legs off the altar, and I am forced to release the woman. I fall onto my breastplate, the metal cracking against granite. The woman's feet wave madly above my head. I reach toward her helplessly. *"Get off me!"* My finger brushes her heel. *"Get off me! In the name of Christ, let me go!"*

Arms grab my waist and yank. I grip the edge of the altar so they cannot pull me away. A dozen hands take hold of my legs. They pull with all their strength. The altar tips backward an inch.

A soldier runs to the front of the altar and draws a dagger.

"She's our only hope!" I shout.

The soldier raises the dagger over one of my gauntleted hands.

"Don't!" I bellow. *"Don't!"*

The man snarls, tenses and—

"Let him go."

The voice is calm, but loud, and it has an immediate effect.

The choir goes silent. The priests stop chanting one by one. Soldiers grow silent and look toward the pews. The soldier in front of me lowers his dagger and looks back.

A young man stands at the rear of the church, his back straight as a cathedral wall, his arms crossed over his chest. Henry Bolingbroke. He glances up at the dying woman. "Take her down."

A soldier pulls himself onto the altar, beside me, and lifts the woman so that the rope goes slack again. Another man bows, edges past the duke, and runs toward the gallery stairs.

The soldiers still have a hold on me, but I nod to the young duke. "Thank you, my lord."

His lips curl into a smirk. "Do not thank me yet. You will take her place."

CHAPTER THIRTY-THREE

SOLDIERS PULL ME UPRIGHT. One pulls Saint Giles's sword from its sheath while the others shove me toward Henry Bolingbroke. The man in the gallery lowers the rope slowly and the woman flops against the soldier on the altar. She wheezes and sucks for breath, coughs and clutches at her neck. I close my eyes and thank Mother Mary for sparing the woman. Or for guiding me here in time to save her.

Protect the afflicted, Edward. And put the cure in the proper hands.

The words Father Peter spoke at the priory come back to me.

And where will I find these proper hands?

On the proper person.

I glance to the dark-haired woman, lying on the church floor, sobbing. I have found the proper person.

The duke takes a step forward and brushes something from the sleeve of his doublet. He wears dark, regal blue, with a chain of office draped over his shoulders. His red beard is trimmed meticulously. "Do I know you?" he asks me.

"We've met, my lord. I am Edward Dallingridge. Knight of the shire."

Recognition lights his face. He is son to John of Gaunt, so I do not know if recognition is a good thing. "Yes! You are Arundel's man. I remember now." He waves his hand dismissively toward the soldiers. "Let him go. Sir Edward is a good man. He fought with my father." He smirks at me again. "And against my father at times. I am sure there is a purpose to his silliness. Walk with me, Edward."

He turns and strides toward the church door, his boots clicking against the flagstones.

One of the priests beside the barrel, a balding man with a wart beneath one eye, clears his throat. "My lord!"

The duke pauses and looks back. "Father Benjamin?"

"We have... there is still the exorcism." The priest waves toward the barrel. "It's not complete."

The knights pull the plaguer's head out of the barrel. The afflicted man makes a wheezing noise and clicks his teeth.

Henry sighs and raises a hand, palm upward. "Please, Father," he says. "I have humored you enough. Every soldier in the army has left his post to come here, as you requested. And look. Look at that poor man. All you've done is moisten him."

"We did not have time to finish the rite, my lord! It was working. These... these men shattered the proceedings with their violence and... and their evil desires for the heretic woman."

"We've had more than an hour of singing and praying and dunking that man in holy water, Father," Henry replies. "The choir is exhausted and, frankly, so am I. Another hour or two will make no difference to the demons. They are not leaving him."

The priest folds his arms, nods. "Very well, my lord."

Henry takes two strides toward him. "You understand, don't you? We've given it a long time and it hasn't worked."

"Yes, my lord."

"I want to hear you say it. Tell me that you understand."

The priest clears his throat. Looks nervously to the sides. "I understand, my lord. You are wise in calling an end to the ceremony. The demons have not left him. Perhaps we erred in our execution of the exorcism."

Henry smiles. "Yes, that's probably it, Father. Look in your Bibles and see if you can't make it work next time." He turns away and calls to one of the men wearing the arms of Hereford. "John, get the men back to their posts. And lock up the alchemist. She's earned a reprieve, not a pardon." He motions to me. "Come, Sir Edward. I want to hear why a knight of the shire would fight an army to save a heretic."

Tristan and the others are disarmed and released. They join me beside the duke, as does Father Benjamin. The two knights who were assisting in the exorcism try to take positions beside the duke, but he waves them off. "Sir Edward is an honorable man. He means me no harm, and even if he did, he would not do anything in cold blood."

An endless stream of soldiers walk back toward their posts.

"Do you know that woman, Edward?" He draws a square of silk from a pouch at his waist and folds it in half. "The heretic?"

"No, my lord."

"Did you think you knew her? Think carefully, because what you did is a serious crime against God." He wraps the square of silk around the handle of a bucket that sits outside the door of the church, picks up the bucket, and walks toward a well on the village green.

"No, my lord," I repeat.

"He did not know her, and yet he tried to interfere with the Lord's justice," Father Benjamin says. "He's either mad or a servant of the Devil."

The duke sets the bucket down beside the well. "Are you mad, Edward?"

"Sometimes I think I must be," I reply. "A sane man in a mad world is insane."

"Although, in these times of madness," Tristan adds, "only madness will save us. But madness in this case would be sanity." He rubs at his forehead. "And so times of madness would be times of sanity." He glances at me. "What were we talking about?"

Henry stares at Tristan, then address me again. "Why were you interfering with the Lord's justice?"

"Because he is a heretic!" Father Benjamin snaps. "He brought weapons and violence into a church! Disrupted a sacred rite and stopped the just execution of an evil woman."

I set my gaze on Father Benjamin and leave it there for a long moment. He shifts and folds his arms, but his stare does not waver. "Because I believe she can save England."

The duke grins at me, but I do not smile.

"I have a message for you," I say. "From Sir George of Brighthelmstone. He is the marshal of Wickham Manor, now."

"Sir George? Heaven's Gate, I haven't heard from him in years. How is the old mongrel? What does he say? He did not speak ill of me, did he?"

I draw out the ceramic statue of Mary and hand it to him. "He said you would know what this was."

The duke studies the figurine and grins. He tucks the statue into a pouch and pulls a pair of gloves from his belt, turning to the well. He pauses before donning the gloves and shows me his hand. A small, red sore breaks the skin on the back of his thumb. "What do you make of that? My surgeon tells me it's from my gauntlet, but it's been bothering me for some time now. You don't suppose … this isn't …"

I look at the sore and shrug. "If you've had it for some time, it's not plague. Probably nothing, my lord."

He nods. "Was there more to Sir George's message?"

"He asked me to tell you that Wickham Market is with you. That they support you as king, and ask for soldiers at—"

"For all that is holy!" Henry slips his hands into the gloves. "Why does everyone say that? I do not want the crown. Richard is king. Not me. I have no right to that crown while he lives. What would the people think of me if I took the kingdom by force?" He yanks angrily at one of two ropes attached to the well. One of the water buckets rises and the other descends as he pulls hand over hand.

"The people want you to be king, Henry," Father Benjamin says. "God wants you to be king. Take Richard the Unholy down from his throne and bring sanctity back to England! You cannot fail, for the power of God is with you! 'The Lord takes vengeance on His adversaries and keeps wrath for His enemies. His way is in whirlwind and storm. He rebukes the sea and makes it dry; He dries up all the rivers; the mountains quake before Him; the hills melt; the earth heaves before Him. Who can stand before His indignation? Who can endure the heat of His anger? His wrath is poured out like fire, and the rocks are broken into pieces by Him.' Richard will burn, and break into pieces, Henry! God will destroy him and set you upon the throne!"

Father Benjamin's hands tremble with passion. I recognize the verse. It is from the times of the Old Testament, when God was murderous and full of wrath.

Henry looks at the priest for a long moment in precisely the same way he looked at Tristan a short time ago, then pours water from the well bucket into the one he brought from the church.

"Tell me about this heretic, Edward. What you did in the church is serious. I must judge your actions and determine your fate. Tell me why you want her to live. I want a truthful answer now, or I swear before God that you will hang."

"You should hang him anyway," Father Benjamin's hands still tremble, but his voice is low and sharp.

"This plague," I say. "There is a cure for it."

The duke lifts the church bucket with a groan and walks toward a row of narrow cottages. A bearded man wearing Henry's arms trots over and tries to carry the bucket for him, but the duke waves the man away. "I can do it. Get the bread, Godfrey. From the church."

We continue toward the cottages, water sloshing in the bucket.

"That is nonsense, Edward. I heard rumors of a cure when I was in France. Everyone talks about a cure, but no one has ever seen one. A man in France told me that the only cure was to eat a spoonful of crushed emeralds." He smiles, but the expression holds little humor. "There is no cure. This is a scourge from God. The best we can do is grant peace to the afflicted."

"We may be able to exorcise them," Father Benjamin says.

"Or drown them," Tristan adds.

"There is plague in France?" Morgan asks.

"There is plague everywhere," Henry replies. "It isn't quite as bad in France, yet. Not like it is here. Louis has been brutal when dealing with the afflicted."

A typical French response to adversity. It seems King Louis has finally found an opponent he can defeat in battle.

"Is that why you came?" Morgan asks. "Is that why you raised an army? To help clear the plague?"

The duke shakes his head. "I came because Richard... that... that prancing *fool*, has sworn to strip me of my lands and titles when my father dies. I raised an army and sailed back to England to make sure that *imbecile* does not take away my birthright."

We walk in silence to the first cottage. Henry glances at Morgan, then me. "Don't look at me like that. I was banished. How could I have known the plague was so bad here? I would have come sooner, had I learned the state of things here."

Morgan nods.

"You see that, don't you?" Henry adds. "You must understand that I would have come earlier."

"Yes, of course," Morgan replies.

"Of course, what?" Henry's gaze is locked on my friend.

Morgan glances at me, clear his throat. "Of course, you... would have come earlier. Had you... had you known, my lord."

Henry beams him a smile. "You are absolutely right. I would have been here months ago. I'm glad you understand that."

The bearded man, Godfrey, returns with a basket of bread. Henry raps on the cottage door and looks at me. "So, Edward, you disrupted a church service and fought with my men because you thought a girl alchemist you had never met could cure a plague sent by God? My father said you were a smart man. You are not living up to that assessment."

"He most certainly is not," Father Benjamin says. "I think he is an imbecile."

"Your father said that?" I ask. The image of John of Gaunt in Richard's cell drifts into my thoughts. Nothing left but a slug of a man, half-plagued, barely able to speak. I realize that he tried to tell me about Henry's titles. Those were the words he could not form when he tried to speak to me.

Death is something that comes to all men, but lands and titles can live forever. Whatever I may think of Gaunt, I cannot deny that he worked hard to give his children a better life. The Lancaster name shines brightly in England because John spent decades polishing it. King Richard could wipe away Gaunt's entire existence with one signature and send the Lancaster family into the shadows of history. I do not blame Henry for his anger. I would have challenged Richard's actions, too.

Henry should be told that his father is already dead. But I am not certain the subtle morality of my role in John's death would be appreciated. Particularly not now, when Henry is deciding my fate.

The cottage door opens. A wizened face peers out. An old woman with filmy eyes.

"Good day, Christina," Henry says. "I'm sorry you could not attend the service. How is your hip?"

The woman clutches a shawl about her neck and smiles toothlessly. "It only hurts when I'm awake, m'lord."

Henry returns her smile. "I've brought you water." He motions to Godfrey, who holds the basket out. "And bread."

"The Lord bless and keep you, m'lord." She takes a loaf of bread as Henry pours water from his bucket into a bucket by her door.

We walk to another cottage, a few down from Christina's, and Henry raps on the door. "Why would you think a sorceress that you've never met could mix a cure for this plague, Edward? It does not make sense."

"Because we have instructions for the cure," I say. "We know the ingredients. We simply need an alchemist to mix them."

"Stop that!" Henry shouts at Pantaleon. The Italian is rummaging through the basket of bread. "If you want a loaf, take one, but stop touching all of them. Your hands are filthy." Henry smirks at me and raps on the door again. "And from where did you obtain these instructions? A peddler?"

"From an ampoule that contains the cure." We did get the cure and the instructions from a peddler, but imparting that information may not be helpful to us. I draw the spare ampoule from the poke at my belt. It is the last one. I show it to the duke, then point to Morgan. "The same cure that healed this man."

The door opens and an elderly man peers out, his face pitted from a childhood pox. Henry does not look at the man. He looks at Morgan. Studies the scabs along his face and hands.

"Good day, m'lord," the elderly man says. "A pleasure to see you, Lord Henry."

Henry speaks to him, but continues to stare at Morgan. "I've... I've brought you... bread and water."

Godfrey extends the basket and the old man takes a loaf.

"You were plagued?" Henry asks. "With this new illness? The demon plague?"

"No, my lord," the old man says. "I'm fit and strong, my lord. No demons."

Morgan clears his throat. "An afflicted dog bit me. But our Heavenly Father brought me back."

"He's lying!" Father Benjamin snaps. "He's a leper trying to make himself seem clean."

"I ain't a leper, my lord!" the old man barks. "I'm healthy!"

Morgan waits for the old man to stop speaking. "I'm not a leper, Father, these are clerical vestments. I was plagued and locked in a nunnery's wine cellar for days. The Lord sent a cure and brought me back." He glances at Zhuri. "And I am eternally grateful to my friends for doing the Lord's work."

"The Lord didn't bring him back!" Father Benjamin hisses. "He was never plagued! And if that foul tincture *did* heal him, then it was necromancy, not the Lord! Alchemy gave him life! He's no better than the sorceress! He's a sinner and heretic, and under the power of the Devil, himself!"

The old man takes a deep breath and grins toothlessly. "You haven't been talking to me, have you?"

Morgan's face flushes but he does not speak. He will never argue with a priest.

But Tristan will.

"Morgan is not responsible for decisions made by others," he snaps. "He is the most devout man I have ever met. If he's a heretic, then we are all doomed."

"I think he has a sound argument, my lord," the old man offers.

"We *are* all doomed," The priest replies. "Look around you. This scourge was caused by alchemy! And you want to use alchemy to end it?"

"That's a sound argument too," the old man says.

"This scourge was caused by monks grinding up dead saints and pouring the powder into the Sacrament dough," Tristan replies. "And you want to use prayer to end it, *baldhead?*"

Zhuri bites his knuckle. "Tristan, no!"

"*Liar!*" Father Benjamin roars. "You are a liar and a blasphemer, and you shall be put to death! *To death!*"

"Enough!" Henry tugs at his tunic and glares at Tristan. "Father Benjamin, if you hear another word of blasphemy from the mouth of this knight, you have my permission to burn him." He takes a long breath and brushes dirt from his glove. "I do not believe there is a cure, Edward. And even if there was, I do not believe God would want us to use it. Our Lord brought this scourge upon us for a reason."

"Amen!" Father Benjamin adds.

"What makes you think it was God who brought this plague upon us?" The thought strikes me like divine lightning. Henry stares at me. Everyone stares at me. I lick at my lips. "Why does everyone assume that God would punish us like this? Why has no one blamed Satan for this? And why wouldn't God give us a cure to save the devout from the devil's horror?"

"Ooooooooh!" The old man in the doorway draws out the sound. "I ain't never thought of it like that."

"God wouldn't use alchemy to defeat the devil," Father Benjamin snaps.

"Christ was an alchemist, wasn't he?" I repeat Father Peter's words from the priory before I think about what I am saying. "Water to wine."

A profound silence falls. A flush paints the priest's cheeks a bright red.

"So... so sayeth the Lord?" Tristan mumbles into the silence.

Father Benjamin points a hooked and trembling finger at me. "You... you will die for those words."

Henry looks into my eyes. "I could have you killed for speaking like that, Edward."

"But you won't," I say. "Because you hear the truth in them. Moses was a sorcerer. He turned a stick into a serpent. Parted an entire sea. God grants power in times of greatest need. And He has given us this gift. When we need it most."

Morgan clears his throat and raises his eyes to the Heavens. "'Every good gift and every perfect gift is from above, coming down from the Father of Lights.'"

"So sayeth the Lord!" the old man in the doorway shouts.

"They must be hanged, my lord," Father Benjamin's voice is a whisper. "They have defiled our Lord Jesus Christ."

"Prayer is the only answer to this plague, Edward." Henry's voice wavers.

"And God has answered our prayers," I reply. "He has sent us a cure. What would people think of you, my lord, if they learn that you could have cured the kingdom, but did not?"

Henry looks up at me sharply.

"Alchemy is a sin," the priest hisses.

"Alchemy... is contrary to the laws of God and England," Henry says.

"*Necessitas non habet legem*," I reply. "Necessity has no law."

The duke stares toward faint wisps of smoke rising in the distance, rising from piles of smoldering bodies. I understand the struggle in his heart.

"I want proof," he says. "I want proof that this cure works."

"My lord!" the priest shouts. "You cannot—"

"Silence!" Henry arms are lance-straight at his sides, hands clenched into fists, as he shouts at the priest. "I have done everything you asked me to. Everything! The exorcisms. The prayers. The lashings and the hair shirts." He jabs a finger toward the rising smoke. "*I have burned two hundred afflicted men, women and children because you said they were demons*! I have listened to every piece of advice you have given, and nothing has worked!" He wipes at his lower lip, breathes a deep sigh, and continues more calmly. "What if these men are right? What if God has delivered the cure to us? Shall we sink the ark because we do not like the way it was built? Shall we refuse to flee through the Red Sea because it was parted with sorcery?" He turns to me. "Can you prove to me that this cure works?"

"I can," I reply. "My wife is plagued. Give me four horses and I will bring her back here, and cure her before your eyes." I try not to think of Richard's wife, the Good Queen Anne.

"I need all of my horses, Sir Edward," Henry says. "St. Edmund's Bury is less than twenty miles from here. You can walk. Keep to the Roman road, and take some food from our stores. We have wine for—"

"I need the horses, my lord. I don't have much time to reach her."

"And why is that?"

I rub at a spot of rust on the steel of my bracer. "King Richard... he... he wants to kill her. He's heading to St. Edmund's Bury with an army as we speak."

"What?" The bucket falls to the grass with a thud.

My companions turn their eyes toward me. There is a labyrinth to be navigated here, and a Minotaur down each path. "I... I upset him. It is a long tale. One I will gladly tell you when my wife is safe, my lord."

"I don't care why Richard is angry with you," Henry replies. "Did you say he is leaving Framlingham?"

I nod. "His army is marching as we speak."

"I spent two days outside Framlingham with my men, waiting for Richard to meet me and he never left the castle. I need you to be absolutely sure of it, Sir Edward. Has Richard left Framlingham?"

"We met one of his men this morning," I reply. "He said the army is mustering."

Henry picks up the square of silk from the ground and folds it neatly. "Godfrey, tell John to prepare the men to travel tomorrow. And remind them that we are not waging war against Richard, we are simply presenting him with an unassailable argument against stripping the Lancasters of their birthright. Go. We march to St. Edmund's Bury tomorrow."

"Hurrah!" The old man grins again. "You will be King Henry IV!"

Henry shakes his head. "I'm not taking the crown from..." He dismisses the old man with a wave and strides back toward the church.

"And Godfrey," the duke calls. "Get Sir Edward some horses."

CHAPTER THIRTY-FOUR

THE ALCHEMIST IS NAMED JOSALYN. She is pretty and shockingly young, with a round face, dark hair, and eyes the color of a forest at sunset—greens and browns and yellows. She does not speak but kneels at my feet and bows her head with what I imagine is gratitude. Her arms embrace my legs, an echo of what I did to save her. She weeps silently. I wonder if she is mute. Or perhaps her throat was injured by the noose.

Henry relented, in the end, and gave permission for her to start work on the cure, but only for today. Because tomorrow Josalyn will accompany Henry's army to St. Edmund's Bury. "And if your wife is not healed by this cure, Sir Edward," he said, "I will put the noose back around the heretic's neck. And this time, the knot will be on the side, not the back."

A noose knotted on the side breaks the neck instantly. There would be no saving her a second time.

I help Josalyn to her feet and we escort her through the village, past rows of cottages and tile-roofed shops. A soldier told us that her home is on the outskirts of Stowmarket, and serves as her alchemical workshop as well.

My pace is just short of a trot. The others struggle to keep up. I want to give this woman what she needs to produce the cure and be on my way.

Armies are ponderous things. There are wagons and pack mules, cattle and armored infantrymen. It will take Henry's forces ten or eleven hours to complete the twenty-mile journey. But I do not have that long.

If King Richard is quick-marching his men—which I have no doubt that he is—and leaving wagons and animals behind, he will reach Elizabeth by tomorrow afternoon. So I must leave within the hour and reach St. Edmund's Bury tonight.

I still have not solved the problem of Sir Gerald and his men. Perhaps they will think they have missed me and simply leave the town. But that is more prayer than possibility. Sir Gerald will wait for me until Judgment Day. No. Judgment Day may already be upon us. Sir Gerald will wait for all eternity.

Two soldiers in leather hauberks walk to either side of the girl. They will guard Josalyn at her workshop until the army leaves Stowmarket.

I give the girl the spare cure as we hustle through the empty village, and explain to her what we need. She studies the ampoule carefully and listens as I relate my experiences with the alchemist from St. Benet's. I explain that the ingredients for the cure are listed on each ampoule. "They are written in Arabic," I say. "But my friend Zhuri will translate the words and scribe them for you before we leave."

"I will be delighted to help you with this task." Zhuri bows to her, his eyes making quick darts in her direction, though never lingering. I believe the Moor is smitten. "I will do whatever you require of me."

"I'm not comfortable with this, Edward," Morgan says. "If she is to do this, then she must do it in the name of God. There should be no question of our piety or motivation. Priests should be there. Any water she uses should be blessed. Crucifixes must be mounted on the wall.

God's presence must be seen everywhere. Everywhere, Edward, or we risk heresy."

"So, as long as the trappings of religion are near, heresy isn't heresy?" Tristan asks. "I'm going to thump Father Benjamin in the nose with a Bible the next time I see him."

"Quiet, Tristan," I reply. "Morgan's right. People will balk at the cure if they think it is the Devil's work. We need this to have the Church's blessing from the beginning. I will speak with Henry."

We stop outside a two-story cottage of wattle and daub. Whitewashed stones form a tidy square around an herb garden beside the structure. A yellow-flowered plant adorns the wooden sign that hangs beside the door. The plant is Saint John's wort, and the cottage is an apothecary's workshop. I have seen four alchemists burn, and three of the four swore at their trial that they were simple apothecaries. That is the alchemist's defense; and the typical answer is a pyre, a grin, and the words, "Of course you are."

One of the two soldiers opens the black-varnished door and the other motions for Josalyn to enter. She glances at the soldiers and gives a short shake of her head, extends the ampoule back toward me.

"I know." I say. "They tried to hang you. But these men will obey Henry. No harm will come to you. You must listen, this is important. The ingredients for the cure, they were written as riddles. For instance, one of the ingredients was called the juice of metal, and the alchemist understood this to mean quicksilver. He said any alchemist could decipher the riddles."

I dig inside my shoulder sack until I find a glass bottle wrapped in linens and bound with leather cords. I use my dagger to cut away the wrappings and show the jar to Josalyn. The sunlight strikes dark red gleams from the otherwise black fluid. "There was only one riddle he couldn't solve, and that's because it wasn't a riddle." I extend the large bottle to her. "*Ad-dimaa ah-teen*. The blood of dragons." I extend the bottle toward her. "This is from a real dragon."

"We slayed it," Tristan says. "Edward and I. We slayed a dragon, and collected its blood."

I shake my head. "We didn't actually slay—"

"*We slayed it.*" Tristan barks. "Edward and I. We are dragon slayers."

The jar is heavy. Josalyn takes it with both hands, looks at the blood, and shakes her head again.

"I know, it is hard to imagine that dragon blood could be used in a cure," I say. "But Zhuri confirmed our belief. Dragon's blood is considered a powerful healing elixir in the Muslim world."

"It is," Zhuri says. "I've heard it said that anything can be cured with the blood of dragons."

I point to the bottle. "I'm certain you understand how rare that is. Have care with it."

She closes her eyes and takes a long breath.

I reassure her as best I can. "I know we ask a lot of you. But you are England's best hope. If you can make this cure, you will rise from heretic to saint. Not a bad reward, is it? Saint Josalyn, patron of alchemists. How does that sound?"

She shakes her head again and extends the bottle toward me. "I..." Her voice squeaks, so she rubs at her throat and tries again. "I..."

A man screams from somewhere behind us. I look back toward the village green. I spot three men in the distance. They sprint across my field of view, laughing, their swords flapping up and down in belted sheaths. And they disappear behind a long, thatched building.

"I... am not..." Josalyn coughs. "I am not an alchemist."

"What?"

Zhuri whirls toward her so quickly that his elbow strikes her hand. I watch for a helpless eternity as the bottle of dragon blood spins through the air.

And shatters on the row of white stones.

CHAPTER THIRTY-FIVE

THERE IS NO SOUND IN THIS WORLD louder than the roar of an iron-barreled, fifteen-foot siege cannon hurling fire and stone at a city wall. I have heard such blasts many times, but my first was at the Battle of Nájera. I remember that first volley. The violence of the gun surged through my blood like ripples through a jostled mug of ale. Smoke stung my eyes and the stench of sulfur burned my nose and my only thought was that not even Satan could have made such thunder when he fell to the earth.

But the clink of a broken bottle in Stowmarket is louder than any cannon in Spain. It is not a gun, and it is not Satan, but the sound ripples through my blood nonetheless.

It is the sound of my own Fall from grace.

I lunge to my knees and scoop at the shards, gashing my hand. My blood mingles with dragon blood upon the spattered stones. I cannot form words. I can only grunt.

"God in Heaven," Morgan cries.

"Mary's tits!" Tristan dives to the ground beside me and scoops out handfuls of blood-drenched earth. Zhuri, Morgan and Pantaleon kneel and try to salvage as much of the blood as they can.

Josalyn covers her face and weeps. "I'm... I'm so..." She cannot get the words out, either because of her injuries or because of her sobbing.

"It is my fault." Zhuri pounds the earth with a fist. "It is my damnable fault! I am a curse! A curse!"

The thud of footfalls sounds, not far from us. People running. Three soldiers approach us. The same ones who distracted us before and caused the catastrophe.

"*Che cosa è questo?*"

The three men who were running and laughing along the avenue stop a short distance from us. Pantaleon rises, holding a rounded shard of glass with a drop of blood in it. He nods to the three men and speaks to them in Italian. "*Questi idioti appena condannati umanità.*"

I am not certain of what he said, but I believe he has called Zhuri an idiot. Perhaps he has called all of us idiots. And perhaps he is right. I should have kept the glass bottle with me until I could set it down in the girl's workshop.

Tristan runs into the cottage and clatters around. He returns with a ceramic jar to hold the recovered fluids.

The bottle of dragon blood would have filled four tankards to the brim. What we recover from the stones and soil of Stowmarket is less than half a mug. I want to roar. I want to howl. I want to tear down the daub walls and curse everyone around me. But I cannot. Because Josalyn sobs at my side.

"It's fine," I grunt. "We can…" I do not know what *we can*, so I brush dirt from my palm. "It's fine."

Tristan holds the jar in one hand and a bloodstained stone in the other. He shakes the stone so that a drop of blood falls into the jar.

Morgan squats so that he can meet Josalyn's gaze. "How can you not be an alchemist? They were about to hang you!"

"And the Church *never* hangs people without reason." Tristan's voice is more sober than I have heard it in a long time. His eyes do not stray from the jar of dragon blood in his hands.

Josalyn turns her trembling face upward and sniffs. "They hung my father," she says. "They said he was an alchemist, but he was an apothecary."

The two soldiers glance toward her and grin. One mumbles, "Of course he was."

"They hung him." Tears glimmer in her eyes.

Zhuri pats her back awkwardly and does not correct her English.

He must truly be smitten.

"He mixed a paste that the plague victims do not like," she adds. "He could walk among the afflicted with the paste on his arms and they would not come near him. And they hung him for it. They said he was a servant of the Devil!"

Tristan and I exchange a look. "Do you have any of this paste left?" Tristan asks.

She shakes her head. "He made only one batch of it. He would have made more. It was very simple to make. Flour, fish-oil and red lichen. But the lichen is difficult to find. He would have found more of it. I know he would have. But they hung him!" She spits toward the two soldiers who escorted us to her home. "He was trying to help, and they murdered him!"

"I don't understand," I say. "Why do they think you're an alchemist?" I turn to the two soldiers. "Why were you hanging this girl if she's not an alchemist?" My voice rings across the desolate town. I take deep breaths to settle the rising tide of rage.

"She... she was practicing alchemy," one of them says. "And sorcery."

I look to the girl.

"My... my... father taught me a little."

"How little?" I ask, edging toward her. "Can you do what we are asking? Can you make this cure?"

The girl stares at her bare feet and is silent for a time. When she looks up, her eyes shimmer with tears again, and behind those tears is something else. Terror. The poor girl is terrified. And I think it is me who frightens her the most.

"I can try."

The rage drains. I draw a deep breath. "Course you can. That's all we're asking. Just try. No one will think worse of you if you can't do it."

No one except Henry Bolingbroke, who will snap her neck.

Why did I think this girl could make the cure? The alchemist at St. Benet's spent months in his workshop—toiling day and night—and could not do it. How can a girl, who looks as if she has yet to see her fifteenth year, succeed? I gaze at the jar in Tristan's hands.

Because she has something the alchemist did not.

"Try. That's all we're asking. Just try." I force a grin. "Unfortunately, I don't think we'll make a great difference either way. How many cures can we possibly mix with such a small jar of dragon blood?"

Josalyn sniffs and looks at the jar. She closes her eyes for a long time, and when she opens them she wrinkles her nose and shrugs. "Twenty-five thousand?"

Tristan scoffs. "What?"

"Twenty-five thousand. Maybe a little less. The numbers are difficult to reckon."

"Don't speak rubbish," I say. Her lips quiver and I take three deep breaths. "I didn't mean that. Please tell me why you believe we can make twenty-five thousand cures."

"It's not rubbish." She rubs at her eyes. There is a hint of petulance in her voice. "That jar measures one gill, and the blood is nearly to the top. There are four hundred and fifty grains in a gill. The ampoule you gave me comes from a large batch of this cure. I know that because it contains dragon blood equal to a fiftieth part of a grain, and no one could measure out such a small amount. So if there is one fiftieth of a grain of dragon blood in each dose, and we have four hundred and fifty grains of dragon blood, that means we can create twenty-five thousand cures. A little less, I think." She shrugs. "The numbers are difficult, so perhaps I am wrong."

"You say he taught you a *little?*" The humor is back in Tristan's voice.

"Absolutely beautiful," Zhuri says.

Josalyn glances at Zhuri, then looks away, blushing.

"Why would you assume that the ampoules contain a fiftieth part of a grain of blood?" I ask.

She holds out her hand. "Show it to me, my lord."

I draw the extra cure from my pouch and place it in her palm. She holds it close to her eyes and rolls the ampoule. "There." She holds it up to me. "See the circle and dot? Next to the words for dragon blood?"

"Stop playing games, girl," Morgan says. "That writing is Arabic. How could you know the words for dragon blood in Arabic?"

"I don't," she replies. "But I know the word blood. And it only appears on the ampoule once. I'm better with Arabic numbers than letters, but I know some words. My father made me learn a little of the language so I could help. Most of the best writings on alch... ah... medicines come from the Muslims."

"I could teach you to read in Arabic." Zhuri averts his eyes when she looks toward him. "If... if you wanted."

Josalyn rubs a strand of her hair between thumb and forefinger. "I would like that. Very much."

I wave my hand between them. "You are saying that we can cure twenty-five thousand people with a gill of dragon blood?"

She smiles at Zhuri and blushes, turns to face me. "A little less I think. But yes."

Twenty-five thousand is more than I ever dreamed we could cure. And yet, all I can think about are the tens of thousands that will not be cured because of our mistake.

We held life in our hands.

I let my gaze fall upon the shards of broken glass among the white stones and close my eyes when I cannot bear to look anymore.

CHAPTER THIRTY-SIX

ZHURI DECIDES TO STAY WITH JOSALYN. He tells me he will travel with Lord Henry's army and rejoin us at St. Edmund's.

"Her father has many papers in Arabic and Hebrew," he says. "She may need to consult them and I am the only one who speaks those languages. I want nothing more than to continue my journey with you, but I must make this sacrifice. For the cure. For England and for Spain."

It is a good pretense. I almost believe him.

We leave him with the girl and her two guards, in the spice seller's cottage, and return to the church. The three Italian soldiers follow, chattering to Pantaleon.

Henry Bolingbroke waits in the churchyard, a gaggle of priests fluttering and squawking around him. Four chestnut palfreys have been saddled and hitched to the gate that borders the church.

The priests grow silent when we approach. I spot Father Benjamin among the white-robed clergy. He sneers in a most unchristian manner and I turn the other cheek of my arse to him as I push in beside Henry.

"I had them pack salted cod and dried hare in the saddlebags," the duke says. "And two skins of wine."

I nod my thanks. "You have done much for me, Lord Henry. And yet, I will ask one more favor, if I may."

Henry crosses his arms and nods for me to continue.

"An enemy waits for me at St. Edmund's Bury," I say.

"I thought you could beat Richard there if I gave you horses," he replies.

"Another enemy," I say. "A knight with a small army. He has vowed to kill me."

"Is there anyone in England who does not want you dead, Sir Edward?"

I scratch at my chin and smile. "There's an archer and his wife, in Norfolk." My smile fades. "But they might want to kill me too."

I think about the bowman in the mill, the one who helped us escape Sir Gerald. I wonder if the cure I left healed their son or turned him into a monster. Life or death. Heaven or Hell. The world forever hinges on two opposite outcomes. And now, my journey hinges on Lord Henry's answer to my next request. "I could use some men. Two hundred would likely be enough."

The duke studies me for a time. Father Benjamin whispers something and Henry nods.

"I'm sorry Edward," he says. "I am in a difficult position. The king banished me, and I was not supposed to return for another eight years. Many would think me unlawful for returning, and for raising an army." He looks into my eyes. "You don't think I'm being unlawful, do you, Edward?"

"No," I reply. "I think you are trying to save your nobility, and to help England recover from this affliction."

He smiles broadly, claps my shoulder. "I'm pleased you see it that way. Sadly, the only way to prove my intent is to offer no strife. To anyone."

Father Benjamin crosses himself. "The last thing the duke needs is to have his men slaughtering other knights," he hisses. "If he chooses to attack the licentious King Richard, he is justified. Otherwise, we shall raise arms against no one. This is a mission of peace."

"A mission of peace?" Tristan barks back. "You're leaving smoldering piles of plaguers in your wake. Hanged men and women dot the countryside like wind chimes because of your *peaceful* mission."

"Heretics and demons must be destroyed," the priest replies. "If it was up to me, you and—"

"Enough!" Henry snaps. "Just stop it. Both of you." He turns to face me. "I cannot send men from my army to fight other Englishmen, Edward. I am sorry."

A silence settles as I consider my next argument, and in that silence, Pantaleon and the Italians laugh.

One of the men shouts, "*Avreste dovuto vedere la sua faccia!*" The five kinsmen burst into laughter again.

Henry points at Pantaleon. "Is he your man?"

I shrug. "I'm not sure. I think he's just traveling with us."

"But he speaks Italian?"

"Many Italians do." The disappointment makes me surly.

Father Benjamin scowls at me.

Henry nods curtly. "I think I may have a solution to your problem."

There are ten Italians in Henry's camp—the remnants of a mercenary company that left France with the duke. They wear brigandine armor—knee-length leather jerkins sewn with overlapping metal plates—and white, padded tunics with the red cross of Saint George upon them. Steel greaves and lobstered metal shoes protect their legs.

I have faced such men in battle many times. Genoese crossbowmen. Once, these soldiers were considered the most dangerous warriors in Europe. Companies of these men can unleash a hail of deadly shafts from three hundred paces—a hail that burns through men, and punches through metal as easily as flesh.

"Those crossbows will make quick work of Gerald," Zhuri says.

"Terrible weapons," Morgan adds. "Do you know the Church once outlawed crossbows? The Pope felt the wounds they caused were too hideous. 'Hateful to God and unfit for Christians.' That's what he said."

"They weren't so hateful or unfit during the Crusades," Tristan adds. "The Pope was quite happy to let our Crusaders use them against Muslims."

"That is because we are irrelevant," Zhuri replies.

"I never said that," Morgan replies.

Tristan smirks. "So, are you calling these Genoese soldiers hateful to God, Morgan?"

"I won't take part in a conversation where my words are constantly twisted."

I walk down the line of crossbowmen, inspecting them as the others continue to prattle.

Our armies were terrified of the Genoese for decades. Until the Black Prince fought a battle in a place called Crecy. On that rainy day, wet bowstrings and poor tactics by the French rendered the Italians ineffective to the point of disaster. And, on that blessed day, the English archers, with their six-foot war bows, emerged as the most feared soldiers in Europe.

The French hold such a fear of our archers, now, that they cut off the first two fingers of every captured English bowman. This ensures that our men will never draw a bow again. It is a custom that does not sit well on our side of the Channel. Whenever French and English armies meet for battle, our archers hold up two fingers, nails out, to show they are still capable of putting an ash shaft through a French heart. The gesture has become the worst of insults.

I study the Italians standing in two ranks before me. They may not be English archers, and there may only be ten of them, but Genoese crossbowmen are a great asset.

"If only we had another fifty," I murmur.

Tristan nods. "And if only we could understand them."

None of the crossbowmen speak a word of English. Their commander knew our language, but he is dead now, or wandering mindlessly across East Anglia. Pantaleon will have to translate between us, which is only slightly better than not being able to communicate with them at all.

"How much does the paid come upon me?" Pantaleon asks.

"You can keep the horse," I reply. "That'll be your *paid* for translating."

"I gave the arse to the horse," he replies.

"*Ass*," Morgan corrects. "*For*. You gave the ass *for* the horse."

"A donkey isn't worth a palfrey," I reply. "That horse is worth three donkeys. Are we truly going to argue about payment? Will you never do something simply because it's honorable?"

"I fight with you," Pantaleon says. "I make the *Italiano* into the English. I bring friends of you from the danger. Many things, I do. The honor is the good on you. The paid is the good on me. And none give me the paid." He shakes his head. "I do not get the justice."

"Get used to it," Tristan says. "None of us gets the justice. Not a bloody one of us."

Henry provides horses for all of the crossbowmen, but makes me swear that I will return every one of his animals when his army reaches St. Edmund's Bury.

Apologies, Pantaleon.

I nod my agreement, thank Lord Henry for his help, and we chase the dying sun out of Stowmarket.

Twenty miles separate me from Elizabeth. Twenty miles, two hundred men, and an army of plaguers. But I have the Virgin Mary guiding my way, and some of the fiercest soldiers in Europe at my back.

The Scourge: Emaculum

The clouds tumble away from the setting sun as we ride, and one of the fiercest soldiers in Europe shreds the silence by shrieking like a woman set aflame. The cry is so loud and so full of terror that Morgan's horse rears. Tristan and I draw our swords and whirl our palfreys.

"What is it?" I spin my horse again, eyes darting to the horizon and back. The Italians stare at me blankly. "*What is it?*"

A tall crossbowmen shrugs, points to a soldier with brown hair, and rattles off a stream of Italian.

"What's he saying?"

Pantaleon speaks with the tall man.

"He is saying the man, Tarviccio, he do that sometime."

"He does what?" I ask.

"He lifts the voice."

"He screams?"

Pantaleon nods. "Yes. He screams."

I look at Tarviccio. A thin man with a long nose, slouching in the saddle. He flashes a nervous smile and waves.

"Why? Why does he scream?"

"It is not known." Pantaleon shrugs and nods toward the tall soldier. "The man there has the name of Frederico Longobucco. He say Tarviccio not make large problem, eh? He scream sometime. Is simple."

"We're trying to sneak past hundreds of men who want to kill us," Tristan snaps. "I think it might make a large bloody problem, eh?"

Pantaleon speaks with Frederico Longobucco and they both nod. "Frederico, he say you not have worry. Tarviccio not does it many time. Very rare."

I sheathe my sword, glance at Tristan, and drive heels into my palfrey's flanks. Tarviccio could not have become a member of an elite class of warriors if he screamed often. It is an annoyance, but if it rarely happens I will not worry about it.

My company moves forward again, rumbling across the shallow hills of Suffolk. The sky is a fiery orange, the land beneath it a honey gold. Stalks of foxglove wave in the breeze, like rows of purple church bells, and another of Tarviccio's shrieks rings out across the plains.

CHAPTER THIRTY-SEVEN

I AM NOT CERTAIN HOW BEST TO APPROACH St. Edmund's Bury. The fastest path would be to follow the wagon road straight to the city's east gate. Or to travel overland until we reach the Sudbury road, which knifes northward to the city's southern gate. But Sir Gerald's men will be watching. It does not matter from which gate we enter, we will be spotted a mile or more from the city.

If we somehow find a way to get past Sir Gerald, it will be a simple matter to enter the monastery. A tunnel beneath the prior's chamber extends out to the banks of the River Lark. It is how Tristan and I entered and left last time, and it is the only way I can get to Elizabeth.

I break my horse's canter and let her walk for a time as I think.

"We'll keep going westward," I say finally. "I want to stay off the main highways to the city."

"If we continue west, we'll hit the Sudbury road, Edward," Tristan replies. "The one we took into the city last time. And Gerald will have men all over that road."

"We'll stop before we reach it," I reply. "I'll send up scouts and get a measure of Gerald's defenses before committing."

Tristan and Morgan look to one another. I know they are concerned about our chances. Gerald could have two hundred men or more around the city. I have no plan. No idea. The only certainty I have is that two hundred men are not enough to keep me from Elizabeth. But my friends should not have to take such a risk.

"Tristan, Morgan," I say. "I cannot make any guarantees about our safety from this point. We may well be riding toward our deaths. I release you of any obligation you have to me. If you wish to return to Sussex, I will think no less of you."

"I do wish to return to Sussex," Tristan replies. "So let's hurry up and rescue Elizabeth."

Morgan nods. "I pity Gerald's men if they try to stop us."

I know I should try harder to make them leave, but I cannot keep the smile from my face. I could not find two better friends in all the world.

"I pity them too," Tristan says. "They'll be washing our blood and brains from their armor for weeks."

"And think how sore their arms will be from all that mashing and hacking," Morgan adds.

Tristan raises his hands as if warding off phantom blows. "No, please, no more hacking! No more mashing. Mercy! Mercy!"

Morgan laughs and slumps in his saddle, as if dead.

I stare at the sky and shake my head. I could not find two more irritating friends in all the world.

I try to gauge the character and emotional state of the Genoese as we ride. It is difficult to inventory men you cannot speak with, so I ask Pantaleon about them. They all hold the same basic rank, but it is Frederico Longobucco who took over the command when their sergeant was killed by plaguers. He is tall with dark hair and green eyes. Sharp-eyed and pragmatic, but with a quick smile that tells me there is far more to him than discipline.

Frederico's opposite is a man named Rigi Coraggio, who is thick-shouldered and stubble-faced. Rigi, or Rizio as the others call him, possesses a rugged handsomeness. He grins perpetually, and the men never fail to return the expression. Pantaleon tells me that Rizio is famed for his inhuman ability to drink.

Joseph Magazzi is the shortest of the crossbowmen, and the best shot. I am told that he can hit a coin at fifty paces, but I will have to see proof of this to believe such a boast.

There is also Nicolo Barezzio—called Magnus by the others. A hulking giant who makes an eighteen-hand draft horse look like a pony. The man's shoulders are like sandstone blocks, his neck an oaken stump. On his back sits a colossal siege crossbow—a weapon that is normally set upon supports and fired from castle walls. A siege crossbow can send a narrow tipped bolt through two knights in full armor. And when using the square-headed bolts—the ones meant for striking concussive blows against armor—the weapon can launch knights from their saddles as if ropes had yanked them backward.

I have never seen a man fire a siege crossbow without supports, but I have no doubt Magnus has the power to do so.

Pantaleon speaks about each of remaining men, adding his own insights and opinions. Antonio lo Grato is thin with murky blonde hair and is, apparently, quite witty. Domenico is fidgety and sweats, and is the most devout of the crossbowmen. Ermolao is thick in every sense of the word. Thick fingers, thick features, and not the brightest of the lot. Francisco is so fat that the brigandine armor he wears had to be cut vertically at intervals so it would fit around him. Zilio is quiet, and Tarviccio … Tarviccio screams.

They are an odd bunch, but they follow Frederico's commands unswervingly and seem to know their weapons well.

They will have to be enough.

We ride until the molten disk of the sun touches the treetops of a distant forest and sets them ablaze with oranges and yellows. To our left, down a shallow bank, is a tall barn and a stone cottage. A half-dozen men and women gather outside the door. Twenty or thirty shorn sheep mill near a stream, a stone's throw from them.

I goad my horse toward them.

"Edward," Tristan calls. "There are people down there. People have not been kind to us."

"We need to know how far we are from the Sudbury road," I say. "And we've got ten Genoese crossbowmen with us. I think we can deal with just about anything we encounter."

Tristan and the others trot to catch up with me. "Have you been on the same journey I have?" Tristan asks. "I would like it known that I think this is a bad idea."

As often as I have been amongst men, I have returned less a man. Father Peter's words come back to me, but I wave Tristan off. The day I fear six unarmed commoners is the day I give up my spurs. I ride down the slope.

"Are you here for the miracle of Mother Mary?" A man calls to me. He wears a thick traveling cloak and holds a crude wooden cross in one hand.

"We just need to know how far we are from the Sudbury road." An understanding of his words comes to me. "Did you say the miracle of Mother Mary?"

The door to the cottage opens and a thick-chested man with a beard that hangs to his stomach steps outside. "Greetings, I'm Alyn," he says. "Orderly row, please. If you want to see the miracle, have your two shillings ready."

"What miracle are you selling?" I ask.

The man smiles at me, but the grin fades when he sees my companions. He holds his hands up. "I don't want no trouble, lord. You and your men can see it for free."

I look to the west. We will lose daylight in an hour. But the Virgin has been my guide and protector throughout this journey. Perhaps this is a message. I smile at the thought. Two weeks ago, I was laughing at Morgan for telling me that Saint Giles had spoken to him. "Show us quickly, Alyn."

We leave the horses with Tarviccio and the rest of us follow the bearded man toward the stream.

"You lot stay there," Alyn calls to the gathered pilgrims. "I'll be back shortly."

"What does the Virgin have to do with this?" I ask.

"You'll see, m'lord." The man picks his way through the mewing sheep. He lays his hands on them, studying each as he passes them. "There it is." He wraps his arm around one of the ewes and lifts her tail high. "Have a look there, under her tail. It's the image of our blessed Mother Mary, so it is."

Morgan's breath is a hiss. "Blasphemer! How dare you! How dare you demean the Virgin by suggesting that her image is on… the arse of a… of a…" His eyes widen. He points silently and falls to his knees. "Sweet angel of mercy. Lord of our Heaven. It's the Virgin Mary!"

I look at the sheep's arse, and I cannot deny the image.

Her face is directly below the tail. A pink circle with wisps of dark tan around it, like hair beneath a hood. Two small discolorations form perfect eyes. Faint lines of darker pink suggest the curve of her mouth. Her shawl and the arms of her robe billow downward, formed by swooping streaks of nearly white skin.

"*Dio onnipotente! Un miracolo!*" One of the Italians—Domenico I think—falls to his knees and covers his face with his hands. "*Un miracolo!*"

"I have no argument," Tristan says. "That's the Virgin Mary. On the arse of a bloody sheep."

"Mind your language, Tristan," Morgan mumbles.

Tristan opens his mouth to offer a retort, but his words die when he looks at Morgan. "Are you… are you crying?" He stoops to have a better look but Morgan turns his face away. "You're crying!"

"Of course I'm crying," Morgan snaps. "We are in the presence of divinity. The Holy Spirit has touched me. I have never seen a more sacred sight."

"It's a sheep's arse." Tristan replies. "An ewe's anus has moved you to tears, Morgan."

"And that's why I will ascend to the Kingdom of Heaven, and you will not, Tristan. Because you see an arse, and I see the Mother of God."

Tristan does his best, but he cannot keep from laughing.

"If that arse is the Mother of God," Tristan says, "it must have been quite a bowel movement."

I do not know what to think of this miracle, except that perhaps the Virgin Mary is chiding me. She did this once before, when she guided me to a horse that was a cow.

"How have you kept these sheep alive?" I ask. "Does the Virgin protect them from the plague?"

"No, my lord," the bearded man replies. "We..." He trails off and rubs dirt from his hands. "No, my lord."

"So why haven't the plaguers gotten them?" I ask.

He flashes yellowed teeth and shrugs. "I know it ain't right, m'lord, but we use the old magics. My wife, Alison, she's a woman of faith. Ain't no one more devout than my Alison. But her family, they come from the west country. And they believe in the old ways, too."

Tristan and I glance at one another. Morgan crosses his arms.

"Show us," I say. "But do it quickly."

We are forced to wait until Domenico and Morgan have finished praying to the sheep's arse. When they finally rise, Alyn leads us across the gently sloping pasture. He points to a circle of squat stones, a fluttering willow at one end.

"The old magics," he says.

Twenty one stones—each as wide around as a shield and rising no higher than my knees—lie in a circle large enough to fit the entire flock of sheep.

I have seen stone circles before. Most of them are in the west of England. Pagan structures made by the ancient druids to venerate forgotten gods. I visited one in a place called Avebury. Elizabeth would not come with me. She would follow me into battle if I asked her, but she would not go near those stones. I chided her for her decision, but when I saw the ominous structures, I could not blame her. There is something sinister about them. Something of dark magic and hidden power. Each stone was as tall as a man. A group of them were arranged in a perfect circle, standing like petrified sentries, looking as if they could spring to life with a sorcerer's word.

I am an expert in the construction of castles. But not even I can fathom how the stones were brought to that field, nor how they were stood on end. They are alien and beautiful and full of mystery. I suppose the pagans would have thought the same of our cathedrals. Perhaps those circles were their cathedrals, built for their gods. Perhaps their gods listened to them, as our God listens to us. The Bible tells us there is only one God, but in the very next sentence, it forbids us from worshipping any others. It is a bit suspect, that.

Elizabeth would flounce for days if she knew I was entertaining thoughts like this. I hope I will see her flounce again. I won't get the chance if I tarry here from much longer.

"This is not right." Morgan looks at the stones and shakes his head. "This is pagan sorcery. And it's a sin."

"So is alchemy," Tristan replies.

"I know it ain't right." Alyn tugs at his beard. "It ain't right, but it works. My wife, she's devout, but she knows the old magic, too. The plaguers don't go near the circle."

Tristan rubs at his face with one hand. "Let me see if I can sift through this. These stones are a pagan magic created by a devout woman. So, if the plaguers have been possessed by demons, and they won't go near the stones, the circle must be good, correct?"

"That's not—" Morgan tries to speak but Tristan shushes him.

"I'm not done. If the plaguers are simply sick people, and they won't approach this circle, then the stones are bad. But if the plague was sent by God, and the afflicted then became possessed by demons as a result of their illness, and the stones warded them off, would we be warding off God's plague, or Satan's demons? And if the stones are evil, but they protect the ewe with the Virgin Mary on its arse, does that make the Virgin a demon? And is anyone hungry? Pantaleon, is there any fish left?"

Morgan shakes his hands toward the Heavens, as if asking God for patience. I have felt like doing the same many times while in Tristan's presence.

Something moves in the distance. I point to a large figure lurching toward us. "Here's your chance to prove that the circle works."

"Aw, that ain't but one illman," Alyn says. "I'll get him with a shovel."

"Illman?" Tristan chuckles. "I like that. Illman."

"I don't want him killed," I say. "You're right. He is an ill man. And he doesn't deserve death. Everyone in the circle."

"It doesn't work so well if it's a woman," Tristan says. "Illwoman. Illoman."

"They're all illmen," Alyn says. "The men and women."

We step over the stones and stand at the center of the circle. I take my gauntlets off and draw my dagger. The scars from a dozen slashes crisscross my forearm. Remnants of a day when I had to coax a plaguer army across five miles of Essex coastline. I add another slash, let the blood flow to the grass. The plaguer in the distance straightens and shambles toward us at a faster pace. He is perhaps the fattest plaguer I have ever seen. And he appears to be naked.

The Italians draw windlasses from their belts and attach them to their crossbows "Pantaleon, tell them they can load if it makes them feel better, but I don't want anyone firing on him unless I order it. Is that understood?"

Pantaleon speaks to Francisco, who nods.

Genoese mercenaries are responsible for buying their own equipment, so all of the crossbows are slightly different. Some of the weapons are made with wood and horn. Others have wooden stocks and powerful steel bows. But almost all of them are loaded the same way—with the use of pulley devices known as windlasses. I watch the crossbowmen crank the handles. They make quick circles, cranking back the bowstrings with a seamless efficiency.

The corpulent plaguer draws ever nearer. A mere thirty paces away, now. A strip of fabric drags from his left leg— probably what is left of his trousers, still looped around his ankle. It is the only hint of clothing on him. His gray, filthy belly hangs down in folds and jounces against his quivering thighs. Boils sprout from his flesh, and seep like rotting mushrooms.

Alyn shifts his weight from one foot to the other and shoots glances toward his sheep.

The Genoese raise their crossbows and aim at the fat man. I hold up a warning finger and Francisco nods. The plaguer draws nearer still.

"I don't think he's going to stop," Morgan says.

"It's difficult to bring that much flesh to a halt," Tristan replies.

Rizio, the champion drinker, chuckles and calls out: "*Suo cazzo non è grasso,*"

The Italians laugh. I look to Pantaleon, who points at the plaguer's crotch. "He is saying the man possess one piece only that is not fat, and this the piece he should want being fat."

Morgan lets out a sharp blast of air. "Tell them to stop being childish. That poor man is sick."

"Or possessed," Tristan adds. "Or sick and possessed. Or, simply cursed by God." He points to the man's crotch and chuckles. "Cursed twice."

The fat man stops abruptly when he is ten paces away. His flesh jiggles. He has breasts. Great wobbling folds of rotting skin that swing when he halts. The stench of him wafts into the circle and it takes all my strength not to recoil. Several of the Italians groan and cover their noses with their forearms. Morgan's nostrils flutter. Tristan winces.

The plaguer stares into the circle with ebony eyes. A gash on one cheek leaks a yellow pus.

"He's not coming closer," Tristan says. "Thankfully."

"The old magics." Alyn pinches his nose, so that his voice is tight and high.

"This is evil," Morgan says. "I can feel it in my bones. It's not right."

"It isn't evil," Tristan replies. "Everyone's coming to this farm to gaze at a sheep's arse. But this circle of stones is the bloody miracle."

I squeeze more blood out of my forearm and wave it in the air. The plaguer hisses, takes a step forward, then recoils. I reach my arm toward him, but he seems to lose interest in the blood and staggers around the stones, toward the sheep.

"I am astounded," Tristan says. "And I don't astound easily."

"The old magics are powerful," Alyn says, his nose still pinched. "Can you tell those crossbowmen to shoot him now? He's making for the sheep."

Tristan unbuckles his sword belt and takes hold of his sheathed sword. He trots to the far side of the circle, steps over the stones and reaches toward the plaguer with the sheath.

We follow him to the edge of the stones. The fat man slows and turns to face us. "Tristan, what are you doing?" I ask.

"Testing the limits of the old magics," he replies.

He draws back his arm and thrusts the sheath at the man's belly.

And the plaguer explodes.

Episode Seven

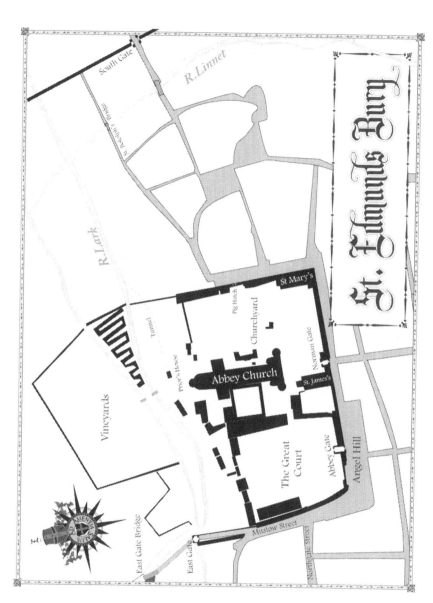

St. Edmunds Bury

CHAPTER THIRTY-EIGHT

WHEN A MAN HAS BEEN TO WAR, his sensibilities change. Death does not hold the same horror that it once did. Pain is tolerated with less fuss. Once you have stared down ten thousand men screaming for your blood, most other dangers seem trivial by comparison. And, once you've been to war, broken, bleeding and rotting bodies no longer make you retch.

But here, on this field in Suffolk, I spill the contents of my stomach onto the pasture. And every man with me does the same.

The plaguer's slime covers all of us. A greasy blend of phlegm, puss, blood and whatever else was inside him. It smells as if a rotting donkey had been filled with feces and left to simmer in a vat of urine. I fear I will never cleanse my nostrils of the scent.

The fat man lies in the grass, writhing. His stomach and one of the hanging breasts no longer exist. All that is left of his torso is a ribcage and a spine. Scraps of gore hang from the jagged bones like his torn trousers hanging from his leg. His remaining breast has been flipped onto his shoulder by the explosion.

Tristan has suffered the worst of the eruption. I cannot see his armor through layers of blood, yellow globs of fat, and ruptured lengths of entrails. He stops retching and glances back at Alyn. "The old magics are a load of shit."

"Why… why he fly in pieces?" Pantaleon asks.

"I… I told you…" Morgan picks something soft and red from his hair, retches again. "I told you… these stones are evil."

"It wasn't the stones," I say. "He was rotting." My stomach muscles clench and I open my mouth, but nothing comes out.

"Oh, Christ and Mary," Tristan says. "Do you think any of that fat man got into my eyes?"

"I don't think I've ever… heard a more peculiar statement." Morgan says.

"It's not a jest, Morgan," Tristan throws off his gauntlets and wipes at his eyes. "We don't know how that affliction spreads."

"I don't think you can get the plague through your eyes," I say. "I'm certain we've all had plaguer blood spatter beneath our lids at one time or another."

Tristan nods, as if trying to convince himself.

"Why did he explode, Edward?" Morgan asks.

One of the Genoese stands, then drops again immediately and vomits. I keep my hands and knees on the ground. "I'm not certain. But I've heard of such things happening. King William, the first one, they said he was too fat to fit into his coffin. When the priests tried to shove him in, he burst."

"I've heard of whales exploding on beaches," Tristan says. "I suppose that plaguer loosely qualifies as one."

Something slides down my temple and onto my neck, just inside my bevor. The sensation makes me shiver, which causes my stomach to clench again. I plant my hands in the damp grass, and retch again beside a magic stone. And when what little I have left in my stomach is free, I stare at the stone. My breath quickens. I run a finger along the crags and smile.

In the distance, Tarviccio decides to scream again, but not even his shrieking can wipe the smile off my face. "Pantaleon." I stand and brush grime from my hands. "Tell Frederico that Tarviccio's screams don't seem rare at all."

But Pantaleon is not looking at me. He draws his sword, his gaze sweeping toward the cottage. The Genoese pick up their crossbows and run from the circle, some retching as they go.

"He not scream without the reason," Pantaleon says, wiping at his mouth. "He scream for the help."

CHAPTER THIRTY-NINE

TARVICCIO IS WRESTLING WITH a red giant—a monster, with long red hair and a jungle of beard that dangles nearly to his stomach.

Nine crossbows lift to shoulders. I cross my arms and wait for the red-headed giant to have his moment of understanding. He lets go of Tarviccio and raises his hands.

"He done attacked me, he did." A thick brogue taints the man's speech. He is a Scottish giant. "I was defending meself. And if you don't mind me asking, what is that stench?"

Tarviccio shoves at the Scotsman and says something to Frederico.

Pantaleon translates. "He say this man, this hairless farmer of carrots, he try and take the horse."

"Hairless farmer of carrots?" Tristan says, smirking. "Looks like he's got plenty of hair."

Pantaleon shrugs. "It not sound so well in the English."

"What in God's Kingdom you got all over you?" The Scotsman covers his nose.

"Never mind that," I reply. "What is a Scotsman doing in Suffolk?"

The giant shrugs. "Just passin' by."

"You Scottish savages should stay in your own lands," Morgan snaps.

"We Scots are savage," the man replies. "But we ain't savages."

"I am a knight of England," Morgan says. "You will address me as sir."

"Bugger your arse with a carrot," The Scotsman replies. "I'll not show respect for you English... you English..." he struggles for the proper insult, "hairless carrot farmers!"

"It has better sound in the Italiano," Pantaleon offers.

"It's rubbish in English," the Scotsman agrees.

Morgan draws his dagger. "You are an enemy to England, and you tried to steal our horses. Why should we let you live?"

The Scotsman unhinges a five-foot war sword from a mount upon his back, sets it point down in the earth, and pats a leather sack hanging from his belt. "Colyne and I were about to ask you the same question."

"No one's going to kill anyone," I say. "What's in the sack?"

"None of your concern." The word *none* sounds like *noon* when he says it.

"I have ten crossbowmen that say it is my concern," I reply.

The Scotsman looks at the raised crossbows. "What a world this is," he says with a grin, "where men must threaten other men to get what they want."

"You're right," Tristan says. "Before long, we'll be attacking each other for horses."

The Scotsman laughs and points to Tristan. "I like this lad."

"What's in the sack," I ask again.

The giant tugs the cords on the sack and draws out a rotting human head. "It's me friend, Colyne. Say Godspeed, Colyne." He uses his free hand to work the stiff lower jaw and speaks in a high-pitch. "*Godspeed, English carrot farmers.*"

Tristan laughs. "This Scotsman is mad."

"He's a vile barbarian," Morgan says. "Why would you keep a man's rotting head in a sack?"

"Well, I couldn't fit his whole body in there, could I, you leper? I'm takin' him home, to his clan. And you're one to talk about disgusting. Walking about with intestines in your hair."

"I'm not a leper," Morgan replies.

"Course you're not. An' I suppose those are just filthy priest robes you're wearin'?"

Morgan crosses his arms and sighs. "I'm tired of this, Edward. I want armor. And a sword." He shakes his head slowly. "Lord, how I miss my sword."

"I thought Christ was your sword," I mutter.

"Don't be absurd," Tristan says. "Christ is soft and fleshy. You couldn't cut anything with him."

"Forgive him, Lord." Morgan gazes upward. "For he is stupid."

"You do not wanting the big armor that is heavy," Pantaleon says. "It make you not fast."

"Don't start on that again," Morgan snaps.

"What's your name, Scotsman?" I ask. "And where are you coming from?"

"Name's Alasdair. And I'm coming from Rochester."

"Rochester? The castle?"

"The very same," he replies. "Colyne and me got let out."

"Colyne and I," Tristan says.

"No," Alasdair shakes his head at Tristan. "Colyne and me. You wasn't there, lad." The Scotsman laughs, a wild, thunderous laugh.

"You were a prisoner?" Morgan asks. "They let you out of the dungeon?"

"Aye. We were prisoners. A guard opened the gates and said we was free. There was hardly no one at the castle. So we started walkin' home. But..." his eyes grow wide. "There are these... these creatures walkin' about. Horrible things.

Colyne got half torn apart. And then he tried to have a bite a'me. I had to put him down." He wipes at his beard and shakes his head. "I had to put him down." He squints his eyes and brings the rotting mouth to his ear, nods several times. "Colyne wants to know if those men over there are with you."

I feel the hoofbeats before I look up the slope leading to the cottage. A horde of armored riders trot toward the farm. I count them.

"Eleven. Pantaleon, I want the crossbows trained on them. We can take eleven men."

As I watch, another three horsemen appear.

"How about fourteen?" Tristan asks.

"Let's hope we don't have to find out."

Another six horsemen ride over the ridge.

"Shut that cavernous mouth of yours, Tristan."

The riders rumble toward us. Twenty of them. Four wear full harnesses, with closed bascinets. The rest wear either leather hauberks or quilted gambesons. They halt within a dozen paces of the farmhouse. One of the knights advances a few paces farther, draws up his visor and immediately touches his nose with his gauntlet. The fat's man's stench still wafts from us like a curse. I finally make out the arms on the knight's tabard.

Three roosters.

One of Sir Gerald's men.

Of course.

"Look who we have found." The knight speaks in a singsong. "Did you think you could hide forever? Did you think we wouldn't find you? You can never outrun justice. And your justice will leave you in agony for days before you die."

CHAPTER FORTY

"TAKE ONE MORE STEP," I shout, "and these crossbowmen will fill your brain with yew."

The knight leading the band of soldiers raises a hand toward me. "Cease your threats. I have no quarrel with you, good sir. Hand over the Scotsman and we will leave you in peace."

It takes a long moment to find words.

"You... you want the Scot?"

"He tried to burn down a church," the knight says. "We must make an example of him."

"Will you give to us the paid?" Pantaleon asks. "If we give to you the red man?"

"Shut your mouth, Italian." I sheath my sword and turn to Alasdair. "Did you try to burn down a church?"

"I'm a God-fearin' man," the Scotsman replies. "What sort of Christian would burn down a church? That English horse fucker's got it wrong."

"Silence!" The knight calls. "You dare speak to a knight of England in that manner?"

"You should hear what he said to me," Morgan replies.

The knight waves his men forward. "Take the Scotsman. I want him tied to a horse and dragged back to St. Edmund's Bury."

Six men dismount and approach. I hold up a warding hand and they halt. "He says he didn't try to burn down a church."

"I didn't!" Alisdair adds. "That knight and his men were rapin' girls. Had them lined up outside the church. I tried to stop them. Not even English girls deserve to be beaten and raped."

"He lies." The knight studies me. "Do I know you, sir? What is your name?"

He waits for an answer, and I stare back, trying to think of one.

Everything hinges on two possible outcomes.

My instinct is to give him the Scotsman and take no chances. But humanity is the triumph of will over instinct, and England needs as much humanity as it can muster, now. I will not allow a man to be dragged to his death. Not even a Scotsman.

"Have you read much of the Old Testament?" I reply.

"I asked you a question, sir." The knight prods his horse forward a step.

I have often wondered why the Old Testament exists in the Christian Church. The priests tell us that we must love our neighbor. Turn the other cheek. Live life as Christ did. So why must we hear about a vengeful God? Why must we learn about a jealous God who destroys his enemies and allows his followers to fall into eternal torment?

I understand now.

The Old Testament was left in the Bible to remind us that, sometimes, forgiveness is impossible. That there is a time for charity, and a time for whirlwind and storm. A time for love and a time for vengeance.

Sir Gerald has chased me the length of East Anglia. He has tried to kill me a dozen times. He has threatened to destroy my wife. And now Gerald's knights stand before me, seeking to take more humanity from the world.

I feel the Old Testament rising up inside of me.

"'The Lord takes vengeance on his adversaries and keeps wrath for his enemies.'"

"Why are you babbling Scripture at me?" the knight asks.

I walk slowly toward the knight. "'His way is in whirlwind and storm.'"

"Are you quite through?"

"'The mountains quake before him.'" My body trembles with rage.

"I will ask one last time. What is your name?"

"'Who can stand before his indignation?'"

"Are you mad?" The knight's horse sidesteps nervously at my approach. "Tell me your name!"

"Who can endure the heat of his anger?"

He glances at the crossbows on the shoulders of the Genoese. Looks back at his sloppy squad of mounted soldiers. His men send glances toward the Italians, toward the foot-long shafts of death locked into the firing grooves of each crossbow.

"If you do not release that man to us and tell me who you are, I will be forced to attack," the knight says. "Is that what you want? Do you want to die here over a filthy Scotsman? Tell me your name!"

I take a step forward and draw my sword slowly. My voice ringing louder with each word. "I am Sir Edward Dallingridge. Husband to Lady Elizabeth Wardieu. Enemy to Gerald of Thunresleam. Champion of the dead. Defender of humanity, and killer of kings. I am the wolf that destroys the lambs, and I will send every last one of you to Hell if you stand down."

"Edward Dallingridge!" The knight pulls on his reins so hard that his horse rears.

"The very same!" I raise my sword toward him. "Now get off your horse, and tell your men to do the same!"

"I'll see you dead, first!"

Tristan's sword joins mine. "The last man I stabbed with this exploded. Do you want to explode? Do you?"

"*Kill him!*" This knight can shout almost as loudly as Sir Gerald. "Kill them all! I want Sir Edward's head!"

"Come and take it." I spit the words.

Tristan's sword glints as he thrusts it forward. The knight jerks back in his saddle, then disappears in a flash of armor and a clangor of steel plates.

No one moves.

Tristan looks at his sword.

The man lies on the ground, beside his horse. A red stain seeps across the grass beneath his head. His men stare silently at the body.

I look back toward the Genoese. Magnus's massive siege crossbow is no longer loaded. A grin spans his wide face. He winks at me. With all the shouting, I never heard the weapon fire. I turn back to the fallen knight. There is no sign of the bolt that killed him—it must have passed cleanly through the skull and bascinet and continued its flight. A siege crossbow is a terrible weapon.

I nod to Magnus. The rest of our enemies are still a dozen paces away. "Is there anyone else who wants my head?"

There is.

One of the horsemen howls. The rest of them pick up the battle cry, kick their steeds, and rumble toward us like a rockslide.

"Fire!" I roar. "*Fire at will!*"

Pantaleon does not have to translate.

Nine mighty cords of hemp—each drawn to a thousand pounds of force—unleash a storm of steel-tipped, leather-fledged quarrels. The bolts streak past me like Hell's locusts. The bolts that strike armor do so with a subtle clank, like pebbles falling into an iron pail. But there is nothing subtle about the effect they have on the mounted soldiers.

Men shriek and fall from horses. Horses cry out and topple onto fallen men. The world erupts into howls and tumbling flesh. Blood has been unleashed. And the Old Testament rises like a thunderclap in my soul. I run forward toward the remaining men, but they want no part of my whirlwind and storm.

A half dozen of them are capable of fleeing, and they do. Several make their escape on horseback. Three of the leather-clad soldiers ride westward, while the last two knights branch northward.

"Get the knights!" I shout. "Get the knights!"

Joseph Magazzi unlatches his windless and steps forward. The other crossbowmen crank furiously, but I know they will not load quickly enough. I run to my horse.

"*Io gli ho*," Joseph says. He sights along the crossbow, lets out a breath, and fires. The bolt disappears into the distance. Neither of the knights falls.

I look at Pantaleon as I vault onto my horse. "I thought he could hit a coin from fifty paces!"

"Maybe he can only hit coins," Tristan offers. He and Morgan leap onto their palfreys.

One of the two knights cants in the saddle, then tumbles from the horse.

A fine shot. I nod to Joseph Magazzi, who grins and shakes his crossbow at me.

"Tristan, take the Italians! Get the three! I've got the knight!" I dig my spur deep. I have only one spur left. I'm not sure when I lost the other. The palfrey lurches forward and gives chase, grunts as it climbs the valley slope. The knight has almost reached the top of the hill. I dig my spur in again and shout at the horse. I cannot allow any of these men to escape. If Sir Gerald knows we are near, we will have no chance of getting into St. Edmund's Bury.

The knight disappears over the crest of the hill. I shout again at my horse and the poor animal picks up its pace. Almost at the top. A few more paces. The horse blows, ears back, but strains harder. We reach the crest. The mounted knight sits only a stone's throw from me. He holds something in his hands. Why isn't he flee—

I hear the sound of the bolt striking my great helm an instant before I hear the bowstring release.

And death's bony hand finally takes hold of me.

CHAPTER FORTY-ONE

STEEL RINGS AGAINST STEEL.

It is the sound of combat, and that troubles me, because I do not think God would allow fighting in Heaven. I open my eyes and see a broken crossbow bolt on the ground, inches from one of my hands. I do my best to focus on it, but my vision swirls, as if I am underwater. A square head on the bolt. A cube on a stick. That is why I am still alive. The bolt was meant to unhorse me.

Death's bony hand cannot seem to keep its hold on me. I thank Saint Giles and the Virgin for that.

A man howls.

I look up. The effort makes me nauseous. If I had not emptied my stomach earlier, by the stone circle, I likely would do so now.

My eyes focus. Pantaleon lies on the ground. The knight who shot me crawls away from him, one leg stretched out behind him and useless. Blood seeps from the knight's armor, beneath one arm. He and Pantaleon have been fighting. I struggle to my knees but the world is a listing ship and I topple to one side. The setting sun is too bright. My helm hurts me. I work the straps and pry it off with one hand. The left side has caved in. I let the helmet fall to the grass and rise to my knees again. Fight a wave of nausea. The knight glances back, sees me, and crawls more quickly, panting. A horse waits for him a dozen paces away.

I rise to one knee, nearly fall over, and decide to crawl. It takes a long time to reach Pantaleon's side. A crossbow bolt juts from his chest. Blood soaks the right side of his brigandine armor.

He grins at me through blood-stained teeth. "To wear the big armor maybe is not so stupid." His voice sounds strange. The words seem to echo. I wonder, briefly, if I am dreaming.

"Why... why did you follow me, you... stupid bastard?"

"I must to watch you," he replies with a strained smile. "So you are not to flee with not giving to me the paid." He looks at the bolt in his chest. "You owe to me..." he winces and groans. "You owe to me much paid, now. Much paid."

My fists clench so tightly that the gauntlet's steel plates dig into the backs of my hands. I lift the slashed brigandine on his side and look at the wound. My eyes cannot seem to focus properly. "Women and... mead and horses. You'll have them all... friend." The knight's sword left a long gash in his side. The wound will kill him, if the bolt does not do it first. I try to smile through a wave of nausea. "Not... bad. Little... Malta fungus. You'll be... buggering arses again."

"Ass." He coughs. "Donkey is ass." He rolls his head to one side so he can see the fleeing knight. "I broke the leg of him. And put the dagger below his arm. But still he go." He looks back to me. "You will to kill him, please."

"With many blood." I reply. The words catch in my mouth. My throat feels hard, as if the skin is stretched too tight.

"With many blood," he replies. "Go. I watch."

I nod to the Italian and try to stand, but the world still sways. There is a ringing in my ears that will not fade. The knight is ten paces away. I crawl after him. He looks back at me and picks up his pace, grunting and dragging his broken leg. I groan at the pain in my head. Claw toward him. The earth seems to roll beneath me. I lean wildly to one side, then to the other. The knight pulls himself forward along the grass, the toes on his good leg digging into the soil for purchase. It is like a race between drunk infants.

I crawl a few more steps, then force myself to my feet. The landscape sways around me. I wonder where Tristan and Morgan are. The knight is only a few paces from his horse. I stagger after him, each step a victory of concentration. There is no Old Testament left in me. Only old bones and new aches.

He pulls himself forward, reaches for a stirrup.

I lumber toward him.

His fingers brush the metal. The horse nickers and walks a few steps away. Pantaleon chuckles again. The knight groans and crawls after his steed.

It takes five more steps to reach the crawling man. I feel for the sword of Saint Giles, then realize I left it back at the farmhouse. I draw my dagger, but it takes great precision or great strength to kill an armored knight with a dagger, and I have neither right now. A war hammer juts from the horse's saddlebag, so I step past the struggling knight and draw the weapon.

I hear the sound of hoofbeats approaching from the valley. I pray they are friendly hoofbeats. I raise the hammer in the air, and stumble back into the horse. The animal spooks and trots away.

"Oh, bugger it all." The knight works at the straps of his bascinet. "Just do it." He throws off the helmet.

"With many blood," I mutter.

It takes all of my mental strength to bring the hammer down in the right place. The thud of metal on bone rings out, but I do not see the result. I fall forward onto the grass as the knight's body slumps to the ground behind me.

Tristan and Morgan crest the hill and ride toward me.

I rise to my feet again and stagger to Pantaleon's side. "He's dead."

The Italian nods. He looks up at me and winces. "I am to die. But I have spoken the lie. I am not come after you for the paid."

My eyes sting.

"Honor," I say. "You die for honor, Pantaleon."

"No." He shakes his head, tenses, leans to one side.

"No?"

He groans and lashes out with a gauntleted fist, catching me in the cheek. The blow throws me to one side. The world dims.

"What... what is wrong with..." I cannot get the words out.

"I die for the justice." Pantaleon chuckles and touches his cheek, where the last fading remnants of my blow still shine. "You deserve the wife. Elizabeth. I hope that you are to get her, Edward friend."

I let myself slump to the grass on my side and look at him, face to face. My cheek throbs.

Fear enters Pantaleon's eyes. He takes my hand and I grip his tightly.

In this plague-swept kingdom, flesh is the new coin. Pantaleon has bought me another chance.

Pantaleon's death is another dark stain upon my soul. If I live, there will be no end to the churches I must build.

I will raise the first one here, where a great lion fell so that a wolf could carry on.

The Italian's grip weakens as the fear fades from his eyes. And when the last glimmer of life is extinguished, I, too, plunge into darkness.

CHAPTER FORTY-TWO

MY ELIZABETH RUBS A WARM, wet cloth across my chest.

I take hold of her slim wrist and smile. My eyes open but it takes a long time to focus, to understand that it is not my wife in front of me. The memories of my journey return to me and my throat grows tight again. "Where... where am I?" My head feels like it has cracked open, and molten steel poured into the crack.

The woman takes my hand from her wrist and smiles. "You're safe."

"There's no such thing as safe." I am lying in a cot. A half-dozen strips of parchment have been pasted onto my chest. "What's this all over me?"

"Protection." She is tall and pretty, with chestnut hair peeking from beneath a wimple. "It is the old magic." She points to one of the strips, near my shoulder. Writing covers the parchment, but I cannot read the words. "This one protects you from steel swords." She points to one near my stomach. "This one from arrows and bolts."

"A little late for that one." I sit up and begin peeling the parchments off. I am inside a tiny cottage. Blackened beams span the ceiling. The smell of honeysuckle and old smoke mingle in the air.

A door opens. "You're awake!" Tristan enters, dressed in a tunic, and navigates the cluttered cottage. "I got tired of your snoring. I've been waiting outside. What are you doing? Those parchments will protect you."

"I have armor, Tristan," I reply. "I don't need paper to protect me. How long was I out?"

"More than an hour," he replies.

"We have to go." I swing my legs to the floor, and the motion makes the cottage spin. My stomach heaves. I grip the cot frame with my hands to steady myself.

"You should rest for the night," the woman says. "You took a terrible blow to the head."

"I don't have time to rest," I reply. "Who are you?"

"I'm Alison," she replies. "With one L. You made an illman explode on my husband today."

Alison. The name is a dart into my soul. I think of a woman by the Meddestane River, her red life pouring out through a slashed throat. Allison Moore was the first of my sins on this journey. The first drop in the deluge of death that would follow.

"Thank you for your help, Alison with one L, but we must go." I rise, using the standing beams for support as I move through the cottage.

"Edward," Tristan says, "Pantaleon... he... he didn't..."

I stare at the threshed floorboards for a moment. "He died saving me, Tristan."

"It was his idea to follow you up that hill. He said you might need help." He shrugs. "At least I think that's what he said."

I fight an urge to sit down upon the thresh and weep.

"What is the name of this village?" I ask Alison.

"Rougham, my lord," she replies.

My first sin was Allison Moore, and my last, Pantaleon di Alessandria. I should have *given him the paid* and sent him away early on. But I kept him with me, because he was useful.

Pantaleon wondered why we have so many churches in England. Perhaps he understands, now.

"I will have a church built here, in Rougham. Devoted to Saint Mary, and dedicated to Pantaleon di Alessandria. And I will have him knighted. He will be buried in my family plot, at Bodiam." I look at Alison. "Would you do me the great favor of keeping his body here, safe, until we return?"

I am forever leaving bodies of friends in the charge of others.

She nods. "Of course, Sir Edward."

I walk toward the door again, stepping over a bucket filled with dead flowers. A thought comes to me when I take hold of the latch. "Alison with one L, I have one more favor to ask."

Moonlight gleams across the battered helmet that hangs from my saddle. It took half of an hour to bang the great helm into wearable shape. We bathed in the river—to wash away the stench of exploding plaguer—then I helped Morgan pick through the dead until we found a suit of chain mail that fit. He winced as we helped him into the armor, but I think he will suffer any amount of pain to never again be called a leper. He took a sword and a dagger as well, and has been standing straighter ever since.

All six of Gerald's knights wore tabards with the three roosters on them. Tristan, Morgan, and I each take one, and I give one to Frederico.

We bind the hands and legs of the few survivors, and leave them locked in the tall barn beside the cottage. I ask Alison and Alyn to watch over them until I return from St. Edmund's Bury. In return, I give the husband and wife all of the remaining armor, and all but one of the healthy horses. If flesh is the new coin in England, then I have made Alison and Alyn rich beyond their dreams.

I give the last horse to Alasdair, the Scotsman. It is a long journey to his homeland. I doubt he will make it, but at least he has a chance on horseback. He claps each of us on the back, tells us we are "not bad folk, for Englishmen," and mounts the palfrey. He rides away toward the north, but not before taking out the rotting head in his bag and working the jaws one last time. "Goodbye, English carrot farmers!"

The moon dangles in the black sky, looking just as battered as my helm. Staring up makes me dizzy, so I look ahead into the Suffolk night, and think of Elizabeth. I will see her tonight. I will feel her arms around me, and listen to her voice again.

We wave to Alison and Alyn and ride up what is perhaps the only steep hill in Suffolk. The dark makes our pace slower than I would like, but faster than we would be on foot.

"Edward," Morgan calls. "Frederico is pointing to his saddlebag and saying things. Does *lanterna* mean lantern?"

"I hope so," I call back. "Tell him to bring it up here."

Morgan speaks loud English to Frederico, who speaks loud Italian back to him. Pantaleon will be missed for *many, many reason*.

I draw my horse to a halt and wave Frederico forward. We may not be able to speak to one another, but we must be able to communicate.

Frederico rides to my side. "*Devo una lanterna.*" He reaches into his saddlebag and draws out a lantern, hands it to me. "*Lanterna.*"

I point to it. "Lantern."

He looks at the object in my hand, then back at me. "Lahn-tern."

I nod, point to the weapon that dangles from his saddle. "Crossbow."

He slaps the weapon. "*Balestra.*"

"*Balestra*," I repeat.

"Craws bow," he says.

I pretend to hold a crossbow to my shoulder and make a motion as if I am depressing the long trigger at the base of the stock. "Fire!"

Frederico unhooks the crossbow, holds it to his shoulder and presses the trigger. The head of the crossbow rises, as if it had discharged. "*Sparare!*"

I make the same motion again. "*Sparare!*"

He presses the trigger. "Fire!"

"That's hardly useful." Tristan squeezes his horse between the Italian's and mine. "Teach him what he's likely to hear." He pretends to fire a crossbow, holds up a finger. "Kill the hairless carrot farmers!"

"Stop it, Tristan," I say. "You'll confuse him."

Frederico pretends to fire the crossbow again. "Kill de haress carrot farehmers."

"Hairless carrot farmers," Tristan repeats. "Kill the hairless carrot famers."

"Kill de hairless carrot farmers," Frederico says.

"That's it." Tristan grins, then pumps his arms as if he is running, looks back with wide eyes, as if being chased. "Flee! Flee for your lives!"

Frederico grins and mimics Tristan's gestures. "Flee! Flee foh you lives!"

"Since you're so enthusiastic, Tristan," I say, "why don't you take charge of training the Italians? But I want it done properly. I need them to understand my commands. Normal commands. Not this rubbish."

"Of course." Tristan's face is too sober for me to feel confident, but I know he will not endanger us. He will have his fun, but he'll make certain the Italians are capable of understanding me.

The two of them slow their pace so the other crossbowmen can catch up, and Tristan begins his lessons.

I sprinkle saltpeter on the lantern wick and dig out a flint and lighting-iron from my saddlebag. It takes three strikes to get a strong enough spark. The lantern flares to life and the dark burns away in a small circle around me. I will have to blow out the light when we approach the road, lest we announce our presence to Sir Gerald before we are ready.

Alison with one L told me that her cottage is less than eight miles from St. Edmund's Bury. If this is true, then Elizabeth is not much more than an hour away. My heart pounds. I remember the feel of her long fingers entwined in mine. They are always cool, her fingers, and the touch of them on my fiery skin never fails to soothe me. She is the cool breeze in summer. She is the ocean spray on a ship's sun-baked deck. She is the wet cloth upon my feverish forehead, and she is so close now that I can almost smell her scent, lemons and strawberries.

The lantern light flickers among gorse and daisies. Has it been a month since my journey began? I feel like I have traveled for an eternity, trapped in a purgatory of endless setbacks. But not even limbo is forever. There is light in the darkness, and my Judgment Day has arrived.

I wave Morgan over.

"We're going to take the Sudbury road north," I say. "The south gate is the closest to the River Lark, and the hidden tunnel."

"If Gerald and his men are here, they'll have someone at the gatehouse," Morgan replies.

"I'm certain of it," I reply.

Somewhere behind us Tristan enunciates for the Italians: "Sir Gerald."

The Italians recite as one, their accents thick. "Iffa you hava cannon pointed atta Sir Gerald, do notta let him a'go." Some of the crossbowmen laugh. They do not understand what they are saying, but they know it is amusing. I think about shouting at Tristan, but that will only tell him that he has succeeded in annoying me.

Morgan pulls at the tabard on his chest. "You think the three cocks will get us past the guards?"

"I'm hoping so," I reply.

"And what if they decide to bring us to Sir Gerald?"

"If we are taken to Gerald, I will put up a bloody uproar while you flee for your life."

"You know that won't happen, Edward. I won't leave your side."

Tristan's voice rises behind us again. "Fire the cannons!"

"Hallelujah!" The Italians shout back.

"Tristan, keep them quiet!" My own shout makes my head throb.

Morgan sighs. "You really want Tristan in charge of the Italians?"

"It didn't seem like a bad idea at the time," I mutter. "Morgan, if it looks like we are going to be taken to Gerald, I need you to promise that you will run. You and Tristan, both."

"I can't speak for Tristan, but I won't make that promise."

I think about Pantaleon di Alessandria.

Is Heaven divided into countries? Do the Italians have their own kingdom there? If by some miracle Pantaleon and I both find ourselves in Heaven, I will take an ark or a winged camel or whatever I must to visit him. I will drink with the Italian, and we will argue about honor and justice and payment, and laugh for eternities.

"Morgan, if I am caught, I need you and Tristan to finish this. I need the two of you to cure Elizabeth and bring her home."

Tristan's voice rises from behind us again. "Morgan is a leper."

"Morgan issa leper," The Italians repeat.

"I'm not a leper!" Morgan shouts back. "Don't teach them that rubbish!"

"You're only encouraging him." I wait until he looks into my eyes again. "I need your oath, Morgan. I need to know that you and Tristan will finish this if I can't."

Morgan is silent for a long moment, then nods. "Very well, Edward."

He holds out his hand and I place one of my hands over it and one under.

"I swear, upon God, and the... the King of England..."

"You can skip that part," I say, smiling.

"I swear, upon God, Saint Giles, and the Virgin Mary, that if anything happens to you, I will not rest until Elizabeth is cured and home, or I am dead."

"I accept your oath, Morgan."

We push farther, through the long pastures of Suffolk. Tristan continues his ridiculous schooling of the Italians.

"Do not taunt bald men!" he shouts.

"Or God willa kill us with bears," the Genoese reply.

I glance at Morgan. He will do whatever he can to help me. He will die for my Elizabeth, if he has to, even though I killed his Matilda.

A cloud passes over the moon, blotting out the fields of Suffolk.

Morgan had a wife once. Margaret. She was killed by plaguers, and Morgan mourned her. But Margaret was his dead brother's wife. His marriage to her was one of duty. Matilda was something else. Matilda was his Eden, and we destroyed her.

"Morgan..." I clear my throat and start again. "Morgan, I can't convey to you the extent of my sorrow for... for what happened to Matilda. My soul weeps for what we did."

He turns his face away from me and does not speak for a time. The moon escapes the clouds again and washes the landscape in silver. When he finally replies, Morgan's voice is low, but steady.

"If we seek ways to fault ourselves, we will always find them. The true measure of fault is intent. Someone I respect very much once said that."

I remember those words. I spoke them to Zhuri when he blamed himself for Morgan's affliction.

"Our intent was to give Matilda peace," Morgan says. "To send her to God. We can't fault ourselves for what we didn't know. All we can do is wait to see her again, after this life." He turns to me and flashes a sad smile. "If I am killed trying to save your wife, I will see my Matilda and my Margaret. And if I live, you will see your Elizabeth. It is a victory, either way."

The breeze picks up, I think, because my eyes suddenly sting. "Morgan—"

A dozen trumpets shriek out across the heaths, echoing beneath waxing Suffolk moon.

And the words die on my tongue.

CHAPTER FORTY-THREE

"WHAT THE BLOODY RIOT WAS THAT?" Morgan gains control of his horse, which spooked at the trumpets and skittered a dozen paces ahead.

I blow out the lantern and stare northward, the direction from which the instruments sounded. "Gerald likes horns, but that sounds like too many even for him."

Tristan's horse clumps to our side.

Morgan stares into the darkness uneasily. "You don't think...?"

I shake my head. "There's no way Richard could have gotten here so quickly."

But there is a way. He could have left with his men in the afternoon, and marched them at full speed, without rest, leaving wagons with equipment and food to travel behind at a slower pace. His soldiers would be exhausted and hungry, but they could make it.

But if it is Richard and his men, not even a forced march will give him victory. Because they are still more than a mile behind us, from the sound of the horns. We will beat him to St. Edmund's Bury. And if we ride fast, we will have time to heal Elizabeth and flee to the South before his army enters the town gates.

My heart thunders again at the thought of Elizabeth. I think about the Good Queen Anne, and about the scampering abomination in the alchemist's cellar. Elizabeth will not suffer that fate. I know she won't. But I cannot banish from my mind the mad laughter of the alchemist's wife. I cannot purge the image of that hairless, withered thing she had become.

My life and salvation now hinge on two opposite outcomes. I shall live in eternal bliss, or I shall die and face never-ending torment. Because if Elizabeth becomes a monster, I will see her off to Heaven and then send myself to Hell.

I hand Tristan the dead lantern. "Stay here with the Italians. I'm going to find out what that clamor is about. Morgan, do you feel up to galloping?"

"No," he says with a smile. "But my horse does."

We gallop.

Our steeds fly through the dark pastures. It is dangerous to ride so quickly. Rabbit holes or large stones can bring a miserable end to such rides. But if Richard is near, we are out of time.

I spot a distant glow after half a mile, as if the horizon is on fire. We slow to a canter and, after another half mile, I glean distant signs of movement. The faint flickers of marching soldiers seen through hedges. They are on the western road, the one that leads to St. Edmund's Bury.

The land swells to the north of the approaching army, so Morgan and I cross the road swiftly and canter up the rise. We hide beside juniper bushes and gaze down at the western road until the army comes into view.

"Sweet Heaven above," Morgan murmurs.

The army has grown.

More than two hundred mounted men lead the long column. One of every twenty or thirty holds a lantern. And behind the horsemen, in an endless stream, march thousands of slouched, heavy-stepped footmen. It is hard to get an accurate count at night, but I would say three thousand at least. Possibly thirty-five hundred. If this is

Richard's force, then he has gained men on his journey. Knights and soldiers joining their king.

Dozens of banners fly above the marching men, but I only need to look at the first pennant to find my answer: Fleur-de-lis and lions.

It is Richard.

We are out of time.

"Go! Ride! Ride for St. Edmund's Bury!" Tristan and the Italians watch me, eyes wide, as I gallop toward them. "Ride!"

Morgan and I roar past, heading southwest toward the Sudbury road. I glance back to see the others slamming calves against flanks, lashing reins and chasing after us.

Tristan raises his sword in the air as his palfrey takes flight, and calls to the Italians: "I am your leader!"

The Italians respond with a ringing warcry: "So sayeth de Lord!"

Thunder rolls across the Suffolk heath as my companions spur their steeds into a gallop. We shake the earth, hooves battering the earth like falling castle walls. Our horses rumble onto the Sudbury road like a flood crashing through a valley. I see very little in front of me, and pray my horse does not turn a hoof. Every step is potential catastrophe. My breath comes in shallow gasps, the reins dig against my palm, through the leather of my gauntlet. But in spite of the terror, laughter rises in me.

I am flying.

My way is whirlwind and thunder.

And tonight, I will storm a monastery.

Tonight, I will howl like a tempest.

Tonight my sword will flash like lightning.

The Old Testament billows in my soul again and, tonight, anyone who stands in my way will die.

With many blood.

My horse froths and blows and, after three miles, breaks its gallop. I allow a respite, and we trot until the southern gate of St. Edmund's Bury rises like a monolith in the distance. Moonlight paints the edges of the gatehouse silver. Torches flickering on either side of the portcullis add an orange hue. Just past that gate is a road that juts, like a dagger blade, toward the monastery. I know a thousand plaguers gather around the walls of the abbey. They are all that stands between Sir Gerald and my Elizabeth.

I wonder where his forces are. Probably locked in fortified buildings, watching the roads and waiting to kill me. The plaguers were once my enemies, and Gerald my ally. But I led an army of plaguers onto an English battlefield, and everything changed.

Champion of the Dead.

It is terrifying how quickly things change.

I tap the reins and pat my horse's neck until he comes to a restless halt. The others gather at my side. I wheel my horse so the others can see my face.

"Once we're in, we will circle around to the tunnel, find my wife, and go home." Fire courses through my veins as I say it. We are a half-mile from Elizabeth, and her cure hangs from my neck. "If there are guards at the gate, I will speak with them. The rest of you will keep your mouths shut. Is that understood?" I stare at Tristan. He sees the resolve in my eyes and swallows whatever comment he was going to make. Frederico looks at me with squinted eyes. I place a finger on my lips. "No speako. *Silenzio.*"

He places a finger over his own lips and nods. "No speako."

We ride at a walking pace toward the town. Spires and towers from the monastery glitter in the moonlight. The portcullis barring my way is the very gate to Heaven, because my eternal bliss lies just beyond. I wonder if there is an earthly Saint Peter guarding this gate.

We come within a dozen yards of the walls before a voice calls out.

"Stop and identify yourselves!"

"I am Sir John of Meddestane," I shout. "Open the bloody gates."

My Saint Peter steps from the gatehouse and stands in the arch. Flickering shadows from the steel portcullis carve his face into squares. He has a jutting chin that makes his profile look like a crescent moon. A baggy suit of mail hangs from his thin frame. "I'll need you to speak the words, sir."

The skin around my neck grows warm. He wants words. Of course they would ask for verification. I am a fool for thinking they would allow us in simply because we wear the three cocks.

"The words?"

"Yes, sir, the words. We can't open the gates without them. That comes straight from the king."

"Which king?" Tristan asks.

"King Gerald, of course."

A few of the Genoese chant together. "Iffa you hava cannon pointed atta Gerald, do not—"

Tristan waves a hand wildly at them. "No, no. We don't need that now. Quiet. No speako."

I stare at Tristan and he pretends not to notice.

The guard either did not understand the Italians, or does not care about them. He sets his gaze on me. "The words, sir?"

Sweat beads on my scalp. "The words." I clear my throat. What words would Sir Gerald use to safeguard his camp? I think about Gerald. Who he is. What he stands for. You never truly know someone until they become your enemy. And then you learn far more than you should.

"The words," I repeat.

The watchman scratches at his enormous chin. If I give the wrong phrase, the guards will sound the alert. There will be no second chance.

Moonlight battles the wavering glow of torches upon the stones. Another soldier peers out of the gatehouse. They are growing suspicious. Richard's army marches closer with each breath and I am thwarted by words. I am pinned between anvil and smith's hammer, trapped between two madmen, and not a single idea comes to—

In these times of madness, only madness will save us.

The words flare in my mind like a burning hedge.

What other words could there be?

I open my mouth, but Morgan speaks first.

"Death to Sir Edward of Bodiam."

"Morgan, no!"

But it is too late. Saint Peter has judged me, and I have been found wanting. The guard motions into the gatehouse.

I send a withering glance toward Morgan, look back at the portcullis and snarl. The Old Testament rises like brimstone in my heart. I will pull down the gates of Heaven if I must. I will tear the bars away, one at a time. I will kill every man standing between me and my angel. I will—

A sonorous clank rings out from the gatehouse. Chains rattle. A wheel clatters rhythmically and the portcullis rises.

My hand tightens on my sword's grip. Tristan's horse sidesteps, and blows. The Italians look to one another in confusion.

Morgan does not move. He and his horse are statues before the gate.

Saint Peter steps aside stiffly. "Thank you, Sir John. The words are correct. You may enter."

Morgan's expression is as close to a smirk as he ever gets.

"God told me," he whispers.

I should have trusted him. If there is a man who knows how to get into Heaven, it is Morgan.

CHAPTER FORTY-FOUR

WE RIDE SLOWLY ALONG SOUTHGATE STREET. My hands tremble against the damp reins. The muscles in my legs twitch with every few steps, and it takes all of my will to keep from driving my one remaining spur into the horse's flank and galloping toward the hidden entrance. Elizabeth is here. Close enough to hear me if I called. Close enough to see me if she stood upon the curtain walls of the abbey. But Sir Gerald's men are close, and so I must plod along as if I have no fire in my veins. Every clopping step of my horse upon the cobblestones is a torture, like water drops from a leaky thatch when you cannot sleep.

Clop. Clop. Clop. Clop.

It is agony.

"Everyone be calm and silent," I say it to the others, but I think I am saying it more for me. "Do not draw attention."

The town is empty. All of the inhabitants are dead. Or gone. Or afflicted. Only the plague lives here, now. The plague, a monk and a nun. Brother Philip and Sister Mildred are the last healthy denizens of St. Edmund's Bury. They live in the monastery and promised me they would watch over Elizabeth. Thousands of plaguers insulate them from the rest of the town, so I doubt they are even aware that Gerald's men hold the gates.

Water gurgles in the distance. Southgate Street crosses the River Linnet somewhere ahead, although I do not plan on crossing the river upon this street. I know of a small bridge to the east, on Raingate Street. Saint Botolph's Bridge. It is small enough that Gerald's men may not be posted there.

I will say a prayer to Saint Botolph himself as I cross. He is the patron of travelers, and with the journeys I have endured these last weeks, I believe I have earned his attention. Perhaps he will—

A scream shreds the silence, echoing across the town and startling me so much that I fumble at my sword's hilt. Morgan's horse spins and bucks. Tristan's blade rings as he wrenches it free of its sheath. But by the time I pry Saint Giles's sword out, I realize that I will not need it.

None of the Italians have drawn their weapons. Frederico rubs at the bridge of his nose. Tarviccio covers his eyes with his hands.

"Tarviccio!" I call. "I said silence, didn't I? I said keep calm, didn't I? Tristan, tell them what I said."

"Yes of course," Tristan replies. "Because while you and Morgan were scouting Richard's army, I learned Italian."

I look at Frederico and point to Tarviccio. "He is going to get us all killed. *Morte*." I add the last word in French in the hopes that it might help.

"*Morte*?" Frederico replies.

"*Morte*." I loll my head to one side and thrust out my tongue. "*Morte*."

"Ah! *Morto*." Frederico holds up his unloaded crossbow and points it at Tarviccio. "Killa de hairless carrot farmer?" He shakes his head. "*Nessuno uccide miei uomini*."

"I don't want you to kill him," I say. "Just forget it. Forget it."

We keep the horses still and listen for approaching men. A dog barks in the distance. One of the Italians belches quietly. A plaguer howls from somewhere near the abbey.

We hear no footsteps. If Gerald's men are coming, they are coming in silence. But I do not think they will come. A terrified scream in the night has become as common in England as the cry of an owl or the shriek of a hungry fox. I mourn for my kingdom.

We slip our horses between a tiny farm cottage and a boat maker's workshop just south of the River Linnet, and ride across overgrown fields to Raingate Street. Saint Botolph's Bridge is as frail looking as I remember. I do not know if it can support horses, but it does not need to. I want to attract as little attention as possible, so from this point, we will walk.

We dismount. I hand my horse's reins to Francisco, the fat crossbowman, and point to a line of oaks along the river. "Tie them all up and wait here with them."

Francisco takes the reins and looks to Frederico. The two Italians look at me.

I make expansive gestures in a tying-up-horses fashion. "Tie them up at those trees." I push my palms downward several times. "And wait here."

They look at each other. Frederico speaks a few words in Italian, and the fat man pulls the first two horses toward the trees.

The River Linnet joins the Lark a few hundred paces from this spot, and the hidden tunnel is a few hundred paces along the Lark. I search in the darkness for the willow that marks the prior's secret entrance, but I cannot make it out from here.

Francisco and the other Italians tether our horses to the oaks. Tristan and I don our helms, and Morgan straps on a bascinet he salvaged from the battle at Rougham. The Genoese begin loading their crossbows. They are a clatter of windlasses against wooden stocks, of chains cranking, and grunts.

"Why are they doing that?" I ask Tristan.

329

"Well, the windlasses are used to pull back the bowstring of their crossbows," he replies.

"Tristan, I'm not in the proper state for jokes. Why are they loading?"

"I'll find out." He turns to Frederico. "Why are you loading?"

Frederico cranks at his windlass and frowns. "*Che?*"

Tristan nods sagely and salutes me. "They are loading because of *che*."

"God's teeth, Tristan, I thought you would learn to communicate with them. Have you learned nothing of their language?"

"I have." He clears his throat and recites in horribly accented Italian. "*inculare tutto.*"

I know I should not ask. "And what's that mean?"

He holds up a finger. "Bugger it all."

It takes a frustrating amount of gestures to make Frederico understand that I want Francisco to stay with the horses. The fat Italian seems to protest at first, but Frederico speaks sharply and the complaints stop. They are a disciplined lot, these Genoese.

We leave one of Sir Gerald's tabards with Francisco, and after teaching him to say, "Death to Sir Edward of Bodiam," we leave him sitting on a stump. He stares after us, arms folded.

Saint Botolph's bridge groans as I walk across it. I stop at the middle and say a short prayer to the patron saint of travelers. I ask that he see me safely through to the end of my journey, and I beg him to allow the Syrian cure to heal Elizabeth. I have traveled hundreds of miles, faced seas of afflicted humans and animals, defeated a French army, slayed a dragon, fled from plagued lepers. So many dangers. And yet, I have not known a terror as great as I feel now, a mere three hundred yards from my beloved. The ampoule that holds Elizabeth's cure feels like a jabbing finger at my throat.

We walk across a field where cattle once grazed. Ranks of curving ribs glint in the moonlight like giant harps, and skulls lie scattered among the high grasses. It is all that remains of the unfortunate cows.

Hooves ring out in the distance, upon the cobbles of the town. We all drop to a knee and wait to be discovered. I stare toward the monastery, but can see only its spires and battlements. A thousand plaguers pounded and scratched at the walls of the abbey last time I was here. I have no doubt they are still there, in the dark.

I wait a long time after the hoof beats fade before rising again and marching toward the Lark. It takes an eternity to cross the field, and another to reach the lone willow. Its branches slump downward, listlessly pointing out the hidden entrance sunk into the side of the riverbank.

I glance toward the monastery. The plaguers are still hidden from me—by darkness and trees and buildings—but I can hear them now. Snarls and howls. They sound like chanting demons from this distance, but I know they are not. Perhaps demons have taken possession of their bodies, but it is sickness that has allowed such possession. And the holy water around my neck can burn the demons out.

Or burn them in.

I force the doubt from my mind and wade into the shallows of the river. The cold water seeps through my armor and trousers. Metal glints among the sedge. The gate. Closed, as I left it. Prior John's tunnel burrows directly under the willow tree and runs several hundred paces underground. A ladder of iron rungs at the end leads into the prior's chamber, inside the monastery itself.

I take hold of an iron bar and pull. Flakes of rusted metal grind beneath my gauntlet. The gate squeals loudly and falls with a thud against the tall grasses of the riverbank. A stench of wet, rotting bodies wafts from the tunnel.

"Get in," I call to the others. "Hurry, before we're seen."

The Italians hold crossbows over their heads as they wade into the Lark. Frederico is the first to pass me. I hand him the lantern and speak to him in Italian: "*Lanterna.*"

He gives me a quick nod and climbs into the tunnel. "Lahntern."

The other Italians follow, several groaning at the stench.

"I hope Brother Phillip is awake," Tristan says as he passes me.

"I hope he has food." Morgan clambers into the tunnel and I follow.

The stench reminds me of Richard's dungeon at Framlingham. The tunnel is wide enough for two men to walk, side by side, shoulders brushing. I push my way past the others and take the lantern from Frederico. The flickering light does little to improve the visibility. There is a suffocating darkness here. My heart races with the memory of the first time Tristan and I entered. Plaguers had found the tunnel. Two dozen at least. We fought our way through them, killing with many blood and shouting hallelujah. We were fools

Dripping water echoes. Lantern light glitters among the flints and stones used to pave the passageway. I take a sloshing step forward, through calf-deep water, then another. A scraping sound rises from the depths of the tunnel. A rat, I imagine. I hope it is not plagued. Lantern light shines upon something pale and slick. A decaying face with no eyes stares sightlessly from the floor, submerged to the cheeks. The first of many bodies. I step past the corpse and walk farther into the tunnel, past skeletons that jut from the water like shipwrecks. I count twenty paces before one of the Italians closes the gate behind us. It shuts with a screech and a thunderous clang that echoes through the darkness.

"*Silenzio!*" I call. "Satan's toe, can you be any louder?"

"Yes," a voice calls out. "Oh, yes, I can."

The voice does not belong to any of the Italians. Nor does it belong to Tristan or Morgan. It is a voice I'd hoped never to hear again. I look back toward the gate, shove Morgan's head to one side so I can see. It was not an Italian that shut the gate.

A group of men stand outside, silhouetted by the moonlight. I cannot see them clearly, but I do not need to. I know Sir Gerald's voice too well. We have been trapped like rats. How did he learn of the hidden entrance? My breath catches and a thought as horrible as plague seizes me. Brother Philip would not have opened the trap door to anyone but me. We agreed on a pattern of knocking. And if Gerald had entered the monastery, he would have ambushed me inside the prior's chamber, where I could not possibly escape.

"Morgan?" Tristan says.

"What?" Morgan hisses.

"I don't think it was God who gave you those words at the gate."

"I regret that it won't be my hand that kills you," Gerald calls from the tunnel mouth. "But I do appreciate the irony of an evil man being torn to pieces by demons."

Sloshing footsteps sound ahead of us. I turn and hold my lantern at arm's length. Plaguers. Their eyes glinting in the lantern. An endless mass of them. Far more than Tristan and I encountered the last time. Far more than twelve of us can handle. Fear seizes my heart, colder than the water about me.

The afflicted snarl and reach for us with rotting limbs. Tristan draws his sword and sighs in his helmet.

"*Inculare tutto.*"

CHAPTER FORTY-FIVE

"ONE HUNDRED AND THIRTY-TWO DEMONS," Gerald shouts. "We let them in, to welcome you. Do you feel welcomed?" His shrill laugh echoes through the tunnel. "Welcome, Edward. *Hell welcomes you!*"

I try to calm my breathing. Gerald and his men could not have entered the monastery. If they had, Elizabeth would be with them. Sir Gerald would not forgo the opportunity to kill her in front of me. They have not been inside. Philip did not let them in, so Gerald let the plaguers into the tunnel out of spite.

The lurching mass of plaguers splash toward us. Their feet churn the water, sounding like a broken water mill. Their groans and shrieks echo madly, like the sounds of a child's nightmare. Lantern light glitters from the shining bone of a man's skull, visible through shredded skin. He hisses, a terrible sound in this tunnel, and lunges at me.

They are not to be slaughtered, Edward.

I kick him backward and he falls against two of his afflicted brethren. All three crash into the water, at the feet of the plaguers behind them.

"Tristan, Morgan, keep them at bay for a moment." I back away. My hands shake so much that it takes three tries to hang the lantern on a flint stub in the wall. I shove my hand cannon at Morgan.

"Keep them at bay?" Morgan holds the gun crosswise and shoves at the plaguers as they advance again. But there are scores and scores of the afflicted. We will be overrun. Knocked down or pushed back to the entrance, pinned against the gate. We will be crushed, our armor ripped away, our flesh torn from us in strips. I try to calm my breathing.

Someone screams behind us. It is Tarviccio. Again.

"Someone shut that Italian's bloody—"

The words die on my lips. An arrow juts from the crossbowman's shoulder blade.

"Death from the front, death from behind!" Gerald shouts. "When I am an old man, I will sit in the sun and smile at the memory of this moment!"

"Tell me that story again, Edward," Tristan says, grunting. "You had... a cannon pointed at him..."

The Italians, all save Tarviccio, turn toward the gate and fire, shouting as one: "Death to de harless carrot farmars!"

The Genoese know their work.

Their sudden attack is so swift that only Gerald and the archer next to him sees it coming. The two men leap to the side, and the eight crossbow quarrels rip into the soldiers behind them. The shrieks of Gerald's men echo in the tunnel.

"Die, Edward!" Gerald's voice is pitched high and warbling with madness. *"Die, miserable wretch!"*

"Keep holding the plaguers at bay!" I fumble through my shoulder sack.

Morgan groans against the weight of the advancing horde, skids backward a foot. A woman clamps her teeth around his gauntlet and he uses his knee to break her jaw. *"How can we hold a hundred plaguers at bay?"*

"One hundred and thirty-two!" Gerald is beyond madness. He is in a state of rhapsodic fury. His cackling fills the tunnel.

"When we get out of here," Tristan says, "I'm going to tie him up and laugh at him for hours. I won't hurt him. Not at first. I'll just laugh."

"If we get out of here." Morgan aims his cross at a woman in a filthy dress and she recoils from it. Tristan uses his hand bombard to shove at a plagued soldier whose livery is so muddy I cannot make out the sigil.

"We will get out of here," I shout, still fumbling in my shoulder sack.

"How?" Morgan screams. "*How?*"

"We're going to walk forward, into that horde, and the plaguers will protect us from Gerald's arrows." I cannot find what I am looking for. Did I lose it? Have I condemned us all?

Tristan and Morgan look back at me, then at each other.

In these times of madness...

"And what," Tristan replies, "will protect us from Gerald's archers?"

I find a ceramic jar in the shoulder sack and draw it out. "This."

... only magic will save us.

The Italians work their windlasses, but archers are much faster than crossbowmen. Another arrow slashes into the tunnel. Another Italian cries out.

Tristan and Morgan are shoved back again, and I am forced to retreat. We are less than fifteen paces from Gerald.

"I hope you have a dozen knights in that jar," Tristan shouts.

"Better than that." I throw off my gauntlet and strip the wax seal from the jar, glance at the pink ointment inside. "The old magic."

"What?" Tristan and Morgan say it together, one with hope, the other revulsion. Both of them stumble back as the plaguers press forward.

"*Shoot again!*" I have never heard Gerald shout so loudly. His cries are deafening in the echoing tunnel. "*Keep shooting!*"

I glimpse more archers outside. Moonlight paints the curve of at least three bows bending back. One of the archers makes a choking sound and falls backward. Tarviccio screams again, this time with fury. He lets his crossbow drop to the waters and slumps sideways against the wall.

"Edward!" Tristan bellows. "We can't hold them back!"

I reach two trembling fingers toward the open jar, but Morgan and Tristan stumble into me and I nearly drop it.

Another Italian shrieks as an arrow finds flesh.

"There are too many!" Morgan calls. "We need more light!"

"I hate this tunnel!" Tristan howls.

I scoop two fingers of paste from the ceramic jar.

"This was worth waiting for!" Gerald screams. "The Lord says good things come to those who wait, and this is surely the greatest thing I have ever witnessed! Are you dying yet, Edward? *Are you dying?*"

The plaguers push against the two hand cannons. Tristan stumbles on a rotting body and falls back on his arse. Plaguers reach for him. He jabs with his sword but one of them, a man with a filthy beard, falls onto him, grabs the bottom edge of his helmet. The plaguer's beard is so grimy it looks like pudding. I reach forward with my bare fingers, thrust the pink paste at him.

And he recoils, tumbles backward and kicks away from me, into the other plaguers. I thrust the paste closer and he shrieks, lunges again and again against the legs of those behind him. There is a madness of colliding plaguers. Bodies fall. I pull Tristan to his feet. Rub the paste along the flat of his sword blade.

"What are you doing?" he asks.

"Enchanting your sword," I reply.

He jabs his blade forward and the plaguers back away from it in a ripple.

"It's a miracle," Morgan whispers.

"It's magic," Tristan says, grinning. He advances, waving the sword. The afflicted in the first few ranks try to back away farther but there are too many behind them. They are shoved toward Tristan and Morgan, howling and hissing at the sword and cross.

Frederico howls at me. *"Ci stanno uccidendo!"*

Morgan glances at his cross, then at Tristan's sword. I know what he is thinking. The same thoughts came to me in Rougham, when Alison-with-one-L helped me prepare the paste of fish oil, flour, and some red lichen from the stone circle outside her home.

Morgan thrusts the cross forward. The plaguers thrash and tremble and hurl themselves backward against the wall of their afflicted brothers and sisters.

I reach into the jar and draw out another dollop. One of the plaguers stumbles forward, shoved by someone behind, and knocks into Tristan. He knocks into me and the glob of ointment flies from my finger onto the wall. I growl. There is not enough of the cream for it to be wasted.

I scoop out more of the balm and smear it onto Tristan's great helm.

"We're going to push into them," I shout. "One at a time. Go, Tristan!"

Tristan looks in my direction and manages to express shock and incredulity with a tilt of his helmet.

"Go!" I roar.

He stares at the afflicted mass for a moment, then lunges into them. The plaguers roar and fall to the sides of the tunnel. He takes another step into the crowd.

I smear the paste onto Morgan's helm and clap his shoulder. He shoves at the plaguers with the staff of my cannon again and they recoil from him.

The crossbowmen unleash another volley at Sir Gerald's men. One of the Italians lies in the water, face down. Arrows jut from several others.

"Frederico!"

He glances at me, his hands fumbling with his windlass.

I do not have time to explain. I smear the ointment on his face. He slaps at my hands. *"Che cazzo stai facendo?"*

I point a shaking finger toward Tristan, then realize that I cannot see him anymore. He is lost in the crowd of plaguers. Only Morgan remains, shoving at the plaguers with the cannon."You have to go in there!"

Frederico shrugs violently and attaches the windlass to his crossbow.

"We have to run," I shout. "Through there."

He shrugs again and steps into the stirrup of his weapon.

I push him and point deeper into the tunnel. He looks at the plaguers, then at me. I smear paste onto my vambraces and step beside Morgan, thrust my arms forward at the afflicted. They howl and fall away from me.

Frederico touches his face, looks at his fingers. I nod.

"Flee!" I point into the plaguers. "Flee for your lives!"

Frederico looks back at his men and shouts to them in Italian. Two of them finish loading, fire a volley toward the gate, and fall back to Frederico. I dredge their names from my memory. Domenico and Ermolao. One devout, the other slow-witted.

I smear their faces with the ointment. There is not much left of the paste.

Frederico shouts at his men in Italian, pointing past Morgan toward the plaguers.

Ermolao shakes his head. Domenico crosses himself. The Genoese are a disciplined lot, but I do not think there is a soldier on this earth who will run into a crowd of plaguers without hesitating.

Frederico shouts again and lunges at the plaguers. They hiss and thrash, backing away from him. "*Ora, andare!*"

The two men exchange glances, then walk gingerly forward. Frederico and I exchange glances, too, and shove the men into the crowd. Ermalao shrieks, but the plaguers leap back from him. The two Italians push their way through the crowd as the next two crossbowmen fall back to Frederico. Tarviccio's face shines with sweat and he grimaces, but I do not think the arrow in his shoulder will kill him. Joseph, the marksman, is at his side. I apply the paste to both of them and we shove them into the horde. I pray I am not sending them to their deaths.

Sparks light the tunnel for an instant as an arrow strikes the wall beside me. The tunnel curves here and the archers have trouble finding a clear shot.

"What are they doing?" Gerald shouts. "What is happening in there? *Where are they going?*" His voice cracks with fury.

Magnus stumbles back to us, the massive siege crossbow hanging from his shoulder. An arrow juts from one side of his chest, another from his thigh, but he drags a crossbowman through the waterlogged tunnel. I smear ointment on his thick, bare arms. The man he drags is Riggio, drinker and jokester. I do not think Riggio finds anything funny about the arrow in his flank. I scrape the last of the ointment from the sides of the jar and rub the paste onto Riggio's face. Frederico makes the plaguers recoil again, demonstrating the old magic, and speaks in Italian. Magnus kisses a cross dangling from his neck and drags his friend into the plaguer horde.

Morgan glances back at me and I nod. He tucks the cannon to his chest and drives into the throng, after Magnus.

I drop the empty jar and look back toward the gate. An arrow strikes the wall and shatters, sending fragments of wood clattering against my helm.

Three archers at the gate draw back their cords. I have no time to unsling my shield. Frederico and I dive to the floor. I try to flatten myself as much as I can. The water gushes through my visor and washes, cold, upon my face.

I rise a moment later, when I am sure the archers have fired, and scrabble toward the plaguers. Frederico does the same. Something thuds against the shield on my back. Another bloody arrow. I am glad I did not have time to unsling my shield.

We dive into the mass of plaguers. They are Heaven's soldiers, and they will protect us, for we are the champions of the dead. They are God's armor, and they will shield us from Gerald's arrows.

I shove my way deeper into the afflicted. A man wearing a hood tugs at my helmet.

"Let go!" I shout.

A woman with one long, dangling earring grabs my breastplate at the armhole and yanks.

"Leave me be!"

Teeth scrape against my helm.

I raise my vambraces toward them. "Fear the old magic!"

A gangly woman breaks teeth on my mail skirt. A bald man snaps at my bare hand and I pull it away at the last instant.

I look at my arms. There is no trace of ointment on them, only beaded water.

Frederico screams.

God's armor is eating us.

Episode Eight

CHAPTER FORTY-SIX

I TEAR MYSELF FROM THE GRASPING PLAGUERS, spin, and fall onto my hands and knees. My palms slide against the sludge of mud and rotting bodies covering the tunnel floor. The afflicted crush against me. Legs and hands and gnashing teeth. I crawl past them, drag myself through a river of death, rip myself free of their clutching hands. Teeth click against the steel of my armor. Bodies fall onto me and slide off the shield on my back.

A plaguer grabs my foot. I kick with my other leg, lashing with the iron spur, and feel flesh yield beneath it. The plaguer howls and releases me. I pull myself forward.

Where is it?

"There!" Gerald shouts. "There he is! Shoot him! Put a shaft in his skull!"

Where is it!

The lantern still hangs from the flint stub, and a patch of pink shines on the wall. Brighter than any stone. I lunge for it. A plaguer grabs my great helm, pulls me back. I slam my elbow into his chin and he lets go. More hands pull at me as I stretch forward. More teeth searching for weaknesses in my armor. My fingers touch the wall, scrape the glob of paste from the stones. I reach back with the ointment and the plaguers pull away from me, then fall forward as the rear ranks shove them. I smear the paste onto the bridge of my helm.

Frederico howls and tears free from the crowd. He falls, with a splash, at my side. Points to his face, where I had smeared the ointment. "*Questa merda non funziona!*"

An arrow drives into a rotting body a foot from my face and an archer outside shouts that there is not enough light to see us.

"Just keep firing!" Gerald shouts behind us. "Don't stop!"

"How did you not get bitten?" I say, rubbing my fingers over Frederico's face again, dabbing the last remnants of the old magic onto his skin. He squints at me and I wave him off. "It doesn't matter."

An arrow slashes into a plagued woman. She screams, the horrible plaguer scream, and tries to back away from us, but she cannot push past the plaguers behind her. Another arrow plunges into her stomach. And then another strikes my shield.

"Edward!" Tristan shouts from somewhere beyond the plaguers. "Edward, we can't see!"

I whirl around in the water and an arrow thumps into the shield on my back. I groan and grab the lantern from the wall, crawl forward. An arrow splashes into the water beside me. Another glances off my helm. I stumble to my feet and push forward, feeling God's armor part and nestle around me.

"Where are they going?" Gerald shouts. "They're killing themselves! Are they mad?"

The plaguers nearest to me back away, hissing. Other plaguers shove past them, then they, too, hiss and back away. They are like eddying waters, roiling about me in impotent rage. Frederico lumbers behind me. We thrust our way through the afflicted, squeezing past endless rows of bodies, nestled so tightly against the plaguers that I can smell their foul breath. They howl and flinch from me when the heated metal of the lantern touches them.

The tunnel opens wider after a dozen paces. Tristan, Morgan and the crossbowmen are huddled at the center of a small chamber. Their eyes are wide, their hands clutching weapons tightly. Tristan lets out a deep sigh, nods to me. He glances at the back wall, now illuminated by the lantern. "There!" he cries. "There's the ladder."

I stride toward the steel rungs but Tristan beats me to them. "You can go last this time," he says.

"You have nothing to worry about," I reply. "The plaguers won't climb after us this time."

"I'm always last," he says, clambering up the ladder. "And there are always plaguers climbing behind, reaching for me. Not this time, Edward. Not this time."

He reaches the trap door, shoves at it tentatively and it yields, rising a few inches. He glances down at me, then shoves the trapdoor firmly. It opens.

A multitude of plaguer faces look down and hiss, their arms grasping at Tristan's helmet.

"God hates me!" he cries, lashing out at the plaguer arms with one hand. "How are there plaguers in the monastery?"

I barely hear his words.

The trap door was unlocked.

Gerald entered the monastery.

Tristan throws his helmet off and pulls the plaguers down one by one, yanking on their arms until they plummet to the chamber floor. He screams in terror the entire time.

I wince each time one of the afflicted strikes the mud, but there is no other way. Most of the plaguers rise from the mud and recoil from the ointment on our armor. The ones that cannot stand writhe and pull themselves along he mud, away from us.

"Hurry, Tristan!" I clench and unclench my fists the entire time. When the last of the plaguers is down, scramble up the ladder, my boots clanging dully off the iron rungs.

Tristan climbs into the prior's chamber ahead of me. I hand him the lantern and climb the last steps into the monastery.

"Wait for the others!" I cross to the door and yank it open.

The moonlight cascades upon St. Edmund's Abbey; a central church, taller than most cathedrals I have seen; a prior's palace as opulent as any duke's; breweries, gilded chapels, a refectory, stables, kitchens. It is a glittering city within a town. But it is not the fine architecture that draws my attention tonight. It is not the statues of saints and bishops, or the studded minarets rising into the night sky that make me stare. It is the half-dozen lurching shapes in the churchyard.

"How did they get in?" Tristan stands behind me and looks over my shoulder.

I do not respond. The trap door was open. Gerald got inside.

My heart hammers against my ribs, a condemned prisoner rattling the gates of his cell.

The trap door was open.

I run across the churchyard, ignoring the shouts behind me, around to the entrance of the great abbey church, where I left my Elizabeth. I dart through an archway, and throw open the mighty doors, remembering the horror that awaited me inside the first time I arrived.

It is too dark to see the chantry, where I left my Elizabeth. A few candelabra are still lit, their candles guttering, but most of the light in the cathedral has been extinguished. I race down the broad aisle, my footsteps echoing to the ribbed ceiling far, far above. The shrine of Saint Edmund sits behind a screen, upon on a raised dais and behind the high altar. I take no heed of the gilded screen, nor the box of marble and gold that lies beyond it. Because a shape writhes upon a feather mattress, in front of the high altar.

My shape.

My angel.

My Elizabeth.

My Elizabeth is here.

I imagine the sound of choirs in this church.

My Elizabeth is here.

I throw off my helm, let it clang upon the flagstones and echo to the heavens. Someone has draped a sheet over my wife. She thrashes against it, makes muffled grunts and moans.

I kneel beside her, draw the cure from around my neck and stare at the ceramic ampoule. Dear God.

How I have dreamed of this moment.

How I have dreaded this moment.

I cannot think overly much about what has to be done. I must give her the cure without a thought to the consequences, or I may never find the courage to do it.

I take hold of the sheet, draw a deep breath, and pull the fabric away.

I stare down at my angel.

A twitchy man with bushy eyebrows stares back.

CHAPTER FORTY-SEVEN

"BROTHER PHILIP?" I ROAR. "What the devil are you doing here?"

The monk grunts and jerks his head back and forth. I draw my knife and cut the gag from his mouth.

"They took all the chickens!" he shouts. "Every last one of them!"

I slap him.

I should not hit a man of God, but the fury is upon me.

"Where is she?" I bellow. "*Where is she?*"

Brother Philip's face is a deep, mottled red where I slapped him. He arches his twitching eyebrows almost to his hairline. "Wh... where... is who?"

I pound my gauntleted fist against the floor. The crack of metal on granite resounds across the chantry. "*Where is my wife!*"

My words echo back to me.

... *my wife!*

Brother Philip licks at his lips. "She's... she's safe. She's here in... the monastery. She's safe."

My shoulders lurch with each breath. "She's safe?"

Philip regains some composure. He frowns at me. "Of course she's safe. I told you we would take care of her. I told you that. I am a man of God. I do not lie. Of course she's safe!"

Elizabeth is safe.

The words are an icy river against my fury. I slump forward, hands on thighs. "She is safe." I draw a long, long breath.

Brother Philip nods. Clears his throat. "I imagine she's safe, at any rate."

The breath catches in my throat. "What?"

He shifts on the mattress. "Well, I assume she's safe. I can't know that for certain, can I? I've been bound and left here."

I take his robe in both hands and lift him off the mattress, roar so loudly that his hair billows. "*Where is she?*"

... is she?

His chin quivers. Tears stream down his temples. "They were cruel to me," he says. "Terrible and cruel! But I didn't say a word. I didn't tell them anything about Lady Elizabeth…"

A swell of pity tempers my anger. Philip resisted Gerald's men. Heaven knows the unspeakable agony he suffered at their hands, and he resisted, so that Elizabeth would be safe. I set him down on the mattress, speak gently. "Can you tell me where she is, Brother Philip?"

"…until they hit me," he adds.

I stare at him. Try to make sense of his words. Footsteps echo in the nave. I do not turn to look. I can only stare at Brother Philip.

"One of the men hit me in stomach," he says. "What was I to do? He actually struck me! I told them. I had to tell them. But I made them promise they would not hurt her. I forced them to swear an oath, that they would keep her safe. So you see? She is safe."

Men take hold of my arms before I can strike Brother Philip. I strain against them, reach for Philip's throat.

"He's a monk, Edward!" Morgan shouts. "He is a man of God!"

…of God!

Philip shrieks and sobs, thrashes against the ropes that bind him. "I had no choice! They were violent!"

...were violent!

"*Where is she?*" I howl, pulling against my friends' arms. "*Where is my wife?*"

"You'd better tell him," Tristan calls to Philip. "We can't hold him when he's like this."

"St. Mary's!" Philip sobs. "Sister Mildred took them to St. Mary's!"

...to St. Mary's!

I yank my arms free and pound along the aisle, my footsteps echoing to the ceiling like war drums. St. Mary's. The church is at the southern corner of the abbey, built along the curtain walls. I leap through the open doors, nearly colliding with Magnus, who still drags Riggio.

"*Attento!*" Magnus shouts. But I am gone.

I race along overgrown gardens and unkempt lawns painted blue by the moonlight. Through orchards of worm-blighted trees. I pass a polished charnel house, where the unearthed bones of the dead are stacked when graveyards need more space. And for a moment, I believe the bones have escaped. A score of impossibly thin plaguers stumble about the base of the monument. Lifeless husks of cows and pigs are scattered around the charnel house, and across the church yard. Plaguers glance up, momentarily, from their bloody feast. They continue eating and I continue running.

Pounding footsteps sound behind me. Tristan and Morgan.

St. Mary's rises at the corner of the abbey walls. It is a magnificent church, but a mere lump among the palatial buildings of the monastery. I skid to a halt at the side of the nave and yank open a small, iron-studded door.

Moonlight streams through the yawning stained-glass windows, painting faint color patterns on the walls. There are no flames in the church. Two dozen carved, wooden angels stare down from the hammer-beam ceiling. A shaft of silver light splashes upon a nun who sits with her back against the altar.

I run to her, kneel at her side. "Sister Mildred!"

Blood, black in the faint light, soaks her habit and pools beneath her. Her wimple has been torn away. The moonlight sets her golden hair aglow. She glances sideways at me and speaks, but Tristan and Morgan's echoing footsteps, as they enter the church, drown out the whisper of her voice. She tries again. "I'm... sorry."

"What happened?" I reach into my shoulder sack, draw out the Malta fungus. But there is far too much blood on the floor. Morgan and Tristan arrive, panting.

"They...raped me." Her voice is a brittle reed. She stares toward the enormous rose window at the far end of the church. "All of them. Fourteen men."

Morgan's breath grows ragged. He tries to speak, but I silence him. A dark, Old Testament fury grows in my chest.

"I am..." my voice breaks, and the Old Testament fades, replaced with a New Testament guilt. This woman cared for me when I went mad. She cared for Elizabeth. Bathed her and sang to her. She cooked for me and Brother Philip. Washed our clothes. It was partly due to her that I returned from my madness. And now, she dies because of me.

Am I a selfish man?

Am I an evil man?

Perhaps Gerald is right. Perhaps I deserve to die.

"I am sorry, Sister Mildred. I will bring justice to those who did this."

Justice.

I think of Pantaleon di Allesandria, and my sorrow grows heavier.

I take the hem of her habit and lift. There is far too much blood on the flagstones. I do not believe I can help her, but I must try.

She pins her habit down with one hand and shakes her head. "When... the last was done. He... used dagger... to... to..." She shakes her head and keeps the habit pinned down.

Morgan stands and paces along the chantry, each footstep an echoing hammer blow. I can see the fury in his eyes, even in the dim light. I feel no anger. Only sorrow. Sorrow and guilt—the cornerstones of Christ's church. Perhaps I am a good Christian, now.

"What... what better place to die." She sobs and gestures toward the church around her. "Mary's bosom."

I look away from Sister Mildred. The arches along the nave are colossal eyes, staring our way. Like an audience of giants. A jury of Gods.

"Do you think... Christ will still want me?" she asks. "After... those men..."

"You will sit beside Mother Mary herself," Morgan says, his voice gentle and quivering. "They will make an angel of you."

Tears sting at my eyes. I take deep breaths to keep the sobs from escaping. "What... what was Elizabeth's fate? I must know."

Sister Mildred slides her hand onto mine, squeezes.

"Did they... did they..." I cannot say the words.

The nun smiles at me. "They... didn't get her."

I rub at the corners of my eyes, not understanding, staring stupidly at Sister Mildred.

"Heard them... coming," she replies. "Brother Philip... screaming about... oath... not hurt Elizabeth." Her voice grows fainter with each word. She points with a trembling hand to the sealed doors of the church, doors facing out into the streets, into the horde of plaguers gathered around the abbey. "I let her out."

I stare at the doors.

"She's... so lovely, Edward. Dressed her... this morning... blue dress. One with... bow on back."

"Out?" I look into the nun's eyes. "You let her out there?"

She nods. "Men wanted... go out... get her. Couldn't op... open door. Afflicted... packed tight. As... as if..." Sister Mildred lets out a deep breath and speaks no more.

We gaze down at her silently.

As if... the plaguers were protecting Elizabeth.

As if... God's army was thwarting Sir Gerald.

As if... Saint Mary herself was sealing the doors of her church.

I kiss Sister Margaret's hand, rest it on her lap. The nun died protecting Elizabeth. More flesh paid to buy my angel's life. I stare at the front doors of the church. My wife is outside, protected by a thousand plaguers. God's army will keep her safe.

They will let no one near her.

I let out a long sigh that echoes in the empty church like a serpent's hiss.

Not even me.

CHAPTER FORTY-EIGHT

THE DOORS OF ST. MARY'S OPEN no more than an inch. The snarling, hissing crowd outside is pressed tightly against the oak. I peer through the crack but I see no one in a blue dress.

"Edward, I hate to interrupt with trivialities," Tristan says, "but should we worry about Gerald's men being in the monastery still?"

Morgan spins swiftly, staring into the shadows of the church. "He's right. Why aren't they still here, waiting to strip the skin from our bodies?"

"And piss on our pulp," Tristan adds.

I, too, glance into the corners of the church. It is foolish to look. If Gerald's men were here, they would have revealed themselves long ago. I slip my arms under Sister Mildred and lift her, laying her broken body on the high altar. Morgan whispers a prayer in Latin, and I add a silent vow to avenge the nun.

"Let's see what Brother Philip knows," I say.

"An enjoyable five heartbeats that will be," Tristan replies.

We leave St. Mary's and run back toward the massive abbey church. There are more plaguers outside now. I count eleven lurching figures.

A scream from the abbey church.

We rip open the great doors and run inside.

The Scourge: Emaculum

Brother Philip sits on a pew, drinking wine from a skin. Frederico sits next to him. Tarviccio and Magnus stand beside the altar. The witty Italian they call Tonso draws an arrow from Riggio's back. It was Riggio who screamed.

I stride to the chantry and set the jar of Malta fungus on the altar, look at the Italian's wound. The arrowhead came out with the shaft, and the blood flowing from the wound is light and a bright red.

"He'll be fine. But put this on the wound," I point to the jar, then to Riggio's bare back.

Tonso nods. I catch a glimpse of Saint Edmund's shrine and walk toward it. The long chest of marble and gold is painted with scenes of saints and martyrs. A candle is lit at every corner.

"They went out." Brother Philip stands at my side. "They went out while I was bound, and I had to light them again. They have never gone out while I have been here."

I think about Sister Mildred and a wave of exhaustion crashes through my body. "Many flames have been extinguished tonight."

Brother Philip crosses his arms and stares at the shrine. "A bad omen, the candles going out. He was England's patron saint. A king who died for his lands a people. A man who would not renounce his beliefs. Keeping the candles lit is the least we can do for him."

"He's not our patron saint anymore." I remember the pilgrims on the road to this very shrine. The ones with their plagued loved ones in a wagon.

"He should be," Brother Philip replies. "Saint George isn't even English. Edmund was an English king. A Wuffinga."

"Wuffinga?"

"It means 'clan of the wolf.' They were one of the first families in East Anglia. Edmund is more English than you, or me."

Clan of the Wolf. I have never heard of the Wuffinga family, but here, standing before a dead king's tomb, I feel a bond with them. King Edmund was a wolf, and wolves protect one another. I kneel and offer a prayer to the Wuffinga clan.

"I just saw Sister Mildred," I say.

Tristan joins us by the shrine.

"Is she well?" Philip sees my expression and covers his mouth. "Did they strike her? Did they hit her in the stomach?"

"They murdered her, Brother." I rise from the floor so that I tower over the monk. "They raped her and murdered her."

"But at least you didn't get punched in the stomach again, eh?" Tristan adds.

Tears well in Brother Philip's eyes. "I don't...understand. Where is Sister Mildred?"

I point to the fresh blood on my breastplate. "She's dead. She's dead because you told Gerald's men where to find her. You might as well have kissed her on the cheek for them."

His eyes widen. He shakes his head slowly. "No... no... where... where is Sister Mildred?"

I take hold of his cloak and lean in so that my nose brushes his. "Listen carefully. What happened to those men? The ones that hit you?"

He blinks rapidly, again and again. "They... they had to leave."

Tarviccio screams.

I do not have to look to know it is him. I have never memorized another man's screams before. Once again, he has reason to scream. Tonso has pulled an arrow from his shoulder. I return my attention to Brother Philip.

"Why did they have to leave?" My hand on the monk's robe is stained with Sister Mildred's blood.

His eyes regain their focus. "They said they couldn't find Lady Elizabeth. And that the king would be angry if they did not."

"The king?" I spit the word. It rings like an insult before the shrine of a martyred king. "Don't call him a king. His name is Sir Gerald."

Several of the Italians murmur: "Iffa you hava cannon pointed at Gerald, do notta letta him go." It sounds like a prayer in the towering church nave.

Brother Philip stares at the Italians, his eyebrow twitching. "Who... who is Sir Gerald?"

I release him, rub at the blood on my hand. "A lunatic knight. The men who hit you and killed Sister Mildred serve him. He was likely in here, himself."

Philip shakes his head. "Those men did not serve this... this Sir Gerald."

"Why do you say that?"

"Because, as I said, they serve the king." He rubs his hands on his robes. "They serve King Richard."

A veil tears away, and the wind that has torn it howls into me. I understand what has occurred. King Richard must have sent men ahead, on fast horses. A sensible thing to do. He knew that I did not have an army, and so surmised there was another way into the abbey. Perhaps he knew about the tunnel all along. He's the bloody King of England. How many times has he been to St. Edmund's Bury? Prior John may well have told him about the hidden passageway.

The men arrived at the town gate, announced themselves in the name of King Richard. Gerald would have had no choice but to let them in, and the men would have ridden directly for the tunnel.

But Sister Mildred thwarted them. Elizabeth slipped through their grasp. Richard's men might be searching for her outside the gates right now. But I do not think so. It is more likely that they are riding back to Richard's army, with news that Elizabeth is among the plaguers now.

And when they left, Gerald set a trap for us. His men are not in the monastery because Elizabeth is not here.

I look at Brother Philip. "Why are the afflicted in the monastery?"

One of his eyebrows twitches. "They are attracted to the cows and pigs, I think."

The urge to slap him again is almost irresistible. "*How* did they get in?"

He shrugs, and his eyebrows twitch convulsively. "I... I let them in."

I stare at him.

"When the men went to St. Mary's, I opened the pig hatch. So the men would leave."

The pig hatch. A tiny door on the south side of the monastery, used to load pigs onto wagons. Plaguers would have to squeeze to get in, but the opening is wide enough. I cannot decide if Brother Philip's actions are the embodiment of stupidity or brilliance. He called on God's army to protect him.

"How many got in?"

"What do you mean?" he asks.

"How many got in before you shut the gate?"

His head shakes slightly, almost not a shake at all.

"I never had the chance to shut it," he replies. "The gate is still open."

CHAPTER FORTY-NINE

THE FIRST BLUSH OF SUNLIGHT paints the eastern sky as we leave the abbey church. There are more plaguers in the church yard. Too many to count. Magnus and I each hold one of Riggio's arms. The others follow behind, swords drawn, heads turning from side to side as they track the approaching plaguers.

We help Riggio past St. James's Church with its stone cockleshell sculptures, across the great court, to the Abbey Gate. This is a massive gatehouse—as big as some keeps—rising three stories. Statutes of bishops and abbots and great lords stand in niches on every side of the stone tower. I pull open the thick oaken door at the side. We climb a set of cramped spiral stairs into the barracks chamber above the arching gate.

There is nothing left in the chamber but a table, three chairs, and broken bits of wooden furniture. A dove flutters madly through an arrow slit and out of the tower. I help Magnus set Riggio down, then run back to the spiral staircase and continue climbing. Tristan and Morgan follow. We do not stop until we have reached the battlemented roof of the structure. I place my hand on one of the merlons and stare out across St. Edmund's Bury. My eyes shut and do not open for far too long. I open them, shake my head to shed fatigue.

Richard's army glows in the distance, marching toward the town. Gerald's army is nowhere to be seen. God's army stands at the monastery walls, growling and hissing, scraping at the stones with bloody hands. Elizabeth must be among them.

I lean through a crenel and stare down into the town square. It is called Angel Hill, that square, but I see no angels. I see no long golden hair. No blue dress with a bow on the back. Dawn battles night in the east, but darkness still sucks all color from Angel Hill. Shadows make it difficult to tell man from woman.

I walk to the opposite side of the gatehouse and stare down into the abbey's great court. Not many plaguers have reached the northern section of the monastery. Only three that I can see. A dozen cows and countless sheep linger in a walled enclosure at the rear of the churchyard. One of the sheep bawls into the night.

"I could live here," Tristan says. "Lovely gardens. Fascinating history. Plenty of alehouses." He glances down at the horde along the abbey walls. "Shame about the neighbors." I look at him, and something in my eyes makes him place a hand on my shoulder. "We'll find her," he says quietly.

An opening in the crenelations leads to a narrow wall-walk that spans most of the compound. We step through the gap and hustle along the battlements until we reach the Norman Gatehouse. I glance down at the yawning arch beneath us, barred by double portcullises. There is as much darkness here as anywhere. I cannot see her.

"Not so many plaguers inside the monastery as I would have thought," Morgan says. "If that pig door is still open, why haven't they overrun the abbey?"

I walk to the opposite side of the Norman Gate and stare down into the church yard. Beyond the charnel house is the great cemetery. The wooden crosses glow in the moonlight. They look like hilts in the night, like swords plunged into sacred soil, like a war between the living and the dead.

Only twenty five or thirty plaguers linger in the churchyard.

"Let's have a look at the pig hatch," I say.

We walk the battlements to the corner of the monastery, where St. Mary's church stands. This was where Elizabeth joined the afflicted throng. I stare down into that throng with such intensity that my eyes water.

Where are you, Elizabeth?

I close my eyes, feel her long, cool fingers against my cheek. Smell lemon and strawberry. See her crooked smile. When she is happy, truly happy, she looks sad. As if the surge of emotion is too much for her. As if she cannot believe that such joy is possible. I see her sad bliss, feel her lips against mine. And I open my eyes.

Moonlight glitters on golden strands of hair. For the briefest of moments, there is a bow, and then it is gone.

"Elizabeth!" I shout down. "Elizabeth!"

Morgan and Tristan pull me back from the crenelations.

"We'll find her, Edward," Morgan says.

"She's going to be coy and difficult tonight," Tristan says. "Let's find her some flowers before we start shouting across the entire town, eh?"

They are right, of course. If Gerald hears my shouts, he will know we are alive. I step back to the crenelations and gaze down once more. Did I imagine the bow? Even if I did not, there must be hundreds of bows in that crowd. Her scent lingers in my mind.

"Pig hatch?" Tristan says.

I nod.

We enter the church tower through a tiny wooden door, and emerge from another, which leads to the abbey's southern wall. Tristan stops after twenty paces and laughs.

I follow his gaze down toward the pig hatch and understand why there are not many plaguers in the abbey. Morgan sighs.

An afflicted woman, fat and draped in luxuriant fabrics, has wedged herself in the gate. She is on hands and knees, half in and half out, motionless like an animal resigned to a trap.

"She's a savior," Tristan says. "If the alchemist girl succeeds, I think we should cure that woman first."

The abbey is safe. Gerald likely thinks it has been overrun, but a portly noblewoman has secured our fortification. I stare back toward the town, across the rippling waves of plaguers.

The abbey is safe, but we are trapped inside.

Elizabeth waited for me in this abbey for months. I travelled a hundred and fifty miles, through demon armies, angry knights and mad kings. I faced every imaginable obstacle to reach this town, with a cure in hand. And now it is I who am trapped in the monastery.

And Elizabeth is outside.

All but one of the Genoese are asleep, on the floor, when we return to the Abbey Gate. Domenic I son watch. He stares at the door from a wooden stool.

Morgan sits against a wall and tries to say a prayer for us, but his words grow further and further apart until they become snores. Tristan turns the old table upside down and lies inside, taps one of the upward-facing legs. "A four-poster."

He grins, and is asleep before I can take three breaths.

I gesture to Domenico and raise a forefinger. "If I fall asleep, wake me in one hour. Understand? *Uno ora.*"

The Italian nods. I sit against a wall and think of Elizabeth. She is outside, alone among thousands of the afflicted, and I do not have much time to find her. Richard's army will arrive tonight and, in the morning, he will set his men to the slaughter. I must... wake early. And...

I yawn.

I must wake early and find... wake early....

I open my eyes. A shaft of sunlight streams through an arrow slit, painting my face. Domenico is slouched on the stool, asleep.

Morning!

I jump to my feet. My bones pop and grind. Muscles burn with yesterday's exertions. Elizabeth is outside. I rush to the battlements. Clouds smother the sky, but the day is bright enough to make me blink. Elizabeth. I will find her now. The blue dress and the bow, the radiant blonde hair. She will be outside the walls.

I lean over the parapets and look for an angel on Angel Hill.

And see no one.

I stare from one side to the other. The streets are empty.

There are no plaguers outside the monastery.

CHAPTER FIFTY

No!

I lean forward so far that I almost fall from the tower. Angel Hill is empty. How can it be possible? Richard! Oh dear God, he slaughtered them all in the night! He slaughtered them and I heard nothing!

I fall to my knees, raise clasped hands to the sky, but can think of no prayer to offer. How can army slaughter thousands of plaguers without—

Faint snarls and howls rise in the distance.

I scramble to my feet and look eastward. The abbey walls block my view, but I can hear them! The plaguers have moved toward the east gate. I run along the narrow battlement and look down toward the town gate. And I breathe a sigh.

Tristan and Morgan emerge from the Abbey Gate and stare down onto Angel Hill. Both of them flinch at the empty street, then run along the battlements to my side.

"Remember when we did that in Falaise?" Tristan laughs and addresses Morgan. "Roger Miller—one of our footmen—fell asleep one day at his post. So Sir Robert moved the entire army to a forest a quarter-mile away. Do you remember the crazed expression he had when he finally found us, Edward?" Tristan chuckles. "Even the French were laughing, up on the walls."

Morgan nods, but does not smile. "Why did the plaguers move?"

I let out a long sigh. "What could lure five thousand plaguers away from an abbey full of livestock?"

They look down toward the East Gate.

"An army of four thousand men," I reply. "Richard is outside the town gates."

We stare down on Mustow Street. Plaguers are packed onto the road, between the abbey walls on one side and the rows of tightly packed cottages and shops on the other. The front of the column is pressed against the town's East Gate, snarling and reaching through the bars of the portcullis. The rest of the plaguers stream back for hundreds of paces, shoving and hissing into the air.

Richard's army stands outside the gates. I stare down at the banners and spot one with three roosters upon it.

"Gerald's with Richard, now," I say.

"I wonder if he makes Richard call him King Gerald," Tristan says.

"I wonder how long they'll stay outside." I try to keep my voice from trembling. "Once that gate opens, it will be a massacre."

"I didn't think he would really do it," Morgan says. "Richard has brought an army here to kill your wife. He's mad. Completely insane. Can't those soldiers with him see that?"

I let out my breath in a quivering stream. "Men will follow anyone."

A part of me admires King Richard. His anger in me is misplaced, but if I thought a man had killed my wife, I would stop at nothing to exact vengeance. I know the Lord tells us that vengeance is wrong. But if infidels violated a church, I would crush them. And if anyone harmed my angel, there would be nothing left of them to bury.

"Not all of Richard's men are outside the gate." Tristan points to a cluster of knights standing at the corner of

Northgate Street. Their armor glints dully in the morning light. The colors of their surcoats seem too bright on this gray day.

One of them points, and shouts something that I cannot make out. They run toward the back of the endless column of plaguers. A knight with a pheasant crest on his helm throws a canvas sack over a plaguer woman and pounds the back of her head with his gauntlet. Another knight ties a rope around her waist, to secure the sack, while the others protect him with spears and pole axes. There is no need for protection. The plaguer army does not even look at the men as they haul the afflicted woman away.

We run along the battlements to keep the knights in view. I watch as they drag the woman along the cobblestones, down Northgate Street, to a wagon. A dozen canvas-draped figures thrash in the bed. Two of the knights lift the plagued woman and hurl her into the wagon. They do it with such force that her body bounces off the back wall and rolls to a stop among the other bodies. The woman's muffled cries reach us, two hundred yards away.

The Old Testament stirs inside me again.

They are searching for Elizabeth. I pull at my sword slowly, my arm trembling. Tristan stops my elbow before the sword is completely free of the sheath.

"That wasn't her," he says.

"They'll keep searching, Tristan," I reply. "And eventually, it will be her. She might be in the wagon already."

"They are doing you a favor," Morgan replies.

I glance at him.

"Let them search," he continues. "If they find her, then our work is done."

I point to the town gate. "Morgan, there are four thousand men out there, waiting for that gate to open. They will storm into the town and hack those plaguers into tiny chunks. Every last one."

"No," he replies. "They won't. Richard hasn't entered the city because his army is distracting the plaguers."

Tristan laughs. "Morgan, you're brilliant."

I steady my breathing and gaze toward the East Gate. The plaguers are not attacking the four knights because the scent of four thousand men outside the gates is overpowering. If the knights are quick and careful, the plaguers will scarcely be aware of them.

"And when I say brilliant," Tristan adds. "I mean that you occasionally say something that isn't completely foolish."

"Richard wants to see her die," I say. "He wants to know he has killed her."

Morgan nods. "Those knights can pick out every woman that looks like Elizabeth, and bring all of them to Richard. But it will take hours. Days maybe."

"And they don't have days," I add. "Henry will be here late this afternoon."

Tristan grins, looking like a child who has hidden a frog in his sister's bed. "But Richard doesn't know that."

I think about King Richard at Framlingham, slaughtering plaguers for the crowd. Raising his sword for their approval, and not receiving it.

I am a crowned heartache, Edward. I am a dead prince's shadow.

"Richard will negotiate with Henry," I mumble. "He will give Henry whatever he wants. He might be insane, but he needs to be loved. If he fights and loses, his shame will be eternal."

I think of the joust, his hands yanking the reins toward me. The collision of horses, and his words to me when we crashed to the earth.

I win.

"He can't allow himself to lose. He'll give Henry back the Lancaster titles. And if he has found Elizabeth, he will turn her over. Because he can exact his vengeance upon us later. When no army threatens him."

I would not do the same. If a man killed my wife, I would not delay my vengeance. But Richard is King, and kings must marry their kingdom before they can love a wife.

"So there's nothing to worry about," Morgan says.

"No." My hand is white upon my sword's grip. "Nothing to worry about." I gaze out at Richard's army. "But we must make certain that Henry and Richard don't battle." I point down to the square. "And we need to watch those knights. If they find Elizabeth, all of our problems are solved."

"Yes," Tristan says. "All of our problems. Except for the *minor* matter of King Richard stripping us of our lands, torturing us for days, and burning us in public. But yes. I agree. All problems solved."

It takes seven hours for Henry Bolingbroke's army to reach the outskirts of St. Edmund's Bury. Tristan spots them an hour after midday, from one of the soaring towers that rise above the abbey church. I send Morgan and the Genoese out to meet him. If Gerald's men still guard the gates, nine men should be plenty to get past them.

"Scout out the gate, first," I call to them. "If there are too many men, come back, you understand?" Morgan nods. It is a small risk, but I need Henry to know that Richard's army outnumbers his own, and that the king's forces are camped to the east.

I stay behind, on the battlements, and watch Mustow Street. A new batch of knights works the afflicted horde. The original knights were relieved during the day, but the cart has not moved. It brims with plaguer women. Sometimes, one of the afflicted will fall out of the wagon bed, and two men will swing the woman back and forth before hurling her back.

It is possible that Elizabeth lies at the bottom of that wagon. But none of the women they have captured under my watch is my wife. The knights ran out of canvas earlier in the day, so they use tapestries and curtains and rugs to catch their prey.

I watch for an hour before footfalls sound on the steps of the Abbey Gate. Tristan and Morgan emerge from the tiny door onto the battlements and say nothing. They simply smile and exchange glances.

"Good news?" I turn back to the square. The knights wrap a tapestry around a woman whose hair is more red than blonde.

"Very good news," Tristan replies. "Henry has been gathering forces on his march. He has three thousand men with him, now. And that's not the best of the news."

I lean against a crenel and cross my arms. They look at one another and their smiles grow.

"Are you planning on telling me?" I say.

A voice calls, echoing, from the spiral staircase. "Planning *to tell* me." Zhuri steps onto the battlements and grins. "And yes, we are." He reaches through the doorway and helps the girl, Josalyn, onto the battlements. She stares out across the town, eyes wide. I doubt she has ever been up this high. She turns and looks toward the towering abbey church.

"So tall," she says.

"They build them tall," I reply, "to serve as an example. So that monks remember not to slouch, but to walk erect before God."

"And they do," Tristan says. "They also walk erect before the whores of Rye, if the rumors are true."

I flash Tristan a glare and turn to the girl. "Do you have something to tell me?"

She curtsies, holds out a glass phial.

I stare for a long moment before taking it. "Is this...?" I look from the girl, to Zhuri, to the phial. "Is this...?"

"She succeeded," Zhuri says. "She replicated the cure. We have done it, Edward!"

Carefully—remembering past disasters—I set the phial aside. My hands tremble. I sweep the girl into my arms and whirl her in a circle, laughing. "I'm... I'm astonished! And... and overjoyed! I... I just... how many have you cured?"

The others stop laughing. Josalyn goes stiff in my arms.

"We... haven't actually tried to cure anyone," Zhuri says. "Henry wouldn't let us try."

I release the alchemist. "So how in the Nine Hells do you know it works?"

Josalyn shrugs. "We don't, my lord. But I followed the instructions precisely. The medium we produced looks identical to the one you left with me. If those instructions were correct, then this cure will work."

I study the phial. "How many do you have?"

"Twenty seven," she replies.

I clench the phial in my hand. "The Genoese locked up the afflicted who were wandering the monastery. There are thirty or thirty five of them in that little chapel by the fishponds. Morgan, take a few of the Italians with you and pull one of the plaguers out. But be careful." I hand Zhuri the phial. "Cure someone. Then we can celebrate."

I look at Tristan. "Where's Henry now?"

"He and his army are a mile out. They'll say 'hello' to Richard very soon."

I look out to the east, but I do not see Henry's army. I stare back down at Mustow Street. The knights are finding it difficult to find women at the back of the column. They have circled around and come out on Scurfe Lane, at the center of the long line of plaguers. I try to look past them, toward the gate, but the abbey walls block my view.

"Let's hope Richard's men aren't itching for a fight."

CHAPTER FIFTY-ONE

RICHARD'S MEN ARE NOT ITCHING FOR A FIGHT.

I watch them desert his army in droves—scores at a time—when they first spot Henry's forces. They run across the East Gate Bridge and disappear among the trees and pastures of West Suffolk.

Henry's soldiers look formidable. He leads with his knights, six or seven hundred of them, mounted and spread in a single rank a quarter mile long. Armor glitters. Spear tips gleam. A dozen banners flutter among the line, catching the afternoon sun in bright flashes of color. Behind them march the footmen. Three thousand men in mail, or leather, or quilted gambesons. Henry has placed the soldiers that wear chain mail in the front, so that his army resembles a wave of steel. A shimmering millstone, come to grind Richard's forces to powder.

King Richard has never been the best tactician. He could not have expected Henry to arrive at St. Edmund's Bury, but that is no excuse for stranding your army on an island. His forces are trapped between three thousand plaguers and Henry's advancing might. And his only escape is the East Gate Bridge. It would take half an hour to get his forces across the Lark. And entering the city would require an hours-long battle against the plaguers. He does not have that sort of time. So he musters his troops and lines them up in ranks on his island.

Henry's soldiers march to the banks of the River Lark, blocking the East Gate bridge and sealing Richard's tomb. A single horseman canters toward Henry's army from the south. It is Morgan, dressed in the suit of mail he took at Rougham. I sent him out through the vineyard gate to tell Henry about Elizabeth, and to ask humbly that Richard include a pardon for us as part of the upcoming negotiations.

Slow hoof beats ring out from inside the town. I run back along the parapets and look out toward Northgate Street. Richard's knights are leaving. The two draft horses draw the wagon of plaguer women along the cobblestones. I wonder if Elizabeth is among them. I think about summoning the Genoese and assaulting the knights, but I know I should not. When two armies meet, any hostility can trigger a war. And war will doom my Elizabeth.

I watch the knights rattle along the street, away from me. And I pray to the Virgin that Elizabeth is not on that cart.

Henry's herald meets Richard's on the East Gate Bridge. The men wear bright tabards, richly woven with their lord's arms, and carry long scepters. I have been witness to the absurdity of heralds many times. They exhibit the ridiculous courtesy of men who know they will not die, should the armies meet in battle. Each tries to bow lower than the other. Each tries to speak with more elegance than the rest. It takes ages for heralds to simply introduce themselves to one another. But it is a tradition of war, and there is no man more traditional than a fighting man.

The heralds are not negotiating Henry's terms. They are simply negotiating how Richard and Henry will negotiate. Such is the way of war.

The parlay ends, mercifully, after an hour. Trumpets sound and Henry marches his army a quarter mile away from the Lark. Morgan breaks away from Henry's army and rides back toward the vineyard.

"Henry's letting the King cross the bridge," Tristan says. "Edward, why is he letting Richard cross the bridge?"

I grip the edge of a merlon tightly, feel the cool strength of the stones. "The king doesn't want to negotiate while he's trapped."

Richard, in the masterful armor that he wore at Framlingham, leads his army across the East Gate Bridge. He wears a crowned bascinet instead of the jousting helm, and a thick red cloak cascades over his shoulders and down the back of his charger. When he is across, he leads his men south, toward the vineyard.

"Where's he going?" Tristan asks.

I point to a pasture at the foot of the vineyard walls. "He'll probably set his army there. It's a sound location. A river and wall at their flanks."

But I am wrong. The king's forces march past the field.

I lean out as far as I can to follow Richard's progress. "Where the bloody Hell is he going?"

"France?" Tristan offers.

Richard and a dozen of his closest knights stop at the east end of the vineyard, where an open gate awaits. Morgan must have opened it for them, under Henry's orders. The King's army rides through, two at a time.

"They're coming here," I mumble. "God in Heaven, Richard's marching into the abbey."

We leave the battlements, charge across the great court, and into one of the towers of the abbey church. I take the spiral steps two at a time until I reach the very top. I double over on the roof; Tristan pants so hard that he cannot speak. It took only two hundred and twenty six steps to silence him.

The views from this height are magnificent. The flat fields of West Suffolk stretch out into the late-day haze. Bright green pastures and monstrous armies of shaggy trees.

The vanes of a mill spin slowly in the distance. I glance down at the churchyard and the world seems to shift beneath me. I clutch at the stone wall and close my eyes. We are a long, long way up.

When I open my eyes again, Richard's forces are crossing a wide bridge, built to support wagons returning from the vineyard to the abbey. I had assumed the king would assemble his army in the vineyard, itself. He is not. He is coming here. To the heart of the monastery.

"What is happening?" I mutter.

Richard's soldiers trudge past winding fishponds and the walled pasture where Brother Philip's livestock live. A few of the soldiers peer into the enclosure at the cattle. Richard marched them with no supplies, and they are hungry.

The army marches past a small chapel and into the churchyard.

"We're being rude," Tristan says. "We should go down and greet them. Perhaps you can offer him another cure."

Richard crosses the churchyard, his soldiers filing through the ranks of wooden crosses of the cemetery, through brigades of the dead, one army passing another. They march past the jagged remains of cattle. Past the granite charnel house, and the overgrown orchard. He does not stop until he reaches the corner of the yard, where St. Mary's stands. The rest of his army settles into ranks, facing the Vineyard. Knights on tired horses and men at arms in filthy breastplates. Archers with unstrung bows on their backs and peasants armed with spears and picks.

A familiar wagon rolls at the very rear of his forces, pulled by two familiar horses. I wonder again if Elizabeth lies inside, wrapped in canvas and buried beneath scores of writhing bodies.

It takes more than an hour for the army to enter the churchyard. The sun droops in the western sky. The king sits on a chestnut destrier, St. Mary's to his right and the wall of the monastery at his back. A dozen mounted knights huddle with him—his elite guard. I squint at the banners of these men. It is too hard to make them out from this height, but one of them is a familiar yellow. Gerald is one of Richard's elite, now. Allies bound by their hatred of me.

A horn sounds in the distance. Henry's army advances.

"Both armies are coming in here?" Tristan asks.

"Sacred ground." I realize the soundness of it as I speak. "Neither of them wants a fight, so they meet in a churchyard."

Henry's troops file across the vineyard, over the wagon bridge, and into the churchyard. Tristan and I spend another hour watching troops move. They form their lines among the graves of the Great Cemetery, with their backs facing the vineyards.

A gaggle of priests march at the very rear of Henry's forces. One of them—who I suspect is Father Benjamin—holds a crucifix aloft. And behind the priests march two dozen men and women in black robes.

"Henry brought the choir?" Tristan chuckles.

"Father Benjamin's idea, no doubt," I reply.

Less than a hundred paces separate the two armies. Heralds from both sides ride into that space and bow. A herald from Richard's army removes a brightly plumed hat, with a flourish, and speaks. I cannot hear what he says, but Tristan provides his own translation.

"We have a very big army, you stupid troubadors," Tristan says. "Far larger than yours. Tell those men to leave the field or we will cut off their phalluses and thread them onto a giant steel hoop, like a great keyring of cocks."

The herald bows with a flourish.

One of Henry's heralds returns the bow and speaks. Tristan provides another interpretation.

"It is true, you hairless carrot farmer. Your army is slightly larger. But if you try to battle us, we shall drive wooden stakes into your filthy canals, raise the stakes over the battlements, and perform a puppet show for the plaguers. Furthermore, if it were even remotely possible for you to thread the phalluses of our army onto a giant iron ring, I would suggest you do not show it to your wife, who would recognize each and every one of the cocks."

They smile at each other and bow again. Richard's herald responds, and Tristan, again, gives me his thoughts on their conversation.

"You farting poltroons. If you dare to attack the King of England, God will defecate on your souls and throw you out upon the gutter of eternal punishment. Not even the pope could save your shit-stained souls."

Henry's herald nods, and utters a short response.

Tristan shrugs. "Which pope?"

I smile, but it is a brief thing. England has a cure. And my journey is at an end. But Elizabeth is still not at my side. I touch her cure, at my neck, and stare down toward Angel Hill.

Footsteps pound up from the spiral stairs. Tristan and I draw our swords, but it is Zhuri who stumbles onto the tower roof, panting. He doubles over, hands on thighs. "It... it..." His words become coughs.

"Steady, Moor," I say. "Deep breaths."

"It... works." He grins for an instant before breaking down into a fit of coughing again.

"The cure works?" I ask.

He shakes his head. "No, the vineyard gate. It squeals a bit, but it opens."

Tristan and I look at one another.

Zhuri coughs again, then grins. "Of course the cure! Would I run up two hundred steps to talk about a gate? The cure worked! One of the plaguers is healed. A fat woman stuck in the pig gate."

I laugh too hard, because tears stream down my face. I turn my face skyward, laughing and crying. The cure works.

England is saved. I stare down at Angel Hill again and search for a blue bow. I do not see one.

I duck back into the spiral staircase. "Let's get down to the churchyard. We must tell Henry. And I want to make sure he includes a pardon for us as part of the negotiations."

CHAPTER FIFTY-TWO

"SIR EDWARD!" HENRY SITS A MASSIVE WHITE CHARGER. The duke shimmers in armor that has been polished to a mirror sheen. Steel besegews dangle on either side of his breastplate, sculpted in the shape of the Lancaster rose. His bright surcoat bears the family arms, trimmed in gold thread, and his bascinet is crowned by a rampant lion.

Father Benjamin sits a dappled palfrey at Henry's side. He looks at me as if he just sucked the juice out of a lemon.

Knights and men-at-arms gather around me, clapping me on the back, smiling and raising their fists in approval.

"We're with you, Sir Edward!" one calls.

"Have you found Lady Elizabeth?" another asks.

Henry goads his horse through the crowd, raises his visor and grins. "Your Moorish friend told us stories of your adventures. If even half of them are true, you are a bloody hero, Edward! A bloody hero!"

"You're right about the blood, my lord," The red of Sister Mildred's blood is still on my hands. So much blood.

"And you were right about Richard! By Satan's knee, you were right! I can't believe he left Framlingham just to kill your wife!"

"Edward has a talent for infuriating titled gentry," Tristan replies.

Henry dismounts and claps me on the shoulder. "Well, he hasn't infuriated me."

"Give it time," Tristan says.

"In fact," Henry says, "get in your harness, Edward. I want you to lead my left flank."

"Lead your left flank?" I ask.

Henry waves his hand. "A ceremonial position. There will be no fighting today. I simply want everyone to know that Sir Edward Dallingridge is favored by the Lancasters."

"There *should* be fighting today!" Father Benjamin snaps. "You have Richard cornered. His army is tired. And God has chosen you! Tell them, my lord! Tell them about the miracle!"

"There will be *no* fighting," Henry replies. "And it was not a miracle. It was...it...I'm not certain what it was. But I do not believe it was a miracle."

"Plaguers came at our army as we marched here!" Father Benajamin says. "And the afflicted would not attack Henry! They recoiled from him as if from the light of the God! He is the Lord's warrior! The new chosen King of England!"

"He hasn't been around any red lichen, has he?" Tristan asks.

Henry and Father Benjamin look at Tristan.

Tristan shrugs. "No, you're right. God's warrior. Chosen King of England."

There are only three things that I know repel plaguers. I do not believe Henry has a holy relic, and I am fairly certain he would not use the old magics.

The duke showed me a small sore on his wrist when we were at Stowmarket.

I do not share my thoughts.

"My lord," I say. "I would be honored to stand on your left flank, but I believe my wife is outside the gates. I must go out and look—"

"I want you on my left flank, Edward. It is not just an honor. It is for your benefit. So everyone may see that you are under our protection. When all this is over, there isn't a man in my army who won't help you find your wife. And when I return home, I will tell the Duke of Lancaster how you helped me corner Richard. Perhaps your silly feud with my father will finally end and the two of you can be friends again."

Tristan glances at me.

I clear my throat, stare out across the sea of wooden crosses. Richard's men are cutting down a cedar tree that grows beside St. Mary's. "You mention your father—"

"Later, Edward. Get in your harness. There's a destrier waiting for you by the little chapel behind us. I'll tell Sir Jason Bidwell that you are taking over for him on the left flank."

Perhaps it is best that Henry does not know about his father. Not today. Angering him when the armies face one another is not wise.

There must be no fighting today.

Tristan and I return to the Abbey Gate and help each other into our armor. The Genoese are gone, returned to Henry's army no doubt.

A page leading a saddled destrier meets us beside the St. David's Chapel. The choir sings behind him, although the voices sound oddly flat in the open space of the churchyard. I mount the horse and we report to Henry's left flank.

A mounted knight wearing reds and yellows waits for me. His helmet bears a small castle upon the crest. "Sir Edward?"

I nod. "Sir Jason Bidwell?"

"Aye," he replies. "You'll be taking over this flank?"

"I'm sorry," I reply. "It's not by choice."

"Nothing to apologize for, Sir Edward," he says. "Your Moor friend told us everything. All of your exploits. And the cure you found. The whole army is talking about you and your wife. It is an honor to step aside for you, sir."

"No reason why you can't be here too, is there?" I ask. "This isn't a battle, it's a parade. Stay at my side and we'll share the honor." He grins. I try to give him one in return, but Elizabeth is still not at my side, so I clap him on the shoulder, instead.

"Well spoken, Edward." Tristan has no horse, so he stands beside mine. "The three of us will take position here and share the honor of leading the..." He sees my expression and hesitates, then grins and jabs his thumb at the men behind us. "I'll... I'll go join Morgan with the rest of the formation."

I stand at Sir Bidwell's side, listen to the choir, and look across at Richard's army. They outnumber us, but their ranks teem with untrained peasants. Parts of the formation look more like a mob than an army, men pressed into service for the king. Richard does not want peasants to fill Framlingham Castle, but he does not mind them filling his ranks. If the armies were to fight here today, I wonder how many of the peasants would rout at the first charge.

Sir Jason looks at my arm and smiles crookedly. "I haven't seen anyone use a shield in years."

I tap my great helm, also a relic of the past. "Sometimes the old things are the best."

When Richard set his army on the field, he left a large gap between two of the ranks. Probably to allow the king and his guards to ride through when he and Henry meet. The gap allows me to see St. Mary's, and Richard, who stands next to a thick stump—the remains of the cedar they cut down. A hulking man with no shirt stands beside the king. The man wears a great helm and holds a massive bearded axe.

Sir Jason follows my gaze and shakes his head. "King Richard has strange tastes. Musicians and poets and..." he waves uncertainly toward the shirtless man. "Whatever that is."

I nod. Strange tastes indeed. I tap my great helm and point to the shirtless man. "He likes the old things too."

Sir Bidwell laughs. "Aye, he does. Looks like a bloody executioner."

I smile, but it is a fleeting thing, a caterpillar crushed by a cold granite block.

An executioner. He looks like a bloody executioner.

Two knights shove a woman toward the cedar stump. A canvas sack covers the woman's head and torso, and is tied around her waist. My breath catches. The destrier seems to sway beneath me.

"Are you unwell, Sir Edward?"

I wave my hand at him and watch as the knights pull at the canvas from the woman's head. They have found Elizabeth. They are going to execute her, here, in front of me. They are going to do it before there are any negotiations. I raise my reins, knowing I will never reach her in time. My vision blurs. The knights pull the canvas away from the woman.

And I release a long, rattling breath.

It is not Elizabeth.

"What are they doing?" Sir Bidwell asks.

Trying to destroy me.

Trying to drive a dagger through my heart.

Trying to damn me for eternity.

"They're beheading that plaguer." Do they think the woman is Elizabeth? "Leave her be!" I shout across the field, but I know my voice will not carry far enough.

I look for Henry at the rear of our army, but I cannot see him through the soldiers.

Richard's knights kick the woman to her knees, then shove her shoulders down, so that her neck rests on the stump. She flails and writhes. I imagine she is shrieking.

"He has to stop," I mutter. "That's a woman. A sick woman."

The executioner's axe gleams in the setting sun. It rises and drops with a brutal efficiency and the woman's struggles cease.

"Murderer!" I shout. "*Murderer!*"

I know Richard could not have heard me, but he steps forward, removes his helm, and looks directly at me. Perhaps he smiles.

And I see, for the first time, the long line of afflicted women standing by the monastery wall. They are tied together in groups, arms pinned to their sides, fabric over heads and torsos. Knights use staves and spear shafts to keep them huddled in place.

"He's going to kill them all." I search for Henry again and this time I glimpse him, far behind me. He is surrounded by priests and knights, his horse facing the abbey church.

I look at the plagued women. The executioner's axe ends the life of another one, and the knights cut another woman free from the queue. They strip off the canvas sack and drag her by the hair to the stump.

I do not see Elizabeth among the plaguers, but the oath I swore stings my eyes. I stare at the crosses rising between the two armies. I imagine a thousand carpenters nailed upon them, each one staring blankly at me.

I am champion of the dead. But I can do nothing.

The heralds are still upon the field. They laugh and bow and make flourishes with their hands while afflicted women add blood to the sacred soil of Saint Edmund.

I watch and offer a prayer to the thousand crosses, ask the Carpenter to forgive my failings. I try to put the oath out of my mind. Try to forget about the promise I made.

But the Lord reminds me.

A blue dress near the back of the first column of plaguers.

The cusp of a bow just visible beneath a canvas sack.

I forget how to breathe.

My Elizabeth.

A red storm rises in my soul.

Who can stand before his indignation?

My sword rings as I draw it free.

Who can endure the heat of his anger?

I made an oath, and the God of the Old Testament is testing my resolve. The voices of the choir rise ever higher, resounding across the churchyard, drawing out one final word: "*Hallelujah!*"

I drive my remaining spur into the destrier with such force that the animal bellows and rears before leaping forward. My voice rips across the battlefield, louder than any choir, louder than any horn, louder than the very thunder of Heaven.

"*Elizabeth!*"

My horse vaults a wooden cross and we are away, galloping across a field of the dead. Across the sacred ground of Saint Edmund. Across the last three hundred paces of my journey.

"*Elizabeth!*"

My cry is the loudest sound on the battlefield, and the echoes of it rumble back at me. I am so focused on the blue dress that, at first, it does not strike me as odd that my echo should rumble. And then it does.

I glance back over my shoulder.

Henry Bolingbroke's army charges after me, like a biblical flood. The steel of their killing tools shine in the setting sun. They howl, and hurdle crosses, and kick through the carcasses of slaughtered cattle. They shout for Henry Bolingbroke. They shout for England. They shout for Saint George and Saint Edmund.

But most of all, they shout for me.

I glance back at them for a heartbeat, then turn and lash my warhorse's reins.

Men will follow anyone.

CHAPTER FIFTY-THREE

RICHARD'S PEASANTS FLEE OUR ADVANCE like mice from the plow. Like dust in a whirlwind. Judgment Day has arrived, and they are not ready.

A plague of locusts fills the air. One strikes my shield with a flat clank. Arrows. Richard's archers.

I duck behind the shield as my horse gallops on, and two more arrows strike. Their bodkin tips drive through the layers of leather and wood, and glint in front of my eyes. I pound the shield with my fist and roar. Sometimes the old things are the best.

My horse cries out and stumbles. Crashes onto its forelegs. The world tips upward and I leap from the saddle. Hit the earth with a sickening crash that sends lightning through my body. I tumble along the ground, clattering. One of my couters sails free from my elbow and bounces away. My left shoulder burns. I cannot draw a proper breath, but I stagger to my feet, wheezing. The sword of Saint Giles lies beside my dying horse. Arrow shafts jut from the destrier's flesh. I do not have time to end the animal's misery. An arrow clanks off my shoulder, spinning me. I gasp for breath, take up my sword. The biblical flood crashes around me as Henry's men finally catch up.

Richard's footmen rumble forward.

And the two armies collide.

I have difficulty focusing on the clashing men about me. Perhaps it is the fall I took. Things happen too quickly. My vision skips, like the words of a stutterer, images seem to halt—as if time itself had stopped—then move forward too quickly. The roar of battle assaults my ears at an impossible volume, then fades to nothing, before rising to an unbearable roar again. Metal clashes against metal. Weapons squelch against flesh. Men cry out for pity. But there is no pity here, only pain. When coin has no value, ransoms cannot exist. Everyone dies like commoners.

Someone shouts my wife's name and drives a war hammer deep into a knight's chest. One of Richard's men-at-arms lunges with a spear, shredding an infantryman's thigh. The infantryman opens his mouth in a howl, but there is no sound. Again my hearing falters and the world returns to silence.

I swing my sword at a footman wearing a kettle helm, my stroke impossibly slow. The sound of my battle cry comes and goes, as if it is tapped out on a broken horn. My blade gashes through leather. Blood sprays leisurely from the wound, like spores floating in the breeze.

Something strikes me in the side, making me stumble. I whirl in time to take the next axe blow on my shield. One of Henry's knights crumples the axe man's helm with a five-foot war sword. The knight has a castle on his helm. Sir Jason Bidwell.

He points to the mark on my shield, where the axe struck. "Sometimes the old things are the best!"

"Sir Edward is not *that* old!" Tristan appears at my other flank, holding a poleaxe.

"This is holy ground, Edward! We cannot fight here!" I do not have to look to know that Morgan is behind me. "It is against the laws of God!"

I shout back to him: "*Necessitas no hab—*"

A spear skims my great helm. Tristan buries his axe in the spearman's shoulder. Morgan lunges with his sword. Drives it under the soldier's chin, releasing a tide of blood.

I shove past a surrendering peasant and look back toward the cedar stump, twenty five paces away. The executioner has not stopped. He has not stopped.

Richard rolls his hand in the air and the knights hurry forward with the next woman, dragging her by the hair.

My left side burns. I glance down. Blood flows from under the fauld at my waist and runs along my right leg. The axeman's blade found flesh. I raise my shield arm, touch my side and find broken mail and more blood.

A man-at-arms with a war sword swings at me. I duck under the blow and explode into him, shield first. He sprawls backward and Tristan splits his face with the poleax.

"You wounded, Ed?" Tristan calls.

I shake my head and press forward.

There are only six women ahead of Elizabeth. My limbs twitch with panic. The Old Testament rises like brimstone in my soul, gives me the strength of fury. Sometimes the Old things are the best.

A man in chain mail lunges at me with a spear. I duck behind a stone grave marker and swing with every ounce of strength I have, howling. Spilled blood takes my footing. I skid and Saint Giles's sword shatters the top of the gravestone.

His wrath is poured out like fire, and the rocks are broken to pieces by him.

Sir Jason and Morgan batter the spearman and I slip past them. My side aches. Blood washes over my right leg, leaves a trail behind me.

Elizabeth.

I throw myself forward, toward my wife. Ever forward, ever onward toward her. There is no battle. There are no enemies. There is nothing but Elizabeth, and judgment for those who stand between us. Saint Giles sings his song of madness, and I dance through the horrors of war. Men fall before me. Blood makes a marsh of the churchyard. The screams of my enemies are a choir, and their hymns are Elizabeth's salvation.

I am the wolf that slaughters wolves.

I am the savior of England.

I am the angel of death. And I kill *with many blood.*

Only five women stand between Elizabeth and the executioner's blade. Richard smashes a gauntleted fist into his palm and bellows at his knights.

A man crashes into me and we both go down. I roll onto my side and crush his throat with my elbow. Stagger to my feet and drive my shoulder into a footman holding a poleaxe. He topples and Tristan pounces on him.

"We're clear!" Morgan shouts. "We're clear!"

War still rages behind us, but a dozen of us have stabbed through the entire army. We have broken through the lines.

Only two dozen paces separate me from my wife.

Less than thirty paces from my Elizabeth. I pound my breastplate with the hilt of my sword, feel the reassurance of her cure.

Richard, guarded by twenty dismounted knights, looks at me and dances, his hands waving to some imaginary rhythm.

My heart pounds. Not because I face the King of England, but because the King of England stands between me and Elizabeth.

Richard gestures to the horde of afflicted women and shouts. There is too much noise to hear him, but I read the words on his lips. "Kill them all!"

Half of his knights turn and advance on the rows of women. I roar and sprint toward them, but one of the knights strides out to meet me. The visor of his bascinet is carved to look like a savage, roaring ape, his tabard bears three roosters.

"This is the last time we meet, Edward!" Sir Gerald twirls a mace in his hand. The sun's rays shimmer along the sharp flanges. He shouts back toward Richard. "I will kill him!" His carved visor turns back my way, then he flinches and adds, "Your Highness!"

"Do it!" Richard screams.

The knights who advanced on the plagued women do their best to help the executioner. They attack at random, crumpling skulls and severing spines. Tristan, Morgan and Sir Jason charge past me, toward the knights, with a half dozen of Henry's footmen at their heels.

I throw my shield aside and try to join them, ducking past Sir Gerald. But Gerald of Thunresleam is fast. He hammers me in the back with the mace. My bones tremble. I tumble to the earth with a groan. Roll to one shoulder. The mace rises high in the air. The ape mask roars at me. I swing my leg, catch Gerald behind the knee and send him sprawling to the earth.

We rise at the same time, both swinging. His mace crashes against my spaulder and my blade clicks off his helm. It is a bone pain I feel. A deep, burrowing agony that numbs my entire left side. Gerald's bascinet has a new gouge, but he seems otherwise unaffected by my strike. I stumble and look at my weapon.

The sword of Saint Giles has saved me more times than I can remember, but an arming sword is a poor choice against well-made plate armor. I consider dropping it and finding a better weapon, but Saint Giles is my saint. He has never abandoned me. So I grip the hilt tightly and send an overhand cut at Gerald's head. He lunges out of the way. My blade clatters off his arm.

I glance behind him while he regains his balance. There are only two women ahead of Elizabeth in the queue. Behind them, a fierce battle rages for the mass of plagued women still bound together. My allies do not realize that Elizabeth is not among the larger group.

"She's in the queue!" I shout. "She's—"

Gerald roars and takes a running swing at me. I drop to a knee and duck beneath the blow. Batter the steel skirt beneath his breastplate. My blade mars the metal, nothing more. Gerald spins and swings in one motion. I dive to the ground and the flanged mace knocks the unicorn crest from my helm.

"Satan protects you!" Gerald clenches his fists and growls. "You are no better than those demon women behind Richard!"

I do not waste my stuttering breath on a response. The wound in my side seethes. I am losing too much blood. My head swims. I rise to a knee. The Old Testament has burned through me. There is nothing left. No whirlwind. No storm. Not even a hint of indignation. There is only terror for Elizabeth.

One woman now. Only one woman stands in front of my wife. The executioner has not stopped. My friends fight a furious battle with Richard's knights. I pray that even one of them breaks away and helps Elizabeth. A few of the plaguer women have gotten loose, or been cut free. It is a chaos of bodies, steel and blood.

Gerald checks a swing and surprises me with a kick to the face when I duck. The world turns red. My nose is burning copper. I fall to one side, unsure of which way is grass and which sky. Gerald's shadow falls upon me. I try to scramble to my feet but the mace finds my side. Armor crumples. Ribs splinter like glass.

Elizabeth.

I crawl toward the cedar stump.

Elizabeth.

"When I am done with you, I will rape your wife with a poleaxe." Gerald kicks at my wounded ribs and I cry out, my voice hoarse with pain. He laughs.

I claw at the earth. Reach with a quivering hand toward my wife.

Elizabeth.

She is next. No one stands before her. Only the executioner. I sniff at the air, searching for the scent of lemons and strawberries. She is so close. So close.

"Tris...Tristan." I try to shout, but only a gasp comes out. I point a trembling, finger toward the cedar. "Morgan. She's there...she's there..."

I put both fists on the grass and push myself up, onto one knee. Sir Gerald raises the mace in both hands and takes a stride toward me. He is faster, better armed, and younger.

I watch him approach. And at the last instant, I tuck my shoulder and roll toward him. He grunts and tries to stop himself, but his momentum carries him toward me. He hops to avoid tripping, and I thrust the blade of Saint Giles upward, under his fauld. I drive the blade of madness with all of my remaining strength. The tip is not sharp enough to cut cleanly. It splits flesh, crushes cartilage and bone, destroys all manhood, and widens his filthy canal.

Sir Gerald is faster, better armed, and younger, but I have fought in more battles than he has even heard of.

Sometimes the old things are the best.

He tumbles to the ground, shrieking like a plaguer, his armor clanking along the grass. He rolls, gasps out a choked scream, his hands clutch at his groin. Blood fountains from beneath his mail.

I stagger to my feet. My breath comes in ragged sweeps. The wound at my side does not hurt anymore, and that is not a good sign. Six of Richard's elite knights stand beside him. I glance toward the plagued women. The small group of my allies has been reduced to Tristan, Morgan, Sir Jason and a man-at-arms wielding a battle axe. They fight a furious, clanking battle against four more of Richard's men. I lurch toward the cedar. The executioner grabs Elizabeth by the hair and drags her off her feet.

"Don't you touch her!" I roar. *"Don't you touch her!"*

I rush toward the executioner but Richard's six knights step forward to block my path. They are a wall of steel and axe blades. My Elizabeth is in the executioner's hands, and a half-dozen soldiers keep me at bay.

"Sing for me, Edward," Richard cackles and twirls in a circle, just behind the knights and only a few paces from the executioner. "If you sing me an apology, I may spare your life."

The executioner, fingers wound in Elizabeth's hair, drags her toward the stump. I duck low to follow his progress behind Richard's men, then hurl myself at the wall of knights. They shove me backward and I topple onto my back. A few of them laugh. The wound at my side burns and more blood washes over my leg. I do not have much time, but Elizabeth has even less. I roll to my side, stagger to my feet.

"Go on," Richard says. "I want you to beg. Sing a song of your wretchedness."

The executioner pushes Elizabeth onto the stump.

I call to God.

I call upon Saint Giles and Mother Mary.

I call upon the clan of the wolf, upon the old magic, and the gods of the stone circles. Upon the stars, and reason, and science, and the Carpenter on his cross. I call upon every one of them and cast my gaze to the skies.

The cross atop St. Mary's glitters gold in the fading light. Swallows fly in circles around the church. Eight more crosses glow orange upon the battlements.

"No song?" Richard shrugs. "Then die, Edward Dallingridge. Speak your last words, troubadour."

I point. My arm shakes like an old man's. The Lord gives me strength for one good scream, and I find the perfect words.

"Kill the hairless carrot farmers!"

A steel rain falls upon the knights. Some scream, but most simply crumple silently. Every one of them is struck, save King Richard, who looks at his fallen soldiers as if God struck them down.

And perhaps He has.

"No!" Richard shrieks. "Those were terrible words! *Terrible words!*" He spins in a complete circle and raises both fists into the air. "*No!*"

I nod to the Genoese on the battlements. Frederico salutes me and shouts down, his voice distant and tiny above the battle, "*So sayeth de Lorda!*"

Beyond the king, the executioner stares at the crossbowmen on the battlements, one of his sweating hands holds Elizabeth down, the other grips his axe. There is uncertainty in his eyes, and that is good. Elizabeth's life depends upon uncertainty.

Richard backs away from me, glancing to either side, his face twisted and flushed. None of his knights are standing. He rips the crown from his head with a roar. His hands curl around the metal so tightly that the edges gash his skin. Blood washes over the circlet of gold.

"A crowned heartache!" His howls turns to sobs. "A dead prince's shadow!"

I barely hear the king. My life is Elizabeth, and her life hangs by a thread.

Tristan limps to my side, his left arm tucked against his chest gingerly. He glances at Sir Gerald. The knight has thrown his helmet off, but still writhes on the grass, blood soaking his crotch. "They should remove one of the cocks from the arms of Thunresleam," Tristan says.

I barely hear him, too.

Richard thrusts the crown out to me. "Take it! Seize the crown, cousin! They wanted an Edward. Give them one!"

The crown glitters at the corner of my vision, but I want no part of that shackle. I shove Richard aside and lumber toward the cedar stump, still trying to soothe the executioner.

My closest friend in the world speaks to Richard. "They haven't had a Tristan yet."

I stumble forward toward the king and the cedar stump, holding my hands up, palms outward, toward the executioner. He tenses as I approach. Raises the axe.

"Wait!" I hold up a hand to stop him, my voice echoing against the walls of St. Mary's. "*Don't!*"

I leap.

The blade drops with brutal efficiency.

CHAPTER FIFTY-FOUR

I HAVE AN INSTANT TO SAVOR the feel of Elizabeth's body against mine, before the bearded axe splits the back of my breastplate.

The pain shatters my mind.

I am back in Bodiam, showing Elizabeth the foundations of our castle.

No one can harm us when this is built.

Pain makes the vision billow, like reflections in a rippled pond. I will die. The executioner's blow will kill me. But I will break death's bony fingers and hold him off long enough to give my angel her cure. And, if she returns to life, I will laugh and drink a toast with death.

Agony enters my bones. It is as if I have tumbled from the abbey tower. I cannot feel my body. Only the reverberations of pain.

I roll to one side. The executioner's axe lies on the ground two paces from me. I follow the haft to his hand. The man lies on his side, his eyes open wide, gazing past me. Blood washes from a ragged hole in his cheek. An eighteen-inch crossbow bolt, thick as a wagon spoke, lies buried almost to the vanes in the earth beside him.

I look toward the battlements. Magnus grins and holds up the monstrous siege crossbow. A terrible weapon. My spine throbs with pain.

Elizabeth is on her feet, hissing, but Morgan holds her tightly, whispers soothing words. I look toward the battlefield. Richard's men are routing. Henry's army roars toward us, the first rank less than a dozen paces away.

Sir Gerald screams. He forms no words, only echoing shrieks. Two freed plaguer women have found him. They kneel beside his head. One yanks his hair back. The other bites a chunk from his cheek. His screams are louder than I have ever heard. He is a few moments from Hell, and the dead and dying men of Richard's army will follow him there.

The king sits an arm's length from me, rocking, arms around knees. No. Not the king anymore. The gold circlet is gone. Tristan kneels beside me, his helmet off and the crown of England on his head.

King Tristan I, of England.

"You're going to need a new breastplate," King Tristan tells me.

But I barely hear him.

It takes an effort to struggle onto my knees. Perhaps I will live, after all. My shattered breastplate falls away, thumps to the grass. Elizabeth snarls and paws at me with long, slender fingers.

Elizabeth.

I work the straps of my great helm, pull it off my head and toss it to the ground. Morgan lays Elizabeth on the grass with a gentle firmness.

My Elizabeth.

My fingers fumble for the cure, draw the ampoule out from under my mail. I yank, hard enough to snap the leather cord. The ground seems unsteady under my feet. I hold the ampoule in trembling fingers and break the ceramic seal.

Dear God. How I have dreamed of this moment.

How I have dreaded this moment.

I cannot think about what I must do, I must simply do it.

But I cannot.

My arm trembles so much that I fear I will spill the cure. I hold it in both hands. Recall the scuttling horror in the cellar of the alchemist's tower. I think of Good Queen Anne, strapped to a cross. Withering, teeth sagging and falling from her gums.

I draw my dagger. If the cure goes badly, I will send my angel to Heaven, and follow Gerald to Hell. I have delivered the cure to an alchemist, and protected the lambs from the lions. But only Elizabeth's life can cleanse my soul.

Mother Mary.

I can only say her name. There are no prayers strong enough.

Mother Mary.

Elizabeth howls and I tip the ampoule into her mouth before I can deliberate any further. Morgan pushes her chin upward and holds her jaws closed.

Oh dear God. What have I done?

Tears come to my eyes. Breaths become sobs.

My Elizabeth. My angel. My wife.

Tristan places a hand on my shoulder.

What have I done?

A voice rises in song beside me.

"*Nowel, nowel, nowel...*"

The mad king Richard.

The crowned heartache.

Elizabeth struggles against Morgan, thrashes her head from side to side, but he will not relent. I gaze into her midnight eyes.

"*Out of your sleep arise and wake...*"

Her throat pulses. She has swallowed the cure. It is too late. Too late.

I stroke her face. She snaps at me, hisses. I take her hand, feel the long, pale fingers against mine. She draws in a screeching breath. Her back arches and she falls to her knees, lurches onto her back and flails.

"... *God has made for mankind's sake...*"

Her thrashing slows.

I stare into her eyes. Are they lighter?

"Eliza..." My voice breaks. I stifle a sob and start again. "Elizabeth, I... I met Geoffrey Chaucer. And... I saw a real dragon."

Her breathing grows softer, more rhythmic. Her eyes close. The snarl fades.

"... *all of a maid who makes me knell...*"

"I'm here, my lady. I'm here, my bride." I run my hand over her head softly.

And the first clump of hair falls out.

CHAPTER FIFTY-FIVE

I STARE AT THE blonde locks in my hand. My punishment is complete. I have made a demon of my angel.

My soul blackens. The Lord gave me one of his Valkyries, and I let Satan take her from me.

I raise my dagger, stare at the blade in my trembling hand.

"I am... so... so... sorry..." a sob breaks my voice.

Tristan seizes my wrist. Morgan crouches over Elizabeth, protects her with his body. I struggle to free my hand. "Let go! I won't see her like this!"

"We can find another cure!" Tristan shouts.

"We can pray!" Morgan adds. "God will save her!"

"... *of all the women she is the belle.*"

"I won't see her change! *Release me!*"

Tristan restrains me, shoves me backward. Are there tears in his eyes?

"Ed... Edward?"

The sound stops my heart. Silences the entire battlefield.

No, it is not a sound.

To call it a sound is to insult God. What I hear is creation. It is the seasons, all of them, together. Sun and snow, bright leaves and rain. It is the full moon and the glitter of stars. It is lemon and strawberries, honey and silk. The song of every bird that ever sang. Fingertips on your back and lips on your neck. A choir of gods.

It is the sound of my Elizabeth.

"She was dragged by her hair," Tristan whispers. "She was dragged by her hair!"

I stare at the blonde locks still entwined in my fingers.

She was dragged by her hair.

"God in Heaven, it works." Henry Bolingbroke stands behind me with a dozen of his knights. "Heaven's wonder, it truly works."

"Send these cures to every corner of England," says Tristan. "My kingdom will begin its recovery today."

Lord Henry holds his hand out.

Tristan stares at the hand, sighs, and takes Richard's crown off. "So ends the reign of King Tristan I."

Elizabeth's eyes brighten to summer blue. They meet mine and my breath catches. The long, pale fingers reach out, trembling. I take them and a tear splatters her skin. "Elizabeth?" I lower my gaze. God lives in her eyes, and I cannot bear to look. I am not worthy of Him. Or her. "You deserve better, Elizabeth. Better than an old wolf like me."

She reaches toward me with her free hand, strokes my face. The crooked smile returns. She speaks, and I fall in love with her once more. "You'll do."

I laugh, or perhaps I cry. I do not know. My nose finds her neck. Lemons and strawberries. A thousand dark sorrows leave my body like crows from a forest. "*J'taime*," I whisper. "*J'taime*."

Her fingers touch the tears on my cheeks, and blue lakes form in her eyes. "Yes," she whispers. "I believe you are." She shivers in my arms. "Where... where are... ?"

"You're safe," I whisper, my voice choked. "You're safe."

A trumpet blares and I glance back.

Father Benjamin places the crown on Henry Bolingbroke's head.

Elizabeth's arms find my neck, and my lips find hers.

A great cheer rises behind me, echoing across the monastery.

Richard laughs, still rocking a few paces away. "Listen to them, Edward," he says. "Listen to them. They love us."

I do not know who the cheer is for, and I do not care.

My wife is healed.

I am healed.

And soon, England will be healed.

My nose finds my angel's neck again, and I breathe deeply. Lemons and strawberry cleanse my soul.

I look skyward, but I do not know who to thank.

Help came from too many places. The Virgin Mary guided my way. The saints helped me cut through my enemies. The pagan gods protected me with their old magic, and the stars above kept me healthy and strong. Muslim and Hebrew wisdom discovered a cure. Alchemy crafted it. A woman reproduced it. And both a priest and the King of England gave it their blessings. It is a time of madness, and only the tempered madness of a half dozen beliefs could save us.

I am still unsure of the affliction's origin. The priests and bishops called it a scourge from God. They preached that the holy hand of the Father was purging the wicked from the earth. But I have heard many other thoughts on the cause of this sickness: the ground bones of saints; buggery; witchcraft; leprosy; rats; bad air. There are too many to recall.

I am a simple knight, so I choose to believe that this sickness was a blessing. The Lord was merely testing me. Setting challenges to see if I was worthy of His greatest angel. I do not believe I am, but through a madness of perseverance, I have outlasted even God. And, for now, my trials have ended.

Hallelujah.

The Scourge: Emaculum

The End

Historical Note: Episode One

Once again we find Sir Edward Dallingridge of Bodiam traveling the slightly altered landscapes of 14th century England. I will try to guide you through Edward's England as best I can, pointing out the monuments of accepted fact and navigating the side roads that a historical fantasy must sometimes take.

Book three strays from traditional history more than any of the previous two novels, mostly because of one event in history that I have had to change (I will discuss that change in greater detail at the end of episodes 3 and 8). As always, I have tried to remain true to established historical facts wherever possible.

In episode 1, Edward and Sir Tristan find themselves running from the relentless Sir Gerald of Thunresleam. Our two knights leave the forest into which they fled and spot a hind that draws Edward's attention to a cart upon the northern road. Hinds, Edward says, are Saint Giles's animal. And they are, but who the hell is Saint Giles?

Saint Giles was a Greek saint who lived in the 7th century. He was a hermit and a vegetarian, and he is said to have suckled doe teats for milk. You hear that sound? That's the sound of Tristan laughing.

Giles was shot by a hunter who was trying to bring down one of the saint's cherished deer, and the saint was forever plagued by this arrow wound. Edward talks about Giles as "the patron saint of madness," and he is, but, because of the arrow wound, he is better known as the patron saint of cripples. Unfortunately, "In these times of madness, only cripples will save us," doesn't have quite the same ring.

The Scourge: Emaculum

I do not know if the real Edward adopted Saint Giles as his protector. I do know that the small church sitting next to Edward's castle at Bodiam is devoted to Giles, so I like to imagine that the saint played a role in our hero's life.

Later in the episode, our weary knights encounter a band of pilgrims on the way to St. Edmund's tomb, on a mistaken premise. They believe Edmund is the patron saint of England. And he was at one time. But King Edward III, as Sir Edward mentions, favored Saint George—A Roman soldier who slew a dragon. And so Saint George became the head of Edward III's new order—the Knights of the Garter—and the symbol of England.

In recent times, there has been a growing movement to change the patron saint back to Saint Edmund who, unlike St. George, was actually an Englishman. More on Saint Edmund later, but a part of me favors the change. Saint George's red cross on a white background is England's flag, but it was the flag of Genoa long before that. And Saint Edmund was not just an Englishman, but one of the earliest English kings. He died defending the English people from the Danish invaders and refusing to renounce his faith. All very good reasons to replace the Roman Saint George, who had very little to do with England. I also spend a lot of time in Bury St Edmunds (as the town is known, now) so I may be biased.

We end the episode at a monastic house that lies on the southeast border of Norfolk. This is Langley Abbey, and parts of it still exist. You can visit the abbey and tour the remains and imagine what it must have looked like, standing upright before God, among the flatlands of Norfolk.

Historical Note: Episode Two

Edward was a knight with many friends, but the Dallingridge family (sometimes known as Dalyngrigge) wasn't always so well connected.

Edward's grandfather, John Dallingridge, earned his prestige the old-fashioned way—he married into it. His marriage to Joan, daughter of Walter de la Lynde, gave John several estates, and, when John's son, Roger, was old enough, he too was married into a more powerful family. Roger married Alice Radingden, who gave him even more estates.

So it was only natural that Edward, Roger's son, should be married off to another powerful woman. And that woman was Lady Elizabeth Wardieu, who brought with her—among other properties—a small estate in Bodiam. But Edward's duties didn't end with his marriage. Like any knight, he was expected to carve out a better status for his family.

And he was very good at carving.

In his day, the ruling class was on the front lines of every war (things have changed quite a bit since then). So Edward was, first and foremost, a warrior. He started his battle experiences at the early age of thirteen, fighting in France under the Earl of Arundel. He was, apparently, a brilliant soldier, because he earned praise from all of his commanders, and received his knighthood before his 21st year. He fought in many different places, on land and sea, in France and Spain, for a number of famous commanders. But it was as a mercenary in Sir Robert Knolles' free companies that he truly carved out a better life. He made enormous amounts of money with Sir Robert, enough to build a castle at Bodiam. Enough to make him one of the most important knights in England.

But Edward was more than a good soldier—he was also a brilliant councilor. This combination of skills were highly sought after in medieval England. It wasn't long before King Richard started taking notice of him. The king and the Earl of Arundel sent Edward to survey the coastal defenses of East Sussex, on the south coast of England. He was called again, in 1384, to survey the defenses of Rye (Tristan's home), seven years after the French burned the town. I have seen no evidence to show that Edward ever inspected Framlingham Castle. In fact, I am fairly certain that he never did (not in an official capacity, anyway). But Edward's keen eye for defenses is a good filter with which to look through when describing a castle.

And while we are on the subject of Framlingham, there is one other inaccuracy, although this time it's one of omission. A very small omission, but it wracks at my historical conscience, so I will mention it. A half-moon-shaped fortification defended the approach to Framlingham at the time this story takes place. It was a fairly major structure, separate from the castle, and Edward and his friends would have had to walk through it to reach the main gatehouse. I omitted it because it added too much complication to the description of the castle. There. I've said it.

My conscience is clean.

Framlingham was an interesting castle. It was the home to the earls of Norfolk, particularly the Bigod family. Roger Bigod built the structure without a central keep, which was not often done at that time. All of the buildings in Framlingham were built along the curtain walls, which, coincidentally, is how Edward's castle at Bodiam was built. Sir Edward might not have surveyed Framlingham in an official capacity, but perhaps he took note of it on his own.

King Richard gave Edward a license to crenellate (build a castle) in 1383 despite the fact that—as Edward points out—there was little reason for the French to attack Bodiam. There were rivers and channels that led from the coast to Edward's home, but the French raids had all occurred directly on the coasts of England.

Edward wanted a castle. And Richard allowed him to have one.

It's good to have friends.

Historical Note: Episode Three

The story begins a slow deviation from history at this point. The final events remain the same, but I have had to make a few changes on the way.

I do not know if King Richard II ever visited Framlingham, and I am fairly certain he never set up his court there. But when a change in history as large as a demonic plague is introduced, things must shift a bit. And, along with the king's geography, the timeline of things has shifted too.

Things have jumped forward a few years. Richard should be out of the country at this point, trying to suppress a rebellion. But an outbreak of demonic plague would hardly be a time to leave one's country. So I have left him in England.

A few more deviations from historical fact have been made in future episodes. I have done this in the name of storytelling, and will, of course, point out the deviations when they are made. But most of them revolve around Richard, the son of Edward the Black Prince.

History has marked King Richard II as a failure.

He is most often described as vain, quick to anger, and even insane. And there is much evidence to support those claims.

Before he came to the throne, kings in England were simply addressed as "sire," or "my lord." But Richard insisted that his subjects call him "Your Majesty," or "Your Royal Highness." He also insisted that subjects kneel before him, and he was the first king to have an official portrait of himself painted. Acts of an egotistical man? Perhaps. Signs of a changing monarchy? Probably.

The Scourge: Emaculum

Richards reputation for quick anger and pettiness stems from dealings with his enemies. When a group of his lords rose up and tried to suppress him, he waited years before exacting his vengeance on them—murdering a few and exiling several more. And his rumored madness comes, most likely, from a flamboyant personality, a love of drama, and a passage in a historical document about a tantrum he had (which some refute as mistranslated).

Added together, these facts paint a bleak picture of a mad king spiraling into failure. My story has perpetuated this image. I hope I have not done King Richard a disservice.

Richard had many failures, but I know from the politics of our modern age how easy it to paint someone in a negative light with just a few well-placed facts. Kings in England (and elsewhere) are like painted layers on a canvas—each new king paints over the last, creating a new vision of reality. If the new king did not like the old, then the old would be painted to reflect this. And so we have layer upon layer of processed reality. It becomes very difficult to strip away each tier to see what king and country were truly like.

Richard was a boy when he became king, and he not only had to fill a large throne, he had to escape the black shadow of Prince Edward, whom everyone assumed would succeed King Edward III.

Prince Edward was the avatar of chivalry (in some ways) and one of the most beloved men of his time. His skill at warfare was only surpassed by his humility and respect for his enemies (the noble ones, at any rate). The Black Prince was massively outnumbered at the Battle of Crecy, but—with the help of his archers—destroyed the French army. At Poitiers, when he captured King John of France, the Black Prince honored the monarch by letting the king have his tent. He also insisted on attending to the king, like a servant, saying, "You are a great man, and it is an honor to serve you."

Like most military men of the time, Prince Edward has a couple of massacres attributed to him (Limoges and Caen). His penchant for burning fields and villages as he marched was also a blemish on his reputation (although it was more a sign of the changing face of warfare). Despite this, King Louis of France—England's bitter enemy—held a parade of mourning when Edward died. A celebration of the man who many considered the finest prince in the world.

That's quite a shadow to live under. And the crushing weight of such expectation no doubt contributed to Richard's downfall.

Historical Note:
Episode Four

There has always been a great paradox among Christian soldiers—the obvious conflict of killing in a religion that forbids killing. The solution, in the Middle Ages, usually involved money. Knights and other soldiers paid monks or priests to pray for their souls. The more they killed, the more they paid. Sometimes, a soldier killed so many people that it was easier just to build a new church or abbey for the monks or priests. Many of the holiest places in England were built as penance for the murder.

William the Conqueror fought one of the bloodiest battles in English history at a place called Hastings. You might have heard of it (although the fighting actually took place a few miles from Hastings, at a place now—helpfully—called Battle). One of the first things William built in England was an abbey, on the very spot where he and his soldiers killed so many Englishmen. And he didn't stop there. He built dozens of churches and monasteries to make up for his sins on that day.

In this episode, Edward and his friends barely escape the horrible maiming that King Richard calls "legging." There was no such punishment in the Middle Ages, of course.

Or was there?

England had, until as late as the 17th century, an interesting punishment for coin counterfeiters. The victim was suspended over a cauldron of boiling oil and lowered slowly. So very slowly. His (or her) feet would burn and bubble, the skin turning soft and peeling from the bones. Next, their shins and calves, then their knees and thighs. Until there was no skin or muscle left. Only a skeleton of legs. After that, the victim was probably unconscious from the pain. I imagine they did their best to revive them before completing the immersion and killing the hapless counterfeiter. I wasn't aware of this punishment until after I wrote this episode, and the eerie parallel once again drove home a point: That there is little that can be done in fiction that is worse than reality.

Historical Note: Episode Five

It is my hope that after two and a half books in Edward's trilogy, readers will realize that the most nonsensical events in the story are usually ones taken directly from history.

The pig trial in this episode is a common representation of animal trials held during the Middle Ages. In fact, many of the dialog lines were taken directly from court records of the time. The trial itself is based on a similar trial that took place in 1492—at the French village of Clermont—although I could have chosen from scores of similar pig trials across Europe and England over several hundred years. In the Clermont case, a young pig was "arrested" for entering a house, killing a small child, and eating parts of the body. At the trial, several witnesses were called and the "porker" (yes, they actually used that word in the trial) was found guilty of the murder. As in the court case Edward witnessed, an aggravating factor in the crime was that the pig committed the offense on a Friday, something prohibited by the Lord.

I wish I could say I made that up.

The hapless church clerk in this episode tries to defend the pigs using a very powerful argument—an argument, in fact, far ahead of its time. A 17th century Jesuit priest named Pere Bougeant philosophized about animal trails and stated that, if animals could be assigned blame, then they could be judged in the afterlife. The clerk from our story uttered the exact words that Bougeant wrote: "*If that is the case, then beasts would be a species of man, or men a species of beasts. And both of these propositions are incompatible with the Word of God.*" The attorney in our fictional trial rebutted Bougeant's words with the true medieval view, which is that misbehaving animals were possessed by demons. And that it was the demons that were being tried.

The Scourge: Emaculum

It is easy to poke fun at the medieval mindset that allowed these trials. They are amusing to us today, but in the framework of strict religious beliefs and a tightly regimented life, these sorts of trials made sense. It is easier to accept that demons have taken a loved one than it is to accept a random bolt of misfortune. A demon can be tried and executed. Justice can be had and the demon can no longer kill. But a haphazard stroke of savagery cannot be controlled. How does one punish fate? How can there be justice if the universe is unjust? And so animals are given a trial, to show that the system applies equally to all. That even demons must face the consequences of their actions.

Although those thoughts are simply my personal ruminations on the subject. No one knows for certain why these trials were conducted. In the story, Edward believes the trials to be a show of force. A shaking of spears, to reassure society that humans are the superior class, and that animals should learn their place. Edward may be right. But I have yet another theory.

Medieval law, like medieval medicine, often focused on both the physical and the spiritual. Perhaps these sorts of animal trials provided a sense of closure to the victim's family, a healing salve for the soul. The entire weight of the law rose up at your side, condemning the creature that took your loved one. Magistrates, villagers and priests arranged an elaborate demonstration of support, and, as a community, mourned one of their own. They shook their fists at the guilty animals, they howled at the outrageous savagery, they shouldered some of the anger and anguish.

The trials might seem foolish to us, but maybe we are the fools for not giving members of our community the same demonstration of solidarity that medieval villages showed theirs.

If you are interested in medieval animal trials, I recommend E.P. Evans' book *The Criminal Prosecution and Capital Punishment of Animals*. The book was first published in 1906, but was reprinted in 1988, so it can be found if you search. Although dry at times, it is a fascinating historical and philosophical text.

Historical Note: Episode Six

Alchemy in the Middle Ages was a topic of much controversy. The Christian Church was, at turns, vehemently opposed to and grudgingly tolerant of it. In 1279, the Franciscan order of monks forbade alchemy, magic and demon summoning. The Dominicans and Cistercians forbade it in the 14th century. And, in 1317, the pope himself issued a papal bull denouncing alchemy and banning the dark arts.

And yet, scholarly monks like Roger Bacon, explored alchemy as a way of understanding God. Kings were known to look to alchemy as well, but they of course used it to gain wealth, not understanding. Edward III hired an alchemist named John de Walden to boost his coffers, and the pious Henry IV was known to hire men of these dark arts. In the 14th century, even one of the popes got involved. He hired a "physician" for "certain secret work." No one knows what that "secret work" was, but the consensus seems to be that the "physician" was an alchemist. And I'll go out on a limb and wager that it had something to do with gold.

There was much religious scorn directed at alchemists, but it seems that they were more reviled for the rampant fraud in their professions than for any spiritual shortcomings. John de Walden, King Edward III's alchemist, ended his days in the Tower of London for failing to turn twenty pounds of silver into a like quality of gold.

Our friend Geoffrey Chaucer, in his *The Canterbury Tales*, tells of an alchemist who cons a priest into giving him £40 to change mercury into silver. The alchemist disappears and the priest never recovers his money, or sees an ounce of silver.

But this episode wasn't just about Alchemists.

Edward gains a dozen Genoese crossbowmen in this episode. The Genoese were, as he mentions, the most feared soldiers in Europe, for a time. Disciplined, incredibly skilled, and capable of decimating the enemy ranks (although the word 'decimate' means to kill one in ten, so perhaps I should say 'annihilate' to be more precise).

Edward speaks about the Battle of Crecy, in 1346, where English longbowmen overtook the Genoese as the most feared soldiers in Europe (although, again in the name of precision, I will call them English "archers", because the term "longbow" hadn't yet been invented). The French outnumbered the English at Crecy to a staggering degree. It looked to everyone on the battlefield as if the English would be annihilated (not decimated).

The French sent the Genoese crossbowmen in first, to soften up the English lines. But several fatal mistakes were made on that day. The Genoese were ordered to attack even though a sudden storm had soaked the bowstrings on the Italian crossbows. And, as we learned in episode 1, wet cords dramatically reduce the range and power of these weapons. The Genoese also were missing their pavises— large shields they use in battle to protect them from arrows fired at them. Apparently the pavises were with the baggage train and the French commanders did not want to wait for them.

So the Geneose were ordered forward, despite their protests, and they fired when they should have been in range. But Just like Tristan's wayward bolt in episode 1, the Genoese volleys were largely ineffective. It was not so for the English archers. War bows can be unstrung quite easily, so, when the rainstorm first swept across the battlefield, the English simply tucked their bowstrings under hats, or into pouches. And when they fired upon the Genoese, their bows were at full power.

The Italians, having no pavises to protect them, and with weapons rendered nearly useless by the rain, routed. This infuriated the French, who charged the English lines on horseback, trampling and cutting down the fleeing Genoese "cowards." But the English archers were not done. They fired narrow tipped "bodkin" arrows that punched through plate armor and made quick work of the knights's horses. The resulting mess of fallen knights, crossbowmen and horses made it difficult for the next wave of Frenchmen to reach the English lines. As these next soldiers picked their way through the dead and dying, they, too, were cut down by the English archers. Each successive wave found it more difficult to get through, and when mounted knights did make it past, it was at a walk and not a charge.

Everyone had expected a massacre at Crecy, and there was one; but it was the French who were massacred. And it was the English archers who made it possible. The feat was recreated 70 years later, at the Battle of Agincourt, when poor tactics by the French and a field of deep mud allowed English archers and a "happy few men" to once again pull victory from overwhelming odds.

Historical Note:
Episode Seven

Edward and his men witness a miracle in this episode.

No, not *that* miracle. The other one—a magical stone circle that keeps plaguers at bay. Thousands of such circles existed across England at one time. They are the Neolithic remains of a culture that no longer exists. A people who worshipped their own gods, and erected monuments for their fallen dead. The most well known of these structures is the one at Stonehenge.

Massive stones were dragged more than two hundred miles to the site at Stonehenge. But how? And for what purpose? There have been many theories developed to answer both of these questions, but it is difficult to know with any certainty. Some believe the stone circles were a monument to the dead. Others believe they were a place of healing, or perhaps a supernatural circle of protection. Edward, in our story, believes them to be cathedrals to the ancient gods of the druids. And I like that explanation.

Most English stone circles have been found in the west, where large stones could be found easily. Suffolk does not have the same geology—it is mostly flint or chalk—so building such great circles would have been even more difficult. But could they have used smaller stones to do the same thing? Some argue, yes.

Take the village of Alphamstone. Some claim that a ragged circle of half-buried stones around St. Barnabas Church was made by bronze-age denizens. If true, this would be the first stone circle found in East Anglia. And, if true, who is to say that there aren't more? That Edward couldn't have found such a circle?

Edward's Genoese crossbowmen see action in this episode—their crossbow bolts make quick, savage work of

Sir Gerald's soldiers. Morgan notes in an earlier episode that crossbows were once banned by the Church for the cruel wounds inflicted by bolts, and this is true. Crossbow bolts were shorter and thicker than arrows, so they tended to pierce armor much more easily. The longer, more slender arrows fired from a bow often shattered on impact. That said, even crossbow bolts sometimes shattered against armor, so the square-headed bolt was invented. This was the bolt that knocked Edward from his horse in this episode.

The crossbow was, at first, seen as a weapon for cowards. Knights railed against the use of this device in warfare, calling it dishonorable and claiming that any man could use it, even without training. Ralph Payne-Gallwey, in his excellent work, *The Book of the Crossbow*, makes a humorous observation about this protest:

"Though the knights, secure in their heavy armor, had no scruples in riding down and killing the leather-clad foot soldier, it is entertaining to read of the fierce outcry they made when the foot soldier retaliated with steel crossbow and arquebus."

Historical Note: Episode Eight

Yeah, that didn't really happen.

The whole battle-in-the-churchyard thing never occurred. When Henry Bolingbroke took the crown from Richard II, there was no fighting; it was a forgone conclusion. Henry had an army, and Richard had just lost his in a disastrous foray into Ireland. There was no armed conflict, unlike the Battle of Bosworth, where a different King Richard (Richard III) lost his crown to a different Henry (Henry Tudor).

But there should have been a battle.

Richard II should have met Henry Bolingbroke on a sodden field somewhere in England. There should have been a clash of soldiers. The hum of arrows in the afternoon sky. The cry of men and horses. If drama and poetry ruled the universe, no crown would ever pass from hand to hand without a battle.

So I created one.

In reality, Richard II fled to Flint Castle, in Wales, when he learned that Henry Bolingbroke had returned and raised an army. Henry met with him there, and Richard gave up his throne to the man who had borne the principal sword at his coronation. Shakespeare's version of the event was dramatic and heart-wrenching:

Here, cousin, seize the crown;
Here cousin: On this side my hand, and on that side yours.
Now is this golden crown like a deep well
That owes two buckets, filling one another,

The Scourge: Emaculum

The emptier ever dancing in the air,
The other down, unseen and full of water:
That bucket down and full of tears am I,
Drinking my griefs, whilst you mount up on high.
...
O that I were a mockery king of snow,
Standing before the sun of Bolingbroke,
To melt myself away in water-drops!
Good king, great king, and yet not greatly good,
And if my word be sterling yet in England,
Let it command a mirror hither straight,
That it may show me what a face I have,
Since it is bankrupt of his majesty.

We know Henry Bolingbroke became King Henry IV, but who was he before that?

There isn't much written about what he was like as a man. We know that he was John of Gaunt's son. A Lancaster boy who grew up as a playmate to his first cousin, Richard Lancaster (Richard II). Henry was a brilliant soldier, and although he was Earl of Derby, and Duke of Hereford, he had no real claim to the throne. But he had plenty of reasons to dislike the king.

During the peasant revolt, the 14-year-old King Richard fled the Tower of London when the mob approached. The king took most of the soldiery with him, leaving a handful of notable figures—14-year-old Henry included—to fend for themselves. It did not go well for two of those notable figures; the Archbishop of Canterbury and Richard's treasurer were dragged out of the Tower and beheaded. It is said that Henry, himself, was dragged out, but that one of his guards talked the mob out of taking the boy's head. I can't imagine that the mob realized he was John of Gaunt's son, or they would likely have dismembered him. The mob hated John of Gaunt above all others.

This event during the Revolt was surely a formative event in the history of Henry and Richard.

Much later, in 1387, Henry was part of The Lords Appellant, a group of nobles opposed to what they saw as Richard's mismanagement of the realm. This group raised an army and marched on Richard—who fled and locked himself in the Tower of London (see the pattern emerging?). One of his men, Robert de Vere, led an army to defend him. The Battle of Radcot Bridge was a victory for the Lords Appellant, but they did not try to strip Richard of his crown. Instead, they held a parliament (the Merciless Parliament as it was called) and accused scores of Richard's closest knights and advisors of treason. Most of those accused were drawn and quartered without a real trial.

Richard watched as all of the men closest to him were murdered by his enemies. He became a powerless king for a year, biding his time, waiting for the right moment to strike. And strike he did.

He exacted a savage vengeance on his enemies, imprisoning or having scores tortured and murdered, one by one. John of Gaunt, Henry's father, actually helped Richard regain his power, and then Richard turned on him too. A mad king? Perhaps. An angry one? You bet.

Henry Bolingbroke was pardoned for his role in the Lords Appellant (most likely because of his father's influence), but a few years later, Richard found an excuse to banish him.

Henry Bolingbroke and Thomas de Mowbray, Duke of Norfolk, accused one another of treason in 1398. Rather than letting the two of them battle it out in a trial by combat, Richard banished them both—Mowbray for life, and Henry for ten years. John of Gaunt, Henry Bolingbroke's father, fell out of favor with Richard a few years later, and died not long after. Richard then took the extraordinary step of stripping Henry Bolingbroke of all his inherited titles and making the banishment permanent.

The Scourge: Emaculum

So Henry returned and raised an army, although it has been said that he swore to all his generals that his only goal was to regain his lands and titles. I doubt we will ever know if that was his true purpose, and, if it was, when it was that he changed his mind. But Henry Bolingbroke seized Richard's crown, the reign of Henry IV began.

Richard was imprisoned in the Tower of London, and starved to death. It's not clear whether he starved himself, or if he was starved under Henry's orders.

Henry Bolingbroke pardoned most of Richard's supporters—something is advisors warned him not to. And perhaps his advisors were right. Henry spent many of his days as king quashing rebellions in every corner of his kingdom. His enemies grew and grew, he developed leprosy, and he died a hated man.

All of this is, of course, only a side-note in our story. Because Edward Dallingridge found his wife, and healed her afflictions. In reality, the two of them lived (happily, I will assume) in one of the finest castles in England. Bodiam Castle, run by the National Trust, is one of England's finest treasures, and I suggest you visit it if you are ever anywhere near Sussex, England.

There are loose ends still in my version of Edward's story, and perhaps someday those ends will be tied up. But I doubt it will be him that ties them.

Because Edward has been tamed.

So sayeth the Lord.

About the Author

Roberto Calas is an author and lover of history. His serial trilogy (The Scourge) is about a 14th century knight fighting his way through a demon-infested England to reunite with the woman he loves. And every bit of it is true except for the made up parts.

He earned a degree in journalism from the University of Connecticut and worked as a reporter, freelance writer, and magazine editor. But his true love has always been fiction.

In addition to The Scourge series, Roberto has written The Beast of Maug Maurai (fantasy), Kingdom of Glass (historical fiction in the Foreworld universe), and Wages of Sin (a historical-fiction short story). He lives in Sandy Hook, Connecticut, with his two children, and visits the United Kingdom on a monthly basis to be with his fiancée, Annabelle. Sometimes he fights demons to reach her.

You can learn more about Roberto on his website:
robertocalas.com

Other Works by
Westmarch Publishing:

Rick Gualtieri:
HALF A PRAYER

Robert Kroese:
MERCURY REVOLTS (MERCURY SERIES, #4)

Stant Litore:
ANSIBLE 15715
DANTE'S HEART
THE RUNNING OF THE TYRANNOSAURS

Angela D. Mitchell:
THE BRIDGE

Melissa Olson:
BLOODSICK
THE BIG KEEP

Richard Ellis Preston, Jr.:
AN OFFICER AND A GENTLEMAN
THE LEAGUE OF THE SPHINX: THE PURPLE SCARAB
(COMING SOON)

Cynthia L. Moyer:
STOLEN SPRING
DROWNING SUMMER (COMING SOON)

Made in the USA
Lexington, KY
12 February 2016